# HIDDEN REMAINS

## BOOK TWO IN THE CRIMINAL ACTS SERIES

# CLAIRE STIBBE

Berkeley Books
Bookpreneur, 10180 S. State Street, Sandy, UT 84070

Berkeley
Square
Books



Library of Congress Cataloguing-in-Publication Data has been applied for
ISBN 979-8-9904871-5-4
ISBN 979-8-9904871-4-7
ASIN 979-8-9904871-3-0

# What's next
# on your reading list?

Discover your next great read.

Get personalised book picks
and up-to-date news about this author.

Visit us online at
www.claire-stibbe.com

*"A sickness had begun to grow within him. It was a sickness of the mind. And where sickness thrives, bad things will follow."*
The Hobbit


*"Stronger than lover's love is lover's hate.*
*Incurable, in each, the wounds they make."*
Euripides

# PROLOGUE

I never meant to hurt anyone, although that opinion is up for debate. No amount of blacking out at the time will ever excuse what I did.

You don't just rip someone's heart out and leave it in the gutter like a piece of trash. No one does.

Have I lied, been unfaithful, made snide remarks, when a tiny word of encouragement would do?

Yes.

This is what I hate the most. But I never intended to cause so much pain.

The sky beyond my shelter reminds me of the colour of my wife's eyes, a rare shade of baby blue. If I pretend hard enough, the memories of our life together rearrange themselves and we start in a different place. One where I wasn't pretending to be someone else.

I love her as deeply as I hate her.

No matter what she did, I could never prove it. Survival matters now.

Every morning, I check the weather and imagine I'm inhabiting the fictional life of a frontiersman. I fish for crabs and dig for clams, and there's plenty of bull kelp and bladderwrack to eat. When I tire of eating fish, I trap squirrels and rabbits. If I pretend it's a normal day and do all the things I normally do, I don't feel different.

Yet I am different, inside and out.

My mind won't stop rehashing the night I carried my girlfriend's body into the sea, hoping she would decompose and become part of the marine sediment. But Nic was as stubborn in death as she was in life, and I should have known she would float back to shore like a piece of driftwood.

It was so innocent in the beginning. A glance, a dare, a dirty little secret. How could I, a former celebrity, do anything without the glint of a camera lens peeking through the trees, or zooming in on my most private moments? Podcasts, TikTok posts, and newspaper articles all scrambled to get a story.

Nic with her long black hair and teasing smile. Nic who loved the beach and the nights we spent there. Nic with her carefully curated social media feeds, hand-on-hip glamour and duck-face selfies. That wasn't all she posted.

I can still feel when the life went out of her. Seeing her face, her unfocused eyes, caused a spasm of panic and breathlessness. Then came the dawning understanding of what I'd done and the terror of what made me do it. It was so real and so sudden I could almost taste it. Yet I knew this day would come. Confession, then absolution.

Nic is gone, a distant nightmare of wet hair and seawater and congealed blood on concrete. Because of her, I have no future. No one knows the choices I've had to make, or how many bridges I've burned to save myself.

I've lost everything.

Do other people retreat inside the shadows of their darkest thoughts, hoping nobody else can see the depths to which they've fallen?

Are they driven by voices no one else can hear?

Acting was something I loved. Something I was good at. When I stepped out in front of the camera as Ethan Holloway, reconstructive plastic surgeon and serial killer, it felt like I was on fire. It's no good trying to drown out his voice. He's still with me, the darkness to my light. He blocks out the good things and leaves me in a haze of self-doubt.

The script is still inside my head, and I silently rehearse. There is a way out of the prison Holloway has forged for me, but I can't find it. It's this stifling existence that has signalled the start of my nightmares.

It gives me time to think – days, hours, months – it's all I ever do. After a while, so many thoughts wind around each other, and they get pricklier, until the whole thing resembles a ball of barbed wire.

Holloway was my final TV role. The character who wormed his way into my head and saw me for who I really was. He was my idol, everything I wanted to be, despite my wife's warnings.

I tried to tell her it was simply a complicated relationship between an actor and his muse. But my immersion into his character forced me to confront the worst reflection of all.

Mine.

# PART I

# THE HUNT

# 1

# LILJA

The March evening creeps against the windows as day melts into night. I grab a coat and move from the heat of the kitchen to the outside grill and carvery, which is closed for the winter.

The distinctive call of the lapwing in its noisy, tumbling flight disturbs the peace of the evening. Since the house is close to the coastal wetlands, it drifts back to us every so often, favouring us with its mysterious presence. I look for it amongst the twinkling lights that wrap the beech trees along the drive, but I don't see it. The atmosphere should be warm and inviting, but somehow, in this magical wonderland, I can't help but feel that I'm being watched.

I nod at our two parking valets, who are admiring a red Ferrari, and I head towards the garage where light spills onto an apron of gravel. The motion sensors mounted above the winery have been flicking on and off for no reason, and I strain to see something that could have activated them. Deer skulking too close to the fence?

Curious, I move past the sitting-room window where guests are drinking and chattering. The social routine should have calmed me, but it doesn't. What I don't see is who or what has set the sensors off. There are no prowling reporters beyond the sign that clearly reads *Private. Residents Only*.

I turn the corner to the garage. On the gravel is a curl of smoke coming from the butt of a cigarette. I look around for the offender, expecting to see a guest or a worker adhering to our strict no-smoking policy inside the dining room. There's nothing but the tail-end of my cat, Ted, as he disappears into the shrubs.

The immaculate lawn and the ha-ha, a ditch that separates the deer park from our garden, are silent. Ducks rest in flocks along the water's edge, heads still tucked under their wings. Nothing appears to have disturbed them.

Three seconds later, the motion sensor clicks off. A gust blows along the drive, a glorious sound if it were not for a cigarette packet that bounces along the gravel towards me. Burgess, my gardener and commis chef, who lives in the flat above the garage, probably had a cigarette break, since he typically takes half a dozen of those per shift. Only he doesn't smoke that brand, nor do our valets.

The only person who did was Zane. Then I feel it – something intangible – like an icy breath on the back of my neck, as if an invisible finger has lightly brushed it. I turn and expect him to say, *Didn't expect to see me, did you, Lily?* But it's nothing.

It's always *nothing*.

Some of our former security detail favoured the same brand of cigarettes, but since none of them work here anymore, I can safely assume it belongs to one of our guests. I pick the packet up and shove it into my pocket.

To all our friends, I had the perfect marriage until Zane confessed yet another indiscretion, a quick fling, as most of them were. A shiver runs down my spine as images flood through my mind. Parties, faces, where a group of women flirted and drooled. It didn't seem right that they were staring at him and ignoring me, and I can still feel my stomach churning in terror. It was all so humiliating.

But a full-blown love affair… hell, no!

Days have stacked up into weeks and months with no word about Zane's remains. When he disappeared over fourteen months ago with ten thousand pounds of our money, he became Britain's juiciest piece of gossip. His fans dubbed him *Gone Boy*, and he swiftly entered the realms of urban legend.

The press intrusion was horrific. They published the vulgar details about our marriage – cut short by Zane's monumental screwup with his assistant, Nicola Gatlin – in every newspaper. It forced me to keep Bizzy, our daughter, out of school until term's end.

I should be angry, but I'm sad. When I think of him, I imagine a smile blooming across his face and, in that moment, the spark that had originally bewitched me. Then I see his body lying in a snowdrift somewhere in the Pacific Northwest, its ribcage exposed to carrion. My vision blurs with tears.

I should pat myself on the back for pulling through. One of my greatest achievements this past year is the sign outside our front gate, which leads diners to *The Brasserie at Barton Manor*. A Georgian country house in Dawlish Warren, with its brick chimneys and double-hung windows, set in its own ten-acre valley. The drive runs through an avenue of beech trees, and the front façade has stunning views of the Devon coast.

Our website describes it as: *"A full-service restaurant on twelve elegant acres, offering an unmatched experience and atmosphere. The gardens provide spectacular settings for private parties and weddings. Stroll through the arboretum, enjoy a breeze on the patio, host an unforgettable event – Barton Manor is the ideal place."*

Alterations had to be done, of course. New cloakrooms and a wall knocked down between the old dining room and the orangery, and a shiny new kitchen extension. What I long for now is a Michelin star and a feature in every top dining magazine in Britain. I've written to *The Great British Bake Off* producers to encourage them to consider Barton Manor's spacious lawns for their iconic white tent. It would put us on the international map.

Footsteps on gravel cut through my thoughts. I turn, expecting to see a valet walking towards the garage, but there's no one there. At the end of the lawn, there is a gap in the trees, and a tiny red light glows in the darkness, blinking on and off as if someone's smoking a cigarette. All I hear is the whisper of leaves and the rippling phrases of a robin.

My eyes latch onto the tree as if I can make out a man leaning against the trunk. Then my thoughts change from terrified to borderline amusement. It's simply a car's brake lights in the distance.

A loud squawk of guests emerges from the house, some studying the front façade, while Stella, my house manager, waves goodbye. Her turbulent white hair is freshly curled, and her signature trainers peek out from beneath a long skirt. Little does she know I roam the gardens like a sleepwalker; a figure dressed in chef's whites, shivering under a coat.

I return to the kitchen. The sound of thumping knives and clanking whisks lulls me for a moment, sauces made, and garnishes set out – mise en place. No one asks where I've been. They're used to my anxiety attacks and my need to be alone.

I wash my hands and stare through the kitchen window. My image hovers above the sink like a hologram projected on glass; ice-blonde hair twisted into a French knot and a face that could do with a few more smiles.

Stella walks into the kitchen with her iPad. 'Last orders. Kunal Bakshi and Sabine Knight-Bruce want the duck. Guess what? Arno Penna is on table eleven.'

We all rush to the small window in the kitchen door and peer out into the dining room. There he is, the hottest golfer in Britain.

'Everyone wants smoked bacon,' Stella says, as she stands behind me on tiptoe to look over my shoulder.

The chefs remark on his muscular arms and seductive eyes, although I'm sure there's some strategic brilliance in there some-where. Celebrities like to be "seen" at Barton Manor. They know that producers, directors and reporters dine here and there's a good deal of posturing and celebrity worship. I have the death of Zane's mistress and his subsequent disappearance to thank for that.

'Hot behind!'

My sister sidesteps me with a piping hot mushroom sauce with herb-roasted beetroot. Her spaghetti-thin limbs, coupled with her waifish beauty, make her appear younger than she is. With a freckled and worry-free face, most people think she's in her mid-twenties. Yet she's thirty-eight this summer and I'm forty, trying to bury my loneliness by working every second there is.

I open the fridge and take out the belly of smoked bacon cured with spices and maple syrup. I slap it onto the chopping board. It briefly resembles a human arm, all fat and no meat. I hesitate, and the knife trembles in my hand.

'Everything okay?' Paul, my darling thug of a brother-in-law, asks.

'Yes, chef.'

I don't want him to think I'm having a hard time keeping up. Paul is Chef de Cuisine. Even though we run the kitchen with a hierarchy; Sous Chef, Chef de Partie, Commis chefs and servers, we are family. We serve lunch and dinner, and in the summer months we open our popular barbecue patio.

I cut several slices and peg four rashers to a wooden frame for servers to flame at the table. Paul barks four orders of spiced duck breast to a chorus of 'heard that, chef,' and the buzz begins. While I'm plating caviar and Wagyu tartare, and my sister is running the pass, I'm bombarded with images of Zane.

He loved me once. Used to stare at me like I was an oil painting. Later, I learned it wasn't because he admired me, but because he was appraising me, sizing me up, asking himself: Will she always be beautiful? Will she be the beta to my alpha? Will there be tears of joy when we make love? Or will there be tears of rage when we don't? Will every frustration, every disappointment, lead back to her?

Had it?

He wanted two children. I miscarried one and had Bizzy, my gifted daughter and greatest achievement, who is now fifteen. I never strayed from the terms of our marriage. My part meant keeping his secrets until the sign above our kitchen door "To Bear and Forebear" became unbearable. He strayed all the time.

'Where are table ten's apps?' Paul's voice drags me back to the kitchen and the appetisers he's looking for.

'Here, chef.'

'Let's clear the rail and get these orders out!'

I'm always glad to see someone has ordered kalops and pickled beetroot, my grandmother's slow-cooked stew. It was one of Zane's favourites, too.

Despite the wind dusting the leaves outside, I can't keep my mind on my work. Perhaps deep down I know I'll never be rid of the monster.

## BarbedWire - Trending #InZane

**@BantaBadger:** So here we are again at Barton Manor. Current mood: sipping tea and reliving every episode of *Play Him Play Her*. Feeling the vibes of Holloway with every sip.

**@CirceAtNight:** Zane Osborne isn't even talented. A legend in his own mind, and a spoilt brat diva on the daily.

**@SherylAdams:** Divo, I think you mean. Why does anyone care about him? I won't watch another Ozzie movie again. I didn't like him before, and I don't like him now. He gives me the ick.

**@HeyWhatsUP:** OMG what are you? Twelve?

# 2

# ZANE

It was a year ago when it happened.

An escape from a scandal and a mad dash to freedom. The last bit of news I gleaned from a library in Québec was that my disappearance came as a shock to the celebrity world.

*No kidding.*

Looking back, I realise now how close I was to being arrested. Arriving in Canada the day before the detainer came through was a stroke of luck. The Sûreté du Québec never caught up with me. I found a website with the tagline: *Tried & Trusted Fake IDs*, delivered in forty-eight hours. All I needed to do was provide the headshot and pay with a gift card. The man was true to his word. He sent the driver's license to me through the mail.

I left England as Zane Osborne and arrived as Theodore Oliver. I bought myself a burner phone and boarded a seaplane. The view from the window confirmed how remote it was, fjords carving through the coastline with dense forests of spruce and fir. During the trip, I selected an accent for Theodore Oliver and called myself Ted, in memory of my wife's elusive cat.

Reports of my death circulated widely in England. Someone started a Facebook group in my honour where fans talked about the "demise" of Netflix's hottest TV doctor. I picture Stan Marriott, *DevonLive's* reporter, brushing a hand over his bald head, dark eyes blinking behind his glasses. He wrote the local angle of my story, which was surprisingly complimentary.

I found myself on the lower reaches of Big River in Labrador, a familiar stretch of land I'd visited many years ago. The nearest town was Makkovik, an Inuit community about twenty-one miles away and too remote for anyone to find me. I bought all the clothing and cooking gear I would need, including items for hunting: fishhooks, trapping wire, a recurve bow and arrows, and a hunting knife and a hatchet.

Once a week, a boat ferried hunters to the village to stock up at the local stores. I took this opportunity to recharge my phone, buy more cigarettes and whisky, and keep up to date with the local news. People said my accent was chantant, a cross between Québécois and West Island, Montreal. I wasn't sure which was better. Having an accent or being visible because of it. Most importantly, I had to use Canadian English. Gas station and not petrol station, parking lot and not car park. It was a never-ending struggle.

On the first day I arrived in the Nunatsiavut region, it rained. Branches and brush were too soggy to light a fire. When they say the eastern coast of Labrador gets thirty inches of precipitation per year, they weren't lying.

Close to the beach was a perfect place to build my shelter, high enough to escape the rising tide and shielded from the river by trees. I cut branches to make an A-frame, using bracken and moss to pack between the cracks. The construction was sturdy and well insulated, with a fireplace constructed of rock. Through my door, I remember seeing a harbour seal far out on the river and beaver tracks on the shore. It was the best view a man could have.

I collected water from the stream, which had to be boiled thoroughly to ward off giardia, a parasite spread by animal faeces and lethal if ingested. I gathered bunchberries from the forest floor, which, when boiled and dried, made a tasty snack to chew on while hunting.

My shelter was well stocked, and I trapped fish in my gill net daily. I made a rod out of a six-foot branch and, after attaching maggots I'd found near the riverbank for bait; I was fishing in fifteen mile-an-hour winds. High tides brought bladderwrack upstream, a brown seaweed rich in iodine and great for stews. Low tides left brook trout caught in pools. When the weather changed, it changed fast, and storms from the west brought hammering rain. But at night, auroras danced across the sky.

Grouse, squirrels, berries and mushrooms weren't enough, and I was losing a pound of weight every day. A week later, I got lucky. I was within twenty yards of a young caribou, quartering towards me near my traps. My first shot hit him in the lung. The second sailed off into the brush. I followed a trail of blood for two hours before I found him. The skinning and hauling were exhausting, and since I hadn't accounted for shooting something as large as that, I had to go back to my shelter to collect my pack frame. Every trip was worth it because I knew I'd be dining out on that thing for months.

Back at camp, I hung the main quarters in my shelter to smoke and left other parts in the trees to keep from predators. But each day, I had a strange feeling I was being followed. Animal or man, it was impossible to tell. Eyes seemed to track me from the brush, never moving or making a sound. Every so often, I looked behind me, thinking I saw movement. But whatever it was had disappeared into the brush. Instead of a slight ache of worry, it was a full-blown tightness which almost stopped me from breathing.

At night, my last thought was about Lilja. She was a natural beauty, fit and toned, with platinum blonde hair over a natural tan. While she was at college, I found out she worked part time at the local gym and realised I wasn't lifting weights nearly often enough. I came in every night, and she became my regular spotter, timed my reps and monitored my lifts. But she wouldn't date me. She said she didn't want to marry someone who might become famous one day.

It was a few years before I saw her again. She was working in an upmarket hotel; her sights set on a career in catering. After hanging around the bar enough times, I made sure her sights were set on me. We were married the following year.

Why did I screw it all up?

Because of the erotic charge the occasional fling gave me.

The following morning, I woke with the worst headache, a mixture of dehydration and shock. The injury, which would have forced me to leave the confines of the forest, happened while peeling a stake for one of my traps. A brief lapse in concentration led to a stupid, costly mistake. It caused a cut in my thigh, which I thought was nothing, except for the blood all over my sleeping bag, which took a while to stem.

A few days later, it swelled, and there was a cloudy, yellow discharge. Whether this had happened with the incessant scraping of clothes against my skin every time I dressed and undressed, I don't know. I used my emergency radio to call Atanarjuat, a local tracker, and the one person I could rely on to keep my location a secret.

When I first arrived in Makkovik, I met him in a coffee shop. He was friendly and curious, and wanted to know what had brought me here. I fed him some lie or another and then told him about my stalker and how I was in constant fear of my life. Atanarjuat made me promise not to fall foul of other hunters, and he kept my hiding place a secret.

It was an hour before he arrived with medical supplies, food, and a bottle of Angel's Envy. He didn't have to tell me the wound was infected. I knew it was. He cleaned it with alcohol and some kind of tea tree antiseptic cream he'd bought at the local pharmacy. It left a sharp burn, and my stomach flip-flopped as if deciding to purge my last meal.

'You'll live,' he told me.

He dressed the wound with an absorbent pad and a bandage that covered the top of my thigh all the way to the knee and told me it would need changing every two to three days.

I offered him my smokes and whisky, which he refused, but he made himself comfortable in front of my fire and ate two bowls of rabbit stew. He gave me an antler bone thumb ring to protect my finger from the bowstring, a gift I'll always treasure. Somehow, we got to talking about his childhood, about the tattoos on his hands and how the boys at school always teased him about his long braid.

'The bullying got so bad I wanted to cut it off,' he said. 'But my father begged me not to. I thank him now because my hair is part of my identity.'

Deep down, my admiration for him increased. It must have been hard for a young boy who was teased for having long hair.

I was ashamed to hold back any information about myself, but I needed to protect him as much as myself.

To get my mind off the pain, he told me a story about a giant stingray caught in Big River. The monster weighed in well over six hundred pounds and was thirteen feet long. We had a good laugh until I knew it was time for him to leave.

'Stay still, my friend,' he said. 'The earth sleeps, and so should you.'

That night, I didn't sleep at all. Every rattling twig and every sigh of wind made me jumpy. It shocked me how much blood stained my sleeping bag, and an idea bloomed, more out of desperation than practicality. Would it be enough to alarm Search and Rescue if they come looking for me?

I had frequent nightmares and visions of death until I realised that living in perpetual fear of law enforcement trackers finding me was a far greater punishment. I was tired of being alone, and just as threatening was the mental toll without human contact. The imaginary Holloway, the sociopath I once played, was the only person I spoke to, and he was grinding me down with every whisper.

My deteriorating mental condition would eventually force me closer to the mainland, even though I was in danger of someone recognising me.

The last straw happened the following day, when the sun came out and I was collecting water from the river. I thought I saw the glint of binoculars on the opposite bank. A visible flicker that caused a sinking feeling in my stomach. I knew what I had to do. It meant leaving a few provisions behind, most notably the blood-stained sleeping bag.

Seeing those binoculars had shocked me to the core. I shouldered my backpack and bow and placed as much as I could on my frame. Getting the hell out of there to a cabin downriver was top priority.

I was hit with the realisation that if I hadn't got out then, I wouldn't have got out at all.

# 3

# LILJA

Here I am. The world's most conscientious worker. Up at six, downing a creamy oatmeal smoothie and my first cup of espresso.

I believe in discipline and routine, which means twenty minutes to stretch, fill my water flask and decide on a walking route. I labour up the hill behind the house, picking up speed along the cliffs and then downhill back home. With fresh air in my lungs and the sting of rain on my cheeks, I feel ready to start the day.

Okay, so I had a horrible night. A noise woke me up, and I wondered if it had come from inside a dream. As my eyes adapted, the open door sliced itself out of the darkness, as moonlight flooded in from the landing. Then the sound of crunching gravel outside. I wasn't imagining it. Nor was I imagining the strobing light from a torch, which briefly lit up the room.

By then, I was fully awake, expecting to hear a disembodied voice telling me it was the ghost of Zane past. I told myself there were no ghosts until the sound of boots scraping against the terrace warned me that this was perhaps the wrong conclusion to come to. I parted the blinds and peered outside, barely able to make out the barns in the darkness, except for the brief jinking of a torch before it died altogether. My heart fluttered behind my ribs, and I felt sick.

*It couldn't be Zane*, I told myself; *it couldn't be*.

I wanted to drown out the voice in my head telling me that unhappy ghosts never rest and that they haunt the living, especially those who had wronged them. I stared at every portion of that view for nearly a minute, wondering if it had been the headlights of a passing car reversing in the lane, its exhaust clouding the night air.

I checked the CCTV but there was nothing but grainy shadows and I wondered if the camera lens was dirty. The footage was unusually dark.

It bothered me in an elusive way, like a window open somewhere letting in a chilly breeze. Nostalgia hit me, a memory stifled by the years. When we were first married, Zane disappeared one night, and I awoke to an empty bed. With the benefit of hindsight, I see where some of my insecurities came from. The fear of being abandoned. How could my husband have left me all alone?

I slumped back against the pillows and decided the crunching gravel outside and the torchlight were Burgess coming back from a party. I imagined his neck buried under the coils of his scarf, cigarette smoke darting from an open mouth.

This morning, I hide away in my study on the lower ground floor to track inventory and make sure all purchases are being done on budget. So far, our website has received five-star reviews with the promise of return visits.

There's a timelessness to the study. Maybe it's the bookshelves that frame a Georgian fireplace and the decorative cornices where the wall meets the ceiling. Perhaps it's the French doors that lead out to the garden where the curtains billow in a warm breeze.

After Zane left, I found myself in there most days, deciding how to change it. I repainted the walls a light coastal blue, giving the room a casual elegance it desperately needed. I packed his books and ornaments away in the stables and replaced them with old English classics and a collection of Herend porcelain. It's very me, and I like it.

Chef Paul serves breakfast every day at 8.00 am for the family. Today, it's ham and gruyere cheese omelettes with fresh berries. No matter where my daughter Bizzy is in the house, she insists on texting me. It's always a back and forth about who is taking her to school. It's Stella's week, I remind her.

I check the lunch menu and make a prep list of all my dishes today. If I record every step and time it, I'm rarely accurate. Paul has a rhythm and an inner metronome. He's honed a sixth sense from years of hotel cooking, every menu memorised, even down to the finest detail. He is everything I want to be.

There's a staff inspection before every meal. Double-breasted whites are starched and laundered daily, and all chefs must wear disposable gloves. Ovens and cooktops are pristine, and floors, walls and ceilings must be sanitised.

When we're done, I corner Burgess and ask him if he was outside last night. He shakes his head. The twitch at the corner of his mouth makes me wonder if he's hiding something from me, like a girlfriend climbing over the wall of our property and staying overnight. He's done it before.

I grab my ingredients and utensils and stand behind my workstation. It's important to have a sense of how to move through a recipe from prep to garnish, and how to measure the minutes. I season the trout inside and out with salt, pepper and cayenne, followed by the court-bouillon with sliced vegetables and thyme. The smell of simmering onions and rice vinegar reminds me of family meals in the orchard. It was something Zane insisted we do during the summer holidays, like Pop Larkin in *The Darling Buds of May*. I love the spring. It reminds me of new beginnings, memories of childhood escaping through a sea of bluebells.

Over the cacophony of kitchen alarms and clanking pans, I hear a phone ring. Reddened, I look around the room. Paul doesn't allow phones at work, and that includes me. I snatch it from my pocket before checking the name.

'Yes!' I shout over Paul yelling for two cheese and spinach stuffed chicken.

There's silence before the call disconnects, and then it rings again. The caller ID shows the number as international. I hate the part of me that still clings to the hope that this is the police with news about Zane's remains. I duck into the boot room and grab a coat.

'Hello,' I say, and race out to the terrace. There's no reply, but I can hear the wind crackling against the mouthpiece. 'Can you hear me?'

I perch on one of the garden chairs and lock eyes with our resident lapwing, who is limping about on the lawn. Then another noise, like someone tapping a mug. It only fuels my frustration, and my voice gets louder, more impatient. But the line is eerily quiet. For a second, my gaze flits from the lapwing to the trees and into the deer park. There's no one in the garden besides me.

No sooner do I hang up; the phone rings again. If it's not the police, then who? I go through the same scenario, the same loud hellos which get no response.

Only the silent calls – which could simply be a computer gathering information about me, or a hacker wanting the details of my bank account.

Something is brewing. I can feel it. Part of me wonders if Zane could have survived.

He won *SOLO*, the British survivalist programme, where they dropped twelve contestants along the banks of Big River in Labrador, leaving them to endure the harshest of climates. He appeared in Season 6 and lasted a whopping seventy-two days. But that was twenty years ago.

While various scenarios cross my mind, there is only one that sticks. Last year, DC Symonds, the officer dealing with our case, told me that a local tracker in Labrador found Zane's camp somewhere south of Makkovik. He brought back a few of his belongings, including a shredded sleeping bag stained with a large amount of blood. The local police assumed a bear had mauled him, yet they never found his remains. Deep down I know this is significant.

How valid was the Canadian coroner's report at the time? In the many police visits I'd had with DC Symonds; she emphasised that finding his remains was a critical piece in this high-profile case.

The next thought chills me to the bone. What if Zane were alive in some pocket of the world, recovering from a gruesome bear attack? What if plastic surgery had restored him? He could be the homeless man in the street, his hand cupped for loose change. Slipping into character, all that pretend-play, was something he was so good at.

Last year, I went through Zane's things at least five times to see if he'd packed any sentimental items, something that might reveal he'd planned this whole thing. What I found was missing money from one of our bank accounts, most of which I retrieved, except for the funds from the Hellman's Trust.

As for the CCTV footage, it was past its retention period and overwritten by fresh recordings. The police could not recover it from the rest of the house, even on the night that Nic disappeared. Zane had turned off sound, motion, and smoke alerts, anything to prevent recordings from going to the cloud.

The problem is, *BarbedWire,* a domestic abuse awareness site with over 3.6 million followers and hosted by the popular chat show host, Andrie Vander-Meulen, is now hotter than TMZ. It's not where you want presumed sightings of your missing husband aired, particularly since my daughter and most of her school friends use it. But several have surfaced within the past six weeks. For reporters, it would make the biggest celebrity story in Britain. For me, the article would propel my husband once again into the limelight and leave my family vulnerable to public attack.

Worse, my social standing in the county has taken a gigantic leap forward. I rightfully belong in the star-studded world of up-market restaurants without having to hide behind a celebrity with a sexual pull impossible to ignore. Especially one who has risen to international stardom as a killer and who could have faked his death.

I've never read my husband's therapy transcripts. They're confidential and kept sealed in his therapist's office. Not a day goes by without me wondering if he'd admitted in confidence to killing Nicola Gatlin. Surely his therapist, Meggy Russell, had an ethical responsibility to report the crime if he had.

I'm hit with an idea. It's something I've been toying with since the messy circumstances of Zane's disappearance became front-page news last year.

Going public.

I don't mean on social media; I mean an interview with Amanda Yeboah of *Celebrity UK.* Why not tell Zane's fans how terrified I was of him and how sorry I was for Nic? Perhaps they would realise what both Bizzy and I went through and stop daydreaming about the possibility that their favourite celebrity is blameless.

My sister's warm hand on my back makes me jump. I turn and see honey blonde hair and a willowy frame, and a kind but searing gaze.

'I didn't think blackened trout was on the menu today,' she says, looking at me like I might be dangerously stupid.

'What? Oh, shit!'

I rush back inside the house and drop my coat on the boot room floor. Paul is shaking his head and wafting grey smoke from the Aga with a tea towel. I'm appalled at the pathetic sound of my voice. 'I'm sorry.' I grab oven gloves and dump the over-baked trout into the sink. It's inexcusable considering how long the guests will have to wait.

Paul sighs, as though he's doing me an enormous favour. He pops open the top button of his white double-breasted jacket and shakes his head.

'For once in your life, can you leave the phone out of the kitchen?'

'Yes, I'm sorry.'

Elin wraps her sisterly arm around me and rests her head on my shoulder. 'Don't get frazzled and bad-tempered.'

I grab a pan, fully aware that my hands are shaking, and feeling everyone studying me, their sympathy not far behind. I keep my mind focused on trout, bouillon and veggies. The kitchen staff becomes a blur of white and steam as voices ring out.

*Don't kill that steak.*

*Heard that chef!*

*I'm firing table fifteen apps right now.*

All the while I'm thinking about how Zane had become so untethered, almost catatonic, where his eyes were dull and held no reflection. For years, I'd acquainted myself with his terrain, studying it and immersing myself in it. I'd been reading scripts with him, selecting the right ones and talking to his director, Simon Berne.

One night, Simon invited us for dinner, and the conversation veered, as it always did, to the best movies of the year. Simon mentioned looking for a screenplay in the thriller genre, a Netflix series accessible to a large audience, and one tailored for Zane.

'A Richard Kimble type gone bad, for instance,' he said. 'No one would suspect Kimble of killing his wife, not just by looking at him. As for corrupt and immoral, a Jed Hill character fits the bill.'

I was familiar with both films. *The Fugitive* was about a vascular surgeon named Richard Kimble, played by Harrison Ford, who was framed for murdering his wife. *Malice* with Alec Baldwin was about Jed Hill, a cocky trauma doc who believed he could do no wrong in the operating theatre. Suddenly, an idea took root. It seemed silly at first, but after a few more glasses of wine, it didn't seem silly at all. Scriptwriters were easy to hire, and I had the perfect one in mind.

Maybe I wanted to see if there was a chip in Zane's self-assured veneer. A crack where pride had taken root. When they chose the script, Zane went Method, where he could get into Holloway's head and connect with him on a deep, emotional level, making his performance more compelling. When he fully resigned to the ugliness of Holloway and all his violent and erratic mood swings, down the slippery slope we slid.

Snapping fingers wakes me from my reverie. Paul, who has been standing over me for the past few seconds, bends down until he's eye level, a disarming gesture which makes me smile.

'Where's that order?'

'Here, chef,' I say, wiping bouillon spatter from the edge of the plate. 'One trout on the fly, beautifully poached.'

I'd like to think I'm in control, but that's no longer the case. My phone keeps pinging. This time, it's a journalist from the *Telegraph* who wants to do a feature on "How Country Estates Thrive." I doubt it's about the income we make from opening the gardens to the public in the summer or the brasserie. Of course, he'll steer the subject to Zane. It's his third request, and I won't be pushed into a corner.

Delete.

Then another ping. Notifications from *BarbedWire*, which are set up to alert me at any mention of Zane. A floating sensation catches me off balance. Like it or not, the hangup call has put a storm in motion, and I've no idea how deadly it is or that it's coming right at me.

**BarbedWire - Trending #InZane**

@BantaBadger: Worst-case scenario, Nicola Gatlin's family may sue Zane Osborne's estate to seek compensation for damages.

@CirceAtNight: Only if there's proof he killed Nic.

@BantaBadger: If there is proof, all assets and property can satisfy a judgement if the Gatlin's win the case.

@HeyWhatsUP: Does that mean they could go after Barton Manor?

@Banta Badger: Anything's possible.

# 4

# ZANE

The steady sound of water drips from the cabin roof into a two-quart pot. Fire glows in the tiny hearth, and a tendril of smoke spills from the chimney.

Sleeping is hard. I can never find a comfortable position. For a second, I doze off again, imagining the jaunty chug of a lawn-mower and the gurgle of fresh coffee on the Aga. My mind snags on the bright halls of Barton Manor and twists through the past. My wife's voice sliding into its welcoming tone and my daughter's chuckles. Then it vanishes into my head, and I wake up with a tear frozen to my cheek.

It's been months since I ate that caribou and months since I've caught anything substantial. Twice, I've thought of walking into the river and being swept under by the tide, but I don't have the guts to take my life.

That sound again. Like a huff of breath, not loud enough to be a bear, but somewhere between a caribou or a man. The forest is full of sounds: pattering feet and the occasional howling of a wild animal, or snow falling from an overladen branch followed by snapping twigs. Now I'm fully awake.

I peel away the aluminium blanket and sleeping bag, and a spill of cold air bites my face. I pull a tuft of moss and mud from the nearest spy hole and stare at the shadows that populate the forest. In the sky, the sharp pinpricks of stars look down between a few wayward clouds. The river slithers like oil, but under its tranquil appearance, the water is freezing. The sun hasn't appeared in over three days. It's so damn depressing out here.

All four sides of the cabin are clear, and there's nothing to see for miles. Then a whisper. *Look through the trees, not at them.*

I've been alone in the forest for over a year, if I don't count my mental roommate, Holloway. He's stuck in my brain, complete with slug lines and a script. I should never have given him a voice.

        EXT: SOMEWHERE ALONG BIG RIVER, LABRADOR
        - NIGHT


        FADE IN:


        CLOSE ON a man stoking a fire in a rock
        hearth inside a small cabin.


        This is Zane Osborne. He's forty-five but
        is looking sixty-five.


        Holloway sits behind him. Osborne can
        neither see nor hear him. Holloway
        exists only in Osborne's mind.

                        HOLLOWAY

                Come on, son, give yourself a
                break. You can't stay out here
                forever.


                        ZANE

                I've already been here a
                year. Another won't make any
                difference.

HOLLOWAY

How long can you survive on
two cans of beans?

ZANE

It's not the lack of food
you're worried about, is it?
It's her.

HOLLOWAY

She set you up. You know that,
don't you?

ZANE

I can't prove it.

HOLLOWAY

Proof isn't everything. My
point is, you didn't deserve
it. The only way to get over it
is to get even. It's not like
you've never thought about it.
The day you go home, walk down
your drive, bypass the alarms,
and watch her sleeping while
you hold a knife. That's the
perfect time.

ZANE
(Over his shoulder)

I'm not killing her!

HOLLOWAY

I hear you, Zane, but you want
her to suffer.


ZANE

Maybe. But neither of us wants
to spend life in prison. Or a
lethal injection.


I pull myself back into the moment and use the centre of my eye, turning my head slightly. There are light and dark tones and grey-ish-blue tones and somewhere in the middle, there's moon glare on snow.

It blew outside all night as wind pummelled the trees, sending clods of slush onto the roof. Yet now, the lull sounds menacing. I remind myself the silence is because snow absorbs about 60% of ambient noise.

I take the recurve bow down from the rafters and inspect my arrows. Some are for big game; three-bladed broadheads, soft steel and easy to sharpen. Others are judo points for small game, which penetrate quickly and put the critters down fast. I slip the axe into my belt and haul on a padded jacket and scarf. The temperature is warmer than it was yesterday, yet there's at least twelve inches of snowfall. Time to inspect my traps.

Outside, jack pines loom like slender giants, and through their branches I can see a star-studded sheet of glass, its demeanour shifting with the seasons. Today, milky films of ice restrain most of it, making it inaccessible by boat. On the horizon, the stars dissolve into a golden layer of sky as dawn creeps in.

This boreal forest is the largest land biome on Earth, extending from the Alaskan border to Newfoundland and Labrador. Swathes of spruce, tamarack, and balsam fir surround the lakes, and I feel a strong sense of humility in the vastness of it. What I fear most is not in these woods, but the darkness inside of me and its unrelenting voice.

A single ray of sunlight slants through the clouds as I walk towards the river. Water no longer laps the sandy shore, and snow covers a curl of grey rocks. Tiny paw prints, likely from a rabbit disturbed by a predator, dart into an underground warren. A sign that danger is near.

There has been three more feet of accumulation during the night and by tomorrow, perhaps a foot more. It's lucky I marked my traps with coloured ribbon as I would never have found them. Most are untouched, and one is scattered with bits of rabbit. It's not the first time something has robbed me of food.

I squint at the faint outline of paw prints, five clawed toes and a big pad, travelling in an overstep walk. When I try to picture the size of the bear that made them, my eyes dart in all directions, imagining drool dripping between surgically sharp teeth. I must remember predators are hunting me as I hunt them.

This was the noise I'd heard earlier. No need to look any further.

When I reach the clearing, I hear the *kuk-kuk-kuk* of a squirrel as it skitters from a branch above. A meagre meal, but a meal I can't afford to miss. One will provide about eighteen grams of protein and a little over one hundred calories.

```
                       HOLLOWAY

          Look high. Move low. Hunt with
          your ears.
```

I scour the branches for movement and see the wisp of a tail as the squirrel retreats towards its drey. It uses the branches to hide behind, and it mimics me as I circle the tree. A minute goes by, and it's about to make a move. The excitement makes my heart flutter like an electric current through my body, and I inch away from the trunk. A quick, easy kill gives me no pleasure, but hunger has taken first place.

I nock an arrow and draw the bowstring towards the corner of my mouth, and I wait for those sharp claws to scrape against the bark. First a tail, then its hindquarters, then its head, and before it disappears again, I release the shot.

The snap of branches and a thud tell me what I want to hear. The yellow fletching is easy to spot on the ground, so I pick it up and study my kill. Nice shot. Right behind the armpit.

I return to the shelter as large snowflakes spin between the trees and turn the forest an eerie grey. After skinning and washing the squirrel, I roast it in a little beaver fat. Best meal in days. I lie back on my bunk and stare at the rafters, where a cobweb hangs in a ropy skein.

A loud snap pulls me back to earth. I drop a half-eaten bone and use my spyhole to locate the noise. It's possible the smell of smoke from my chimney has drawn a bear to my cabin, six hundred pounds of hair, muscle and teeth. Most are hibernating, and although lethargic in the winter, some are active in harsh conditions.

The branches of a nearby tree buckle under the weight of snow, each limb depositing its load. The sound makes me jump. Then I see a silhouette emerging about seventy feet away at the water's edge. Not a curious bear on two legs. I would have heard the woofing and grunting from here.

I shrug on my jacket and bow and creep through a collage of brown leaves and snow.


HOLLOWAY

Be as brittle as the pines and
as sharp as a gyrfalcon.


It's not the first time a hunter has come through here, snooping around my patch. It happened six months ago when a man, who stank like rotting flesh, began creeping around at night. At first, I thought a wolverine had discovered my food cache.

I was smoking fish when I heard the twig snap – a trap I'd set to catch animals sneaking up to my bear hang. The fault was mine. I'd left the ladder up so I could store the rest of the meat I'd trapped. Only something had beaten me to it. I grabbed my bow and nocked an arrow.

There he was at the bottom of my ladder, a man, taller and bolder than me, about to take off with enough food for weeks. I'd never seen eyes like that. A sparkle of hate, hiding something unknown and deadly, and his clothes were blood spattered from the kills he'd made. There was no polite hello, no exchange of names. He panicked when he saw me, dropped his load and drew the axe from his belt, playing it from hand to hand as he circled me.

We stood there in the frigid air, the snow spinning around us. There was something sinister about him. With his jaw clenched and his focus locked tight, his body slinked in and out of the light. It was this same terrifying image that lodged in the back of my throat.

It all happened so fast. The glint of the axe and a loud *whomp* as it flew, barely missing me as I lurched to one side. I tasted bitter panic, and somewhere in those few seconds, my arrow tore through his jacket, no doubt an involuntary response to the threat.

The air squeezed from his lungs, and he staggered backwards, hooking his boot in a tree root. As he fell to his knees, an electric current of opportunity passed through me. If I didn't finish him, he'd get to me first. I rushed at him, and my hunting knife took care of the rest.

Burying him was the worst part. It was cold that night, and my knuckles turned blue as I hacked the ground with his axe. It took hours of precious calorie-burning time to lay him in a hole that wasn't deep enough to cover his nose.

Now I have a new guest, someone who didn't happen on this stretch of beach by accident. It raises the question: Is he looking for me? Or for the hunter I'd killed?

He picks his way along the shore, sometimes sliding, sometimes staggering, until he reaches the fringe of trees. I can make out a fur-lined hood, under which would be a tuque and scarf much like my own. The butt of his rifle hangs across his back.

While he appears to be scoping his surroundings, I lower my bow and turn a full circle, expecting to see the shadowy forms of the SAS well concealed within the forest. But nothing else moves. Nothing human, that is.

I wait a full minute until he changes course, walking inland and scrambling up the rocks towards the trees. I shoulder my bow and creep down the embankment to the stream, which runs parallel to my camp. There's my marker – a tree with a naked crown blistered by lightning – showing where the flat rocks I'd laid in the summer should be. I scramble to find my balance, and I'm almost to the other side when my boot teeters and slides through a thin layer of ice. The crack echoes like a gunshot.

I grip onto roots and brush and scramble up the other side. I try to focus on the last sliver of hope that the man is gone. But he's standing a few feet from the treeline, trying to get a bead on what he might have heard. The rifle is no longer on his back but out in front, muzzle lowered slightly as if the threat he'd perceived is real. Then he backs up into the trees and disappears.

Fear takes centre stage as I creep along the shore to the place where I'd seen him. I crouch and press my hand against the indentations, where sunlight hits the highest verges, leaving deeper depressions in shadow. Possibly a size ten boot. Tactical, like mine.

I move off the path, staying low behind a snow-laden thicket. I pause for several minutes to listen until the exposed parts of my face are completely raw and my feet are numb. Although he can move slowly and quietly, I wonder if he is familiar with the terrain. Why walk through a dense forest in the snow with the threat of frostbite screaming with every step? A knot of anxiety pulls so tight I can barely focus.

There, in the shadow, leaning against a tree, is a figure, so elusive it's as if he's melded to the trunk, his flesh taking on the qualities of bark. I stay down and wait for him to move. The itch to know if he's still there drives me insane, and I inch forward so I can scratch it.

He's gone.

Footprints are the first thing that alerts me. They seem to pass behind the tree and continue for about 10 yards – an unlucky number – because he's still in range. A man could walk and still be alive from a single hit, depending on the wound. A second hit and he'd be struggling to stand. Only I don't want the forest stinking like an abattoir and inviting every non-hibernating beast to my patch.

Or the police, for that matter.

Is he a neighbouring tracker? The trouble with that notion is there are no other cabins or shelters around here, where symbols are notched on trees warning outsiders to keep out. The footprints are widely spaced out as if he was walking at a clip. I decide that following a man with a gun is not a good idea. Minor tasks like filling up my cooking pot and collecting firewood burn too many calories; thirty minutes outside is my max. My store of pike and trout has all but depleted, and there's no sign of fox and wolverine.

The ice will stay on the lake until late May, at which time blue-winged teal and northern pintail will fill the skies, and the otters will return to the cove. There are no more boats to take me to town for supplies. Only a seaplane, if I'm lucky.

I walk back to the cabin and close the door. Through a spyhole, I peer out at a dark cluster of trees. The light is different, and the wind has a melancholy tone.

I search for shadows between the tree trunks. It's just me and an army of towering sentinels, branches scratching and scraping, and tips bending in the wind.

HOLLOWAY

Well, that was exciting,
wasn't it?

ZANE

About as exciting as a cat
facing a car ride to the vet.

HOLLOWAY

So what if there are other
hunters around? You're not the
only person on the planet.

ZANE

Easy for you to say.

A stout northeaster blows through, its timbre sliding and warbling like an eagle-bone whistle. In the hush between frozen gusts comes the snapping of twigs. For a moment, I feel a tinge of annoyance that it might be a fox looting my traps. Then I remember the traps are empty.

I hear a thin, scraping sound followed by a deliberate *crunch, crunch, crunch* of footsteps in the snow. Then nothing.

Someone unfamiliar with the surroundings would need to duck under low-hanging branches to get to the cabin. Had he knocked himself out? Or is he travelling towards me, using the slow, sliding steps of a hunter?

It could be Atanarjuat coming to check on me or a sudden urgency that brings him here. Except he would never venture out this far, not on a whim. Nor would he travel under the trees where roots and boulders would snag him. No, he'd walk along the beach to the gap in the trees and take the path to the clearing.

The shadows and the sudden stillness make the intruder invisible. I realise with a flash of shame that my legs are frozen, while the rest of me shudders in terror. How many minutes have passed since I heard the noise? Two, tops.

Think. Breathe.

Would Atanarjuat rat me out to the feds? The rush of blood deafens my ears, and terror makes me weightless. It's not a nightmare or an overactive imagination.

HOLLOWAY

Maybe you're seeing things.
Why not give that skinny little
rump a pinch?

This isn't a joke. No one walks through a storm during the early hours. No one in their right mind, that is.

# 5

# LILJA

It's late afternoon when I complete the place settings and flowers and check off all my other to-do items for dinner.

I retreat to the study with a cup of Earl Grey tea, and I'm surprised to find that the French doors have blown open, bringing in a chilly breeze and the bitter smell of wet leaves. The theory I put forward in my mind is that the doors hadn't latched properly. I study a shaft of morning sun as it gilds the lawn. The rain is coming down faster, droplets inflating as they fall, and bursting apart against the patio flagstones.

I secure the lock. As I turn back into the room, I notice the mouse and keyboard are angled slightly to one side and my chair is not pushed under the desk. The thought of an intruder slipping inside the house unnoticed lodges itself so firmly in my mind that I feel something akin to terror.

My phone lights up with a text. A series of numbers followed by the words. *But we loved with a love that was more than love—*

It's probably just spam or intended for someone else entirely. Yet I can't stop looking at it and wondering why someone has sent me a line from a poem by Edgar Allen Poe. I realise my anxiety has gone on long enough. It's time to do something.

I call Stella, glad that I can get a signal from downstairs. 'Were the French doors open when you were down here?'

'Not as far as I know. Why?'

'They were open, that's all. I was wondering... I just thought you might know.'

She doesn't laugh like she usually does. Instead, there's a drawn-out breath, as if she's tired of taking the blame. 'It wasn't me if that's what you're thinking.'

Yet she is forgetful. We both know she is.

She hangs up. Blood pounds in my head as if the temperature has crept up a few degrees. I look around the study, reminded of the noises I hear at night and the haunting scent of Zane's cologne. Calling the police over an open door is a waste of time, and I can't go on blaming Stella, or anyone else for that matter. Barton Manor needs security, the sooner, the better.

Inside the desk drawer are business cards I keep for all the CPOs we've ever employed. The words Lambeth Security remind me how professional these close protection operatives are. I call the number and ask them for someone we've used before; someone I can trust and someone who knows the layout of the property.

The CPO they recommend, and who is available, is Ryan Mc-Kellan. I remember his face, not only as one of Zane's most trusted confidants but also for his clean-cut good looks and sharp wit. The assistant tells me she'll draw up an open-ended contract and send Ryan over with it in an hour.

I change into an off-the-shoulder sweater, cream stovepipe trousers, and ballet pumps. It's easy to create a lean and elongated silhouette when wearing neutrals. Zane always loved my natural blonde hair and toned stomach. He said it was one of the many things that drew him to me. But now, those same dimensions have sagged, and I need a lot more than built-in shapewear to keep everything sucked in.

Fifty-five minutes later, the Ring Doorbell chimes on my phone, and I glance at the screen. Stella greets Ryan McKellan, tall, dark, and with his signature languid smile.

Voices pour into the house, one high-pitched and welcoming, and the other warm and deep. I apply fresh lipstick and sit at my desk as if I've been there all morning.

'Knock, knock,' a voice says from the doorway.

I'd pictured the muscular heft of a security guard, but when I look up, this man has the impeccable dress sense of a *GQ* model. Great teeth, great legs and jeans that fit like a second skin.

'Good morning,' I say. 'Good to see you again.'

He stretches out a hand over the desk and throws me a brilliant smile. 'You look amazing, as always.'

I lower my eyes to his raking gaze, noticing how his shirt fits him tightly around the biceps. What I can't get out of my head is how wildly attractive he is. I haven't had a jolt like that in a while.

'I'd like to say it's a pleasure to be here again,' he says, setting a large brown envelope on my desk. 'But it sounds like you've got a lot on your hands.'

There's something about his soft Scottish lilt that grounds me. His excitement at returning to Barton Manor sends a flutter through me, and I can't help the corresponding smile that spreads across my face.

'I never got to thank you for all the hard work you did for my husband,' I say, noting the gold signet ring on his little finger, a ring Zane had gifted him. 'My *late* husband.'

'The pleasure was entirely mine. He was a great guy to work for.'

I take a breath and launch in. 'Since his disappearance last year, I've had a few silent calls, possibly a fan who's got hold of my number.'

His gaze locks with mine, the smile diminishing into seriousness. 'How many calls?'

'I don't know. A few. They don't talk, but I know someone's there.' I catch his eye and let out a grimace. 'There's something else. Someone's been creeping around the grounds at night. It scares me. Especially for my daughter. That's why I need a CPO to make sure the property has the best surveillance.'

'I can definitely help you with that.'

I gesture to the package he's left on my desk. 'It may be a long assignment. A few months, maybe more, if that's okay with you.'

'You're asking me to stay on indefinitely?'

I'm locked between a yes and a *shit yes* and settle for a nod.

I'd like to go over the perimeters for weak spots, run the CCTV and decide which cameras to upgrade, but he changes the subject.

'I hope this doesn't sound intrusive, but what led to Zane leaving?'

I'm not surprised he brought it up. It's probably been on the tip of his tongue since he arrived. My eyes skim the David Beckham lambskin jacket he wears, which is identical to Zane's, and I wonder if fashion is all they shared.

'I don't know where to start,' I say. 'You knew Zane. He was funny, generous, and kind. Everyone liked him.'

'But something changed.'

'It was during the filming of *Play Him Play Her*. I found a character file on his desk. A profile of Holloway he'd created. It wasn't unusual to hear bursts of typing, like he was in high gear for several hours. He rarely saw me in the doorway, watching him, immersed in whatever scene he was doing. When he left for work, I looked. There were comments in the margin that creeped me out.'

'What type of comments?'

My arm intuitively circles my stomach. 'Gory things like using cuffs versus rope, and lethal injections of opioids. He'd have all these windows open on his computer, interviews with serial killers and photos of victims. It was gruesome stuff.'

'He was researching this for his role?'

'Initially, yes. But when he became obsessed with Holloway, it lit a fire in him. Zane wanted stardom. It didn't matter who it hurt. Including me. It started when we read the script together. He'd snap his fingers and fist the table if I didn't get it right. It was his temper that scared me. Explaining how vicious he was would take hours to unpack and is best explained by reading my police statement.'

'Was he always this volatile?' Ryan's eyes seem warmer than before, and there's the promise of loyalty in the air.

'No. It was the role. That's why I employed an assistant. Someone to keep him on track, coordinate his ever-changing schedule, and be the buffer between him and his agent. Nicola Gatlin was a good listener; someone he could rant to about which actor was raking in a whopping seven figures for a memoir without even changing out of their pyjamas.'

Ryan rests his elbows on the arm of his chair, his smile dropping for a moment. 'Was their relationship professional at the beginning?'

'I thought so. She had an agent and was bound by a contract. So was he.'

'But she fell in love with him.'

Thinking about the affair makes my chest hurt. But I shove it down. 'He drove her around in his BMW 6 Series, put her up in our Holland Park house, bought her clothes and jewellery, and gave her a glimpse of the life she never had. Of course, she fell in love with him, but Zane dumped her long before she reached any significant milestone. Her pictures on social media threatened his public image of a dedicated actor, loving father and faithful husband. Love is the most threatening emotion to a married man, one who had no intention of leaving his wife.'

'Did she get… was she—'

'Pregnant? No, she never pulled that card. But her Instagram posts showed how determined she was. I'm sorry she died. Especially sorry that two children found her remains on the beach.'

I wonder if Ryan is comparing what he believed then with what he believes now and weighing up the cost of that loyalty. If he can imagine Zane's leering grin and the nub of a joint burning in a nearby ashtray, he's three quarters of the way there at understanding the real Zane.

All the headlines chalked my husband up as *a multi-faceted talent whose role in* Play Him, Play Her *showcases his exceptional versatility.* When they should have continued *at the cost of abandoning and neglecting his family.* Maybe *abandoned* is too strong a word, but the adoring public would get the idea.

His eyes make a cursory sweep of the room. Visually, the study has changed since Zane was here. I've removed all the cinematic photographs and special editions and replaced them with cookbooks. He must think I've expunged every memory of him after he left.

'It was after she died, he disappeared, correct?'

I nod. 'The one thing we all agreed upon was that he was eluding the police. Not retreating to Scotland to escape the press as his agent suggested.'

'You've seen the comments on *BarbedWire*?' he says. 'The ones that hint that he'd faked his death.'

I wince. 'Can't miss them.'

*Faked.* A word that seems so out of place compared to the news we've all been believing, but a word that might carry a frightening ring of truth. Ryan knows the police received intel about Zane's entry into Canada. He knows about the gruesome discovery of a man-made shelter with a bloody sleeping bag inside. All I could see were teeth and blood and shattered bone. Whether Zane had stumbled across a bear and its cubs outside his shelter, or if a bear saw him as a food source, no one knows. Morbidly, I'd found a website depicting injuries from bear attacks and nearly threw up. As for Zane faking his own death, his fans will keep pulling at that single thread until the police find his body.

'Hypothetically speaking,' he says, 'Let's say he is still alive. Do you think he'd contact you?'

'We weren't on good terms. So, no.'

My comment borders on personal and finding myself being so open surprises me. Am I flirting? Am I sending out the wrong signals? He's what… five years younger? What am I thinking?

I gave up dating a few months ago, disappointed with men who turned out differently from what they advertised. They were mind-numbingly boring and made intrusive comments about how much my business was worth. Probably the biggest turnoff was the lack of dress sense. Creased shirts and frayed trouser hems, and eyebrows pinched at my refusal to talk about Zane. Here I am, sitting across from a man who is eminently dateable, a man I can't allow myself to get involved with.

'This may seem like an odd question.' His eyes drop to the Persian rug, as if studying the Mina-Khani floral motifs. Then his head comes up, and his eyes catch mine. 'Did your husband's fame bother you?'

'What do you mean, bother me?'

'The attention he was getting.'

I strive to keep my tone even. 'If you mean the servers at the country club, fans outside restaurants and the mums at Bizzy's school pawing him every chance they got, it was mildly embarrassing.'

'So, it did.'

I shrug and don't smile, although I'd like to. And yes, I *am* flirting with him.

'His social media exploded when he became Holloway,' he says. 'Three million followers, one hundred and fifty thousand likes, several thousand comments. Mostly women.'

Ryan has done his homework. 'It's not like his name was the answer to a question on Jeopardy.'

'But he was popular.'

'Okay,' I concede. 'He was a national treasure. But there's shit you just don't do in a marriage, and abusing your wife and child tops the list. That shouldn't be a surprise, should it?'

'No. Except for the part where you stayed with him.'

His impertinence staggers me. What does he want me to say? It was the high cheekbones, the dark eyes – all the rare qualities that marked Zane as a leading man. Or the effortless flattery, and the way I felt he focused his attention solely on me. Zane was the route to a life I wanted, a life I would kill to have. I'm not telling him that.

He leans back and purses his lips, a tiny cluster of lines forming around his mouth. 'I'm trying to learn everything about the real Zane Osborne.'

Then he should ask himself, as I have countless times, was Zane's marriage to me simply an extended movie? It's impossible to know what's genuine when you live with an actor.

Ryan wants to know more about the man who won hearts with his unforgettable performance as Holloway. The couture-worthy stud, the man every woman swooned over. He wants to get to the heart of who Zane Osborne was. He wants to *know* the monster behind the mask.

Who better to tell him than me?

## BarbedWire - Trending #InZane

@CirceAtNight: I'm not understanding why there hasn't been a huge push to get more evidence in the Nicola Gatlin case. It's all so eerily hidden and quiet.

@Titmouse: They've no actual evidence or that Zane Osborne's even dead. All we have are lies and fake videos uploaded on social media.

@SherylAdams: Unless that dude had like a year's worth of food and proper gear on him, I'm pretty sure he's done for.

@HeyWhat'sUP: All of you need a hobby. Your obsession with Zane Osborne is creepy.

# 6

# ZANE

A faraway yowl wakes me. I unzip my sleeping bag and stagger to the window and unhook the shutter. Flakes spin like a vortex and then flutter down onto my covered wood storage.

The stillness of the moonlight settles over the lake, bleaching the water a silvery blue. I suspect it was simply a detached branch that had fallen onto the forest floor or the wind jostling the trees.

I've spent my time setting traps, perfecting knots, singing and telling jokes. Well, I sing, and Holloway tells the jokes. Bad ones. Aside from the bone-chilling cold, the isolation and scarcity of food, there is always the threat of other hunters. Speaking with anyone sends a ricochet of terror down my spine, for anyone could recognise me.

I wedge a cigarette between my lips, and the lighter trembles in my hand. After a deep drag, a stream of smoke escapes my mouth, along with the adrenaline that has been buzzing inside me. I look up through the dense canopy at branches scraping against one another, and I wonder if Lilja is looking up at the sky and staring at the same moon.

Something moves in the periphery of my vision, a flicker of light so minor that I might have missed it. I wipe my eyes with my sleeve, and it appears to be a pinpoint of light on the opposite shore that bobs up and down like someone walking over uneven terrain carrying a torch. It's hard to judge distance in the dark, but I'd guess they'd be here in under forty minutes given the hard slog through roots and potholes.

The tiny hammer in my ear pulses out a rhythmic message of terror. There's no hiding when you're living in a cabin with smoke eking through the roof. If they're downwind of that smoke, they'll easily find me.

There are two things I can do. Look them in the eye and offer them the last of my rations: a mug of hot black coffee and a cigarette. Or I could get my bow and send a warning shot in their general direction. But that's just as stupid as the first idea.

What if they have a gun?

HOLLOWAY

> If you were smart, you'd get
> the starter fluid you insisted
> on buying from the store and
> set fire to the cabin. Whomp!
> The forest would be boiling
> red, and you'd be out the back
> door running for your life.

The idea was flawed in so many ways. Too much attention would bring a hoard of Canadian firefighting crews to the area, who might consider it suspicious during the snows. What if this hunter is the same man I'd seen at my old shelter?

Secondly, there's no back door. But there is a window.

HOLLOWAY

> Odd though, don't you think?
> Him tracking you a few miles
> downriver first and then finding
> you here.

The idea of him sitting outside for the past few days means that he's been scoping me. It also means he's adapted to the cold and the terrain, and he's dressed to blend into the surroundings, even down to his warm breath, which is likely caught behind a scarf. He's been observing me and my habits and every tiny eccentricity, making sure I'm the one person he's come all this way to find. Yet I never knew he was there.

HOLLOWAY

> Looks like it's every man for
> himself. Are you ready to fight?

If I move now, he'll hear the snapping of twigs underfoot, smell my sweat, and possibly see me through his night vision goggles. Like a wolf, he'll move faster and quieter and more sure-footed than me. If I run, there's a rusty spring-loaded trap about half a mile away and buried under several feet of snow. If I don't see the marker I left on the nearest tree, it will cost me my leg.

I quietly radio Atanarjuat. There's no answer. He's probably sleeping soundly while I stand here, shitting myself. I decide to let the fire burn itself out, giving me enough time to run before the chimney stops smoking.

HOLLOWAY

> Why run like a pansy every
> time you face a threat? Why
> not confront it like a man!

ZANE

> I'll pass, thanks.

I came out here with a backpack and the will to survive, but admitting failure is the nobler way. After winning *SOLO* all those years ago, I had to eat small helpings to keep myself in starvation mode, counted calories and watched my water intake, so I didn't throw my electrolytes off. This is not a TV challenge, nor are there any winnings to give me an incentive. The cash I keep stuffed in the inside pocket of my coat is barely enough for a month. It means finding work in Quebec. What type of job is a noncitizen likely to get?

                    HOLLOWAY

          Grunt work, son, and a few
          bucks paid under the table.


                    ZANE

          Forever the pessimist.


                    HOLLOWAY

          I have an idea. You're going
          to love this!


                    ZANE

          Forget it. Whatever it is, I'm
          not doing it.


It's time to gather up a few belongings and make it to the ferry without being followed. I take my backpack and bow and unlatch the back window. The cold hits me like a slap in the face. The only sound the hunter might hear, if he hears anything at all, is me dropping over the sill. But I doubt he can hear anything over the stout wind, which shifts the snow and covers every track I make.

As I trudge deep into the forest, the occasional cry of a gull breaks the silence, and so do creaking branches. A low-lying mist wraps itself around the base of the trees and hangs like ghosts above the brush. My head buzzes with exhaustion, and I feel like crap.

<br>

HOLLOWAY

How about I cheer you up with
some verse? Who wrote this?

This is the Wild Huntsman that
shoots the hares

With the grass-green coat he
always wears:

With game-bag, powder-horn and
gun,

He's going out to have some
fun.

ZANE
(snapping his fingers)

What was his name? It's the
guy who wrote *Struwwelpeter*.
Heinrich Hoffmann.

HOLLOWAY

Very good.

I try to raise Atanarjuat on the radio again. This time he picks up. The bad news is he can't use the boat to come and get me. There's too much ice on the river, which means a helicopter is the only alternative. I'm to meet the pilot at the clearing above the ferry and pay him $1,000 in cash if I want it kept between us.

I scuff through pockets of snow and take a meandering path that hairpins towards the clearing, careful not to trip on bedrock that peeks up between the scrub. The sky is now streaked with yellow, and the trees are amber-tinged.

My skin crawls with the sense that something watches me

from the trees, and my gut creeps with fear over the presence of a practiced hunter. For every four steps, there is another sound, timed to sync with my own. Something about it seems familiar, like someone labouring to breathe in the cold. Yet I doubt this person is labouring at all.

I duck into the undergrowth and scan the forest for movement. There are animals that stalk and keep close to the ground, only to maul a man when he least expects it, and there are hunters like the one I'm trying to avoid. My eye catches movement, and I remove the bow from my shoulder and nock an arrow.

My heart gallops in my chest. I don't know where he is. Every part of the forest is different, and this part seems to have unusual proportions, as if the tree trunks are wider. My fear is so suffocating and so profound I can't move.

I spot him well beyond range, using the shadows to his advantage. While I calculate distance, fully intending to burn a hole in him with everything I've got, he disappears behind a thicket of young spruce, branches swishing and flopping closed behind him.

I look one way to study the expanse of forest that leads to the clearing, and then the other to scan the way I'd just travelled. Although there's no sign of him, I sense he must be circling me. I forge ahead and pick my way through the snowdrifts in an unconscious mimicry of his measured steps.

The wind seems to carry the fresh dirt-like aroma of wet wood. There's something else too, something coppery and distinctly unsavoury. I spot the source, a dead bear lying in a dark patch of blood on the forest floor. Steam hovers over a webbing of muscle and viscera, telling me the kill is recent. I scan the surrounding forest. Nothing moves. It's not only the gruesomeness of the carnage that makes me cover my mouth, but that a gunshot was the sound that woke me. The proximity to the hunter's kill fills me with anxiety that even the clearing between the trees cannot ease. If his shelter is around here somewhere, it's less than half a mile from mine.

I give the carcass a wide berth. My boots slide on a thick layer of snow-covered brush, and I grip my bow in my gloved hand and grab a branch with the other to keep from falling.

HOLLOWAY

Bet you don't know this one.

"Like one, that on a lonesome
road

Doth walk in fear and dread,

And having once turned round
walks on,

And turns no more his head;

Because he knows, a frightful
fiend

Doth close behind him tread."

Zane

The Rhyme of The Ancient Mari-
ner. Now, can we have a little
silence, please?

A few seconds pass, and I conjure an image of a loose-limbed man winding between the trees like a phantom. I try hard not to break one of the cardinal rules. Don't run.

Light filters through the branches and turns the quality of the forest a lighter grey. My arms are trembling with exhaustion, the bow quivering in my grip. I whip my head around at the sound of a high-pitched howl, which seems to vibrate on two notes, like the sound a wolf makes when pursuing prey. Only it isn't a wolf. It's too human for that.

I turn a full circle, my bow drawn. Sweat runs steadily down my face as I listen for the slightest sound.

                        HOLLOWAY

            It's...behind...you.


There's that terrible moment when I turn just in case Holloway's right. Another shriek makes me tingle all over, knowing that whoever is out there is mimicking an animal caught in a trap. If it weren't for the sun stalking in through gaps in the canopy and clearing the mist, I wouldn't have glimpsed him at all.

My breath catches, and my heart rate rockets. I crouch amongst the rotting ferns and study the tree trunks. At first, all I can see is white upon white and tiny patches of brown. There, in the middle of it all and about thirty yards away, is a man lying on the ground, his leg caught under him at an unnatural angle.

He's faking it; I can tell. His gloved hand rests on a standard bolt-action rifle, which lies in the snow, its muzzle pointed right at me. A gun like that holds five to ten rounds, and I doubt he'd miss.

He's watching me and waiting, and that's what scares me. Just lying there with his fingers creeping closer towards the trigger, ready to blow my head off.

What do I do?


                        HOLLOWAY

            There's only one thing you can
            do.


                          ZANE

            I'm not killing him, if that's
            what you mean.


                        HOLLOWAY

            If you don't, he'll kill you.
            You're well within range and
            you're a damn good shot.

ZANE

You might be right.

I creep closer and pull my bow to full draw, tuning out every thought and every sound. The bow vibrates, the arrow rushes through the air, and a deep, guttural howl tells me it found its target. His gun fires recklessly without aiming, and the loud boom drives me lower to the ground, the sound penetrating my scarves and hood. The bullet rips through a tree behind me, and bark and twigs rain down on my back. Motion slows, and there's a high-pitched ringing in my ears.

My trembling hands run over my torso.

Nothing hurts.

Nothing bleeds.

I'm panting like a thirsty dog and too terrified to look up.

It's minutes before I risk a glance between blades of grass and see the man lying on his back with the gun by his side. I want to get the hell out of here.

Holloway's voice sounds muffled.

HOLLOWAY

Not so fast, my friend. What
about the arrow?

ZANE

The arrow?

HOLLOWAY

It's the last piece of evidence that will link you to
the kill.

                    ZANE:

        Shit!


                    HOLLOWAY

        It will be if you don't pull
        the broadhead from that throb-
        bing artery.

Keeping my movements steady, I crawl forward on my hands and knees, hoping he isn't playing dead. There is no escape of breath between the fur-lined trapper hat and scarf, and his chest is still. Embedded beneath his chin is part of an arrow, the shaft of which has broken off inches before the fletching. Possibly because of the fall, but more likely because he pulled a glove off and tried to wrench it free. Blood arcs from his neck and soaks into the snow, and I recoil from the ferric stench of it.

His fingers are slightly curled, and on the wedding finger is a thin gold band. Instinctively, I hold my breath, and my lungs tighten, because at the tip of each finger is the distinctive gloss of nail polish.

Through my confusion, I register that this is not a male, but a female. She doesn't move, doesn't twitch, her extravagant glasses flung to the ground. The spring-loaded trap is locked around the bottom half of her leg, its teeth meeting inside her calf.

Everything moves slowly around me, each snowflake separating from the others. The trees, the slanting sun, and the woman's hand, are all cast in sharp detail. I wonder if I'm going mad. I take deep, shaky breaths, but there's nothing to stop my heart's frantic racing.

The crucial minutes following the release of my arrow and the gunshot had cost her life. Guilt claws at my stomach. It's always terrible when anyone gets killed, but especially a woman who may have young children.

*Shit! Shit! Shit!*

But this someone has a police logo on the sleeve of her jacket.

Did she know who I was? Had she reported my whereabouts to the police? Unease worms its way through my body.

I listen for the slightest sound that will tell me if there's anyone else out here. But there's nothing. Rather than get too close and attempt to remove the buried broadhead, I leave it where it is. There's no sign of the yellow fletching, not in the surrounding brush or gripped in her hand. Panic hits me like a punch. Please don't tell me she's lying on it because I'm sure as shit not going to roll her over.

Still on all fours, my eyes search for it, tracking her footprints and two deep indentations where her knees hit the ground. She would have lurched backwards after the gun went off and felt the barb in her neck. Which means the fletching isn't under her.

As I scan every bracken frond and thicket, I spot it almost hidden in a mound of snow. The relief pours out of me in a sigh. I stagger towards it and stuff the damn thing in my pocket. My arms are shaking, and so are my legs, and I'm hearing the steady thud of helicopter blades overhead. The sudden rush of air tells me I need to get going.

HOLLOWAY

> Her phone, you idiot. Her radio.

Holloway is right. She could easily be located if someone were tracking her GPS. It kills me to do it, but sliding my hand inside her jacket, where the last of her warmth still permeates, is a necessary evil. Her phone is in one pocket, volume on silent, and the radio is attached to her belt.

I switch them off and stuff them in my backpack. I try to walk, but my knees buckle under me, and it's minutes before I can get any traction. The question is where to bury my bow and quiver.

It takes a good ten minutes to stumble towards the clearing, where I find a fir tree with a bald crown. I stuff my weapons between its branches and emerge from the trees onto a path studded with rock.

I feel a strange twinge of fear. Not just from the dead woman, but from what has been trapped in my thoughts for the past few minutes. What if the British public knows that I'm still alive? Going back to England in handcuffs fills me with a palpable sense of shame, particularly confessing to another crime. I can already see my wife's face tinged with disappointment and irritation. She's worn that expression for years.

I keep my eyes level with the helicopter's landing skids, which have touched down. My muscles feel like rubber bands, and my heart hammers so heavily I'm afraid it might explode. I glimpse the pilot waving from the cockpit, and I wave back.

After boarding, I keep my eyes fixed on the slowly vanishing land, where sheets of ice thin at the outer limits. For once, I'm grateful I'm leaving. The sky is coarse-grained like basalt, promising another layer of snow tonight. I can only count on scavengers to scatter the markswoman's bones, keeping the ecosystem clean.

'Looks like you had a rough night, eh?' the pilot says.

I cup my ear with one hand, still deaf from the gunshot. 'Sorry?'

'It looks like you had a rough night,' he shouts.

'Yeah," I say, peeling off my gloves. "Well, my shelter was hardly a five-star hotel.'

He grins. Mimicry was a gift I'd discovered as a child, impersonating celebrities and politicians to make my schoolmates laugh. I do my best with my faux accent. It helps me to blend in.

'Not much in Makkovik but crabbin',' he says. 'How long are you staying?'

'Not long. Got a friend on PEI.'

'That so. Whereabouts?'

I've no such friend on Prince Edward Island, but telling him my destination is Quebec is too risky. His gaze sticks, eyes dark as slag, and panic prickles up the back of my neck. I struggle to think of the name.

Which house did Romeo belong to? Think. *Think!* I'm mentally snapping my fingers, and then it comes to me.

'Montague,' I say.

The tracker nods. 'Nice place. Got a niece who lives there.'

*What's the betting…* As we land, I have more time to rehearse how I would answer questions because someone is bound to ask me where I'm from. As I search for a list of likely options, the pilot turns to me and smiles.

'What did you say your name was?'

I want to say, 'I didn't,' but I remain polite. 'Ted.'

'Good to meet you, Ted. You'll be back this way, I hope.'

I feel a deep frown forming and quickly smooth it away. 'Yep. I'll be back.'

'See you, then,' he says, taking my cash.

'You will.'

I wave as I walk towards a small hangar. Another low simmer of panic takes hold. There are two officers studying a pile of paperwork. One has a long braid down his back, and the other, who looks like George Peppard, is talking French too fast for me to understand. But a few words stand out.

Criminel… dangereuse… meurtre.

The last word *murder* seems to hang in the air. They could only accuse me of Nic's murder. Only I didn't kill her. What I did was disturb a crime scene, dispose of a body and bury evidence – despicable transgressions and worthy of time behind bars. Not to mention fleeing the country, which spikes my anxiety levels.

I can't help but wonder if I missed something, but so, too, has every mental health professional I've talked to. Meggy Russell, my long-suffering therapist, suggested hypnosis and dream analysis and encouraged me to describe the event in graphic detail. Nothing sparked a memory of why Nic fell back against the cellar steps without my help. Perhaps the recurring nightmares are simply a jumble of scenes from the many characters I played, rather than any suppressed flashbacks of the past.

I stare at my feet, suddenly dizzy. Please don't let me draw attention to myself by throwing up. I need to find a motel for the night so I can bathe and hopefully recover most of my hearing before boarding the plane to Quebec.

While I'm imagining soaking in a bath for the first time in over a year, an officer approaches me, his eyes running up and down my body, pausing somewhere around my waist.

'Got time for a chat?'

# 7

# LILJA

I drop onto the couch and listen to water dripping from the gutters as the clouds roll across the fields. The gentle whir of a distant plane high in the sky verges on hypnotic, but it doesn't calm me.

I pull out my phone and open the camera, switching it to reverse lens. My face has no blemishes, but the lines around my eyes are deeper, as if I've gained a few years without realising it. I have everything I've ever dreamed of. A daughter, a successful business, money to hire all the staff I want and give them bonuses, and all the little luxuries that remind me how well I've done. But somehow this success feels like it's resting on a precipice. With one small nudge, it could easily come crashing down. I flick the camera closed.

The comments on our website either lift my mood or dash it. They love the ambience, the food, the setting, but they wish their favourite actor would return and regale them with amusing outtakes from his latest film. Even *BarbedWire* seems adamant on reminiscing about Zane's best film roles, as if he is still the most important person in their worlds.

An unexpected scent captures my attention. Citrus, not lemon, subtler and laced with rosemary. It stirs a memory in the periphery of my mind, close enough to know it's here, but too far to make sense of. My ringing phone snaps me out of it. It's Ryan with a question he'd rather ask in person. We agree to meet at The Boathouse for brunch.

There is less than an hour to run. I pull on black leggings and tie my hair into a ponytail, pulling it through the loop of my baseball cap. I change my routine and run along the lane and into a stubble field, as a few cumulous clouds drift above me. About half an hour in, I sense movement behind me, someone else labouring to keep up. I'm not aware of any other runners in this secluded world of mine, so it must be the farmer and his dog, sprinting along the field's margin towards the gate.

As the man passes, he looks at me, eyebrows bunched. A young man, early twenties, with a phone thrust in my face.

'Any news about your husband?'

Anger knots in my stomach. Who is this lanky stalker who thinks he can invade my private space just to get an exclusive? Then I realise the field isn't a private space but very public, the last place I should be.

'Do you know if he's still alive?' he asks. 'I mean, if he was, that means he faked his death, right? How do you feel about that?'

Instead of completing my usual two circuits, I double back and make a mad dash towards the house.

Lanky follows me, lumbering through the stubble, hoping to cut me off at the corner. But stiff stalks of grain slow him down, and I inwardly smile at my daring.

Once I'm jogging down the lane, a van cruises beside me, the back door sliding open and hurried footsteps as someone races to catch up.

'Ms Osborne. Lilja!'

A woman's voice. I press in the code to the gate, and it swings open. Just as I slip through, a camera clicks, and she shoves a microphone in my face.

'Ms Osborne, what do you think about the rumours about your husband being alive? Will you be making a statement?'

I jog down the drive where she can't follow me. I'm grateful it was only one van and not a fleet of them, especially without a bodyguard here to create a barricade.

Satisfied, I look over my shoulder before opening the front door. The gate has automatically closed, but the reporter is still there, filming the long drive, the house and the tiny speck that is me.

It takes a long shower to calm me down, and I coil my hair in a loose bun and dress in a wide sleeve chiffon blouse and new skinny jeans. With the price tag dangling from a belt loop, I snip off the label with nail scissors and toss it into the bin.

Paul is cooking huevos rancheros for breakfast, and the smell of sautéed onions and simmering tomatoes brings the family downstairs one by one. I wish I could join them.

'You're nice and early,' I say to Bizzy. 'Got everything?'

'Yep.'

Paul looks Bizzy up and down. 'You look smart. Is that skirt new?'

'I've had it for ages,' she lies, giving me a side smile.

I'm not having the usual argument about whether the skirt is regulation uniform. The style and colour are close enough. It's the length I question.

I check the drive through the CCTV. There's no sign of life beyond the gate. That's not to say the press isn't hiding somewhere down the lane. I tell Bizzy to hide under a rug in the back of the car while Stella drives her to school.

I excuse myself to make calls in the study. A stout wind bellows from the northeast. Windows rattle and raindrops slide down the panes. Every winter, I make a note to secure the inside shutters on the north side of the house, and every year I forget.

Elin has agreed to cover me today. My sudden "appointments" are making everyone uneasy, especially the ones I can't talk about. On my way out, she meets me at the stairs.

'You okay?' she asks.

'Yeah, I'm fine.'

Her gaze falls on the car keys in my hand. 'Is it Zane? Have they found him?'

News travels fast. 'No. It's nothing like that. I'm going to meet Ryan.'

'You will tell me if he says anything?' She looks closely at me, her eyes scanning my face. 'You will tell me if they've found him.'

'Of course I will.'

I give her a hug and run out to the garage. On the drive over to the restaurant, I keep thinking I should do my share of the cooking. Instead, my erstwhile husband is on the edge of every thought, sharpening instead of fading. Paul has pulled me aside more than once. He hates everything to do with Zane. He doesn't like the attention, the noise, and how it distracts me. I know he and Elin only want what's best for me, but I'm feeling self-conscious under their watchful eyes.

I park in the restaurant car park. This is only the third time I've been here, but I've seen countless lunch dates in Zane's diary for him and Nic.

Ryan is waiting for me outside the door. I try not to look too impressed but dressed in a tailored suit and crisp white shirt, he's athletically chic. Where Zane was striking in a classic sense, Ryan is more rugged, his jaw shadowed with stubble, and with a focused expression I find myself drawn to.

He leads me to a table by the window and pulls out a chair, his hand warm against my back. I'm shocked to be thinking that he is one of those men I could watch all day.

The server arrives with two glasses of iced water and two menus and tells us about the brunch specials. I order a luxury prawn omelette, and Ryan orders sausages, eggs and bacon.

I lean forward and brace myself for what's coming next. 'So, what did you want to ask me?'

He chews his bottom lip. 'I was wondering if you'd consider letting me live in.'

My mind winds back to the hounding reporter at the front gate, and I nod. 'I don't have to consider it at all. I think it's a great idea. What about your family?'

'It's just me.'

I refrain from allowing a smile to stretch across my face. 'We have a flat in one of our stables. Nothing special.'

'Sounds perfect.'

When I tell him about the torchlight I'd seen arcing across the deer park at night and the press intrusion this morning, he doesn't hide his irritation.

'Bunch of circling crows. Just let me catch them messing around.'

'I'm sure it was nothing,' I say.

'You can't know that for sure.' His eyes drop to the deep V of my blouse and the sheer fabric sleeves, which do nothing to hide the lacy strap of my bra. 'May I ask a few questions?'

'You always do.' Forever the ex-cop, although I'm not opening myself up completely.

'What happened on the night of Zane's birthday party?'

My mind slides back to that night, and I try not to leave anything out. 'He arrived late. Before nine. I remember him looking at his phone and going back into the house. It was around forty-five minutes before I excused myself to find him.'

His gaze turns rigid. 'You say he was downstairs for about forty-five minutes?'

'Correct.'

'Didn't his guests find that odd?'

'I suspect the firework display was a distraction, and so was the booze. There were plenty of other celebrities to gawk at.'

He smiles. 'Where was he?'

'In the study, smoking, like he was avoiding the crowd. I asked him to come upstairs to cut the cake.'

He sees me frown, and my eyes make a circle over his head.

'What?' he asks.

'Well, it was odd. I remember the evening being unusually warm, and Zane was wearing a jacket. He kept one hand in his pocket, like he was hiding something.'

Memories reel and spin as I try to think it through. The morning after his birthday party, he was red-eyed and angry. There was sand on the floor outside his study and a tiny spatter of blood on his shirt. When I pointed it out, he responded with a string of swear words that would make Glen Quagmire from *Family Guy* look like an angel.

'What about Nicola Gatlin?' he asks. 'I remember reading that a server recognised her from her picture. Meaning she was in your house that night.'

'That's the thing. No one else saw her. If there had been some kind of confrontation, someone would have reported hearing screams or cries for help.'

'Not with all those fireworks.'

'I hadn't thought of that.'

Ryan also reminds me that there was trace evidence belonging to over seventy people. That's not counting the servers and the company we used to bring tables and chairs. There were plenty of suspects to choose from, most of them improbable at best. The police investigated everyone, and no one showed any reason to hurt Nic.

'I don't see how anyone could have killed her, mopped up the mess and hid a body without someone seeing,' I say.

'You'd be surprised.' He smiles and I catch myself smiling back.

After our order arrives, instead of attacking his plate as Zane would do, he rests his back against the chair.

'By now,' he says, 'we both agree that Zane is the likeliest suspect because of his relationship with Nic. As suspects go, you could be a close second. A motive to do away with your husband's mistress. What foreshadows tragedy more than a woman scorned?'

I do a double take, trying hard not to care that Ryan might think I'm a murderer. 'I might be thoroughly pissed off that my husband cheated on me, but I'm not a murderous hag.'

'What about the housekeeper?'

'Stella? Hardly. She's five feet tall with early signs of arthritis. Dozens of witnesses saw her sitting at the bar after dinner, nursing her third glass of Baileys and slurring to the barman.'

'What time was this?'

'Around 6.30 pm, an hour before kick-off. I'd given her the night off.'

'As far as you know, did she stay at the bar?'

'That's what the barman said. Then she came outside for dinner, and during the fireworks she went upstairs for a rest.'

'What about Bizzy?'

'She was outside the whole time with a bunch of friends from school. They were screaming at every rocket.'

A bigger smile breaks across his face. We eat in silence for a few moments, and then I think of something else.

'I don't know if you're on *BarbedWire,* but one commenter said the police may have found what they were looking for. Something about DNA?'

'I believe they were alluding to your cellar steps.'

So, he is on *BarbedWire.*

'The best thing about grout,' he says, 'is that it's porous and absorbs all kinds of spills, like wine and blood. Perhaps that's why your husband had the steps removed.'

I lower my voice when a server seats a couple at a nearby table. 'We removed them because they were cracked and chipped. With staff in the house, we had to do something before someone had a serious accident.'

He leans even closer. 'Nicola Gatlin was the person your builder spoke to when he arrived for the first inspection. Three weeks later, when he came to do the work, it was Zane he saw and Zane who requested he remove three more flagstones. Any idea why?'

'No.' The word comes out as a whisper.

'I did a little research,' he says. 'The builder couldn't prybar the original flagstones out in one piece, and most of it was rubble by the time forensics caught up with it. They found a spot of blood on the wall that matched Nicola Gatlin's DNA. When I say a *spot,* I mean a pinhead. They also found traces on the edge of a writing pad in her desk drawer. Not enough to say she died on your property or that your husband killed her.'

I let out a rush of air. The only thing that makes this bad news better is the person giving it. I shouldn't be looking, but I can't help noticing how striking he is. I feel the colour flush to my cheeks, and I'm angry at myself for looking.

His gaze trains on me, and our eyes immediately clash. 'You said in your statement that Nicola Gatlin wasn't on the property or in the house.'

'I didn't think so, but now… well, now anything's possible.'

'Obviously, no one saw her enter the house. But what about a back entrance?'

'She always used the French doors to my husband's study.'

'Did they regularly meet there after hours?'

'I'm not sure I follow.'

'Did they conduct their intimate relationship on-site or off-site?'

'Both.'

I tell him about Nic, the day she started working for Zane and the day I saw them kissing. How gutted it made me feel, how insignificant. I recount the steamy text messages Nic had sent him on his phone and on his computer.

'It's not the first time he'd had an affair, was it?' The gentle tone of his voice takes me by surprise.

'No. There were a few others.'

'If your husband was inclined to wander,' he questions, 'don't you think it was a little dicey to hire a woman like her?'

'How do you know I hired her?'

'You were listed as the primary contact at Nicola Gatlin's agency.'

I feel my fingers digging into the palm of my hand, anything to stop the surprise showing on my face. 'She had good references. Her previous employer was also an actor in the same series.'

'Exactly, and Ms Gatlin had a relationship with him. See where I'm going with this.'

Reluctantly, I do.

His phone rings, and he glances at the screen but doesn't answer it. 'Did you like her?'

'She was very efficient.' I refuse to list all her talents, for there were many. 'What's not to like?'

I want to tell him that behind the gloss and phony devotion, a hardness lurked. But coming from me, it would only look off. I decide it's time to turn the conversation to him.

'Tell me about you,' I ask. 'How long have you been working at Lambeth?'

'Three years. As you know, I was in law enforcement before that. I liked the variety and the opportunity to make a difference. Then there's the corruption.'

He gives a rueful smile, his voice telling me about some incident in a car park fading over my thoughts. I've never seen eyes as blue as his. Maybe I have, but they seem bluer in the sunlight. Zane's eyes were so dark they were almost black, and the last time I saw him his face was full of hate. I realise that most of what Ryan is saying is becoming a blur, and I'm too embarrassed to ask him to repeat it.

'You've made quite an impression on me,' he says. 'A beautiful widow who wants to put everything behind her. It can't have been easy being married to a celebrity. While you may not be comfortable telling me everything, I want you to know you can trust me.'

Do I trust him? Only time will tell. I can't help but look around a busy restaurant. Anyone could be watching us from a dark corner, taking notes, and feeding the press.

'Last year, they mentioned…' He takes a long breath, lips circling around the exhale. 'The police mentioned your daughter was afraid of her father. That there may have been some child abuse.'

It hits me all at once. The terror… the fear… that everyone knew. I lower my voice to a whisper.

'The last thing she remembers is being chased around the house by a madman, and again in the car. It must have been terrifying for her. But that was the only time he ever… ever did anything like that. I'd rather not talk about it now.'

It's all I can do to stop myself from grabbing my handbag and bolting between the tables to get outside. But that would only bring more attention to me.

After lunch, he insists on paying, and we scatter to different sides of the car park.

Once I'm locked inside my car, I pull my phone out and check the latest comments on *BarbedWire*.

**Trending #InZane**

@CirceAtNight: These new rumours seem sus. Why would anyone believe Zane Osborne faked his own death?

@BantaBadger: Look at Elvis Presley? People still think he went into hiding. Trust me. There'll be a Sighting Society for Zane Osborne too.

@CirceAtNight: I keep thinking that maybe he was injured, and that someone had been taking care of him.

@BantaBadger: Don't you think everything related to Zane Osborne is shrouded in the darkest secrecy?

@HeyWhatsUP: He's dead. Why are we even talking about it?

# 8

# ZANE

I have all the time in the world to chat, but not with the police. Even though I have no obligation to go with them, it might seem rude if I don't.

'Is there something in particular you wanted to talk about?' I ask.

'Can I buy you a coffee?'

I'd rather he let me go so I can throw the markswoman's phone and radio into the sea. 'Sure.'

The lieutenant points to a small coffee shop, the one I'd frequented a few times to recharge my phone. Two officers standing in front of the counter turn and stare as we walk in.

The lieutenant points to a carafe filling with its first trickle and hands me a mug from the shelf. I want to say, "No thank you, I won't be staying," but I'm too scared to say anything at all.

'Name's Lieutenant Tulimaq,' he says.

Since he waits a beat, I tell him mine. 'Ted.'

I must have ogled the sandwiches and protein bars a few times before he hands me a plate. I grab a BLT, only I'm not tasting it as much as inhaling it. He places a second sandwich and four protein bars in a bag and pays the barista.

'Something for the road,' he says, studying both sides of my face.

I realise my voice is too loud, and he's searching for hearing aids, but the intensity of that gunshot still rings in my ears. The more I nod at his questions, the easier it is to appear unfriendly. He studies me, curiosity fighting his concern, and there's something about his look that scares me.

'Were you camping upriver?' He gestures to the table by the window.

I lower my voice. 'For a few months, yes.'

He watches me as I place my backpack on the floor. 'Whereabouts?'

'About five miles from the ferry.'

His eyes have an uncanny smile to them, although I suspect anything he says will be far from funny. He offers me sugar and cream from the caddy on the table.

'Like living on the land?' he asks.

'Yeah. For the same reasons as any hunter. To challenge myself.'

He nods slowly as if wondering why I hadn't come up with any of the clichés, as in bonding with nature. 'You like killing things?'

'Not for killing's sake, no. Taking the life of any animal deserves respect, and any man living out there would be grateful for the meat and skins.'

'Not every man is like you.'

He looks down at my backpack, and I suspect he's wondering why I don't carry a firearm. Provided the markswoman's police radio doesn't magically crackle into life, he won't ask to look inside.

Then his gaze alights on my thumb ring, which I'd forgotten to take off. 'You use a bow?'

'Yeah. Only it was stolen recently.'

'Sorry to hear that. Did you fill out an online report?'

'Not yet. No.'

He pulls a pad from his top pocket. 'Any idea who might have taken it?'

'No,' I say, maybe too quickly.

He studies me for a second. 'I'll need your full name, description of the bow and how many arrows. We'll open a file.'

I rattle off the answers. Every word feels like it sticks in my throat, because I don't want the bow to be found at all.

He snaps his notebook shut. 'I'll transfer your details into the system. Call me, because you're going to need the occurrence number.'

I take his business card and shove it deep in my pocket.

'So,' he says, threading the pen between his fingers. 'Where were we? Oh, yeah. I wanted to ask you how many shelters you've built?'

'A few.'

'Hard going, huh?'

'A while back…' To shake him off the track, I leave out the part that it happened to another contestant on *SOLO*. 'I built this stone fireplace with a good draft system. There was hardly any smoke, and with the overhang of stone at the top as a spark arrester, it worked great. Until one night, something started throwing sparks like the 4th of July. The boughs caught fire and, poof, the whole place went up in flames.'

'Tamarack,' he says, nodding. 'Burns *real* hot.'

'I even tested the wood to see what burned hotter than others, changing the boughs, dusting off the char.'

'You weren't tucking into a few mickeys?'

'I don't drink.' Another lie follows the last. I've seen hunters buy flasks of alcohol from the grocery store over here – yep, mickeys – only the thought of consuming that much makes me want to puke. 'String of bad luck, I suppose.'

'If it were me, I'd make an opening big enough for an unsplit log and some rocks to cut off the air. If I found a flat rock, I'd use it as a ramp and make another air access from outside. Easy to say in this subarctic climate. Long, harsh winters and brief summers, but of course you know that.'

I know spring is from March to May, and then there's a lag with August being warmer than July.

He gives me a look, half-way between pity and confusion. 'Can't say I ever saw chimney smoke in your neck of the woods.'

My neck of the woods? How far does his beat stretch?

He leaves the table briefly to grab the carafe from the counter for a refill. I notice his fingers are tattooed with two straight lines and a dot above each knuckle, like Atanarjuat's.

He gives me a top-up. 'Did you see anyone else out there?'

'Not so much seen as sensed.' I'm thinking of the first huntsmen I'd seen.

He stops mid-pour. 'Sensing is powerful.'

'I never got a good look at his face. It was too dark.'

'When was this?'

'A few times over the past four months.'

I realise why he'd detained me. Not because my face is doing its rounds on *Canada's Most Wanted*, but because someone else's is.

'So, this guy,' he says. 'Anything special about him?'

'Stocky, bundled up in winter gear, had a rifle slung across his back. Couldn't see what type.'

He ignores the conspiratorial stares from the other two officers. I hope the discomfort doesn't show on my face, but it's there, this unbreakable, ever-widening wall I've put up between us.

He shows me a mugshot of a bearded man with thick eyebrows and an aquiline nose, all the while studying my face. I shake my head.

I can't stop thinking about how long a body can last out there before a hungry pack of wolves picks the bones clean, digesting any evidence of foul play.

HOLLOWAY

Bones have their own story to
tell. You're not out of the
woods yet, pal.

I ignore Holloway and I ask the lieutenant the question he's hoping I'll ask. 'Who is he?'

'Gabriel Camphaug. Killed a few women over the years.'

'Sounds dangerous,' I say, hoping I'd done everyone a favour.

He gives me a slit-eyed look and then nods. 'Ah, well, if anyone's going to sniff him out, it's Sylvia Pedersen.'

I stiffen. The air seems to vibrate with insects that aren't there. He must see me swallow, because his eyes study my neck and then my hands right down to the dirt under my fingernails.

He rattles on about Pedersen being a sniper in the Marines and the cost of training people like her, but that can't be right. Then he nods like he's agreeing with himself and then turns to the others and nods at them, too. I try not to think of Sylvia Pederson buried under four feet of snow. I look out of the window at the dark grey clouds.

Make that six feet.

His head goes back a little, his eyes fixed on mine. 'You like living on your own?'

'I like the solitude. Gives me time to think.'

'You came here to get supplies? Or are you heading out somewhere?'

'I'm hoping to get to Prince Edward Island for a few weeks. Got a friend in Charlottetown. I hear it's nice this time of year.'

'Everywhere is nice this time of year.' A flicker of a smile. 'What does this friend do?'

'He runs art workshops from his gallery,' I say, knowing he's going to run any story I tell him through the system as soon as he gets the chance. 'Well, more of a shed in his back garden.'

'Does he have a website?'

'Rebel Studios, I think it's called.'

I've already done my homework. The place exists, and so does the guy. The only problem is I don't know him.

Tulimaq drones on about the harsh winters and mild summers and how it's something to do with the Icelandic Low and the Labrador current. As much as I like it here, a population of under four hundred is enough to tell me everybody knows everyone, and they're already getting to know me.

'If you don't like fish, there's always caribou, seals and dolphins,' he says. 'And snow crab. Probably not a usual menu item where you're from. Did you know that some of our European settlers came from Scotland? My sister married a McDonald.'

The mention of Scotland brings a vaguely threatening mood. While I don't have a Scottish accent, it summons a dozen scenarios – him assuming I'm far from home and whether I have a wife and child – but he doesn't. He goes off on another tangent about settlers and French-Canadian fur traders, and a young boy who froze to death over twelve years ago.

'So, where are you staying tonight?' he asks.

'Got any suggestions?'

He glances at my beard and my tattered jacket. 'There's a nice place around the corner. I'll give you a ride. It's the least I can do for hauling you off like that.'

His eyes drop again to my waist, and I glance down to see what he's staring at. It's a toss-up between the tear, which is spewing a cloud of down, or the flap of my pocket, which is tucked inwards, and where the yellow fletchings from the broken arrow have made an appearance. Bile squirms in my stomach, and I feel light-headed. Rather than try to conceal it, I drain my coffee and stand.

'Ready?' he asks.

He escorts me past two police cruisers half buried in the snow, the RCMP crown logo barely showing on the door. I catch sight of myself in one of the wing mirrors and the horror hits me. I look nothing like I used to. My cheekbones are enlarged, and dark circles have formed under my eyes. It'll take months for the healthy bloom to return.

The lieutenant beckons me over to the snowmobile, and I sit behind him with an undefinable sense of dread. Amid the roaring of the engine and a high-pitched whine, I find myself desperate for sleep. I can't remember the last time I was warmer than a cat in a sunny window.

The problem comes a few minutes later when I'm nudged awake as the Lieutenant pulls into a car park. I look up at a red-painted building with a white trim. He wasn't kidding when he mentioned the hotel was just around the corner.

'If you're flying,' he says, sitting tight on the snowmobile as I hop off. 'Hacker fares will save you some Loonies.'

I realise a Loonie is a Canadian dollar, but hackers?

'Good deals,' the Lieutenant clarifies. He drops a few coins into the palm of my glove. 'You'll need some change for the laundrette. The real world doesn't take kindly to bums. Even designer bums.'

He's right. I need a good scrub, and so do my clothes. A man like him must see a lot of things, but not a homeless person in a Burberry quilted jacket, recognisable by the rubber logo on the sleeve.

'Thank you. I don't know how to repay you.'

'When you're back on your feet, look me up and send me a care package for the next guy. Sound fair, Ted?'

'It does. I appreciate the coffee.'

'Good luck out there.'

It's clear to me that Lt Tulimaq knows I'm running from something. You're either a hunter or a crabber here. I'm neither. If he finds Pedersen's body, he'll naturally attribute her murder to Camphaug.

Unless he finds Camphaug's body first.

# 9

# LILJA

We all know how everyone loves the tiny spectre of mystery that exists within celebrity lives. I just wish it weren't in ours.

If I seriously believe Zane is trying to contact me, like some secret tapping signal from beyond the grave, that's my business. I keep coming back to one simple thing. If Zane lied about his death, was it because he couldn't live with the truth?

A strange orange dusk fills the room. Rain sheets against the French doors, a hard *tap, tap, tapping* sound as if a thousand tiny fingers are knocking on glass, begging to be let in. Because of the damp, the study smells faintly of wet brick and old tobacco – Zane's touch, which I have tried and failed to scrub from the room. None of it separates me from the decision I've made with Ryan; an open-ended contract where he'll provide personal protection to the family, including event and residential security.

I sink into the leather chair behind the desk and study our signature dishes tonight: filet mignon, roasted halibut, duck breast, Wagyu beef bourguignon and spring vegetable risotto. I'd be licking my lips in anticipation if I weren't so anxious.

Stella enters with two mugs, her hands steady, though I see the tremor in the porcelain when she sets them down.

'Chamomile,' she says. 'Thought it might help.'

'With what?' I ask.

'The stress of running a house and a restaurant all by yourself.'

'I've got you, haven't I?'

She gives a small, clipped nod and perches on the edge of the armchair opposite, smoothing her skirt with deliberate care.

She peers over her glasses. 'You've got that look.'

'What look?'

'Like you've done something.'

I resist the urge to smile. 'Ryan is moving his things into the stable flat. Before you say anything, let's not pretend he's here for anything other than security.'

She stares at me for a few seconds, long enough that a part of me thinks she can see right through me.

She puffs the air from her lungs. 'I still don't see why we need someone traipsing around the property. You've got locks and cameras. And, as you say, you have me.'

'Do I detect a little jealousy?'

'I just don't trust men with keys to other people's lives.'

'That's poetic,' I say. 'Also, a little dramatic. I won't be handing him the keys to the house.'

She doesn't laugh. Instead, her gaze drifts beyond the window to the hydrangea bed Zane tended so diligently. The sight of it used to bother me, but not anymore.

'I want you to feel secure here, Stella,' I say. 'You've looked after this house longer than I've lived in it. But things are changing. The press is circling, and someone's been in the garden at night. I'm not imagining it.'

She flinches, a slight shoulder twitch, nothing more. 'Wasn't there a reporter who ran across the lawn last year?'

'Stan Marriott, *DevonLive*,' I say

'Even I know he has legal procedures to follow, and breaking into a person's property isn't one of them. You should have called his boss.'

'Duly noted.' I walk around to the front of the desk. 'I can't predict how this new wave of information will affect us. Or for how long. But Ryan coming here will keep the press at bay.'

'It's…'

'Brilliant?' I suggest.

'I was going to suggest *expensive*. How much is all this going to cost?'

'We can afford it,' I say.

'As long as he's not planning to take pictures of the house and staff and sell them to the papers.'

'It's all in the contract,' I assure her. 'There will be no picture-taking of anyone or anything.'

Stella isn't known for her subtlety. She's uncompromisingly protective, which is why we all love her.

'You think Ryan will make you feel safer?' she asks.

'I think he'll make whoever's watching think twice.'

'Did you check his references?'

'I did. Impeccable.' The words *how impeccable* hangs in the air. 'Why? Do you think he's hiding something?'

She laughs softly. 'Isn't everyone?'

I draw in my breath, hardly able to believe I've just threatened her with the very thing she fears the most. Being replaced. I want to tell her it isn't what I meant, that there's no one else I could trust as implicitly as her, that all I want is for her to feel comfortable and loved. But my mind races ahead to her lack of focus and her tendency to be shut off from the rest of us.

'You've not been yourself lately,' I say. 'It's, well, it's just that you're not the same Stella anymore.'

She gives a start of surprise. 'What do you mean?'

'You seem to be distracted. It's difficult for me to reach you sometimes.'

'It's not my fault if I can't sleep!' she snaps. 'Sorry, love. I didn't mean to shout.'

I lean forward and take both her hands in mine. 'It won't do any harm for you to see Dr Wiesendanger, just for a check-up.'

A frown furrows her brow. 'What's he going to do? Give me a few sleeping pills and a pat on the hand.'

I know what she's worried about. She's worried that the doctor will find something wrong, like dementia. But it's far more likely to be burnout.

What happened last year affected all of us in different ways, and I can't expect Stella or any of us to be normal after that. I won't make an appointment behind her back. She might see it as a betrayal.

'All right. But you will tell me if you need anything?'

'I'm fine.' Her voice cracks slightly as she stands.

I slide my arms around her neck, and the tears that always seem just around the corner fill my eyes. 'I can't believe I've been so selfish. What must it be like for you to have to put up with all of us?'

She hangs on to me tighter than usual, her cheek resting against my chest. I want to recommend she takes the rest of the week off, but I daren't suggest it in case she thinks none of us want her around.

She pushes away from me gently and brushes an imaginary wrinkle from her jumper. 'When's Ryan coming?'

'Tomorrow. He'll walk the perimeter, maybe ask a few questions. Nothing invasive. Whatever happens, we'll get through this together.'

She nods and looks at her watch. 'Time you were upstairs.'

'I don't know what I'd do without you.'

I feel a strange tightening in my chest as I change into my chef's jacket. Not sadness. Something far deeper, a road I don't want to go down. I dread the day when my seventy-three-year-old house manager finally tells me she's retiring. There will be no one to gatekeep. It's comforting to believe that Stella will always be here, even when I feel I can't cope.

There's an accumulation of delectable aromas in the kitchen, chefs tasting and wowing each other's dishes. I retreat to my station to cook duck breast and Banyuls gastrique. While the sugar is dissolving for the caramel, I realise my decision to hire Ryan has more to do with my daughter's security than my own. He can drive her to school and ensure the press doesn't form a tight crush at the front gates and hurl obnoxious questions.

*How do you feel now your dad's secrets are out?*

*Were there any signs your father was losing it?*

*Did your dad kill Nicola Gatlin?*

I don't want Bizzy sticking her head out of the car window. Her answers range from deadpan to sarcasm, and her hand gestures are worse.

Of course, the past intrigues the press. National papers and

TV stations have requested interviews, all of which I refused to protect my family and my business. Whenever reporters crowded me outside the bank, they dubbed me the Ice Queen. But my face was frozen in terror, not glacial indifference. What they really want to ask is, when did everything unravel between me and Zane.

When I think back, I realise it's been years since we stumbled down the corridor like drunk teenagers, ripping at each other's clothes until we found a bed or a couch. I can't remember the last time he kissed me. I mean, really kissed me.

We became like two flatmates sharing a house, covering our bodies with towels in the bathroom and apologising for getting in each other's way. When we were together, I couldn't have felt more alone. We didn't hold hands; we barely touched, and sex was routine. When he blathered on about his acting, I simply zoned out. I hated the way he looked at women at parties, his eyes brazenly stalking them as if I didn't exist.

These same reporters will want to know if I still love him. I think about that question all the time. I loved who he used to be. Not what he became.

Stella's right. I need someone. Ryan's face flashes through my mind as a possible someone. But I don't have time for a man in my life. Forget the heartbreaker with the piercing blue eyes. Being single is the safest way to be.

Suddenly, I realised what I was feeling when Stella left the study. I would miss her more than anyone if she weren't here. The pain is so acute; it leaves me breathless.

I wish I could take her hand in mine and tell her that everything is going to be all right. But sometimes I'm not sure that it will be.

**BarbedWire - Trending #InZane**

@BantaBadger: You know what really breaks my heart? How people give so much airtime to Zane Osborne and ignore the Gatlins. So what if someone's seen him in Canada?

@Titmouse: Then you have the cast of *Play Him Play Her* to blame for that. Not one of them spoke out in support of Nic. NO ONE. Despicable.

@Banta Badger: I'm tired of anything Zane Osborne. Now he's playing the main character in the news! #InZane egotistical arsehole.

@HeyWhatsUP: He's probably sitting under a tree in Hyde Park, throwing back a bottle of whisky, half crying, half giggling.

@MiloMorales: Imagine his poor wife and family. That's who I think about.

# 10

# ZANE

I'm woken by a door slamming. The first sensation is my skin prickling from scrubbing off layers of dirt from the shower I had taken earlier. The second sensation is the feel of clean clothes against my skin and the smell of detergent in the fabric.

My head is thick, and I can't seem to untangle a knot of thoughts. In the silence that follows, the markswoman is foremost in my mind. Sick to the stomach doesn't come close to describing how I feel. I'm lucky to be alive, *lucky*, because if she hadn't fallen victim to the spring-loaded trap, she would have split my head open with a single shot. It seems like several days ago when it happened, but it was during the early hours of this morning.

The gun she carried reminded me of Lilja. Long, huffy silences often punctuated our arguments, and then she would verbally attack me for some trifling misdemeanour, firing both barrels with no warning. I was tired of her saying my work meant more to me than our marriage. If I'd done something different then would things be different now?

Okay, so I spent time with my scripts and my characters, and maybe, just maybe, got a little more enthused about them than I was with her. But it didn't mean I didn't love her. I get she had abandonment issues because of her father dying when she was little. Everyone has childhood issues; it's almost a rite of passage. Look at me.

Dad walked out when I was ten. Packed a bag and came out here to survive on the land. I tried looking for him in those very woods, imagining the notches on the trees were ones he'd fashioned all those years ago with his pocketknife. I thought I heard him yelling my name, but it was only the wind.

Atanarjuat told me that an Englishman had built the cabin a long time ago, but no one knew his name. According to Stan Marriott's news article from last November, they found Dad's remains along the banks of Big River, so I'll bet a bottle of Angel's Envy the cabin was his.

<pre>
                    HOLLOWAY

          That's all very entertaining,
          Zane. Don't you think it's
          time to get going?

                     ZANE

          Now? I've only just arrived.
</pre>

My phone rings. I sit up in the darkness and pause, staring at the screen with eyes gritty from sleep. It's 10.07 pm, which means I've slept through the entire afternoon and well into the evening. As soon as my bare feet hit the floor, the warmth seeps through my soles and up to my calves. Unbelievable bliss.

I accept the call and croak out a hello.

'It's me, Atanarjuat.'

The reason he's calling rattles around in my head. *Why is he calling now?* I jam the phone between my chin and shoulder while I pull on a sock.

'Everything okay?' I ask.

'The police were asking after you.'

My fingers tighten around the phone. 'You mean Tulimaq?'

'Yeah.' He exhales loudly. 'Seen us having coffee together a few times. Thought I knew you real well.'

I pause for a moment to catch my breath, trying to keep a lid on it. 'They're looking for some guy, right?'

'Yep. Killed a cop is what I heard.'

'They must be canvassing the area, trying to get information.'

I don't know who I'm trying to convince, him or me. There's a long silence before he speaks. When he does, his voice wavers as if it's about to break.

'Whatever you're looking for, I pray you find it. Look after yourself, Friend.'

After I end the call, I stare at the screen as a sweep of emotions takes me by surprise. The reason he called wasn't simply to see how I was. It was to warn me. The reality suddenly hits me. If Tulimaq questioned Atanarjuat, then he must suspect me. If he suspects me, it explains why he suggested this hotel to monitor me. If he's monitoring me, he doesn't want me leaving anytime soon.

'Shit!'

I can't breathe. I can't move. Keeping my head down is the most important thing, same as getting out of here on the next flight to Quebec tomorrow.

I throw my clothes on and ram the rest into my backpack. I'll have to make a mad dash for the airstrip, but the thought of hiding out in a tiny building until morning doesn't sound like a sacrifice I want to make.

I throw open the window, and an icy breeze blows off the rocky outcrops and ruffles my hair. I look up at the arching night sky and down again at deep banks of snow, which cover the property's outer perimeter, reducing parked cars to vague humps. Boulders and pine trees pockmark the ridge, and somewhere among them a man shoulders a gun, looking out over the harbour.

Seeing the man gives me the worst kind of anxiety. What if he's looking for me? Makkovik isn't the best place to hide with its small-town vibe. Which is why I need to leave now.

I creep downstairs and take the corridor leading to the reception area. Peering around the corner at the junction between the front door and a small conference room, I see a young man behind the check-in counter, his chin on his palm, watching the police out of the window.

His name tag reads Spencer Aua. What confuses me is distant laughter from the dining room and clinking glasses. Surely, the guests wouldn't be acting so nonchalantly with a burgeoning police presence outside.

There's a narrow passage to the left of the reception desk that leads to a rear car park. Since Spencer stares at the activity outside as if he's lip reading every word, I could simply slink past unnoticed, like a shadow brushing at the limits of his focus. If I did, would he remember anything about a guest with a backpack? Would the police come in and interview him, asking the inevitable question, had he seen me?

*Wait. There was a man. He was running to the back door. Middle-aged and with dark, wavy hair.*

It sounds too easy and insanely risky. Rather than err on the side of optimism, I stay put. Then what I've been dreading happens.

Two police officers enter the hotel, one male, one female. Lady Cop moves around the room, her gaze alighting on different objects, while Man Cop hovers next to the front desk, chewing gum and tapping his hand on the counter.

'Just routine,' he says. 'Nothing here, but we had to make sure.'

'Where do you think he went?' Spencer directs his question to Lady Cop.

'Probably up there.' She points at the ridge, which leads to a line of fir trees. 'It's curious to me how he got into the hotel and took off again. Are you sure it was him?'

The young man shrugs. 'It looked like him.'

They can't be talking about me, a bona fide guest who'd signed in earlier, ID and all. Otherwise, they would have pounded on my door and dragged me into one of the waiting cars.

She adjusts the radio on her shoulder. 'Do you do nightly inspections? You know, checking windows and doors are locked.'

'No.'

'Okay, because that might be a good idea. It's common courtesy to your guests.' She walks towards the front door, pauses and turns back. 'Was he armed?'

'I don't think so.' Spencer shrugs again.

'You say it was definitely him?'

'Yeah, that's what I said.'

Both officers exchange a look and then proceed back outside.

Spencer picks up his phone and starts talking to a friend. I assume it's a friend with the *you'll never guess what just happened* banter. He ducks into the office behind the front desk and shuts the door.

Now's my chance. As I make headway down the corridor to the glass door at the rear of the hotel, I notice a police officer standing outside with his back to me, his head angled to his radio, and blocking my only means of escape.

I back up slowly, and my backpack slams into a door wedged open with a shoe. I stumble inside and catch the door before the hydraulic hinge slams it shut. I search for a sliding door on the balcony, but there's only a window. To my right is a closed door, presumably to a bathroom, and on the opposite wall is a full-length mirror. Beyond that is a large double bed with a suitcase on a luggage rack.

The top layer of my conscious mind wonders why the occupant purposely left the door ajar. The second layer senses I'm not hearing what I should be hearing. Running water from the shower. A squeaky hinge forces me to back up towards the wall beside the bed, and I'm expecting the occupant to find an intruder in his room and raise the alarm. But it's not the bathroom door opening. It's someone entering from the corridor.

The mirror by the door reveals the reflection of a young woman, who pauses outside the bathroom. Wisps of black hair escape her ponytail, and she grins as if this is the most fun she's had in weeks. She shrugs off a full-length coat and reveals a leather bikini, if a few straps could be called a bikini, and slips into the bathroom.

While the occupant delights in his casual one-nighter, I run to the window and find the latch is jammed and no amount of jigging it back and forth will open it. I'm paralyzed with a unique form of terror. There's only one way out.

I creep past the bathroom and try not to look inside, but it's like the kitchen sink scene from *Basic Instinct*, and I can't help it.

At that moment, the man turns his head and looks at me, his face pinched in disgust. Rooted to the spot, all I can say is, 'Sorry, wrong room.'

I rush down the corridor to the rear door and teeter on the step and look out at swathes of snow as if I've entered a different dimension. The officer has disappeared, and all that remains is a subtle scent of tobacco. If hidden eyes follow me along the back road and I'm walking into a trap, I should know about now.

But no rough hands yank me back, and no one reads me my rights. I'm free to slip and slide down an icy road towards a white house, whose lawn is still wearing its stripes from last season's mowing.

There's an argument screaming in my head. *Where are you going to sleep now? A cowshed?*

Right now, sleeping on a bench in the airport sounds tempting. But the sound of tyres on gravel and the flash of headlights force me to duck behind a tuft of snow-covered grass. My stomach feels an undeniable tug of fear, and my head swims.

I squat in breathless agony as a car continues slowly down the lane towards me, the electric whirr of an opening window forcing me to keep my head down. Torchlight arcs over me and jabs the bushes, circling the area several times before the car stops. The static of a police radio crackles through an open window, but I can't decipher what they're saying.

Is it my story that has hit national and local news? Or has the press not judged me worthy of so high-profile publicity? I console myself with knowing that there are at least a billion other messed up people in the world who have made worse mistakes than I have. But those billion people aren't here in this tiny little town. I am.

Though frightening enough to cause me to shiver, my instinct tells me the police might not know much – if at all – to pursue a deadbeat like me. I can only assume that the case they're building is against Gabriel Camphaug; otherwise, Lt Tulimaq would have arrested me when he had the chance.

The car continues down the lane, brake lights flashing on and off as the officer's torch jinks from side to side. Then he speeds up and turns left to meet the main road.

Below me is a flat rock, sturdy-looking but easy to lift. It sits in a puddle of snow and mud, the perfect hiding place for what I have in mind. With gloved hands, I fumble in my backpack for the markswoman's radio and phone, and lifting the rock, I kick them underneath.

I quickly glance over my shoulder and start walking down the lane. I take out a packet of cigarettes and light one. My head swims with a fresh drag of nicotine, and I think twice about flicking the dog-end into an icy puddle. I stub it out on a rock and return it to the pack. Between the hotel and the main road, a siren wails, and I catch glimpses of blue flashing lights in the distance.

Somehow, through incredible odds and a good dose of luck, I'm a free man.

# 11

# LILJA

It's one thing to forget potatoes. It's quite another to receive a summons from a guest in the hall and not for a missing dish.

An unscheduled visit from DC Symonds is always unnerving and explains the watcher in the restaurant. Her navy jacket looks a little threadbare, and dandruff brushes her shoulders.

'Sorry to interrupt your busy evening.' Her eyes flick over my chef's whites. 'But I wondered if we could have a chat.'

She glances through the glass doors at the dining room, her eyes pausing at what would have been the portrait of a hare carrying a musket but is now an empty wall.

'How can I help?' I ask.

She exhales slowly, meeting my gaze squarely. 'The sightings of your husband in Labrador, which I'm sure you've seen on *Barbed-Wire*, aren't as farfetched as you might think.'

'I don't understand.'

'The owner of a café in Makkovik described a man who came in occasionally to charge his phone. He also bought cigarettes and whisky. Then he stopped coming. A few months later, one of the local hunters bought the same brand of cigarettes and whisky.'

'What's strange about that?'

'Bought by somebody who doesn't drink or smoke. I'd say it was strange. Apparently, this hunter regularly took food and medical supplies across the river to a friend out there. Someone who'd been living rough for quite some time. Someone who had lost a lot of blood.'

I feel numb, and sick, and confused. 'Are you implying that after being mauled by a bear and bleeding profusely, my husband is still alive?'

'I think we should look at all possibilities, don't you?'

A year ago, she brought me the remaining pages of Zane's diary, salvaged by the police. The more I think about it, the more I realise this kind of ruse had Zane's name written all over it. There was me thinking he'd died alone on some spit of land in the Northwest Territories, when all along he'd had help.

'You don't have any photos of Mr Osborne,' she says, while swiping through a few photos on her phone. 'Preferably one with a beard.'

'I hate to state the obvious, but can't you find a character photo of him on the Internet? Or use the ones the police have been circulating?'

'I'm interested in a close-cut moustache and goatee, like the one in the silver-framed photo that was on the table over there but now isn't.'

I know the photo she means, the one where Zane wore a ghutra and agal, and wore his hair long. He was actor Tekin Farouq's understudy in the West End stage production of *Tomorrow's War*. Tekin had a distinctive beard, almost as unique as Seneca Crane's in *The Hunger Games*. Why does DC Symonds need it?

Far from it benefiting her in whatever investigation she thinks she's doing; it benefits me, too. I need to know if Zane is alive and whether he's changed his appearance to something none of us have seen before. Like a shaved head with a single plait running down the full length of his head to his shoulders.

My hands are trembling, and I see she has noticed it, too. I hurry to the hall table and rifle through the drawers, but I already know it's downstairs in a box.

'Don't worry,' she says. 'You probably had a good clear-out after he left. Oh, I'm sorry. I didn't mean it like that.'

'No, of course you didn't. It's just awful. I'm in shock. We all are.'

Then I wonder if that's why she's here, to see how much of his stuff I've got rid of. The last thing I need is another whiff of a scandal to fuel the British public's imagination.

'Could it be in his study?' Her eyes dart towards the lower ground floor stairs.

My mouth goes dry, and fear squeezes the air from my lungs. His study? The last thing I want to do is let her loose in *my* study, but I don't want to appear uncooperative. She points to the stairs, asking for my approval without asking, and I nod and follow her. She clocks the empty corridor walls, which no longer hold Zane's film memorabilia, and which now display three floral watercolours.

'Lavender, cornflower and… What's this one?' she asks.

'Plumbago.'

She makes a satisfied little "Hmm" and continues into the study, where she makes an abrupt halt. 'Well, this is a change. Much more elegant than when he had it.'

My stomach flutters with panic. It seems I can't hide these alterations any longer. She doesn't want that photo any more than I want to explain why I needed to redecorate.

'I found every excuse to put it off,' I say, attempting a deep frown. 'Grief, work, exhaustion. But I had to address the damp. The smell – that awful mouldy smell – had got into everything, including his books. I had the fireplace updated. Rather cosy, don't you think?'

She nods. 'Very.'

But is it? Does she suspect it was a desperate attempt to widen the months between my husband leaving and now? I wish I could tell her everything and be done with it. But there are parts of my life that should remain private and not be laid bare for the public to read about.

For a moment I stare at the desk as if I see Zane sitting there, typing furiously on his computer, oblivious to me but the words in his head. I want to scream at him for not noticing me. He never *noticed* me.

'Lilja?'

I blink the memory away, and DC Symonds comes back into focus. 'Yes, I'm sorry. What were you saying?'

'The Tang horse.' She points to the top shelf of the bookcase. 'Herend porcelain, isn't it? Wonderfully witty ceramics.'

Although my mind says yes, my head barely nods. I can't stand the Zane noise anymore, what with the police officers going through all his papers last year – one of them demanding Nic's laptop, which I couldn't find, and then Zane's.

I told them he had become accustomed to deleting all personal correspondence, including emails to his therapist. Her last communication with him stood out above the rest. *Please don't contact me.* He was already beyond repair.

I'm surprised by the depth of my anger at his selfishness and how he'd left us to suffer the publicity. How can I tell DC Symonds that he wasn't the tall, handsome, charismatic man his movie photos made him out to be? That he had become a Charlotte Brontë character, austere and depressing and tragic. I found him lying on the study couch once, eyes open and staring at the ceiling as if he was locked in a cataleptic trance. Impossible to rouse.

Not that I didn't try. There was Bizzy's water gun.

Of course, his fans continue to regale each other with stories about his magnetism, his devilish sense of humour and his natural joie de vivre. What they don't know is how wicked he was to us.

I felt DC Symonds' hand on my arm. 'You okay there, Lilja?'

'Yes, I'm fine.'

'You look like you've just received some bad news.'

'I'm sorry, it's all so…'

'I know,' she says. 'With your husband gone, you must be feeling terrible.'

Terrible? What a bland word. I don't feel *terrible.* I feel ashamed. While she scans the room, I can't help thinking she might blame me for Zane's disappearance. That somewhere, inside that head she's saying, "It's always the spouse."

Then I remembered we came down here for the photo and somehow, she distracted me with watercolours and a tang horse. Next, she'll ask me about the portrait of the hare with a gun, which is stored in the stables with the rest of his stuff.

I make a show of going through every desk drawer, jolting a

mug of lukewarm tea over onto the fine blue leather blotter, and frantically mopping up the spill with a handful of tissues. All the while, she's watching me closely with those sharp eyes of hers.

'Nothing from the set of *Tomorrow's War*, I'm afraid.' I stalk to the bookcase and open a cupboard beneath. 'But here's the picture we used to have upstairs.'

She holds out her phone. 'Mind if I take a photo?'

'Not at all.' I take it out of the frame and lay it on the desk.

She takes her time. 'That kills two birds.'

Two birds? What was the second?

'I wanted to ask you…' She pauses for a few seconds. 'Have you received any strange calls or texts?'

I suspect she knows I have, and I nod.

'I'd like you to be very brave and talk to the person, engage them in conversation. Just in case it's Zane. I don't have a clear picture of his movements, so I can't say anything more. But I know this. If my source is right, your husband may try to contact you. He can't stay off the grid for long. He'll need a job, which means,' pointing to the photo, 'a new face.'

If Zane is alive, he could come after me and do irreparable damage to all I've built in the year he's been away. I need more information than, "I can't say anything more."

'Did your colleague get a description?' I ask.

She swipes through her phone and lands on a single photo, which had been taken in a car park with a large stand of spruce trees in the background. It's grainy and hard to make out, but the subject, freeze-framed against a dark sky, had been photographed covertly. He wears a padded jacket and carries a backpack, and over his shoulder is a bow. There's something about his hair – the colour, the thick, wavy texture I can still feel between my fingers, and a beard streaked with grey.

It is him.

It's definitely him.

I don't want it to be. The horror of my husband, the perpetrator of such a violent crime, being alive is too awful to stomach. I stand very still, staring at this strangely familiar man.

'I expect this is bittersweet,' she says.

'Surely a much more likely scenario is that he's dead.'

'Because you're afraid he is, or because you'd rather he was?'

I must be staring at her blankly, my whole manner on high alert. Is she hoping to uncover secrets that aren't hers to share? Is she silently accusing me of setting something in motion to betray Zane?

It's no use trying to defend myself. Because it's true. I have.

**BarbedWire - Trending #InZane**

@CirceAtNight: Am I the only person who has absolutely no desire to watch *Play Him Play Her* now that Zane Osborne isn't in it?

@Titmouse: I suspect you've seen little of Ozzie on TV then, or you'd probably not make that statement.

@CirceAtNight: OMG it's like the worst ever series with the worst ever actors. It's so bad it would be over the top for a parody!

@Titmouse: Good grief! Let the rest of us enjoy a good crime series without your comments coming into our feed. But I'll block you anyway!

# 12

# ZANE

I walk along a narrow road, where a few houses and service buildings are lit by lanterns. In this pristine wilderness and under the northern stars, the airport is little more than a two-storey steel garage and a small waiting area, its runway lights flickering over coarse gravel.

Anthracite clouds blow in from the north, and the first drops of rain fall, hard as pellets against my cheeks. I duck inside the airport's front door, my boots skidding in the snow. An empty bench by the window looks enticing. I place the backpack next to me, toss my coat over it and find a charging port for my phone.

There's a press article published last year about my death, including a few obituaries, which I find odd since they don't have a body. Then a news piece about the definition of incapacity, which apparently includes being missing.

Claudia's Law, named after a chef, Claudia Lawrence, who went missing in 2009, allows families to manage the financial and property affairs of their loved ones, even if no human remains are found. It's now possible for the courts to issue a declaration of death after 90 days. I hadn't thought to appoint a financial power of attorney to handle my personal affairs, so when my undemonstrative and chilly wife applies to the court, she will inherit.

THE TIMES
**Celebrity Zane Osborne's estate
overseen by his wife**

Zane Osborne, celebrity of the Netflix hit series *Play Him Play Her,* is thought to have died along the lower reaches of Big River, Labrador, about twenty-one miles south of Makkovik. Every effort has been made to locate his remains, including a local team of investigators.

Osborne was embroiled in a clandestine affair with his assistant, Nicola Gatlin. After she disappeared and was later found dead, his agent says he had 'withdrawn from his role in *Play Him Play Her* and was recovering in a cottage in Scotland.' She also says, 'his actions have come close to ruining him and his marriage.'

Two days later, The Sûreté du Québec confirmed he had passed through immigration, making his actions appear suspicious to police. A tracker located a man-made shelter south of Makkovik and found a ripped sleeping bag stained with a large quantity of blood. DNA matched it to Osborne and concluded he must have died from a bear attack. His diary was also recovered at the scene and has been confirmed by his wife, Lilja Osborne.

After 90 days, Osborne's wife will become legal guardian of his estate, estimated to be worth several million pounds.

Well, shit. I stare at the article, believing things couldn't get any worse. Rereading the piece makes me feel uneasy. I've never been able to reconcile the image I portrayed to the press with the real me. Even my co-star Marschōne Robinson referred to me in the past tense, commemorating my accomplishments on social media. His comment – *Suddenly - tragically - Zane is assumed dead, mauled by a bear* – seems overly dramatic. But wasn't that the point?

I grab a protein bar from the care pack Lt Tulimaq gave me and wash it down with a slurp of coffee. There's no one around except for staff and two pilots making their way out to the car park.

                    HOLLOWAY

          See the woman over there? The
          one with the blue shirt and
          the badge? She's been staring
          at you for the past fifteen
          minutes.

I doubt anyone's been staring at me, least of all ground crew who are busy checking people in.

                    HOLLOWAY

          Maybe she's checking to see if
          your ID is valid. Maybe you
          should take a look.

I stare straight ahead and line her up in my peripheral vision. She's petite and dark, rather like Nic. She's typing something on the computer and talking to a young man with a backpack.

                    HOLLOWAY

          I bet the thought of her look-
          ing worries you.

The thought of her looking makes me shit scared. End of story. Either she was looking, or she wasn't, but she isn't now. I take repeated glances at the check-in desk, psyching myself up for an officer to ask me to step into a private room. The hairs on the back of my neck itch with the certainty that there are eyes on me.

I think of Nic and wonder how furious her family are with me. I had committed an unforgivable act, and because of my cowardice, they will always have Nic's washed-up remains lodged in their imagination.

My head whirls with images of home. The long sweeping drive, the elegant façade and the fairy lights at night. There was magic in it. I'd thought I'd been careful with the home security footage, eradicating all evidence of my comings and goings, not to mention Nic's. I knew how to cut, pause and loop, and I'd altered all the dates of the footage. Although I'm not naïve enough to pretend forensics haven't pieced it all together.

I wish I could go home. But Lilja must hate me for being irresponsible and so utterly selfish.

HOLLOWAY

```
Be realistic, Zane. You can't
go back. If you did, they'd
throw you in a tiny little
cell and nail your privates to
the wall.
```

The one thing I was determined to avoid last year was Bizzy seeing her father being handcuffed and driven to the local nick, like all those felons we watched on TV. If Lilja wants me to stay away – and I'm pretty sure she does – I will.

It's time to go off-script. I lean my head against the seat and watch the sky light up in the storm. I'm lulled by the patter of rain against the window and drift off.

It seems like only seconds later that I'm jerked awake by the hum of activity, and my hands instinctively reach out to clutch my bow. Then I remember where I am.

A woman stands in front of the window, wearing a red jacket and thick-framed glasses, her phone pressed to her ear. She turns and glances at me before walking away.

My heart pounds, and I'm holding my breath. Had she taken a photo of me while I was asleep?

<pre>
                 HOLLOWAY

        Calm down! Nobody wants to take
        a photo of a scruffy old man
        cowering on an airport bench.
</pre>

Now that the rain has stopped, orange streaks slice through a navy sky, and I can see white-capped peaks in the distance. It's almost time to board.

I go in search of the check-in desk and ask if my backpack needs to go in the hold. The woman smiles, although I can't quite read her expression. She must have seen plenty of men with long beards and unruly hair, but not one with ill-fitting clothes and cheeks sliding into jowls.

'Sir, just board with your pilot from gate 1.'

There's only five on our flight, and while I wait, I scroll through old comments on *BarbedWire*.

> @CherylAdams: Zane vanished after Nicola Gatlin's body was found. Now we know why.

> @Titmouse: He's not guilty. He can't be.

> @CherylAdams: Then why didn't he stay and fight his case?

> @CirceAtNight: It doesn't look good for him, all this running and hiding.

> @HeyWhatsUP: If he really is dead, what a waste of a brilliant career.

> @MiloMorales: Ye of little faith. Why are you so suspicious?

Blimey. Milo is the only one in my corner. If he only knew…

A week after I'd left the country, my wife's Instagram page had one post with a selfie of us, our cheeks pressed together. The comment, *why couldn't it have always been like this?* elicited hundreds of questions.

*Had Zane ever shown any aggression during your marriage? Was he moody, inclined to get his own way?* These first two questions got a no from her, but it was the third that makes me shudder. *Were you ever afraid of him?*

Lilja responded. *When he got into character, it terrified me. He was so convincing, so terribly dark. Nic put up with a lot, but where she had the experience to talk him down, I didn't. I'm so sorry about what happened to her. To think anyone could do something so vile, so utterly inhumane to another human being deserves the death penalty.*

My wife was punishing me in the cruellest and most elaborate way. If living in another man's skin, with another man's name, isn't a death sentence, I don't know what is. She can't keep it up forever unless she says I attacked her and has photos to prove it.

If she suspects I'm alive, will she set me up on social media for something I didn't do?

My mind skitters back to Christmas two years ago when I smothered her herby Hasselback potatoes with HP Sauce. The look of horror she gave me… I could have aimed a large Brussels sprout into her open mouth.

She often accused me of shirking my responsibilities and checking out of our marriage. Punishing me for the slightest offence. Okay, shagging another woman isn't a slight offence, it's a deeply wounding one, and I deserved to be punished for what I did. But pushing her against a wall isn't attacking her. Nor is shaking her like a rag doll to stop the hysterics. How many times had I done that? Once? Twice? It wasn't like it was a regular thing. The word 'sorry' rages like a pinball inside my head, but now it's too late to tell her.

I can't seem to fill the gaps in my memory. It's like layers and layers of mousetrap cheese where the holes don't line up. She's in the thunder and the lightning and in the mizzle after a storm. A

Nordic blonde – graceful, slender, single-minded. Her voice doesn't stop grinding in my head, a voice that insisted I was chasing dreams I'd never catch.

But I caught one. The dream I manifested loudly to the universe was when we were walking together on the beach after we got engaged. Fame. There are photos of me with my co-stars or doing the red carpet at a posh hotel, pretending to look engaged at press junkets and smiling into a journalist's lens.

'Over here, Zane.'

'Left side. Give us the left side.'

'Big smile, Zane. Let's see those pearly whites.'

It seems like ages since my last photo shoot. Where I would stand on a street in a Tom Ford suit, posing in front of the camera.

I felt special.

I felt strong.

I felt excited.

Everyone else had to park in the shitty spots outside the studio, but not me. They reserved my parking space and washed and detailed my X6 once a week.

I had many good years of it until my agent dumped me. Now I don't know what to do without a script. I try to be careful not to fine-tune myself to Holloway's normal, but now I'm wearing it like a fingerprint.

Then I hear him laugh because I'm talking to myself again.

Judging by the airport lounge, which is slowly filling up with passengers, so did everyone else.

# 13

# LILJA

I look out of the bedroom window at the frost-glittery lawn. The lapwing is by the pond, standing in one-legged silence. Even in the grey light of day, the plumage has a bluish-purple sheen, as if the bird has preened itself in time for Ryan's arrival.

While doing my hair and makeup, I listen to the news on my phone. *20/20* and *Prime-TimeLive* are running a special about Makkovik, a small fishing village in Labrador, and how someone may have spotted Zane there. There's a photo of a clean-shaven version of him taken a year ago with an accompanying press release. But I doubt he looks like that now.

My imagination tries to present an image of him emerging from a gunmetal mist, running through the long grass of some meadow, free at last. Then the vision separates into tiny pixels and *poof!* – it's gone altogether.

As I turn back into the room, I hear a creaking floorboard from somewhere down the corridor leading to two spare rooms we rarely use. The sound is deliberate, as if whoever caused it had changed their mind.

A shiver crawls under my skin.

When I walk along the corridor and peer into each room, everything is quiet and empty. I tell myself the house creaks, stiff as old knees, but can I be sure?

I listen for the sound again to set my mind at rest. Nothing. I let out a sigh that's a little disappointed and annoyed, but mostly relieved.

After breakfast, I take my coffee and sit on the front steps. The air is damp, and fog has drifted inland, obscuring the beach from view. Ryan's car, a sleek black Range Rover, cruises up the drive. He gives me a broad grin through the open window and asks me where he should park.

'Just follow the signs to The Forge,' I say, pointing to a curve in the drive. 'I'll meet you there.'

I find his car in front of the flint and brick barn with a stable door for an entrance. The top half is open, and he's leaning in to get a better look.

He hears my footsteps on the gravel but doesn't turn. 'Nice place.'

'It's got a large double bedroom and bathroom upstairs. Just watch your head on the beams.'

His eyes cut to me, and he grins. 'Big double bed, you say?'

'I said large double bedroom. It runs the entire length of the barn.'

'Good,' he says, 'because I haven't slept in weeks. Well, you don't when you're sleeping in a single bed and your roommate's drumming until the early hours.'

He wears a light blue shirt, which matches his eyes perfectly, a jacket slung over one shoulder, and a tasteful tie. He stares at me for a second longer than necessary.

'It's been a long time since I've lived on my own. About two years. I was living with my girlfriend until things got tough.'

I want to ask about the girl, where she is now, and if they're still in touch. My expression must register interest because he answers for me.

'She ran off with someone else. It wasn't the first time.'

'I'm sorry.'

I don't want Ryan wondering why I have an intense interest in his ex, so I don't ask more questions. But he tells me anyway. A few words stand out: *flighty, exotic, impossible to pin down.* The type of woman you can't compete with. The type that exudes the mystery all men dream about.

'I'm mad at myself,' he says. 'Mad for dating a blonde bombshell and mad for not listening when my gut was telling me something was off. You think you can change them, but you can't.'

The subject is strangely personal for his first day at work. Before my brain can summon up any words, he looks across the lawn to the deer park and scrunches up his nose.

'Holy shit, I'd forgotten how big this place is. How many acres?'

'Roughly ten.' I point out the nursery garden, the east and west lawns, and surrounding fields. It's important that he learn the full scope of the land for which he's responsible. 'Need any help unloading?' Not that I want to help, but it seems impolite not to offer.

He waves it off. 'No, it's fine. It won't take me long.'

I'm curious about how much stuff he has in his car, but the back windows are tinted, and I can't see anything inside.

'I just have one rule,' I say. 'No smoking indoors.'

'Oh, I don't smoke.'

'Glad to hear it. If you drink coffee, I'll have a pot ready in the study.' I'm about to leave when he asks me another question.

'Who lives in the other barn?' He points to the old stables diagonally opposite his new home.

'No one. It's just storage.'

My daughter insisted we consign Zane's extensive wardrobe to one stall, and I'm not in the mood to tell him. Or that his furniture and books are slowly gathering cobwebs. Bizzy won't have anything in the house that reminds her of her father. Not even the Tiffany lamp he used to have on his desk.

'Do I call you Mrs Osborne?'

'Everyone calls me Lilja. My mother's Swedish,' I add, as if it should make a difference.

Then, I give a parting smile. As I walk away, I don't hear the clatter of gravel under his feet. Either he's scrutinising the grounds or me. While he knows all my backstory, and Zane's, from stalking our social media accounts and learning everything there is to know about us, he is uncharted territory. Best to keep dancing out of his reach for as long as I can.

The thought doesn't stop me from drifting into a reverie where

Ryan and I become friends. Close friends. We go for walks on the beach, and I cook, and we stay up late, drinking wine. What impresses me is that he's the type of man who'd open doors for you, pull out your chair and hand you a rose from the vase on the table. He's also the type to handle a high-powered rifle and make you feel safe.

I try to see him as an asset, someone who will be with us for many years to come. But it's nothing but a foolish daydream.

**BarbedWire - Trending #InZane**

@BantaBadger: What does everyone think about the Makkovik sighting? I think it could be a genuine lead.

@Titmouse: I'm excited and drooling openly. It could be him. It really could.

@CirceAtNight: So, you didn't block me then? @ Titmouse.

@SherylAdams: The guy in that photo looks like Jase from *Duck Dynasty*.

@HeyWhatsUP: To be fair, we only know what the press has told us, which is going to be a HEAVILY skewed version of the truth.

# 14

# ZANE

The plane – a DeHavilland DHC6 Twin Otter – is half full, and I grab a seat next to the left propeller, my backpack stowed in the nose. It's dark outside, and ripples of grey clouds cover the sun.

I stare out of the window and watch as the land recedes. By the time we're airborne, I need a stiff drink, but something tells me there's no alcohol on this flight. Just a few snacks. With several stops, each on gravel runways to drop off parcels or pick up a passenger, sleeping isn't an option.

I try to scrape away the remnants of the day, but the images remain like ghosts. While the scenery changes around me, it remains the same for the dead markswoman. The towering trees above were her last visual of earth.

The thing about killing someone is the continual pause and replay. I don't know how many minutes I lay there after the gun went off, a window of time where I blanked out, staying down in case she pulled the trigger again. When she didn't, I assumed the first shot was accidental. A sudden reflex at seeing movement.

I push the visuals out of my mind. As my life on Big River fades into the background, I try to prepare for my new future.

After we touch down at Natuashish, the pilot announces break time to refuel the plane, and off we all trot into another tiny airport building to take a leak and grab a snack. Once aboard again, a woman walks down the aisle and sits next to me, silver-grey hair and red lipstick, strikingly beautiful. She wears a fur-lined jacket,

Louis Vuitton, at a guess, and now and then I smell traces of Jean Patou. I'd say she was early fifties, give or take a little cosmetic help.

We take off again, and I watch my pale reflection in the window, eyes sunken into their sockets. My secrets have transformed me from family man to villain, and I don't feel safe talking in case some word, some tiny facial tic, gives me away.

I take a sip of water, my eyes straying to her phone where a book she studies catches my eye. *The Demon of Unrest* by Britain's favourite celebrity interviewer, Amanda Yeboah. A man's face dominates the front cover, with dark eyes and a strong, symmetrical jawline. I'm blindsided by how familiar that face is, impossibly youthful, how his life had led him to stardom because, unlike me, he isn't a wanted felon. The subtitle: *Life with the Invincible Marschöne Robinson* gives me a jolt.

HOLLOWAY

Since you're dead, you can't
blame Amanda for writing about
someone else. Better hope none
of these carefully curated
chapters hint at your involvement in murder.

Beads of sweat break out on my forehead, and a wave of heat rolls up my neck. I would have done anything to be the face on the cover of that book. *Anything.*

Just as I'm pulling myself together, the woman turns her shoulders slightly, angling herself towards me. I hope I won't have to endure her gaze for the next few hours, as it flits over my tatty jacket and threadbare jeans. I freeze, waiting for her to say – you're the man who killed Nicola Gatlin – to say *something*.

'Marjorie Harper.' She holds out a hand.

'Ted.' I study baby blue eyes with a dark limbal ring.

'Are you a hunter?'

'Occasionally, yes.'

'Anything worthy of an award?'

'Afraid not.'

She locks eyes with me for a second and then smiles. 'I don't know how you people do it. Must be freezing out there. At least you won't have to kill your dinner tonight.'

I return the smile and then rest my head against the seat. My head is throbbing, and my anxiety is really warming up now. Out of the corner of my eye, I watch her swiping through the book's front matter to the first chapter, where the words *Dead In The Water* produce a shimmer of sweat on the surface of my skin.

<pre>
                    HOLLOWAY

          I'll bet she knows who you are.
          If she does, there's only one
          way to shut her up.


                     ZANE

          What do you mean?


                    HOLLOWAY

          I wouldn't let her off the plane
          if I were you.


                     ZANE

          Oh, great. So now you want me
          to snuff the life out of her.


                    HOLLOWAY

          Hell, yeah! Haven't you always
          wanted to strangle an arsehole?
</pre>

                    ZANE

Not this arsehole.

                  HOLLOWAY

Come on, you've done it in your
head countless times.

              (snorts)

Remember that horrendous review
you got in *People Magazine*?
You must admit, the visual
you implanted in my brain was
quite graphic and quite brilliant. Covering a journalist's
head with a plastic bag and
taping him to a chair for an
entire weekend takes great
imagination.


                    ZANE

It was obscene.


                  HOLLOWAY

As for Ms Harper, she's probably a PI sent to find you.
That's one dangerous travel
companion.


                    ZANE

How original.

```
HOLLOWAY

For heaven's sake, stop sweat-
ing.  You're  giving  yourself
away.
```

I'm too wound up to sleep. My brain is still chugging, and my body is on edge. I stretch out my legs and sit up a little, and Marjorie takes it as a cue to keep talking.

'Awful about the woman that went missing. The problem is serial killers look just like everyone else. You never know when you could be sitting next to one.' She laughs a little too forcefully and taps me on the arm. 'Oh, I didn't mean you. That would be silly. But you know what I mean.'

Then I think: *I'll have to throw in some fake smiles here; otherwise, a blank stare will only invite distrust.* There is something about her laugh that reminds me of Nathan Lane's character in *The Birdcage*, and my grin comes naturally.

'The dead giveaway, of course, is that they don't have friends,' she says. 'They're always inserting themselves into the investigation. That's what John Walsh said, you know, the guy on *America's Most Wanted*.'

I nod and give the briefest of smiles. My wife doesn't have any friends, well, not since I did what I did. Does that make her a serial killer?

While she taps her phone and tells me all about Marschōne Robinson, how utterly absorbing, and how magnetic the son of a bitch is, I'm so tempted to put a hand over her mouth and silence her for good. But there are too many witnesses.

Something in her book must have distracted her because she goes eerily quiet mid-sentence and brings the phone closer to her face. My limbs feel heavy as if I'm wading thigh-deep in water, and my hands, which were flat on my lap, are now curled into tight fists.

HOLLOWAY

You know what's weird. She's
no idea she's sitting next to
a serial killer.


ZANE


Not now, Holloway. *Please* not
now.


HOLLOWAY

Look, she's turning over another page. What if it's the
one with your TV series poster?

I torture myself with thoughts of how my life would have panned out if I hadn't run from sunny Dawlish Warren and simply kept my past sins a secret. Why hadn't I owned up to the police about arguing with Nic in the cellar and then blacking out? There's nothing wrong with arguing and not remembering.

Now I'm sitting here, working up a sweat and waiting for the inevitable. Marjorie will turn over that page and see one of my headshots and blab to the pilot that there's a deadly killer on board. The thought presses down on me, crushing me with its force.

I face the window, hardly daring to breathe, watching a bed of fluffy white clouds and wondering if this is the last time I'll ever see them. My eyes feel heavy, and my chin dips to my chest, and I'm aware of a sensation of falling.

Suddenly, I feel someone grabbing my arm.

'Sorry, I didn't mean to wake you,' Marjorie says. 'But we're landing.'

'We are?' I try to gain control of my racing heart.

'That was some dream you were having. Something about a sniper. You poor thing. PTSD?'

'I nod.'

'Vietnam will do that to you.'

I look that old?

A voice comes over the loudspeaker, announcing Sept-Îles. Marjorie throws her phone into her handbag and buttons up her coat. She sees I'm not buttoning up mine and naturally assumes this isn't my destination.

'Well, good luck,' she says. 'It was nice talking to you.'

I watch her crossing the tarmac with her bags. Worry gnaws away at me. She could have seen the movie poster. Even if she had, would she have made the connection between a smooth-faced young man and a bearded one with sagging skin and protruding bones?

If so, how can I know she won't alert immigration, let alone tell the police?

# 15

# LILJA

I set a tray of coffee and mugs on the table, plump up the cushions and print out a copy of our former security report. There are bound to be blind spots and rusted-out camera housings to take care of. It's a full-time job.

It's almost 10.00 am. Time to plan a quick tour of the grounds, depending on how many questions Ryan has. Where he thinks it best to set up his security equipment, assuming he has quite a selection in that large SUV of his. We can visit the pub for lunch, and I can show him around the village, or we can walk on the beach.

Then I realise how stupid it all sounds, an invitation to bond, get closer, like someone who doesn't realise how much they love pork and apple sausages until they've tried them.

Yet there's no denying the attraction between us. Daydreaming or not, I'm simply acknowledging how lonely I've been feeling, how shocked I was at Zane's death, and even more shocked at the possibility that he's still alive. Perhaps I'm not in the right place to consider a new relationship, even if Ryan were open to it.

I need to stop fooling myself. This is the life I've always wanted, and I won't lose it all now.

There is something about my reflection in the bathroom mirror. For a moment, it's another face I see, the younger me, the me I thought I'd lost. I was so used to seeing the dowdy, unhappy version that I had given up ever seeing anything else. Somehow today, I look young, as if my skin holds an ethereal glow.

There's a knock on the door, and Ryan walks in holding a note-pad and pen. He wears a jacket over a polo shirt, his security badge hanging from a lanyard. I offer him a cup of coffee and a seat on the other side of my desk.

'Keys,' I begin, handing him a set for The Forge. 'The wine cellar is on a fingerprint lock. Only my family are authorised. The outside door by the garage is the same. There is an old key in the lock, but it's simply for aesthetic purposes.'

Ryan takes notes. 'Any other structures on the property?'

'Not ones that need keys. The nursery garden and shed are easily accessible.'

'What about gates?'

'The front gate has a PIN, but any others leading to the mead-ows and deer park aren't padlocked.'

'Then they'll need to be.' He scribbles something on his pad. 'What about cameras for the entire perimeter?'

'Absolutely, if it can be done.'

He nods, tapping his pen on his pad. 'Have you always lived here?'

'I was born here. So was my sister. We lived in this house until my mother remarried, then we all moved to the beach house. It took a long time to get over the death of my father. I think this place often reminds her of him. She and my stepfather do the finances, and my brother-in-law runs the restaurant. We all help in our own way.'

He shuts his notebook. 'You've done amazing things with this place since…'

'Since Zane left?' I feel the oddest sensation in my gut, like a fist squeezing all the life out of me. I suspect my face must be going through several expressions before I land on the right one. Relief. 'Yes, we have. Keeping busy helps.'

I look at his sallow skin and long dark eyelashes and wonder why I feel so drawn to him. I try not to let my gaze linger because if he returns my stare, I won't be able to break the spell.

'I knew Zane very well,' he says, 'although I was told recently that he had some kind of personality disorder.'

'I suppose you could put it like that.'

'Either he did, or he didn't.'

'Not in the way you think. It wasn't dissociative identity disorder in the sense of multiple identities. It was the acting, the role, the whole sordid world of Ethan Holloway. Yet, for some unfathomable reason, Zane wanted to *be* Ethan Holloway. When he was in the thick of it, rehearsing the scene where Holloway drugged his patient and hid her body, those were the worst months of my life. After his assistant died, I couldn't help but think it was him mimicking the same scene. I know how awful it sounds, but he was angry she was taking secret pictures of him on her phone and publishing teasers on social media.'

'Teasers?'

'Partial images; hands, feet, blurred backgrounds, so her followers had to guess who she was with.'

'How did you find out about his affair?'

How much of Zane's womanising does Ryan know? He could conceivably have driven Zane and Nic to our house in London. He could have seen them kissing on the back seat and kept all those images locked in his head, sworn by a confidentiality agreement to keep everything secret. If so, Ryan must hate himself for asking that question.

'I saw them kissing right there on the floor,' I say, pointing to the Persian rug, which I have yet to replace. 'They were reading lines to prepare for intimate scenes he'd be doing with his co-star on a closed set. He told me it meant nothing, that it was all part of the script, a necessity to make his role more believable.'

'You weren't buying it?'

'No. They were sleeping together well before she started working here. They met at a party I was too ill to attend. Something must have happened because when he came home, instead of coming upstairs to bed like he usually did, he came down here and slept on the couch. I know because I checked.'

The memory unsettles me. Nic wanted Zane all to herself. Only I was in the way. A mental question scratches itself into my subconscious. If Zane had been in love with Nic, if he had taken the relationship as seriously as she had, would he have got rid of me instead? I realise Ryan is studying me, his head aslant, his eyebrows knotted. To shake him from his reverie, I continue talking.

'The press was brutal, camping in the lane for days, doing unethical things like calling out to my daughter in the garden, anything to get a story. Now, all I want is for her to feel safe. That's why you're here.'

'To make sure the press doesn't make a habit of it.'

'Right. I'd like you to drive her to school and back. She also has football practice for a school match coming up in a couple of weeks. It's all on the schedule.'

Ryan stares at me long enough for my cheeks to flush. 'It'll be my pleasure.'

Good, I think, because there will be plenty of chauffeuring, especially now the country is interested in Zane Osborne again, media attention spreading out as far as Canada.

I take a deep breath to compose myself. We talk about the surrounding acreage, the trail hikes and where I like to go running. All it takes is a look from him to throw me into overdrive, and I wonder if my heart will ache if I don't get to see his gorgeous smile every day.

He puts his coffee down on a coaster. 'I hope I'm not being intrusive, but when I was here last year, I often wondered if you were happy.'

'Why? Did I walk around with a sour look on my face?'

'Not sour. Sad.'

I don't know why I'm suddenly confiding everything. His smile is infectious, and I can tell after a few minutes of talking that he's easy-going, someone appealing to be around. Everything Zane wasn't.

I tell him how Zane and I met. How I went into the marriage blind to the red flags. Zane was a wonderful storyteller, and every conversation brought us closer. We even enjoyed the same music, the same movies and read the same books.

I can't remember the last time I had a deep conversation with a man. It takes everything in me not to keep telling him how much I adored Zane. But was he worth risking my entire life for? He may have been a husband and a father, but he was an actor first.

Every so often he'd subject me to blind-drunk arguments, where in the morning he'd forget where he'd been and who he'd been with. The thought of spending a lifetime with him in sickness and in health, till death us do part, became unbearable, and I don't know how I put up with it. Then we'd have sex or spend a wonderful afternoon on the beach together, and I'd forgive him all over again.

After Bizzy was born, I employed an au pair. She was happy with the baby at first, reading and playing and constantly wanting to take Bizzy out for walks like it was a fresh adventure. We'd pack a lunch, and all go swimming and sightseeing. There was so much I wanted to show her.

She was the youthful presence our family needed. She put a smile on everyone's face, Zane's more than most. He couldn't stop himself.

Finding out was the worst part. I spotted them in a coffee shop, two happy customers sipping drinks and laughing. I knew then that everything would change, and it would be impossible to stop it. One coffee date turned into a Saturday morning ritual, and soon he was loitering outside her bedroom door. I don't know at what stage his attention became unwelcome, or why. But she left us after that.

Zane sabotaged everything I loved, and now I'm left with nothing.

Ryan's eyes lock onto mine, and all my fears evaporate. I realise I've discarded my coffee in favour of talking to him, running his head ragged with all my marital problems. All the while, I'm looking at how attentive he is.

'Here I was, envying both of you for such an amazing lifestyle,' he says. 'Sure, everyone has their difficulties, but I imagined underneath it all that you always had each other's backs.'

Though I hadn't wanted to admit it, Zane's work made colossal demands of him. The thorough analysis of each character, the inevitable deep dive. He kept promising me that after he finished *Play Him Play Her*, we'd have more time for each other. We'd travel and fulfil our dreams. He definitely travelled and fulfilled his.

I shake my head. 'You imagined wrong.'

'So it seems.'

'What do you think about these "sightings" in Canada?'

He drains his coffee and places the mug on a coaster. 'It's certainly interesting given the witness statements last year, one of which stated that on 27th November, a man, thought to be celebrity actor Zane Osborne was seen leaving Jean Lesage International Airport in Quebec. We know Interpol swooped in, but he evaded its grasp. After that, his fugitive status was just rumours.'

'More than a year later, and they still haven't found him.'

He ignores my comment and rattles on about a sighting in Dubai, where Zane was purportedly spotted playing tennis on the world's highest court at the Burj Al Arab, which is strange because my husband never played tennis.

*Crimestoppers UK* reached out to me, saying that although some people wanted to lynch Zane, his fans fully supported him. What they wanted was balance, someone who could describe the "real Zane" to viewers back home. I refused to talk to them. Now I wish I had.

'Are you saying some of these might be worth investigating?' I ask.

Ryan hesitates for a few seconds. 'Might be.'

'On a scale of one to ten.' I stare at him, looking for something in his eyes that might show how high up the scale it is. But there's nothing there.

He leans forward, a frown making itself at home on his face. 'I'd say a good nine.'

**BarbedWire - Trending #InZane**

@CirceAtNight: Looks like they've found ZaneO. Not literally as in arrested. But found as in sighted.

@Titmouse: Pity he wasn't found in my bedroom.

@CirceAtNight: If it is him, his survival skills definitely paid off. He should earn a merit badge for this.

@HeyWhatsUP: I don't think Boy Scouts are a thing anymore.

# PART II

# THE PRETENCE

# 16

# ZANE

Quebec is every bit as beautiful as I'd imagined. I find a studio flat on Rue des Frênes, overlooking a church named Saint Albert le Grand.

The landlord, who is nibbling French fries amidst a mess of papers and magazines, and who clearly functions better in chaos, barely looks at my ID. Two grand in cash speaks volumes to him.

The flat is nothing noteworthy. The walls are painted a warm cream, which turns to pearl when the morning light hits it. There are two chairs and a table, a faded armchair and a sofa that needs reupholstering, and there's an odour in the shower that reminds me of the men's toilets in a Dawlish pub.

For the first three days, I stayed inside, eating Chinese food and watching films on the unpaid channels. There's an emptiness to the place that feels wretched, and I listen and watch, and nothing happens.

It's hard to keep out of sight, evading patrols and trying to navigate being in a city as opposed to the relative safety and anonymity of the wilderness. Unlike other fugitives, I'm a celebrity, a face many have ingrained in their minds. It means keeping my head down in the event Quebec is as lethal as London with CCTV.

I meet homeless men, play cards and drink cheap wine. There are singers and buskers and storytellers, and my new friend, Jean-Marie Grenier, has been both. His impressive vocal range proves he was a great tenor in his prime, or so he tells me. The wild hair and bulbous nose (his words, not mine) put him in the Cyrano de Bergerac category, and he tells me women don't see the brilliant romantic inside. His beard is as full as mine. The only difference is that dirt and sweat add to its filth, and his clothes are dusty and torn.

To say he sought me out would be an understatement. When I first met him, he kept grabbing my arm and dragging me to the park for someone to talk to. I was happy to oblige. After all, he was better than a tour guide.

Today, he wants to show me the Hotel Le Montagnais. He's a skilful pickpocket as he is a hotel connoisseur, and parts a hedge fund manager from his wallet in the foyer. He pulls me outside and we run through the crowds, acutely aware of the pulse of many feet and the tantalising smell of food.

It's easy to find high-end bistros, where Jean-Marie shows me how to clear the remnants of a leftover meal and a bottle of half-drunk wine from empty tables before the servers come. I'm embarrassed to admit that I've stooped to the level of a common thief. Yet, I see no other way to survive. The thing that stays with me now isn't the hurt or the rejection, but my unshakable determination to make it work.

Down by the river's edge is another restaurant with an outside seating area and awnings. I spy a table for ten, emptying of its occupants, and where a bison burger with a generous portion of chips catches my eye. As my hand reaches through the railings, the guest, having barely left the table, sees fit to return with a takeout box and gasps at my outstretched hand.

I stammer, 'I'm sorry. I thought—'

'Take it. The portions here are more than generous.' He piles the chips and the burger into the box and hands it to me. 'Do you need money?'

I must be giving him a look because he repeats the question. The truth is, I've barely spoken to another living soul since leaving England, least of all one dressed the way I used to dress. A lot has changed since then. Hell, even I've changed.

He peels a hundred-dollar bill from his wallet and holds it out.

As I take the money in a shaky hand, a shadow appears behind him, a server with a stern look, mumbling apologies about the filthy vagrants in the city. That's when I realise the time has passed for niceties. I duck into an alley and head towards the river; the preassigned meeting place Jean-Marie has selected.

I see him with his beanie and frayed coat, sitting on a bench with a wine bottle tucked under one arm. He carries all his possessions in two plastic bags, and it's then that I see the third filled with two takeout boxes, exuding the aroma of garlic and pasta.

He takes a grubby cup from his coat pocket and shares his Cabernet Sauvignon, giving thanks to the Almighty for His amazing provision. Garlic bread, a wedge of lasagna and two meals of chicken carbonara. He doesn't speak; he merely inhales the food, as cheese hangs from his mouth like string.

I look out across the water, where sunlight bounces off the waves, and wonder if that's a whale I see in the distance. You can disappear here, in a city so big that individuals fade away and all you see are crowds.

I remember the hundred-dollar bill in my pocket and press it into his hand, but he throws it back at me like it's contaminated.

'Walk with me,' he says, pressing his hand to his side and flinching.

'Are you okay?'

'Ah, ça va,' he says, dismissing me with a scowl.

He takes me down an alley behind a row of restaurants and pulls me behind a dumpster. He takes a freshly rolled joint from his pocket and lights it. I'm looking this way and he's looking that, and we're puffing on that tiny reefer like our lungs depend on it. He tells me the pain in his side is from a bruised rib. Here's me thinking he's a stoner, but the weed he smokes is to soothe his pain.

The sound of clattering heels on concrete makes me jump, and my heart speeds up to where I feel dizzy. Jean-Marie mashes the joint under his heel while clutching my arm. We see a woman with bleached blonde hair and a phone pressed against her ear, yacking about a hair appointment to touch up her roots. She hurls a bag of trash into the dumpster with an overarm throw before returning through the back door of a bistro.

How did it come to this? That the sight of another person, or any sudden movements, makes my heart race? When had I become so terrified that I'd let the tiniest thing get to me? As Jean-Marie leads me down the alleyway and back into the crowds, sweat gathers at my hairline, and I rub my palms against my trouser legs.

Fear and guilt have become constant companions now, and I can't remember what it's like to live without them.

The beauty of the architecture takes me by surprise. Jean-Marie tells me that Celine Dion, considered Canadian royalty, got married at the Notre-Dame Basilica. A fact I did not know. He points at the Chateau Frontenac, built on a cliff with its pitched roofs and polygonal towers rising above the city skyline, and tells me he used to work there as a barman. I now understand where he got his love for fine wines, which sadly marked the end of his career.

'It was originally the site of a military fort,' he says, muttering something about Winston Churchill, President Franklin D Roosevelt and Canadian Prime Minister Mackenzie King meeting here in the forties. 'You should see Bistro Le Sam at sunset. Beautiful views.'

I'm filled with an acute sense of emptiness, a sense of exclusion. In my old life, I could have stayed at the Chateau, dined on cold Saguenay salmon while being mesmerised by the glint of the St Lawrence River. Now, all I can smell are rich aromas reserved for the privileged, knowing I'll have to beg to taste it.

'Perhaps you will find a job there,' he says. 'A butler, perhaps.'

'I hate interviews, and I would never agree to one.'

'Why? You can't speak French? Everyone speaks English, well, most of them,' he says. 'But other neighbourhoods outside Old Quebec and Vieux-Port speak very little of it.'

'I have a smattering of French from my school days, enough to get by.'

'Paris French? Or Quebecer French?' He sees me frown. 'Probably best you don't speak at all.'

Being on the run has shaken me, and it's hard not to feel depressed at the crowds who sidestep me in the streets. Even a car cruising slowly to avoid pedestrians seems full of foreboding, especially those with dark tinted windows. What if four officers get out with guns and pin me to the floor? There's no mistaking the feeling of being duped by an undercover police car. For the past few days, I've been watching my back. It's as instinctive as breathing.

I think about trust and the comfort it affords. Can I trust Jean-Marie? How do I know he won't trade me in for a reward?

As for comfort, I've got used to being in the same clothes, but I yearn for a new wardrobe like the one I had at home.

HOLLOWAY

```
First, you don't have a home.
Second, your wife has probably
doused your clothing in gaso-
line and set it alight. Let's
not pretend she is keeping ev-
erything as it was in the hope
you'll return.
```

My wife is the least of my problems. Every time we pass a shop window, I glance at my face and see too many crevices. I doubt anyone would recognise me.

Jean-Marie shoulders his way through the crowds and then runs, and I run, too. When I burst out the other side, Jean-Marie is nowhere to be seen. A loud siren and a sudden flash of colour pull up beside me. A police car screams to a halt, and I freeze. I don't know why, but my legs won't move. Two officers rush towards a boutique with outside tables laden with merchandise. I slowly exhale, feeling stupid to have believed they were after me.

Every step I take puts distance between myself and who I used to be. I follow the dusty street as it winds downhill, spotting Jean-Marie several yards ahead, his hand pressed against his side. Then we're running again. Him, with his bags slapping against his legs, and me, with my battered ego all the way to a park.

We find a path thick with trees and bursts of yellow leaves on the ground. We sit in a burrow of roots to catch our breath. In this tiny nook are remnants of pizza boxes and broken twigs. He arranges them into a neat mound with a few twists of newspapers curled into balls. He strikes a match, and the flames lick at the kindling. Soon it's giving out enough warmth for me to consider taking my jacket off.

That's when I look at him, I mean, really look at him. One eye blinks a lot, like he has a facial tic. I wonder how long it will be before he asks me if I've ever hurt anyone.

When I bring up how I'd like to live in Toronto, he says skyscrapers aren't his thing and that I'd hate it as much as I hate not having nice things.

I stare at him, wondering how he knows I like *nice things*. Looking at him must make him uncomfortable because he keeps digging a twig into the fire as if it needs poking.

Then he says, 'I know who you are.'

I feel faint, and the ambiance in this tiny burrow is askew. I wait for the greyness in the periphery of my vision to clear and hope the leaves and the bushes stop swaying.

'They say you killed a woman,' he says.

I'm all ears.

'Anyway, someone identified you.' He shakes his shaggy head. 'If you're thinking of taking the bus or a subway, don't. There are cameras everywhere.'

As if I didn't know. 'Who do you think I am?'

He twists his knuckles into the corners of his eyes and yawns. 'Someone who doesn't use his own name.'

When he says my old name, each consonant and each vowel so carefully pronounced, I lose it. My fists lash out, and the tiny little grotto lights up like a disco ball.

It's true what they say about anger. You really see red.

# 17

# LILJA

I make a pot of tea in the downstairs pantry and take a tray to the terrace. It's my day off, and I decide to make the most of it.

A gust of wind catches my hair, and the flames crackle and pop in the fire pit. The sun moves behind a cloud, and I shiver at the drop in temperature.

I text Bizzy and tell her about my decision to go public, but with some reservations. Her thoughts on whether it's a good idea are important to me, and she tells me to go for it.

It's terrifying to think that my marriage was like stepping on landmines left and right. I'd always known Zane was smart, but it took me a while to realise he was a narcissist. He made all his Google searches at night, histories cleared by morning, and there was an app for untraceable emails. All this points in my favour.

I'd seen enough evidence of Zane's lack of empathy, his manipulation and cruelty, and realised the dangers. I regret that my delay put Bizzy in jeopardy before I acted. There are things that could cast reasonable doubt if this makes it to a trial. Only the police, who seem to take their sweet time, have all the answers.

As a firm supporter of local news, I decide to call Stan Marriott. His articles about the house and gardens have garnered national support. Only this feature won't depict any Prue Leith-type kitchen hacks. It will be a tell-all.

When Stan answers, I dive in, knowing that whatever I say

will be hyped up and taken out of context. It's time to turn up my emotional metre and give the public a taste of the truth.

'You asked me if I wanted to talk about Zane, about the marriage and how we managed for all those years. I've been thinking it might help his fans to understand how I feel.'

'I think so, too,' he says. 'Who doesn't want a "behind the scenes" reality show of the Osbornes hard at play in the splendour of Barton Manor? Just kidding. How about we use your study? We can talk about the days leading up to Zane's disappearance and then take it from there. Nothing too intrusive, but enough to satisfy public curiosity. I'll send you a list of general questions, although there will be follow-up questions.'

I hadn't expected a physical interview. I'd assumed that a telephone call and a written article would suffice. But he's right. Photographs of me in my study would give the interview a more personal touch and convey to Zane – if he is alive and has access to the internet – how important my side of the story is.

It will focus on Zane's privileged lifestyle and how he preferred to shack up with his assistant in the cramped confines of her dingy little flat. If I can swing it, I'll make sure it delves into his state of mind and how it affected me. Zane at his most pretentious, Zane at his most brutal, so his fans get the full measure of the abuse he dished out. Stan sets a date for next week, and I can expect his email questions this afternoon.

My insides twist as if the voice inside is warning me that something bad is about to happen. Just as I'm thinking this, Ryan stalks across the lawn and takes a seat beside me, his hands thrust into his coat pockets.

'Everything okay?' he asks.

My face is trapped in that strange limbo between confusion and doubt, and I give him a reassuring nod. 'I've decided to do an interview on *MarriottLive*.'

'Wow. That's brave. Are you sure you want to do it?'

'I think it's important, given these so-called sightings.'

'People might get the wrong impression.'

'Of Zane or me? Please don't say me.'

He sighs in frustration as if his nerves are worn paper thin. 'Call it gut instinct, but you don't understand the players the way I do.'

This stops me cold. 'Are you saying it would be risky to do the interview?'

He pauses long enough to let me know he does. 'For you, perhaps.'

I hadn't thought of that possibility. We sit in silence for a moment, both contemplating how bad this could be. Apart from the usual critical comments on *BarbedWire*, will photographers rush us and scream a bunch of questions every time we go out?

Finally, he says, 'I'd limit questions about your feelings.'

I turn towards him. 'My feelings? The reporters didn't take those into account when they stopped me in the street last year. The papers referred to me as *The Ice Queen*. Now you're saying my feelings are none of their business.'

'You were married to a celebrity, someone his fans adored. Of course, it's their business. This community stands by you, regardless of the shady things you've been accused of. Hell, you're one of Britain's favourite restaurateurs. This could damage your business.'

The prickly feeling of dread, which I'd had moments earlier, wraps itself around me like a cloak. I hunch forward; my hands cupped around my face. Now I feel bad that he thinks I'm taking an unnecessary risk.

He scoots closer, his hand resting on my shoulder. 'I hope you know how to skirt the obvious trap of saying too much. What happened last year is confidential.'

'Not if it's in my police statement.'

He fixes me with a look of such intense scrutiny I feel myself shrivel. 'You're avoiding the question.'

'I'm not sure I know what the question is.'

'Do you want to paint Zane in such a negative light? Because when the shit hits the fan, his fans won't thank you for it.' He looks at me earnestly. He's also sweating a little.

'I don't see how we can avoid discussing every unkind word, every dismissive comment, and every enforced silence. What made you bring up my feelings?'

'I'm sorry?'

'You advised me to limit questions about my feelings.'

'Probably because you don't want people knowing everything about you, especially if it's going to be taken out of context.'

Somehow, between his appearing on the patio and me talking on the phone, I wonder if he'd overheard my conversation with Stan. But that's not possible, not if he walked across the lawn from the stables. I scold myself for being so suspicious.

He stands and holds out a hand. 'Want to come with me to pick up Bizzy from football practice?'

I massage my forehead with my fingers. 'Probably not. I've got a bit of a headache.'

After I go inside, I spend the rest of the afternoon downstairs on the couch in my study, googling maps of Canada on my laptop and wondering where the hell Zane could be. His absence feels different this time, not a ghost flitting around the earth, but a living Zane, which sits in my gut unpleasantly. I feel restless for things to do.

Where would he likely live? Surely not some downtown squat, unwashed and unloved. No, he'd be living the high life with a rich widow who had access to the finest dining Canada offers. The only problem with that scenario is how well he could blend into the scenery. If he has access to stage makeup and wigs, then he'll be impossible to find.

Something tells me the old Zane would have to put away his expensive tastes and live under the radar. Every image of him spools around in my brain like a film reel, creating an impossible collage of Zanes with beards and moustaches and long, dark hair. A façade of Zane that has never been revealed to the public or to me.

Perhaps, DC Symonds wasn't being so far-fetched when she requested a particular photo of him, for he could impersonate an Emirati and not live in Canada at all.

My stomach roils at the thought of him milking another woman for everything she's worth. Zane can make people do anything he wants them to do.

He's always one step ahead.

**BarbedWire - Trending #InZane**

@Titmouse: Hey guys, did anyone see that announcement on *MarriottLive*? Lilja Osborne's doing an exclusive with Stan the Man.

@SherylAdams: Seriously? I don't think that's a good idea.

@CirceAtNight: Why not? She should totally go live. I heard Zane Osborne wasn't the charming Mr Nice Guy everyone thought he was.

@HeyWhatsUP: You know what they say. Method acting uses personal experience to develop a character. Ask yourself why he was so convincing as Holloway.

# 18

# ZANE

I wake up on the couch with the blanket pulled up to my chin. Rain rattles against the windowpanes, and the wind is a constant bombardment. The clock tower moans as it clings to the stable roof.

The clock tower... the stables... Then I remember, I'm not in my study in Dawlish Warren, but in a grimy one-bedroom flat. I woke up twice in the night to the sound of someone running lines for the last season of *Play Him Play Her*, only it wasn't me because I'm no longer in it.

Fear awakens an urgent craving for a new identity – urgent – because there's a reward attached to the name Zane Osborne in the sodding newspapers. My knuckles are sore and coated with dried blood. I must have done a number on Jean-Marie.

He was knocked out cold when I left him. Shit knows where he is now, but a good guess would be in hospital. Or at the police station.

I grab my phone and access the dark web through CyberShark and find a man called Julius Bedard, whose ID services include running a café on the ground floor of his building.

HOLLOWAY

    I hope this isn't a trap. You
    could find yourself in a little
    cell before lunchtime.

ZANE

I wouldn't go that far.


HOLLOWAY

Alone is safe. Alone is free.
Alone is exactly what you want
to be.


Holloway bursting into a whimsical Dr Seuss-type rhyme is getting on my nerves. I wish I could simply shut him off.

A wide band of sunlight falls through the window onto a worn grey carpet. I open the latch to a brisk breeze wafting in. Across the street are a couple of women and a child, hugging a limp stuffed bear, their voices rising to an excitable babble. Behind them is a row of houses glazed a molten gold, their sun-fired windows reminding me of home. As the conversation dies away, so do the colours, leaching into a stormy grey sky.

I close the window and rummage in the fridge, finding a wedge of brie with a coating of mould. After scraping most of it into the sink, I wrap it between two slices of bread.

I choose a thick woollen shirt and jeans and put on a jacket and a baseball hat. At this stage in the game, a man fresh on the run is a sitting duck. But with my hair flopping over one eye, too wild and woolly to behave, and a fake accent, I'm ready.

Slipping out onto the icy pavement, I make my way to a bus stop and sit there for a quiet half-hour. My mind compares this clean world to the wilderness I'd left behind, while the markswoman's flesh moulders into leaf litter, becoming part of the riverine wetland.

A front door slams, sending up a rocket of crows from the tree in the front garden. A woman crosses the street, heading for the vintage Volvo in front of me, which is in surprisingly good nick. She unlocks the door and glances up at the sky. Mid-forties, well-dressed, short hair neatly styled. She reminds me of Deborah Kerr in the 1957 film of *An Affair to Remember*.

'Looks like a storm coming,' she says, glancing at me before throwing her handbag into the passenger seat.

'Yep, certainly does,' I say, adopting a North American accent.

Before she asks me another question, I pick up my phone and pretend to be focused intently on something. I can feel her stealing glances at me as she ducks into her car and opens the passenger window.

'Can I give you a lift anywhere?' she shouts.

'No, but thank you.'

She puts up a hand, offers a friendly smile and speeds off. I'm impressed that she wasn't afraid of me. For a moment, I imagine she sees the old me, the elegant and exotically dressed me, and we drive into town together, reminiscing…

```
             HOLLOWAY

   Reminiscing  about  what?  The
   murders  you've  committed.  She
   probably  works  for  the  gov-
   ernment.  Security  and  Public
   Safety  would  be  my  guess.
```

Some of what Holloway says rings true, and some of it is a downright lie. I'm having trouble telling one from the other. Thinking people know me, suspect me, have an inkling of who I might be is wearing me down. How can they know? A characterless person sloshing around in worn-out boots is hardly someone they'd remember.

I've gone to great lengths to become anonymous and to find a little of the solace I crave. Changing my identity and creating a new character from scratch is next on my list. I can't be Ted Oliver for another day.

HOLLOWAY

I would limit travel to abandoned cars and public trans-
port from now on. Where are
you going, by the way?

ZANE

None of your business.

I take the bus to Saint-Paul Rue, ploughing through a riot of pigeons to get to the place I'd Googled last night. The sensible thing to do is to find work, the type of job where I can avoid being seen. A graveyard shift, perhaps. Working as a delivery guy or an Uber driver.

HOLLOWAY

You don't want passengers
saying, 'That's the man in the
news. The one who murdered a
CSIS markswoman, and he really
got off on it.'

ZANE

I didn't get off on it. I was
extremely sorry about it.

HOLLOWAY

It's time you stopped playing
the idiot and listened for a
change.

                    ZANE

          I'm listening.


                  HOLLOWAY

          Get the hell out of the big
          city. Work on a farm or in
          the fields. Stay away, do you
          understand?

Anxiety creeps into me, and I'm desperate to run for the nearest alleyway and shove my head between my knees. Images of Canada's Security Intelligence Service keep closing in, and everything in me comes to a dead stop.

I walk along snow-speckled streets with my hands thrust deep into my pockets, my eyes searching for CCTV cameras on the buildings. I give each shop window a sideways glance to examine my reflection. Shit, I look like a character from *Slumdog Millionaire*.

Fresh scents rush me; slushy wet pavements, competing perfumes and the underlying musk of damp coats. City sounds are louder than I remember; hissing air brakes as a bus stops, passengers flying from the open door like a siege of cranes.

There are plenty of menswear stores along Rue Petit-Champlain. I imagine an Italian designer fitting me with cashmere knitwear and cotton shirts. For a moment, I'm transported to Europe with its narrow streets and red brick façades. There's even a life-sized poster of Pierce Brosnan in a shop window to make me feel at home.

I find an outdoor market with clothes hanging in rows, nearly new jackets and coats, something I should invest in. But with less than $1000 in cash, I'm limited. Looking unremarkable is better than looking grungy and unwashed, so I buy a black wool double-breasted coat and a few long-sleeve casual shirts.

I pause outside a pâtisserie, which offers an array of decadent pastries and flaky croissants and where the scent of strong coffee tempts me. What tempts me more is the modest arrow leading upstairs to a first-floor storage room, which is filled with unopened boxes of coffee and condiments, and shelves of brewing equipment. I hear shuffling feet, and a hidden door opens. I'm pleasantly surprised to see a man who must be all of seventy years, tall with dark grey hair. His foot nudges a French bulldog to one side, and he comes forward to shake my hand.

'Julius Bedard. How can I help you?'

I clear my throat, hoping he doesn't catch a whiff of my homicidal past. 'Ted Oliver. We spoke online.'

'Ah, yes.' He smiles. 'You understand that with a new ID comes a new everything. Bank account, email login, driving license. A resumé on LinkedIn. Where are you from?'

'Hampstead,' I say, knowing he won't have the foggiest notion where it is. Then quickly add, 'A suburb of Montreal. My mother – British, of course – emigrated to Canada when I was sixteen.'

*Mother. British. Emigrated.* He's forming a character profile for me to play. Locking the door from the inside, he leads me to a back room with painted-out windows and a skylight. He tilts the chair in front of his desk and makes a *pfft* noise as he wipes dog hair from the seat and motions for me to sit.

'Our IDs have holographic images and magnetic strips. They pass all blacklight tests. If the police stop you, any information that populates their computers will match the information on your ID. Tell me, what kind of work are you looking for?'

Something flips in the pit of my stomach, and my face is burning. Too many things could go wrong. Holloway's idea of working in the fields is too obvious. Surely, if the FBI were looking for illegals, they'd look there first?

I tell him I'd seen something at Fairmont le Chateau Frontenac and what it would mean to me to work there. Starting at the bottom, of course. Although I'm capable of a *lot* more than washing dishes and emptying bins. What about a junior butler position? Surely, it doesn't require a PhD.

Julius' eyes slide to the ceiling. 'Then you will need an enticing resumé.'

He wakes up his computer with his mouse and begins typing, and while he's occupied, Holloway gives voice.

<pre>
                HOLLOWAY

        Do you realise what kind of
        trouble you're in? Obviously,
        you didn't hear me the first
        time. Chateau Frontenac is ex-
        actly where you don't want to
        work. A butler? Seriously?

                 ZANE

        No, but it's where I want him
        to think I'd like to work.
        It gives me a wider scope of
        qualifications.

                HOLLOWAY

        You mean from fruit picker to
        casino floor runner.

                 ZANE

    Exactly.
</pre>

It's a minute before Julius continues speaking. 'To give you an example, the head butler is a member of Les Clefs d'Or de Canada, an exclusive society of hotel concierges. He and his team – a role for which you may one day apply – provide an exceptional service that takes years to learn. Although I can list some excellent qualifications on your resumé, it would be quite an accomplishment for someone of your *inexperience* to pull it off.'

I almost roll my eyes. How hard can it be? If he means there are no crash courses on how to be a butler, he doesn't realise that I am an actor. Of course, this isn't a Netflix series with full set rehearsals, script repairs, and re-shoots. It's real, and it's live. To *pull it off* convincingly, as Julius says, might be tricky. But not impossible.

'Do you have a name?' he asks.

It would be too risky to use the names of any characters I've played. I think of the first name Beckham – Beck for short – but it doesn't fit. On the bus, I had seen a woman reading a romance novel by an author whose last name was classy but understated. Choosing the middle name of my dead son, I decide on…

'William Rivière.'

Julius studies me for a moment. 'Age, height, weight, address.'

I make myself five years younger, six foot one (an inch shorter than I was) and pack on a little more meat. My address won't be my address for long.

'How would you describe yourself?' he asks.

'Conscientious. Professional. Committed.'


                    HOLLOWAY

        Others would say you were a
        killer.


Am I, though? Haven't I thrown away that mantle by burying Theo Oliver?

If I try to recall any part of it, I get brief snatches of the transitional period between night and day when the sky was slashed in purples and golds. The sound of breathing. A man, who I later found out was a woman, whose leg was almost severed. Between the two states of being threatened and seeing the threat, I took the only action available to me.

Self-defence.

Julius' rapid typing pulls me out of my thoughts as he fakes my life from birth to present day, with no political or religious affiliation. We forge an entire biography from one blank sheet of paper to seven pages of convincing backstory.

'If you rent an apartment here,' he says. 'The landlord will ask you for proof of salary or two months' worth of bank statements, a government-issued ID, and a social security number.'

I assume he means here in the city, since the landlord at Rue des Frênes barely skimmed my ID. I open my mouth to ask if paying cash is the best way to go, but before I can, Julius points at the phone in my hand.

'You will need a new one of those. Don't forget to activate it in a public library, turn off location sharing and opt out of Google tracking. Make sure you sign up for a temporary email service.'

My anxiety, which had plummeted to almost normal levels, comes rushing back, and I know I won't get far until Ted Oliver has been erased.

'Since it's policy to require a minimum salary of at least three times the rent, I will cover it by adding a few more zeros to your pay stub. I will also include a fake contract from human resources at the Chateau Frontenac, assuming you get the position, of course.'


                        HOLLOWAY

          Before you open your mouth, be
          warned that he may wait for
          you to leave before alerting
          the police.


                          ZANE

          Come on. Look at this place.
          He's hardly going to call the
          police.


                        HOLLOWAY

          What if Monsieur Bedard is an
          informant? What if, on his way
          home tonight, he pops into the
          Sûreté du Québec to collect
          the reward? Surely, you hav-
          en't forgotten about that.

My instinct is to run, to leave this dingy room as quickly as I can before Julius raises the alarm. Then I calm down. He doesn't care who I am or what I've done, because his business thrives on anonymity and not asking those types of questions. But Holloway has a point. A *what if* point that cannot be ignored.

Julius takes me to the camera on a tripod. 'No smiling.'

Then comes a blinding flash and soon, two passport-size photos are spewing out of his printer. After paying my bill, I'm out the door with a manila envelope tucked under one arm.

Having bought a coffee and a chocolate croissant downstairs, I examine the contents. A driver's license – Permis de conduire – the hologram shimmering in the sunlight and all the paperwork a Canadian resident would need.

Finally, Will Rivière is born.

## 19

# LILJA

The lights flicker, and a clap of thunder shakes the home. At 11.45 pm, the restaurant is now closed, and the guests and servers are gone.

Ryan hunches over his phone while Stella and Bizzy laugh over a cat video at the kitchen table. Elin and Paul are in an affectionate embrace, with his arms around her shoulders and his cheek against her neck. It's been a long time since I've felt that kind of love, and I try not to stare.

I move into the sitting room, take the remote and stretch out on the couch to channel surf. My phone pings with an email. Stan has listed over twenty questions, some of which I veto, especially the ones pertaining to Bizzy. Sod Ryan's advice, I intend to steer the conversation away from Zane and focus instead on me.

'I've warmed up some leftover brownie and added a dollop of ice cream,' a familiar voice says, handing me a bowl. 'My treat.'

Ryan takes off his jacket and drapes it over the arm of the sofa. I don't know if it's the motion that stirs a recognisable scent, but I could have sworn his jacket carried a waft of tobacco. Not surprising if he's been talking to Burgess outside on one of his breaks.

I take one of the offered spoons, and we eat together in an intimate silence. He throws occasional glances at me when I look up from the TV.

He's wearing snugly fitted jeans and a shirt that is open at the second button. The fabric is so fitted that I can make out the shadow of a tattoo; a dragon or something on his upper arm.

'It's Alien,' he says, watching my gaze. 'A chitinous exoskeleton. I thought it was beautiful.'

I hide my grin. 'So, what part of Scotland are you from?'

With the TV droning in the background, he tells me about his childhood and how he and his brother were brought up in a small fishing village called Ullapool.

'My mother was a Red Cross volunteer, and my father ran a holiday cottage business in Gairloch.'

'What made you come here?' I ask.

'My grandmother. Mum sold all the holiday cottages and moved here to look after her. She had dementia by then.'

'That must have been hard.'

'I was only eleven. You dream about the sunsets, the locks, and the mossy smell of heather when you're away from it.' He turns to look at me, an even wider smile curling at the corner of his mouth. 'Don't get me wrong, it's beautiful here, too.'

What was that if not an invitation to flirt?

His thigh almost touches mine as we scoop out the remnants of chocolate and ice cream. Occasionally, his lips tug up at the corners, sending shivers along the back of my neck.

'I've something to show you,' he says.

He helps me into his jacket and offers his arm as we walk outside. The soft crooning of classical music still radiates from the speakers, competing with the ethereal symphony of a robin.

We take a sharp right across the lawn and walk to the lantern overlooking the swing gate that unites the wall with the lane. He points to the gap between the post and the hedge.

'This is how an intruder could get in.' He stands sideways in the gap as if showing me how easy it is. 'I suggest a dummy post. Rock or concrete would do it.'

I realise he's showing it to me to make me feel safe, to give me confidence in his skills. Like anything that needs immediate attention, I'm desperate to get it done.

'I won't pretend this is going to be cheap,' he says. 'We need to secure this property, so you and your family feel safe. If you suggest a budget, I'll know what I'm working with.'

I hadn't thought about money, but you can't put a price on safety. 'Whatever you need.'

'Okay. So far, there are rusty camera housings on the barn, three motion sensors out above the stables, and the front access cameras need attention.'

'Zane used to turn them off. He had a bad habit of forgetting what was important.'

Ryan listens intently, making me feel as if he's absorbing every detail. 'You'd think security would have been the most important thing.'

'Not to someone with drama embedded in his DNA. He was too involved in Holloway's life to live his own.'

Despite my simmering resentment, when I look up at Ryan, everything that happened last year seems like a bad dream. Suddenly, I forget all about Zane.

Zane who?

'It's not my place to interfere,' he says. 'But if you torture yourself, if you think that whatever you did or didn't do would have made any difference, don't.'

I try to muster up a comment, but the tears are coming fast, and I can see by his drawn brows I'm failing miserably. I don't know why I want to cry around him, whether it's simply a need to talk to someone about how vulnerable I'm feeling. Or his disappointment at my agreeing to do the press interview.

A gust of wind blows hair across my face, and he lifts a steady hand and pushes it away with a finger. A weird sensation rolls up my spine, and I think that he's going to cup my jaw and kiss me. I take a few steps back to put some distance between us, stumbling on a mound of grass, almost losing my balance. He rights me with an arm thrown around my waist. I'm fascinated by the feel, giving in to a flicker of excitement and the sense that something new, something explicit, is about to happen.

Somehow, he swings me around, one of those moves that reminds me of a sensual bachata, and we're in the shadows like two teenagers at a school dance. I feel something I don't have the words for. I'm barely coming down from an indescribable high when he stifles the mood.

'We'd better get back inside.'

To his credit, he looks briefly humbled, as if this is something he shouldn't have done. He strides back across the lawn, and I have to pick up the pace to keep up with him.

'You must be freezing,' I say, realising how cold he must be without his jacket.

'No more than you.'

I shrug at his infuriating politeness. His mood is the mirror opposite of what it was a few minutes ago. Embarrassment burns my face and sweat sticks under my shirt. I'm not technically single. I'm not technically divorced. Just because I don't have a certificate to prove it doesn't mean I don't feel my marriage is over. It is. So, what the hell does it matter?

Somewhere between the time he arrived and the attraction that was budding between us, I've allowed myself to hope. A stupid schoolgirl crush that has already shattered, and now I look like a fool.

He doesn't so much as look my way or sense the disappointment thrumming through me. As many times as I glance over, he doesn't meet my gaze. He doesn't take my arm like he did on the way out here. Nor does he steady me when I stagger off the grass and onto the drive. I could ask him what's the matter, I could demand an answer, but I get the weirdest sensation that he won't tell me.

He opens the front door, and I know he won't come inside. I hand him his jacket, and he slings it over one shoulder as if the cold no longer matters.

'I'll do a last walk around.' He goes painfully quiet for a few seconds. 'If there's anything worth reporting, I'll text you.'

I listen to his boots on the steps and the reassuring crunch of gravel as he heads towards the barn. The only other sounds are the soft click of the front door as I close it and the slide of the deadbolt.

When I return to the couch and the droning TV, all that's left of us is an empty bowl and two spoons.

**BarbedWire - Trending #InZane**

@Sheryl Adams: If only celebrities could just be happy with success and not shove themselves in our face every chance they get

@CirceAtNight: People resent him for flying the coop prematurely. I don't think people hate Zane himself.

@HeyWhatsUP: They don't?

# 20

# ZANE

**Sylvia Pedersen, a former marine and sniper, has gone missing**

Locals believe Pedersen was tracking Gabriel Cam-phaug, whose reign of terror began eight years ago with the deaths of Angela Madison and Sila Umiak...

The anxiety I feel makes it hard to think straight. TV and news articles are talking about Sylvia Pedersen. I try to get hold of my nerves before my heart thunders in my ears.

I walk a mile and find a small café down a side street with three people sitting outside. A man on his own and two young women, making off-colour remarks about the food. One tips her head back and gives her neck a good spray with perfume. Tiny particles mist in the sunlight and then sink away.

I sit at an empty table and pretend to read my phone, keeping my eyes trained on the half-eaten burrito one of them has left on her plate. My focus drifts to the man's newspaper with the headline:

MANHUNT FOR SYLVIA PEDERSEN GOES COLD

Trail goes cold in manhunt for Captain Sylvia Peders-en as authorities reach breaking point.

"A multi-agency manhunt has been launched," Lt

> Tulimaq said in a statement. "Despite repeated calls
> to her radio, we have been unable to locate her."

I feel a sharp pain in my gut, and I'm shaking so hard I can barely breathe. I had turned her radio off, but could it still transmit any traceable signals? What about her phone? Surely, she would have enabled location services so police could find her in case of emergencies. But how many cell towers are there along Big River?

None that I saw.

But there will be one near the hotel where I buried it. Hopefully, this will take the police as far from Pedersen's body as possible.

As the man spreads the paper out, I can see Sylvia Pedersen's face on the front page. A beautiful face that displays deep thought, her dark eyes narrowed as if trying to bring a distant object into focus. The horror of her painted fingernails won't go away. It's at times like these when I want to reach for a joint or a glass of whisky, and since neither are on hand, I take two packets of sweetener from a bowl and tear them open with shaking hands.

Sugar always gives me the jitters, and I'm jittering all right. My knee is bouncing up and down, and my foot is tapping on the cobbles. The man with the newspaper gives me a worried frown and then goes back to reading. No doubt he'd love to know what is triggering my meltdown or any other worrying behaviour I might be exhibiting.

I take a deep breath to steady myself, hoping there are no references to Zane Osborne in the small print or another photo to give me away.

HOLLOWAY

> Why would there be? No one
> knows you had anything to do
> with Camphaug's or Pedersen's
> death. Listen, I know you're
> upset, but you need to get
> over it.

                    ZANE

        How can I get over it when it's
        my DNA they'll find?


                    HOLLOWAY

        You wore gloves, didn't you?
        What do you want me to do?
        Snatch the newspaper out of
        his chubby little hands and
        hurl it in the nearest bin?
        Because if you do, just tell
        me and I'll do it!


Holloway's voice becomes a distant murmur as I watch the two women leave. I try to remain calm, but I can't help feeling smothered by the thought that Tulimaq questioning me in the café has something to do with this.

It's hard to remain composed when hunger is robbing me of my last bit of hope. I train my focus on that leftover burrito, take one last glance at the man with the newspaper and grab the meal.

I'm suddenly aware of someone staring at me, and my senses sharpen, and the stress I'm already feeling increases. Newspaper Man is staring right at me. Unperturbed that he's been caught, he fishes his phone from his pocket and swipes the screen. He takes a long time to study whatever he's looking at, then he pleats his paper, hooks it under one arm and drains his demitasse of espresso. When he's striding down the street, my lungs drain of air.

Anonymity isn't easy. I can only bear silence for so long before I'm screaming for company. Not the talking kind, the kind that takes me on a walk, so I don't feel so alone. No one has given me a second glance until now.


                    HOLLOWAY

        You don't think he recognised
        you?

ZANE

Looking like this? You've got
to be kidding.


HOLLOWAY

But he was staring. That can
mean only one thing. Number
one, he was comparing you to
something on his phone. Number
two, he thought you were tweak-
ing at the end of a meth binge.


Now I'm feeling as worried as Holloway. Rather than Newspaper Man being a concerned customer, he's on to me. Reality comes crashing in, and I know I need to make myself disappear.

I can't hitch rides because the police have ghost cars that pick up random travellers on the highway. There must be another way.

I walk along cobbled streets, nibbling at the burrito, and feeling more miserable than I usually am. The crowds have thinned out a little, leaving me dangerously exposed. Perhaps it's the scent of rain or the distant rumble of thunder that makes me relive shitty memories of the incident at Big River.

I can't stop rehashing the Pedersen incident. The way I look at it is that she mistook me for Camphaug and, sensing the threat in my raised bow, aimed and fired. I can't blame her for that. The one rule I'd learned from my father is that no one points a gun at you without meaning to shoot. I did what any man would do. I defended myself. But the kill notches on my cupboard door are adding up, and now I'm losing all sense of right and wrong, as well as my mind.

In a way, this is the perfect setup. Unless they find my bow, they can't implicate me. Of all the things that have happened in the past year, not even I could have predicted *this*.

# 21

# LILJA

I'm trying not to watch Stella, but she sits at the table and stares out of the window as if somewhere, in an isolated part of her brain, a memory returns. I don't know if it's the silent caller I'd told her about or her awkwardness around Ryan. She hates the press that keeps clustering around the front gate like visitors at a zoo.

'Is there anything I can do?' I ask, crushing lavender leaves and dropping them into the tea strainer.

'No, love. I'm fine.' Stella puts on a brave smile and focuses on the tea leaves. 'You know that's my favourite.'

'I thought it might cheer you up.'

She reaches for a jar of honey. 'If you must know, I've been thinking about how things used to be around here when it was just us. You said I was the only who could defuse every argument and put everything back together again. Now I feel everything's too broken to mend.'

It's true. She was the only one who could neutralise the fever pitch of arguments we sometimes had. While Bizzy clamoured for her favourite true crime shows, Zane would insist on watching a boring documentary on Ponzi schemes. Somehow Stella would find something we all liked, and everything was calm again.

'How long is *he* going to be here?' she says, pointing at Ryan who is outside, scraping the mud off his boots on the terrace.

'A few months. Why?'

She leans forward and lowers her voice. 'The one thing I've

learned is not to trust anyone, not even the people you're closest to.'

'Noted,' I say.

I count all the months backwards, trying to work out how many times I'd spoken to Ryan when he worked for Zane. He'd drive Zane back from some gig or another, and I'd see his cheery face in the kitchen and offer him a quick coffee before heading home. There was never anything more than a polite, "Goodbye Mrs Osborne," and a friendly wave. No lingering stares, nothing to make me think he was someone not to trust.

The kettle clicks off, and the water bubbles in a rolling boil. I fill the teapot and let it sit for a while.

'I've seen you flinch whenever a car comes down the drive because you think it's Zane,' she says. 'He won't come back, love. He'll *never* come back.'

'Yes, you said that a couple of weeks ago.'

'Well, I'm saying it again, because I don't think it sunk in the first time.'

I fill two mugs and hand her one. If anyone can help me get back my peace of mind, it's Stella.

'It breaks my heart to know how deeply he's wounded you and Bizzy,' she says. 'He destroyed all of us.'

'But we will recover.' I put my hand across the table and cup Stella's inside mine. 'We will.'

'Are you sure about that?'

'Aren't you?'

A wave of nausea passes through me. This brave woman, who looks at me with compassion and concern, is now full of doubts. The realisation of what she's saying is a massive wake-up call and snaps me out of my selfishness. None of us will fully recover from the death of a young woman whom Bizzy adored and whom Zane had taken advantage of. None of us will come to terms with the fact that she's dead.

'I'll never know for sure,' she says, so quietly it's almost a whisper. 'I feel like I've let you down.'

'You haven't let me down.' Her eyes mist with tears. 'It's… it's just that people won't leave us alone. They won't.'

I take a clean hanky from my pocket and hand it to her. She uses it to wipe the smear of tears and mascara from under her eyes.

'Sorry, I just need to be on my own for a moment,' she says, pushing her chair back.

I want to tell her to take all the time she needs, but the words are stuck in my mouth.

I put my head in my hands and close my eyes. Another tainted memory brings the rumble of Zane's car, the jingle of his keys, and the squeak of his shoes on the hall floor. I remember glancing up from cooking, expecting to see the flash of his smile. Instead, I got the shadow of his body as it darted upstairs without saying hello. Sometimes, his footsteps were hollow, thudding through the house as he yelled my name, his hand rattling the bathroom doorknob, screaming at me to let him in.

All those years of catering to his every whim and navigating his escalating temper are hard to unlearn. Slamming doors, kicking chairs, flipping over coffee tables, swiping ornaments off the book-shelves and shouting curses. I was sick of trying to decipher his mood, all while I teetered on the edge of terror.

When they told me Zane had died in the wilds of Labrador, I didn't believe it. I thought he'd come back. He always did. We'd carry on as we had before, maybe getting better, maybe getting worse. As the months went by and there was no sign of him, I became broken inside, my heart racing for news, nausea rushing through my body, making me dizzy and desperate for air. I kept slogging through all the memories, punishing myself with *what ifs*.

What if I'd been kinder, more attentive, more... sacrificing.

Instead of bawling my eyes out, instead of starving myself into a stack of bones, I went against all my natural instincts and became numb. Somehow, his death was like a balm to my broken heart. I wasn't likely to bump into him in the supermarket with another woman or picture him pushing her up against a granite countertop, their bodies shiny with sweat. No, his death guaranteed my safety until someone spoilt the whole thing by saying they saw a man just like him in Canada. For someone who's trying to forget a husband, I think about him an awful lot.

'Hey you?'

I look up at the sound of Ryan's voice and realise that at some point in my musings, he'd walked in on silent feet.

He sinks onto the chair opposite and slides the vase of flowers aside that currently blocks my face. 'I know something's bothering you, and maybe it's me.'

I make a loud huff filled with impatience. 'What makes you think it's you?'

'I'd like to apologise.'

'For what?'

My stomach clenches into a thistly knot. I take a sip of my tea and don't answer, but my expression tells him I'm listening.

'I shouldn't have touched you. At least, not in that way.' He looks down at the table and caresses a knot in the wood with a finger.

'You barely touched me,' I correct, knowing full well he means brushing the hair out of my face when we were inspecting the swing gate. 'You simply stopped me from falling over.'

'It was more than that. You looked upset, and I wanted to help.'

'You did help and I'm grateful.'

'You know what I mean. I think the world of you. I've watched every news clip, every article about you, and I feel like I already know you.'

Studying brief clips of me on the news and social media is a little creepy. Anyone can form an unhealthy bond with someone in the media. Then I realise, I can talk. I'm stupidly besotted, and it needs to stop.

His gaze finds mine. 'I want to make it right.'

'Which part? Stalking me on the news or thinking the world of me?'

He grins. 'Both. Because I don't want you firing me.'

I consider what I'd want if the situation were reversed. Would I want my boss to give me another chance?

Ryan looks at me for a moment and lets the silence linger. 'I'm not asking you to forget what happened, but I'd like to continue working here. I know I could help you.'

I stare at him across the table; my expression is that of someone making a tough decision. How much is Ryan worth to me? How much liberty-taking is too much? I need him, and I hate myself for this dependency, a craving to hold on to friends even if they're people I should shy away from.

Perhaps it developed after my father died – the insecurity that comes from rejection. I wish I were more emotionally stable without the periods of self-hatred that had happened when Zane found other women. I don't want to be the widow that people rarely invite to parties because I can't be trusted around their husbands. That's why I have the restaurant. Everyone knows I'm married to my job.

I give him a bland, businesslike smile. 'Let's forget it ever happened.'

# 22

# ZANE

Rain needles down in silver sheets, sharp enough to sting. The sidewalks shine like a mirror, reflecting every neon sign and every passing headlight.

I keep my head low, my collar up and my cap shadowing my face. I tell myself I'm just another tourist with a backpack, invisible in the city's swarm. But every sound cuts too close. When a bus hisses to a stop, my heart skips a beat, its tyres shrieking on wet asphalt. I flinch before I can stop myself.

Someone laughs, and the sound punches through me. I steal a glance over my shoulder and see a drunk with his friends.

HOLLOWAY

```
You already look guilty. You
didn't even tell the landlord
you were leaving. Just wrapped
up, packed up and buggered off
to who knows where.
```

Holloway's voice slides into me like a knife between my ribs, steady and controlled, everything I'm not. I shake my head hard, as if I can rattle him loose.

HOLLOWAY

> They see the way you walk.
> The way your head jerks, your
> shoulders hunch. They'll clock
> you for a felon and take pic-
> tures of you.

A couple passing under an umbrella glance at me. Their eyes say it all: unstable, dangerous, someone to avoid.

Shit! The police aren't fools. By now they'll be combing through the apartment camera feeds, collecting witness statements, and every scrap of evidence I left behind in my panic. My face is burned onto their monitors, and into every patrol briefing. If they don't already know I'm here, they will soon.

No more rash moves. If I want to live through this, I need control, patience and strategy, strengths that have never belonged to me. Every pair of eyes feels heavy, like a weight pressing on me, and my skin prickles with fear. Fame has done this to me. I regret chasing it and feeding on it, and now it's a noose around my throat.

I glance over my shoulder again. The street is alive with night-shift workers hurrying home, loners leaning in doorways smoking, and a few strays stumbling around drunk. No tails that I can see. I shift the backpack higher on my shoulder and walk a little faster.

HOLLOWAY

> This is who you are. Every
> choice, every tiny slip-up,
> this is the real you. You think
> you're an actor, but you're
> just a fool in your own play.

The streets thin into warehouses, and lamps buzz overhead, bleeding yellow light onto the slick pavement. I see a sign to the train station, the Gare du Palais. There are too many cameras and too many checks on passenger trains, but freight trains slip through gaps no one notices. For a second, I almost feel as if I have a plan.

HOLLOWAY

```
If acting has taught you any-
thing, it's not to overact.
Right now, that's what you're
doing.
```

My hands ball into fists so tight my knuckles pop. I want to smash the nearest window just to shut him up. I shake the dark thoughts from my head and walk faster, as if I can separate myself from his shadow.

As I'm about to cross the street, blue light washes over the pavement as a police cruiser glides around the corner, its headlights pinning me like a spotlight. My body goes rigid. I'm sure the officer inside will see me, know me, slam on the brakes and shout the words: *That's him! Zane Osborne. Get him!*

The cruiser slows. I consider standing in someone's driveway and waiting till the coast is clear, but I hold my nerve and force myself to keep walking. My eyes drop to the pavement, my stride loose and lazy, like a man simply going home.

The seconds stretch, thin and unbearable. Then the cruiser turns away, tires hissing on wet asphalt, and its red taillights fade into the rain. My breath comes out jagged, and my knees almost buckle, but I don't stop. To stop is to crumble, and that means being caught. The closer I get to the station, the harder fear presses down. Not just fear of cuffs and sirens, but the intense fear of bringing the wrong attention to myself. One glance is all it takes. One stranger frowning because my eyes look familiar, and they remember me from a Netflix billboard, the type of recognition that kills.

The station rises out of the night like a chateau with its slate roof and ornate towers, and its clock displaying a few minutes past six. I'm desperate for a pee, but the only available tree is in the park opposite, and I don't want to be arrested for exposing myself.

My gut tightens, and I push the doors open and step inside. The air is heavy with coffee, the kind that's been sitting on a hot plate since morning, and fluorescent lights glare down on plastic seats, faces lit by phone screens.

I force my pace into the rhythm of the crowd as they shuffle towards the ticket counter. This is a performance; one I can't afford to screw up.

My stomach knots. How much will it cost? Probably every dime I have.

The man ahead of me reeks of sweat and cheap cologne, and the woman behind sighs into her phone, muttering about delays. I keep my hands loose at my sides, though my pulse is hammering loud enough to drown out the announcements echoing overhead.

HOLLOWAY

> You don't belong here. They can
> smell your sweat and fear. One
> wrong blink and you're done.

My jaw tightens. I tell myself not to answer him out loud, but my lips twitch anyway. I'm second in line. The clerk barely looks at the man in front of me, her fingers tapping against the keyboard and her eyes glazed with boredom.

'Destination' she asks him.

'A single to Toronto.'

When I hear the price, I almost gasp. I don't have enough money. As the man in front slides his card across the counter, I step aside and follow the signs to the bathrooms.

That's when it happens. A voice, high and insistent. 'Look! There he is.'

My blood turns to ice. I glance sideways and see a young man, no more than fifteen feet away, cheeks red from the cold, pointing at me. His companion, a woman with a scarf wrapped tightly around the lower half of her face, tugs him back, whispering sharply, but his eyes stay fixed on me.

Does he know who I am? I turn away, pulse detonating, and every muscle in my body is on high alert, urging me to run.

                    HOLLOWAY

          Do it! Give them a show!


Running will only confirm what the young man thinks he's seen, and I need to be smarter than that. I force my legs to move at a steady pace, as though I haven't noticed. My chest feels too tight for air. As I head for the Men's, I noticed a man rushing towards me, jumping over someone's briefcase and then sidestepping me at the last moment. I turn and watch as he hurls himself into the arms of the young man and his female companion, shrieks of pleasure filling the air.

Shit! I thought…

                    HOLLOWAY

          You thought he was heading to-
          wards you. Get a grip, Zane. For
          crying out loud, get a grip!


I duck inside the Men's before my self-control shatters. The air is thick with disinfectant, which doesn't quite mask the smell. A man stands at the sink, washing his hands, and talking to someone on the phone through a hands-free headset. I grip the basin so hard my knuckles blanch, and my reflection stares back, a face that still carries echoes of the man I once was.

'Breathe,' I whisper to the mirror.

The man shoots me a look, and I hurry into a stall.

                    HOLLOWAY

          What the hell are you doing?
          You want your arse burned?

My breathing stutters. I squeeze my eyes shut as I try to drown him out. He's nothing but dead air in my head.

HOLLOWAY

```
Think man, think! Before you
take a leak, you're leaving
your DNA behind. The police
will do an analysis of that
urine, and guess what? It's
got your name all over it.
```

ZANE

```
Seriously? How many other men
have peed in here? How much
DNA would the police have to
trawl through to find mine?
```

When I'm finished, I head for the sinks and splash cold water on my face, flinching as it runs down my collar. For a moment, Holloway is silent, and somehow the silence feels worse.

I step back into the station and weave between travellers, keeping to the shadows and dead spaces. On a vacant bench, I see a man with his back to me shrugging off a backpack and leaving it on the bench beside him. When he bends down to retie his boots, I see the phone peeking out of a side compartment. It awakens a need that had been dormant since the last call I made. If I don't take the phone now, the chance will be gone, even if it means moving into the main trajectory of the station's CCTV.

I creep towards him, keeping my head down and the crowd in my peripheral vision. Most are too busy looking at their own phones to see a man stealing someone else's. I crouch and draw the phone carefully from the side compartment and slip it into my pocket.

As I turn, every nerve ending in my body fizzes with shock. I can't believe I just did that. I expect to hear a loud yell and a clatter of feet behind me, but there's silence.

The man hasn't noticed yet. But he will. When he does, the station monitors will pick up a grainy image of a man whose face they can't identify.

HOLLOWAY

```
Of course, they'll identify
you. The place is crawling
with witnesses.
```

I slip quietly into the crowds, staying away from the turnstiles where cameras are at eye level. I'm almost at the opening of a narrow passage when I hear the echo of distant yelling. My pace increases as I slip inside.

Everything reeks of damp concrete and musty coats, and my shoes scuff against the floor, each step too loud, too sharp, like a perpetual countdown. A flickering bulb buzzes overhead, stuttering light across the walls like a heartbeat.

I push through the heavy door at the end, shoulder-first, and emerge into the night. The rain has softened to a mist, and the air is cold enough to bite. Ahead of me stretches the freight yard with its endless tracks, where iron hulks rest on steel and engines sigh in their sleep. This is it. This is where I vanish.

I crouch low, hugging the shadows of the chain-link fence line. Every movement counts.

HOLLOWAY

```
Let me help you with a thought.
You think climbing a fence and
boarding a freight train is a
good idea?
```

                          ZANE

            Got a better one?


                        HOLLOWAY

            What about stealing a car?


                          ZANE
                     (sarcastically)

            Let's not kid ourselves, Hol-
            loway. It could take all night
            to find one with an unlocked
            door and a key in the ignition.

The fence stretches high in front of me, barbed wire curling at the
top like teeth. Beyond it is a line of boxcars, their wheels groaning as
if they're about to move. There's a section near the far corner where
the barbed wire sags. It's not much, but it's better than nothing.

I move fast, my breath coming out in clouds, rising and vanishing like smoke. Then I hear the voices of two men, their footsteps
crunching on gravel. I hold my breath and press myself flat against
the fence while their torches sweep the yard in lazy arcs, beams
gliding too close and then pulling away. The guards shuffle past,
their laughter fading into the hum of engines. Only then do I let
myself breathe.

I reach the corner of the fence and grip the links as I climb.
Everything rattles under my weight, loud enough to make me
pause halfway. The rain soaks my palms and makes me slip, but I
hang on. As I swing one leg over, a barb tears at my jeans, snagging
and biting into flesh. Pain flares hot in my thigh, and I wrench it
free, ignoring the rip of fabric and the sting of blood.

I drop hard on the other side, and my knees slam into gravel,
and white sparks burst behind my eyes. I crouch, my ears straining
in the silence. There are no shouts. No footsteps. No lights turned
my way.

I huddle in the shadow of a boxcar, my mind hoping that what I'm seeing is correct, because the sliding door is open, giving me about three feet to squeeze inside. The train looms over me, and the smell of grease and rust fills my lungs, acrid and metallic.

```
          HOLLOWAY

     Even if you make it onto that
     train,  what  then?  Another
     town,  another  night,  another
     lie? You can't just vanish.
```

My pulse thunders in my ears. For a second, I want to scream, to let it out, to drown him with noise.

Instead, I whisper back: 'For once, I'm doing it my way, okay?'

A dog barks in the distance, and the sharp command of a man's whistle follows. My body goes rigid, and my nerves are firing. I flatten myself against the freight car, every muscle locked, every breath shallow. The beam of a flashlight cuts across the yard, searching. This is it, the knife-edge between freedom and ruin.

My pulse spikes, my whole body screaming at me to climb onto the first step. The dog barks, closer now. This is it. I've got seconds, maybe less, and scanning the length of the boxcar, the ladder is just out of reach, but it's my only shot.

I suck in one deep breath and launch upward. My fingers slap against the rung, slipping on wet metal, and the train shudders beneath me, a low groan that rattles up through my bones. Behind me, the flashlight beam sweeps back.

I freeze, body pressed tight to the ladder, praying I've melted into the darkness. Rain drips down my nose and stings my eyes.

```
          HOLLOWAY

     You'll fall, or they'll drag
     you down, and instead of pre-
     tending to be dead, you will
     be dead.
```

I climb the last rung and haul myself through the gap, sliding the door almost closed. I find a narrow platform at the front of the car and press myself into an empty corner. The train lurches, metal screaming against metal, and a slow, thunderous shudder runs through the length of the cars. Through the gap in the door, I see the yard sliding past, and lamps smearing into streaks of gold. The train picks up speed, and the city lights fall away.

For the first time in weeks, maybe months, a ragged sound tears out of me, half laugh, half sob. Against all odds, I've made it.

# 23

# LILJA

Yesterday, *BarbedWire* was praising Zane as a Method acting genius. Today everyone is having a roast fest about him seducing women half his age.

The thought has me putting my head between my knees and trying to restore blood flow to my brain. My interview with Stan Marriott today won't cause a small ripple, but a thermonuclear explosion. I've already studied the questions.

I'm wearing black tailored trousers and an ivory top – understated chic. Mum has styled my hair in a smooth beehive bun, like hers, and tells me not to be nervous.

'You'll be brilliant,' she says, fastening my pearls. 'Won't she be brilliant?' She turns to look at Frank, spilling out of a pink embroidered chair.

'She's always brilliant,' he says, lowering his newspaper to give me a once-over. 'Deep breaths, my darling. There's my girl.'

Mum thinks the light shines out of my arse regardless of how inadequate I feel. The reflection in my bedroom mirror tells me to keep a lid on my emotions and not to get fired up. Stan may mention Zane's ornamental girlfriends – relationships that only lasted a few weeks – but the public will side with me. Despite everything, I have some happy memories tucked away in the fractures and crevices that tore us apart. We weren't always the people we are now.

It's past 2.00 pm and there's a bristle of lunch guests in the hall, each admiring the flowers and asking Stella questions about the history of the house. She has become quite the flamboyant tour guide, embellishing stories about a ghost she has seen in the garden.

I slip downstairs unseen. A shaft of sunlight streams through the French doors, dappling the carpet a soft gold. My study makes a beautiful backdrop, and one I hope Zane's adoring audience appreciates. I check my laptop for updates and see an unfavourable comment piece about him in the *Guardian;* written by a journalist we all know and rate. My eyes skim over the relevant paragraphs.

> When Zane Osborne took the lead role in the Netflix series, *Play Him Play Her*, many viewers commented he would become the most bankable actor in the movie industry. For a while he almost was until he trashed the life of a beautiful young woman.
>
> Why should we care if Zane Osborne has been sighted in a small fishing village in Labrador? Isn't it more important that we care about the injustice he wreaked on Ms Gatlin and the effect of his behaviour on those whose lives he ruined?

The piece gives me confidence that not everyone is a supporter. Perhaps my interview won't come as a shock after all.

I spy a smudge of a figure running across the lawn towards the gate. Black ski jacket, dark hair, and well-toned legs. I move closer to the window. Bare branches afford some view of the road where I'd expect to see a swarm of reporters' headlights. But there's only one *MarriottLive* van cruising down the drive. When I hear footsteps on the flagstones, I open the French doors.

'Afternoon,' Stan says. He's wearing a grey suit and a burgundy tie. 'You look adorable. Do you have a jacket? We might need a lapel to pin the mic to.'

He introduces me to Vikki, the producer. While the camera operator and a sound technician adjust lighting and cameras, I grab a beige jacket from the back of the chair and slip it on. Vikki suggests we use the two wingback chairs by the fireplace, and they rearrange the furniture, and then we get settled.

'We'll do a twenty-minute warmup,' Stan says, looking at his watch. 'Then jump right in.'

To stop me from feeling nervous, Stan entertains me with tales of tracking Zane to the Stover Country Park one afternoon and how he collided with a tree and broke his camera.

'Of course, then the game was up. There I was, face down in a pile of leaves, and your husband comes trotting over and asks if I'm okay. He was very kind. Offered me a few fingers of whisky from his flask and sent me on my way.'

'Was he always so chivalrous?'

'There was another occasion. It was late afternoon, and I was sitting in the beach car park as one does on a warm day. There he was, walking in the dunes, waving at me like a long-lost friend. He offered me some water. Of course, I accepted. He leaned in through the window of that nice BMW and took two expensive-looking bottles from a cooler in the console. We had a friendly chat.'

'Dare I ask what about?'

'His father. It was long, as you might have suspected. Seems he both revered and feared him.'

'Sounds about right.' There is a knife of truth to that statement.

'There was another time,' he says, leaning a little closer. 'Same place, same time of day. You get good at celebrity routines. There they were, sitting on the bonnet of his car.'

'Him and Nic, you mean?'

Stan nods. 'Didn't look too friendly. In fact, it looked as if he was trying to give her the old heave-ho. There were a lot of tears and carrying on.'

'Was he shouting?'

'No, but she was. You've got nothing to worry about. Everyone knew what a horny bastard he was.' He leans forward and taps me on the knee. 'I'll introduce you to the camera and you can pretend you're talking to your sister.'

'I won't, if you don't mind. I tell my sister everything.'

'Exactly.' He grins. 'Chin up, chest out.'

He glances at the producer, who places a box of tissues on the table between us, and nods. There's a small countdown to what I assume is simply a pre-run, and Stan faces the camera.

'It's been well over a year since Zane Osborne, star of *Play Him Play Her*, disappeared. Audiences have been long awaiting an exclusive interview with the woman closest to the star. Now, wife and entrepreneur Lilja Osborne finally tells us her side of the story. Welcome to *MarriottLive*.'

'Great to be here,' I say.

'So, Lilja, I'm sure you know that there has been talk of your husband possibly having survived that terrible bear attack in Canada. Do you believe he's still alive?'

'There have been so many false sightings, I don't want to get my hopes up.'

'I'm sure you're remaining cautiously optimistic, although excited for news.'

Instead of my face crumpling in on itself like a rotting apple, I smile. 'Absolutely.'

'Let's go back a few months to the time when Ms Gatlin first started working for Mr Osborne. I understood she started sometime around June?'

'Yes.' My insides loosen, and my heart ricochets. This is no warmup.

'At what point did you find out about the affair?'

I try to compose myself. Saying anything negative about Nic doesn't get me brownie points. Her family could be watching.

'I found texts mostly. His were professional, asking her for his schedule and to set up meetings. Hers were…' This is it, my turn to ratchet up the tension. 'Salacious.'

Stan seems to consider the implications. 'Are you saying Zane wasn't complicit?'

'Not at first, no. He mentioned to me that Nic was a little handsy, and he wasn't comfortable with it.'

'Did he tell her?'

'No.' I give a rueful laugh. 'He left that privilege to me.'

'That must have taken some courage.'

I run a finger below one eye as I catch a tear. 'I started by asking her if she was happy working for Zane. Her words were, "Blissfully happy." I suspected by then she was already in love with him.'

*Love…* Ouch. It seems such a pitiful word to use when it was lust that drove them on. But the word love would encourage empathy among the viewers.

'I applauded her for being such a fabulous assistant and suggested she turn the dial down on the flirting. She just smiled, as if it was already a secret the two of them shared.'

There are a few seconds of silence where I can almost hear the audience gasp behind the cameras.

'Do you think the affair had already started by then?' he asks.

I want to say that her intrusion into our lives surpassed all professional norms. That she was a snake. A vicious, side-winding *snake*! Instead, I simply say, 'Yes.'

'How did you know?'

The air shimmers with images of Nic and Zane, images I don't want to see. Two people caught in slow motion: their passion growing in excitement, their kisses more savage. I refuse to be cowed by it. No matter what I say, any warmth for Zane will vanish quicker than frost on a window as I get to the heart of his infidelity.

'I overheard Zane and Nic running lines. They were laughing about something. What made me pause before knocking on the door was my husband's voice. It didn't sound as if he was in character.'

Stan's forehead pinches in a frown. 'What was he saying?'

I feel a sob push up my throat and swallow it down. 'He asked her if what she'd said about him was true. That a personal invitation to work for him was paramount to an Oscar nod. She said yes. He was every celebrity assistant's dream job. Every woman's crush, including hers. Then it went horribly quiet. The door was ajar, and I saw them kissing.'

Stan's eyes are giant pools of warmth. 'How did it make you feel?'

Perhaps it's the effort of not betraying my anger and frustration at Zane's wrongdoing that makes me hesitate. The audience will finally witness the tears I've kept locked up inside me.

'I couldn't believe what I was seeing. It tormented me for days.'

Stan doesn't flinch. 'Was he in love with her?'

'That was the thing. He treated her dreadfully. It was easy for Zane. He had his life and his career. He had choices. But Nic was in love with a married man who denied they had ever dated. For her, it was as if she had never existed.'

'What was it like for you?'

'Ironically, the same.'

My emotions flare, knowing that I'm sharing my most intimate struggles and secrets to the public, and I want to curl into a ball right here on the carpet and break into tears.

'Did your family know about Zane's affair?' he says.

'I made sure my daughter wasn't aware of it.' My composure wavers. 'But Zane and I had struggled for years over his affairs, most of them short-lived. This one seemed different. I think the biggest factor for him was having a persistent woman interested in him. He loved the attention.'

'Do you think Ms Gatlin contributed to your separation from Zane?'

'Our marriage took its worst hit when she came to work for us. Then it snowballed. They were spending a lot of time together, going for walks, staying up in London. Of course, it affected me. When you're busy paying bills, looking after the house, cooking meals, going to your daughter's sports events and trying to manage a cooking channel online with no input from your husband, you feel undervalued. I asked him why he was seeing her. What he said still haunts me.'

'Do you feel comfortable sharing that?'

I nod. 'He said the irresistible urge of an affair tempted him. He'd fantasised about secret meetings, and the illicit nature of hot, passionate sex, the type you don't want to have with your spouse. For him, it was all about the performance. Making Holloway believable.'

I look straight at Stan, the man with the million-dollar question on the tip of his tongue. He has a sense of right and wrong, enhanced by the signet ring engraved with a cross on his wedding finger and a Sunday school education. He must be feeling as awkward as I do.

There's a long pause while Stan looks down at his notes for the first time. 'Some people have mentioned that Holloway took over his life. That none of this was Zane. Would you say that was true?'

'I think blaming anything on a fictitious character is a copout. But whatever scenes he was studying for *Play Him Play Her* seemed to reflect his mood.'

'So, whatever happened in Holloway's world, happened in his?'

'That's the gist of it. Yes.'

Stan flips over a page, drawing out the anticipation. 'We all know Holloway is a very dangerous character. Were you ever afraid of Zane?'

My voice slows and gives way to a whisper. 'All the time.'

Stan's forehead furrows in a deep V. 'Was there anything in particular he found triggering?'

'Nic's obsession. She kept following him and posting photos on social media. Although the photos were blurry, her readers recognised her mystery man. It made him angry enough to drive out to see her. To put a stop to it.'

The colour rushes to Stan's face, his eyes flitting to the producer with some silent communication. 'When you say *put a stop to it*, what do you mean?'

'To tell her to stop posting things. Also, that she was fired. It was horrible, because soon after his birthday party, her family reported her missing.'

He pauses for a few beats. 'After she was reported missing, how did he react?'

I force a scowl from cracking across my features. 'His whole demeanour changed, as if someone had flipped a switch. He'd fly into rages and spend hours locked away in his study. Things weren't the same between us.' I sigh, as if it's too painful for me to talk about. 'When I asked him where Nic was, he kept saying he didn't know. I believed him.'

'Where do you think she'd gone?'

'I think all of us assumed she was staying with a friend. But days turned into weeks, and none of those friends had seen her. I'm sorry,' I take another tissue. My tears are rolling now. 'I can't… I just can't imagine what her family was going through.'

'How did you feel when you heard the news that she'd been found dead?'

Although my heart clutches tight, I'm powerless to stop the onslaught of words. 'I didn't believe it at first. I thought it was a mistake, a horrid mistake. Until I saw the news.'

He breathes deeply; his face lined with determination to tackle his next question head on. 'Do you believe he had something to do with Ms Gatlin's death?'

I sense a frisson run through the room, and my scalp prickles. 'If he hadn't, then why did he run?'

Stan looks at the camera and then at me. His mouth drops open.

**BarbedWire - Trending #InZane**

@BantaBadger: That's the first time I've seen her so jangled and teary. Normally, she's quite blasé about everything.

@CirceAtNight: We've already established that Nicola Gatlin disappeared after Zane Osborne's birthday party. Ergo, he did it. But what about another scenario? What if Lilja was angry with him about the affair? What if she was out for revenge?

@HeyWhatsUP: That's the stupidest thing I've ever heard.

# 24

# ZANE

I sit on the floor with my back against the wall, knees drawn tight to my chest. My breath fogs in the dark, and every creak of the boxcar makes me flinch. I tell myself I'm safe here, at least for the eleven hours I estimate to Montreal. But the sting of a cold draught makes me unclip the sleeping bag from my backpack and wrap it around me.

I wish I'd stolen a car instead.

Holloway sits opposite me, his cheeks as hollow as mine and twice as pale. My foot almost touches one of his outstretched legs. But he's not shivering in the cold like I am, and there's a smokiness about him that contradicts anything tangible, as if my hand would slice right through him.

<br>

                         HOLLOWAY

             You think you're safe now, do
             you? Hiding in here like a
             rat. You can't hide from your
             memories.

'Not now. *Please,* not now.' I press my palms against my ears; my voice sounds ragged and unconvincing.

HOLLOWAY

Plenty of time to think about
Nic. Want me to remind you how
she sounded right before she
stopped breathing?

My stomach lurches. I squeeze my eyes shut, but that's worse, because images of Nic appear, her face pale and startled, and her lips parted in a half-formed word.

I dig my nails into my arms. "No. That wasn't—"

HOLLOWAY

You? But it was your hands,
Zane.  Pushing,  slapping,
punching. It was your shadow
on the wall. Do you think you
can scrub that all away?

ZANE

It wasn't me. You were there.
You saw everything.

HOLLOWAY

Well,  not  quite  everything.
Apparently.

The images blur as if smeared by dirty glass. I keep asking myself whose hands were on her shoulders and whose fist had grabbed a lock of Nic's hair. Something shifts. A shape moves at the edge of the memory, and for a second, I could swear those hands weren't mine.

My mind races back in time to my birthday party, the time I arrived at the house and the time Nic texted me. Hadn't I greeted the guests first? Hadn't I seen my wife and my daughter standing on the patio under the glare of fireworks, looking so... beautiful?

It was the last time I saw my wife like that, with one side of her face in shadow and the other half lit by the patio lanterns. It reminded me of a technique used in film noir called "hatchet lighting," as if I was witnessing her menacing side for the first time.

Had she been in the cellar that night?

I'd gone downstairs, hadn't I? I'd rushed down there because Nic sent a text asking me to meet her there. I was freaked out because I hadn't invited her. Nor had Lilja.

I was tired of Nic trying her darndest to spoil everything and to expose what we'd done. I was terrified she was going to give me some bad news, like she was pregnant or something, anything to make me reconsider, or that she'd made a statement to the press.

I ran through the gardens to the French doors, which were open. There she was, sitting on my couch. I thought we'd ended everything, but she was crying.

She said, 'Did you ever love me?'

I remember my head aching and wishing I'd taken an aspirin. She said something about my wife hating me and destroying my life, and I remember thinking that was odd. Why would Lilja try to destroy me? Nic, yes. But not me.

Okay, so I was a coward, a filthy piece of shit, or whatever it was she called me. The words went on and on, getting louder. At some point, I took her downstairs to the cellar.

```
                    HOLLOWAY

          You took her down there to
          kill her.


                    ZANE


          No! I took her down there to
          keep her quiet. There were
          servers in the pantry, don't
          you remember?
```

                         HOLLOWAY

                    Oh, I remember.

Nic asked me to marry her, and I must have said no because something set her off. She began punching me. Not girlie punches that don't really hurt, but big pounders that took me by surprise. I didn't hit her back.

                         HOLLOWAY

                    Are you sure about that?

                           ZANE

                    Quite sure.

                         HOLLOWAY

                    Then what happened?

She pulled my hair and kneed me in the groin. I remember curling into a ball on the floor, and I'm sure she was still kicking me. It had to have been a minute or two before I staggered towards the cellar steps, desperate to get out.

I thought I saw a shape up there in the doorway. Maybe a server, someone who'd heard all the noise. Then Nic grabbed my arm and pulled me backwards. I don't know if I hit my head, but there was a missing piece of time where everything went black, and all I can remember is her body arching backwards before she fell.

                         HOLLOWAY

                    It's not exactly a sound you'd
                    forget, is it? The snapping of
                    bone on stone.

There's a second when I know something terrible is about to happen, and I'm too late to do anything about it. I run through every detail, recalling the dress she was wearing, as if that might clear away the mental cobwebs. Was it a white background with yellow daisies? Or was it a yellow background with white daisies? I blink hard, gasping, as though I've surfaced from deep water.

                    HOLLOWAY

          You're    finally    remembering,
          aren't you?

Bile rises from my throat, but I swallow it down. Time slows to a painful standstill, punctuated by the *rat-a-tat-tat* of the train's wheels on the tracks. I don't really want to go back in time with Nic again, but I don't have a lot of choice.

I can't seem to stop shivering, and my eyes feel heavy. Sleep takes me like a chokehold, and I'm dragged under. No warning, no fight left in me.

Nic's here beside me, her hand in mine and her laugh cutting through time. I see her hair falling across her cheek, the way she tucks it back, her eyes catching mine with a quick flicker of lust. Then everything tilts and the walls squeeze in. Her laugh dies, replaced by the thud of her head against the steps. And my hands… my hands are on her, pressing and squeezing, my fingers tight around something soft and fragile. Her breath hitches and breaks.

Then the image slows down like a car screeching to a halt.

                    HOLLOWAY

          Don't look away, Zane. This is
          what you did.

But something's wrong. I'm looking down at her, and my heartbeat is off, and somehow faster and heavier. Nic's eyes find mine, not with fear, but searching and pleading. Her body jerks, and the sound she makes is awful and final. In my dream, I stumble back and stare at my hands. There's no blood.

I wake with a scream stuck in my throat, the taste of metal on my tongue. My shirt clings to me, drenched in sweat.

                    HOLLOWAY

          Haven't we been over this
          before?


                    ZANE

          No, there's something different.

                    HOLLOWAY

          Good. Doubt is good. But tell
          me, Zane, if it wasn't you,
          then who was it?

The question slams into me harder than any accusation. And for the first time, the fear isn't just about being caught. It's about what I've forgotten.

I sit up too fast, and the inside of the boxcar is spinning. The boards creak beneath me, and the train sounds faster. My hands won't stop trembling. They're pale and harmless and couldn't have…

                    HOLLOWAY

          But they did. You felt the
          fight leave her. You felt the
          heat drain away. You killed
          her, Zane.

'No.' My voice cracks in the darkness. 'I saw someone. I wasn't the only one there.'

                    HOLLOWAY

        A convenient trick of the
        mind, old boy. Explain how she
        died in your arms if it wasn't
        you. Explain the silence right
        after she fell. Explain the
        way you ran. The way you hid.

I grip my hair, digging nails into my scalp, trying to ground myself. The dream flashes again behind my eyes: her lips shaping a name, not mine. A shadow with shoulders too broad, moving with a rhythm that isn't mine.

                    HOLLOWAY

        You're chasing ghosts. Now
        you want to play the victim.
        Pathetic.

But the seed is planted, and it writhes in my chest like a living thing. For over a year, I've carried the weight of Nic's death as if it belonged only to me. But I've been living with someone else's guilt.

I stand, pacing the boxcar, running my palms over the corrugated metal walls, needing something solid to feel, something real. It's obvious Holloway doesn't believe me – I'm starting to doubt myself – but I must try to get him on my side.

Fear is still there, the fear of being caught. But underneath it runs something new. Not relief or hope.

A name. And it terrifies me more than the fear ever did.

# 25

# LILJA

I try not to expect the public's response as each strand of my interview unravels on *BarbedWire*. The house is quiet in the early morning, the kind of quiet that makes me feel more alone than I already am. The icy knot in my stomach worsens.

Zane's alleged involvement in Nic's murder is trumpeted widely. Fans blow things out of proportion, rehashing old facts and spinning rumours into motive. Some believe that Nic was killed by an ex-boyfriend in a fit of jealousy. Knowing her insatiable appetite for sex and her infatuation with Zane, he followed her to our house, struck her with a heavy object and made my hapless husband take the blame. Perhaps Zane stumbled across Nic's body, panicked and tried to hide it. It's as good an explanation as any.

The point is, Zane tried to sneak off without telling anyone. If the police hadn't found a charge on my credit card – a card I kept at our Holland Park house in London – for a flight to Canada, they wouldn't have known where he'd gone. All I can do now is sit back and watch it all unfold.

I go through today's email on the sitting-room with a cat pressed between me and the back of the couch, his paws desperately trying to push me off. Four requests for interviews, a traditional publishing house offering me a contract to write a tell-all book, and a well-known magazine wanting photos.

Delete, delete, delete. Although… the tell-all book does sound intriguing.

Bizzy walks in wearing a skirt dangerously shorter than the one she wore yesterday. She's the one person who has remained unwavering through it all, trying to be strong and trying to shield me from the negative comments.

'Hey,' I say, patting the seat beside me. 'Did you sleep okay?'

'Yep,' she says, her mouth opening wide in a yawn. 'You were really brave yesterday.'

'I didn't feel brave.'

'You were. You told the truth, and that's what matters.' She places her phone on the table and taps the screen. 'I've been reading the comments from fans and they're—' she bites her lip as though gathering the right words, 'Amazingly supportive. They're saying how strong you were, that you handled it with such dignity. George and Saneh think you're an inspiration.'

I'm complimented that her two best friends are my biggest cheerleaders. 'They don't know how we feel, Bizz. They don't know what it's like to have someone you loved—' I stop myself from taking a sharp breath.

'But they do. They know what it's like to stand up after they've been picked on by a bully.'

I pull her towards me into a hug. I hear her words, but it's hard to feel them – hard to accept that during all the hurt, there is something stronger than the pain. There have been moments in the past when I thought she might collapse, when the weight of Zane's wrongdoing seemed unbearable. Even in her brokenness, she's remained resilient.

'You know what else,' Bizzy adds, her tone suddenly lighter. 'People think you're *really* hot.'

I laugh and shake my head. For a moment, there's a quiet strength brewing inside. Not the kind that comes with grand gestures or dramatic displays, but the small, unspoken kind found in the way Bizzy can lift my spirits without saying much at all.

She swipes her phone, which is still open at the *BarbedWire* site.

**BarbedWire - Trending #InZane**

@MiloMorales: Shame on those who've said derogatory comments about Lilja Osborne. She has shown great courage and grace. My heart and prayers go out to her.

@BlueJay: She's suffered mentally and physically. ZaneO should have treated her like the leading lady she is - not a sodding extra! She's soooo hot!

@BantaBadger: I don't understand how an actor we all raved about inflicted so much pain and trauma on his family. Absolutely #inZane!

@LiteraryParody: Hats off to Lilja. It must have been horrific living with all this pain. If ZaneO is found alive, I hope he gets life in prison. Total coward!

@HeyWhatsUP: She's utterly brilliant and blows my mind.

'I think *you're* utterly brilliant,' I say.

She waves off the comment and tells me she's going upstairs to get her football kit. I want to mimic her ability to live in the moment and ignore the all-pervading queasiness in my stomach. I look out of the window as the storm clouds turn the sky to ash. It's not the peace I'd expected to find, but it's enough.

I go into the kitchen and try to focus on the day ahead. But the steady sound of footsteps behind me makes my heart skip a beat.

'Morning, Lilja.'

'Morning, Ryan.' I force a casual tone. 'Coffee?'

'Yes, please. What's for breakfast?'

'Eggs, nothing fancy.'

'Let me help you.'

'I've got it, thanks.'

But he reaches up to the hooks above the island and takes down a pan, his arm gently brushing mine. I tell myself to calm down and take control. Every movement feels overly conscious, every glance a little too charged. I can see the faintest hint of amusement in his eyes. Is he teasing me? Or is it simply the effect he has on me?

He glances into the sitting-room, and I catch a flash of concern in his expression before he moves a little closer and lowers his voice.

'Lilja, I know things are a little crazy right now. But everyone here is worried about you. What you're going through. They're worried about what happens if Zane comes home.'

'Obviously, he'll go to jail.'

'If there's sufficient evidence, yes.'

'There has to be—' I stop myself because there's nothing to link Zane to the crime. At least, not yet.

'Why don't you take some time off?' he says. 'Nobody expects you to be running at full capacity, least of all Paul.'

'Did he say something?'

'No.' He leans two fists on the counter. 'Are you really going to make me say it? This interview has stirred everyone. Your being here will incite more press.'

'I think you're missing the point, Ryan. The press isn't interested in me. They're interested in Zane.'

He comes forward and places two hands on my shoulders. 'Look, if it were just Zane we were talking about, that would be one thing. But it's not. Every article is about you now. The public's focus is on *you.*'

I move away from him, his words boiling under my skin. 'Come on, Ryan, you know I can't leave. I have a business to run.'

'Just a few days until this all blows over.'

'Meaning what? Until Zane is found and in custody? That could be months!'

Thank God for Stella; her presence is very much needed, and suddenly here. Her face beams with good mornings, while pretending she hadn't been hovering outside, listening.

I grab a carton of eggs from the fridge and busy myself with mushroom, caramelised onions and goat cheese omelettes. I lose myself in it – the tap of the beater, the gentle thud of a knife on wood – while the voices behind me become more distant. Then I start on crème brûlée French toast.

By the time I've finished, the family is downstairs, food is plated, and everyone chats about my interview without so much as a glance in my direction. Except Ryan, whose gaze doesn't waver from mine.

I think about how this may end up backfiring on me and how stupid I was to have agreed to do the interview. Ryan's idea of time off may sound like a good idea, but I have no intention of leaving now.

Just as I'm about to take a bite of omelette, my phone lights up with a private number. I'm equal parts curious and suspicious, and I accept the call.

This time I don't say hello. I simply listen to the blustery rattle of wind and static, and the intermittent sound of rain against a hard surface.

Then the line goes dead.

My breathing, normally calm, is now shaky with fear. My eyes instinctively make a sweep of the room, and no one is looking at me; no one is in the least bit anxious.

I'm too wound up to eat, so I leave the room and start walking towards the front door. Now more than ever, I don't want my silent caller to be outside, standing with one hand raised to ring the bell.

I open it rapidly, expecting to see a man leaning against the tree with a cigarette pinched between his fingers. There is no one there, only the beating of wings as the lapwing takes off, disturbed by my sudden appearance.

It doesn't mean that someone wasn't here a moment ago. A prickle of unease tears down my spine as I scan the lawn and the drive. Everything seems as it should be, yet I know that it's not.

I know that since Zane left, everything has changed.

# 26

# ZANE

The air is stale, pressing against my lungs like a weight. Every vibration of the train judders through my bones, and every creak feels like a flare fired into the night sky. I can sense something evil wafting on the breeze, as if it's followed me all the way from Makkovik.

I blow warm air through the cuffs of my gloves and scrunch my toes. My mind drifts to the stolen phone in my pocket, and the temptation to search for Zane Osborne is too great to ignore. A wave of relief rushes up from my stomach, rapidly followed by nausea. There are thousands of hits.

I scroll through the top five links until I find a familiar name. *MarriottLive*. The seedy little man has got his own chat show now. I've never been much of a fan. The taped episode shows him interviewing my wife, who should have been looking like a crack addict, but is young and fresh, like a cross between Kate Moss and Grace Kelly.

My heart thrums as I watch the captions. Stan's jagged questions, her weepy answers – and the diabolical misrepresentation of a once brilliant star. Me.

The interview took place in my study, or what's left of it. The walls are light blue, and the picture above the fireplace shows Bizzy wrapped in Lilja's arms, just the two of them, as if I've been swept under the carpet and forgotten. I can't help feeling a spike of anger.

I check *BarbedWire*. People are offering stories about how I broke my wife's heart and killed my mistress without blinking an eye. The only person categorically disagreeing with all the accusations is Milo, a young fan I'd met briefly outside Blundell Street Studios last year and who has loyally protected my corner ever since. He insists there is no evidence, either physical or historical. No police reports provided by Lilja or any other witnesses that might hint of assault.

> @MiloMorales: He is a very much-loved husband and father.

I appreciate Milo keeping me in the present tense, even after comments from armchair detectives, debunking theories I was mauled by a bear.

> @CirceAtNight: Zane Osborne's death is utter bull-shit. Nobody's buying it. We all know his marriage is on the rocks because he's a serial cheater. Since his affair with Nicola Gatlin went south, so has he.

Don't be a dildo, Circe. Canada is northwest of the UK. Look it up.

I find another article on CNN titled *Lilja Osborne Gives Tell-All Interview*, which means most of the major networks are airing the same story.

Small grey dots cluster at the edge of my vision, and I take deep breaths, waiting for the sensation to pass.

HOLLOWAY

You've really outdone yourself
this time. You were clearly born
to be locked up. Oh, and let's
not forget the little misdemeanour of calling long distance
on someone else's phone.

He's right. I shouldn't have done it. I shouldn't have listened to the familiar chatter of home. The image of my daughter scraping every smear of yoghurt from the carton and speed texting her best friend comes to mind. I could see Stella knocking back a few Baileys while watching *RuPaul's Drag Race,* and my wife walking around the herb garden, holding a little willow basket full of lavender and other herbs like some country girl in the 1800s.

<pre>
                    HOLLOWAY

          Only this time, she was hold-
          ing the phone to her ear and
          listening for any signs of you.
</pre>

The train groans as it takes a corner, and my balance tilts, and I slam my hand against the side of a crate. Sounds echo louder than they should, and I freeze, heart banging so hard it feels like it's bruising my ribs.

The rhythm changes, a subtle drag in the momentum, and the grinding complaint of steel under strain. The train is slowing, wheels screeching as the brakes clamp, and sparks hissing in the dark.

There are voices outside, muffled at first, then clearer. Men shouting to each other and boots thudding along the platform. I hear the clang of something heavy being dragged, and the low bark of an engine idling somewhere beyond the freight line.

What if they find the boxcar's door unlocked? They'll see me crouched here like an animal, sweat-drenched and wide-eyed.

<pre>
                    HOLLOWAY

          This is it. This is where the
          curtain drops. They'll haul you
          outside, your hands raised like
          a criminal on stage. Finally,
          everyone will know the truth.
</pre>

There's a crisp thudding sound as someone walks along the platform. The flat of a hand slaps against the side of the car ahead. Then, the latch shifts and clatters.

A thin blade of light slices across the floor, cutting through the dust, and glinting like a knife. The door is no longer closed but open a crack. Anyone walking past, anyone with a flashlight, could see the glimmer of my face inside.

Silence presses in, as if the walls of the boxcar are leaning closer, listening to the madness rattling in my skull. An impatient voice calls the men to empty the front two cars. Boots run along the platform, retreating to who knows where. The air leaves me in a ragged, shuddering exhale.


                    HOLLOWAY

       Someone unlocks a door and
       you're wetting yourself.


'Piss off!' My voice is hoarse and raw, and it's louder this time. I don't care if anyone hears.


                    HOLLOWAY

       Or what? You'll silence me
       like you silenced Nic?


I slam my fist against the floor. The hollow thud reverberates through the car, louder than I had hoped. My knuckles scream with pain.

But Holloway drowns the thought out, his voice getting louder.


                    HOLLOWAY

       You'll never outrun it. With
       every mile of track, every
       stolen breath, you're just
       dragging the corpse with you.

I hear doors rattling and the whine of a forklift. The air feels thinner, collapsing in on itself as I crawl towards the door with the intention of quietly sliding it closed. But someone is walking past, a man with his head down, reading his phone. The sight of him coming to a stop about five feet from the open door shocks me.

Can he see me?

I need to get out of here, not that I know where I am, but if I find a stream, it must lead to a town.

Seconds stretch into torture as he stands there, tapping out a text. Sweat drips from my hairline and slides down the back of my neck. He has only to turn a fraction to see my quivering white face and a pair of startled eyes. I grip the edge of the door as if it's the only thing stopping the floor from creaking under my weight.

The whistle of the engine and the clank of chains save me. Slowly, mercifully, the train jolts forward. The beam of light through the crack in the door narrows, flickers, and fades, and I sag back against the wall, shaking. The wheels bite the track again, and the train gathers speed.

HOLLOWAY

> Lucky. But luck runs out. When
> it does, you'll be on your
> knees permanently.

Holloway is right. Every mile feels like it's taking me closer to the end. For the first time, I wonder if they've already trapped me or if the only cage left is the one in my head.

HOLLOWAY

> While we're on the subject
> of who killed Nic, if you're
> looking for an excuse, you
> could go for incompetency to
> stand trial. Might be easier

to escape from a mental health
facility than a prison.

ZANE

You're wasting your time. I'm
not incompetent.

'I'll prove it,' I whisper, as the train thunders on. 'I'll prove I didn't kill her. I'll prove it to everyone. Even you.'

I have a mental flashback, and my brain tries to process what my mind is seeing. That's when the pieces of the puzzle fit together, and now there's an image to go with the name.

It feels like a small, fleeting victory.

# 27

# LILJA

When the phone rings the next morning, there is an unfamiliar name and a number that doesn't appear to be national. The only thing that sets it apart from a nuisance call from a call centre is the area code of five-one-four.

This time the background noise is different. It seems calmer and not fraught with the pitter-patter of rain and static. Out of nowhere comes the sound of metal grinding against metal, and then the line goes dead.

I look down at my phone as if it will somehow tell me who it was, and my head reels again. It could be innocent. If it were, wouldn't the caller have tried talking to me or at least, calling back? Isn't that what normal people do?

I walk out of my bedroom and onto the landing as I try to decipher the sound. Perhaps it was someone in a garage, standing too close to a high-powered wrench or whatever they use to tighten lug nuts. Only it wasn't as strident as that. It was smooth and intermittent, and I can't place it.

When everything points to my silent caller being someone who might have information on Záne, I feel sick. He must have heard how nervous I was, and suddenly I'm so angry, I want to call the number back.

I walk downstairs and begin dialling the country code and then five-one-four, when Ryan greets me in the hall with a flash of curiosity on his face.

'Anything the matter?'

I put a hand on the banister to steady myself and show him the caller's number on my phone. It sounds crazy asking Ryan to imagine Zane talking to me. God forbid my husband is wreaking some kind of chilling revenge.

'After all these weeks, it never occurred to me that the dropped calls must be from Zane.'

The muscles in Ryan's face tighten. 'He's an idiot if he doesn't suspect covert surveillance on your phone.'

'I'm not kidding, Ryan. Weird stuff's been happening. Strange sounds at night, footsteps on the gravel, the smell of his cigarettes and his cologne. It's like he's outside the house trying to scare me. When I check the CCTV, there's no one out there.'

Ryan shakes his head. 'If it is him, he'd be freezing his balls off.'

I manage a faint smile, trying to hide the depth of my distress. I'll be cleaning or shopping, and some memory rears up. The sound of Zane's footsteps, the tone of his voice, that awful feeling of terror. He's got away with so much.

Ryan must sense my scrutiny, the way my eyes skid up and down his face. I can't keep my eyes off his neatly trimmed hair and his intriguing expression. I get the impression he takes it all in his stride, that women staring at him is a given. But today, the vibe is different.

'I'm sorry. I get scared sometimes.'

He exhales, a short laugh without humour. 'I can imagine.'

'And yet…' I say, trying not to sound paranoid, 'it could be him.'

His brow furrows, just a fraction, but I catch it. 'We both know he's in Canada.'

I look down at my phone, and so does he. All I want to do is listen to the voice on the other end, only I'm too sick with apprehension.

'You want me to talk to him?' he asks.

I nod and hand him my phone.

He dials the country code first and then the number, but it comes up unavailable. Shaking his head, he tries again before hanging up. 'Maybe the phone doesn't accept long distance.'

As he hands me back my phone, something occurs to me. Before Nic came to work for us, there was a night where Zane didn't come home. The following morning, Ryan was standing in the kitchen, drinking coffee and talking to the two other CPO's. I asked him where Zane was. Ryan said he'd driven him to the Southernhay House Hotel in Exeter the night before to meet with his male co-star for dinner, and that Zane insisted he would get a taxi home.

The whole thing tasted sour to me, because when I called the hotel, the house manager had no such booking. Not even under Collins, a name we frequently used for private dinners. What if Ryan had lied to me because he knew exactly where Zane was that night?

'You never talk about your friendship with Zane,' I murmur, 'and it makes me wonder what you're not saying.'

He's suddenly wide-eyed and smiling. 'Zane employed me because of my discretion. So have you.'

I'm still not convinced. It feels as if everything is crumbling around me, and I don't know who to trust. Panic suddenly builds, and my eyes fill with the threat of tears.

'Don't overthink it,' he says, reaching out and touching my shoulder. 'Trust me, there's nothing to talk about.'

His eyes track from me to the sitting-room before pulling me into a hug. Instead of being characteristically cautious of the family watching, I allow my body to be swallowed up by his. For once, I let myself breathe. His presence has a way of quieting the noise in my head, of anchoring me when the world feels like it's tilting.

The sound of footsteps brings me up short, and I push away from Ryan. Stella stands framed in the doorway, her eyes fixed on us, and the warmth drains out of me in an instant.

I smooth my blouse with nervous fingers. 'Oh, Stella,' I say, the words tumbling out. 'I was just…'

'Sorry to interrupt.' Her head tilts the slightest fraction, as though assessing me. 'I was just wondering who was taking Bizzy to school.'

'Me,' Ryan says, running a hand through his hair. 'If that's okay.'

The smile I paste on feels stiff and unconvincing. 'That would be great.'

Stella watches him dart out of the front door, her head turning as he walks past the window. The silence between us stretches until it prickles. There's something faint in her expression, not quite disapproval or concern, but something buried beneath that thoughtful exterior.

'I'm grateful he's here,' she says softly. 'But he ought to know his place.'

The words sound tender, but her eyes are flat and unreadable. For a moment I think I see the corner of her mouth twitch, not towards a smile, but with restraint.

'He was just being kind,' I say.

'I wouldn't classify a hug as being kind. Inappropriate, more like.'

My heart skips a beat. 'It wasn't anything like that.'

'That's what they all say.'

'Is everything all right?'

'I'm not sure. You tell me.'

There's an appalled silence. 'There wasn't anything in it, if that's what you mean. I seem to have a silent caller, and he was…' I lift my arms in the air. 'Helping me.'

'Fine. But I just want to make sure you haven't forgotten you're still Zane's wife. At least publicly.'

She turns at last and walks back into the kitchen. The air suddenly feels thinner. Her words echo in my mind, and I replay the stillness in her body and the flicker in her eyes, and I feel the smallest crack of doubt.

I tell myself it was nothing. I'm simply being foolish, seeing shadows where there are none. She has been with me since I was a girl, and knows my habits, my moods, and my flaws. She knows I wouldn't do anything to shame this family.

I rub my arms though the room is warm, and a strange chill lingers under my skin. I turn it around in my head, looking at small things from every angle, things I may have brushed aside.

Zane complained Stella was always listening on the study staircase, always appearing when he least expected her. The way her gaze followed him as if she suspected him. Things I'd refused to believe. It could all be in my head. God knows these past weeks have stretched my nerves thin.

But alone with my thoughts, I find my heart racing with fear. In the silence, I strain my ears and hear the murmur of her voice and Paul's on the patio. Even if I try to open the French doors to listen, the hinges will squeal loud enough to give me away.

They must be terrified that Ryan is getting too close to me and that I might allow him complete access to the house and to the business. As I sit there on what used to be Zane's couch, with my hands clutched around my phone, I make a decision.

Now more than ever, I need my family to believe in me. I need them to trust that I will fight for them, no matter what it takes.

**BarbedWire - Trending #InZane**

@SherylAdams: I'm done letting this shit fly. All his past posts about love for his wife seem like a joke now.

@CirceAtNight: Yep. You hit the nail on the head.

@SherylAdams: He's just another dog that cheated on his wife. Pretentious, arrogant dickhead. All hail Lilja!

# 28

## ZANE

The train groans as it slows, and the boxcar shudders. A sliver of light seeps through the crack in the door, and the dawn sky is a dull shade of grey.

My breath fogs in the cold Canadian air, and my stomach growls with hunger. I can't put off eating or drinking for another day. I try to focus, but my head feels light, and my legs are wobbly. If I can't stand, I can't walk. If I can't walk, I can't run.

In the gentle *clackity-clack* of the train, I feel more at peace. Hearing Lilja's voice on the stolen phone, saying hello once and then staying as silent as I was, gives me hope. I indulge in the fantasy that I might go home and get back with her. Surely after I explain how much I've changed, she will understand. For now, I gain pleasure simply by casting myself in the role of a remorseful husband, who, in all his messed-upness, is desperate to make things right.

```
                    HOLLOWAY

So,  you  believe  that  your
wife's  mental  health  hasn't
taken a battering? You assume
that she's simply shaken but
unscathed?
```

ZANE

A man can use his imagination,
can't he?

HOLLOWAY

If your focus hadn't been on
playing out my sexual fanta-
sies, we wouldn't be in this
shithole, would we? There is a
healthy balance, you know.

ZANE

You wanted me to be believable. You wanted me to be you.

HOLLOWAY

Next, you're going to tell me
you committed yourself deeply
for the cause. That this,
without the aid of pride and
vanity, it was something you
simply had to do.

ZANE

I played you well, didn't I?

HOLLOWAY

At great cost to you, yes.
Sooner or later, the true
nature of what you did with
Nic's body both before and
after death will become clear

<pre>
            to your daughter. I doubt some-
            one so absorbed in social media
            would miss it. Until then, we
            have an agonising wait for the
            local police. They'll be  at
            the next station. You watch.


                    ZANE

            I wish I could talk to her.


                   HOLLOWAY

            No. You don't.
</pre>

The screaming brakes pull me out of my trance. I don't know how much more of this freezing monotony I can take. Rather than ride the train all the way into central Montreal and risk capture, I decide this is my last stop.

I shrug on my backpack and crawl towards the door. Sliding it back takes the full force of my body, and the runners make a deep-throated growl. It takes superhuman effort to restrain myself from squeezing through. Since the pistons are blowing steam and the engine is chugging at a standstill, they will drown any suspicious noise. There are no signs of any uniforms.

Ahead, the train curves towards a small station, which is illuminated by a weak pool of yellow thrown from a single lantern. To my left, there's a break in the trees, where the ground slopes down to a winding road, running parallel to the train tracks and curling towards a building with a neon sign.

I climb down from the boxcar, and my boots crunch loudly against the snow-hardened gravel. My heart slams in my chest. Anyone could spot me from the station – a dark figure with a backpack, darting for the trees – and any tracker would recognise the tactical imprints I've left behind.

I slip and slide down the bank, taking care not to snap any tree branches along the way. By the time I reach the bottom, the road glimmers under the streetlights where a row of cars sits along the curb outside a brightly lit restaurant. Sweat stings my eyes as I cross the road, and I can see a few men seated inside, drinking coffee and eating breakfast. Their padded jackets hide their size, but they're not men I'd pick a fight with.

I crouch, my pulse thundering in my ears. There are no pedestrians, but there are a couple of houses set back from the street, door lanterns glowing. I need distance and I need cover. The only way I can get it is by stealing a car. The knot of dread in my stomach pulls so tight, I can barely breathe.

I creep towards the first car. The LED light on the dashboard tells me it's alarmed. The second and third cars are older, and all their doors are locked. I peer through tinted windows, careful not to touch anything in case the shock sensors trigger a siren.

My heart leaps as my eyes land on the dirt track behind the restaurant. There's bound to be a car parked outside one of those houses, something I can hot-wire. Approaching the first house, I see an old Ford Escort parked in the driveway. It's locked. Pent-up frustration rages inside me. It's not until I try the fourth house, where a rusted-out Corolla sits under a carport, that I feel hopeful.

I check the street, then pull on the driver's side handle. No luck there. My stomach knots, and I look around for a rock to smash the window.

```
                    HOLLOWAY

        Don't even think about it!
        You'll wake the neighbours.


                      ZANE

        Wait... What about tugging my
        sleeve over my fist and smash-
        ing the corner of the window?
        Surely, it'll crack and spider
        and then shatter.
```

                    HOLLOWAY

          It's  tempered  glass,  son.
          You'll  need  a  battery-powered
          saw.


I roll my eyes, but don't argue. Looking in through the passenger window, I see a toddler car seat and a tub of disinfectant wipes on the right side of the car. My eyes sweep around the interior, and that's when I see it. The lock at the base of the window frame is up. What child ever locks a door? The sight of it sends my heart thudding hard.

The door creaks open, and I reach into the front seat and pop the lock. The smell of spilled coffee hits me. My hands shake as I yank the steering column shroud loose, plastic giving way under the pressure.

Battery cables are red, the starter is yellow, and the ignition is brown. Is that right? Holloway doesn't answer. I fumble with the wires and strip them with my teeth. All I can remember is red to red and yellow to yellow because if I cross them, I'll fry the circuit. When I twist the wires together, sparks jump, and the dash lights flicker to life.


                    HOLLOWAY

          Quickly!  Touch  the  starter
          wire.


The engine coughs and then roars louder than it should. I pull out from under the carport, not daring to look at the man on the porch, silhouetted against the glow of his living room. Slamming my foot down, the car lurches forward, tires squealing and headlights flaring across the dirt track. He runs after me, screaming, 'Hey! What the hell are you doing!'

My chest is tight and my vision tunnels, but the car moves. That's all that matters. The track suddenly becomes a road, and I turn the wheel and head downhill.

HOLLOWAY

You've won, rabbit, won rabbit,
won, won, won. Look what you've
done, what you've done, done,
done.

It's ten miles of forest and meadows, the heater cranked up as far as it will go before the engine stutters and the car jerks like it's about to die. I feather the gas, trying to keep the revs steady, but every flicker of the dash lights feels like the end.

I turn onto another dirt road, tyres spitting gravel. My hands ache from gripping the wheel, and the car stutters again but doesn't stall. When the track turns into smooth tarmac, I pick up speed, driving past farms, thinning out to dark pine trees and empty stretches of road.

The Corolla growls as if it's on its last breath, every sputter rattling through the frame. I tear down a narrow road that snakes between the trees, and the car's headlights carve thin tunnels of light through the dark.

Behind me, sirens wail faintly in the distance. I grit my teeth, pressing harder on the gas. The road forks ahead, one lane paved, one dirt. I wrench the wheel right, tyres bouncing wildly, and dust and pine needles exploding in my wake. Branches scrape the sides of the car, and the suspension groans as I urge the junker forward.

But the Corolla doesn't like the terrain, and the dash lights flicker as though the whole thing might shut down any second. The car lurches once – twice – then roars stubbornly back to life. I can smell burning oil, and my stomach knots.

The road twists deeper into the trees until I spot an abandoned logging turnout. It's the perfect cover. I kill the headlights and coast into the shadows. Silence crashes down, broken only by my own ragged breathing. I listen for sirens, but there's nothing out here but me, the forest and the wheezing car.

I lean back, eyes burning, and force my lungs to slow. For now, I'm alive and hidden.

The Corolla ticks as it cools, and the smell of hot metal and oil chokes the air. I stare at the steam curling off the bonnet, and I know it won't last another mile. Anyone driving this road will see the car. When the cops backtrack, the broken Toyota will be the first thing they find.

I shove the wires free, killing the engine completely. After ditching the car, I hike downhill. After half a mile, I see headlights cutting across the intersection of a two-lane highway. On the far side is a gas station with three rows of pumps and a convenience store. I swallow hard, and my pulse thunders.

                    HOLLOWAY

        See that large semi? I think
        it's got your name on it. Think
        of a wolf testing its prey.
        Assess for weakness, then iso-
        late and capture.

The semi chugs towards the diesel pumps, its engine giving off a deep, rhythmic hum. The driver exits the cab and runs into the store, possibly for a coffee or a pee, both of which I need. I doubt he locked it, but I wouldn't have heard the remote over the noise. Besides, a semi is not something I can manage.

The place is filling up, cars turning in from the highway and stacking up beside the pumps. At the far corner of the store, a new black Dodge sits idling next to a Jeep, its headlights off. The driver stands by the open door, smoking the remains of a cigarette. He waves to a young woman driving a Civic as she pulls in at the first pump. He grinds the cigarette under his heel, pushes his door closed and runs towards her car, waving his wallet. I'm sure he didn't lock the truck's door, and the windows are too dark to see if there is anyone else inside. The only way I can tell is to move closer.

I watch the driver as he talks to the woman, his back towards me, and then, like the true gentleman he is, tells her to stay inside while he fills the car with gas. For a moment, I wonder if I can steal his truck so unashamedly.

<pre>
            HOLLOWAY

      Think of it this way. It's
      like skinning one carcass to
      wear another.
</pre>

I don't have to think about it at all. Head down and hood up, I creep between the jeep and the truck and open the door. The mixture of coffee, new leather and grilled cheese greets me. Better yet, the keys are dangling from the ignition. In the man's haste to help the young woman – his daughter, his young wife, whoever – he had no time to lock his car. I feel like a shit for taking advantage, but I'd feel like an idiot if I overlooked it.

I slip into the seat and pull the door towards me quietly. The click is barely audible over the roaring semi as it backs into the diesel pumping station. All I can think of is the wide-open highway, the coffee nestled inside the cupholder, and what looks like a burrito wrapped in silver paper.

Slotting the gear into drive, I reverse out gently, narrowly avoiding another truck wanting to take my space. My eyes flick down towards the side mirror as I slide out of the parking lot and onto the highway.

<pre>
            HOLLOWAY

      Now you should be humming The
      Ride of the Valkyries.
</pre>

# 29

# LILJA

Since my interview with *MarriottLive*, the press has been camping outside the house, obsessed about Britain's "it" couple. I open the window and tell Bizzy to stop dribbling a football in the garden and to come back inside. I can almost hear the hum of camera motors from here.

Most days, Ryan drives me to budget and marketing meetings with Mum and father-in-law Frank, and team-leading lunches off site. He helps me with deliveries and inventory, and wards off any lurking reporters. Today, he's taking me to the farm for supplies.

I change into jeans, a black turtleneck and trainers, and brush my cheeks with a little highlighter. My phone rings, and I look at the number, which, by the arrangement of digits, appears to be long distance. *Engage him in conversation,* I say to myself.

'Hello.' I wait for a voice.

The background gives nothing away, and I hang up. A few seconds later, it rings again, and it's the same nobody who doesn't want to speak.

Anxiety bubbles up through my body, scorching and painful. I want to dismiss it as a wrong number, but something tells me to call the person back, just to be sure. When I do, there's a recorded message that tells me the number I'm calling is not available and to dial again. It may be the arrangement of numbers I'm using or the wrong country code. But a text from Ryan asking me if I'm ready tells me there's no time to waste.

I grab a warm ski jacket and run downstairs. Stella holds the front door open and points to the drive where Ryan stands by his SUV, his hand ushering me into the back seat.

He tells me to keep down, and I feel the car cruising smoothly down the front drive.

'Two press vans,' he warns.

He pauses as the automatic gate opens and glides through. As we pull out into the lane, the press swoops down on us, questions barking through tinted windows, flashes rolling off the side of the car.

Ryan keeps his eyes forward and heads for the church. Soon, we're cutting through the countryside, windows open a slit to catch the fresh air.

He looks back at me through the rearview. 'You okay?'

'Fine, thanks.' I crawl over the console into the front seat and snap on my seat belt. 'I got another of those silent calls.'

There's a determination in Ryan. I sense it in the stiff brace of his shoulders and the tightness of his jaw. All I can think of is that he's just as concerned about it as I am.

'Every arm of law enforcement is on the lookout for him,' he says. 'When they find him, shit's going to fly.'

'What if he comes back from whatever ratty little hole he's been living in and demands his life back?'

'Before you get too jazzed, Zane can't demand anything.'

I rest my head back against the seat. 'A hundred pounds says they'll find some minor technicality and get him off.'

'Hardly. Just because he's a celebrity doesn't mean he's untouchable.' He squints out of the rain-spattered windscreen. 'I want you to relax and forget about it for now. Think you can do that?' He looks over at me. 'Say yes, Ryan.'

I roll my eyes. 'Yes, Ryan.'

I'm buoyed by the mood and the scenery. How can I doubt a seasoned bodyguard? He won't let anything happen to us. Of that, I'm sure.

'Have you ever done any modelling?' His voice breaks through my thoughts.

'I'm about two inches shy of the preferred height.' I cast a glance at him in profile. His nose has a slight bump, possibly broken doing sports, and there's a small scar above his eye. Apart from that, he's perfect.

'How about you?'

'Not a chance,' he says. 'Although I did ballet when I was about five, which was a source of ridicule amongst the school rugby team. They said I had a walk. A kind of glide.'

'I don't see it at all,' I say. 'Well, maybe a little.'

He laughs, his hair ruffling in the breeze. He flips on the radio, and *Cheri Cheri Lady* blasts through the speakers. I can't help grinning at him, his head bobbing and voice rising, looking as high on the beat as I am.

A slice of fiery orange bathes the hills, and a skein of geese flies under a grey sky. I'm feeling better than I have in months. By the time we get to Hynards Farm, I've laughed myself hoarse.

The market is well stocked, Highland and Lincoln Red beef, all native breeds, grass reared and local. I can't resist a homemade cheesecake and a few other tasty treats for the family. We haul my order into the back of the car, including boxes of eggs and milk.

I ask him to stop at a florist on the way home. We select blue jacket hyacinths and creamy narcissi for the hall, and wands of deep violet muscari for the tables. We buy coffee and pull into the beach car park, sipping our espressos while watching a jostle of runners streaking past the car, wearing black tracksuits with the emblem of their school emblazoned on each chest. They follow the curve of the seawall and are quickly lost from view.

'If this is a good time, I'd like to show you something.' He unlocks his phone and leans towards me. 'One of my friends sent it to me. He said they went through thousands of surveillance footage of men leaving the airport on the same day and time Zane arrived in Canada.'

By friend, I assume he means a cop. He presses PLAY and, in the centre of the frame, a man darts from a shop to a waiting cab. The image is grainy and hard to make out, but it captures a view close enough to make out scruffy jeans and a baseball cap, a padded jacket and hiking boots. Even though the man stoops to give the cabbie directions, the newspaper he carries over his head to ward off the rain makes it impossible to see his face.

Ryan rewinds the video and pauses it at the part where the man peers into the taxi driver's window. There's a small gap between the edge of the newspaper he's holding and his chin. I freeze as I watch this eerily recognisable man.

'It could be him,' I say, studying the sharp angle of the man's jaw. 'But there's not enough of his face.'

'The car picking him up is not a cab. It was a private car, an Uber, and one without an active website presence. They charge top dollar and leave no digital footprint. But to the passenger, they appear like any other Uber.'

'Where did the driver take him?'

'He dropped him off somewhere along the Boulevard Champlain. Unfortunately, he didn't see where he went.'

I watched the video with a horrid sense that these images were the last the police saw of a man who looked uncannily like Zane. It is as if he'd been taken beyond the lens of the camera and spirited away into the Twilight Zone.

'Somebody must have seen him,' he says, starting the car. 'If that somebody exists, they haven't told the police yet.'

'What kind of person wouldn't tell the police?'

'Someone unknowingly harbouring him or someone who believes they're in a relationship with him. It takes only one person to call it in.'

My spine tightens as we pull back onto the road. 'What if they never find him?'

His eyes turn dark suddenly, like a field when a cloud has passed in front of the sun. 'I'd give the police a little more credit than that.'

I close my eyes, pushing away my frustration. News like this is unwanted on a day like today. This was supposed to be our time to connect, to have a few hours without my husband cropping up in every conversation. Seriously? Could Zane make this any more about him?

An unexpected swell of anger hits me, and I gaze through the window at a row of gardens with the first flowers of spring. Ryan's voice is layered beneath my thoughts, not loud enough to be heard, except for the last sentence.

'Was he physically abusive? I mean, had he ever hit you?'

I sag against the seat. 'He hurled books and ornaments across the room, smashed cups in the sink when he was angry. He wasn't violent as much as acting out, like a child if you didn't give him his favourite toy. When I confronted him about his affair with Nic, he grabbed me by the neck and slammed me against the wall. It was the only time he ever did it.'

Zane's temper bubbled under the skin and erupted at unpredictable moments around the time I'd found emails between him and a young actress. It was babe this and babe that, and I remember staring at the words until they blurred into hot prickly tears.

For him, it was the ultimate control, the ability to know how to manipulate me to his advantage. When Zane used to pull me into his arms and promise me it was all nothing, I believed his reassurances and swallowed my doubts. The part I keep to myself is how his fury would disintegrate after a good home-cooked meal and a steamy session in the bedroom. The penance was worth it until his behaviour became odd and erratic. Of course, by then, it was too late.

Ryan turns into the drive, his hand suddenly warm against my shoulder. 'Are you okay?'

'Yes,' I say, leaning away from his touch. 'I'm fine.'

He presses the code, and we're coasting down the drive as Stella comes out to greet us.

'Can I help?' she says as we unload.

'Thanks.' I hand her the flowers.

Instead of the usual chatter at lunch, everyone seems subdued, eating and scrolling through their phones as if they're glued to the latest headlines.

Stella's gaze settles on Ryan. 'How well did you know Zane?'

All faces turn to him. 'Pretty well.'

'I assume you must have shared confidences.'

'Yes, I suppose we did.'

All faces turn to her now. 'So, you knew about Nic, then? You saw them together?'

He looks at me, but my face gives nothing away. 'Yes, I did.'

The effect on the family is immediate, a surge of open-mouthed awe that ripples around the room. I flinch, unable to form a reaction.

'I can't even—' She inhales sharply, casting me a withering glance. 'I can't imagine what that must have been like.'

'For whom?' Ryan asks.

'For you. I mean, you took him to parties, you drove him everywhere. It must have been… awkward.'

I know we're past the first anniversary of Zane's "death", but it feels like Stella's being overly intrusive. Or worse, that she's interrogating him. Thank God for Bizzy, who always fills embarrassing silences with humour.

'Stella has a long questionnaire for you to fill out, Ryan. Fifty questions of what my dad did, with whom and where. It's required.'

Ryan looks momentarily appalled, and then his face breaks into a wide grin. 'You're shitting me, right?'

Paul shakes his head. 'All the sordid details, Ry. Rather you than me.'

Everyone laughs, except for Stella, and I feel the weight of her eyes on me. She pushes back her chair and stands.

'It's not a laughing matter.' She points at Ryan. 'We know nothing about him. He could sell everything we say to the press.'

'Come on, Stel.' Bizzy gives her a playful smile. 'It's not like he's a complete saddo and needs the money. Right, Ry?'

I interrupt. 'I don't like the word saddo, Bizz, and I don't think any of us should assume he's here to take advantage of us.'

'No, Stella's right,' he says. 'You know nothing about me beyond what's in my resume. There was a time when I used to live in a dive on Bermondsey Avenue. I struggled financially and had to borrow money from my dad. It took me four years of gruelling overtime and shitty jobs, but I paid back every penny, including interest.'

'How much interest?' The question is out of Bizzy's mouth before she can stop it.

'£200, which back then was a lot.' Ryan smiles. 'He was simply teaching me the consequences of borrowing money. As for confidentiality, that comes with every job.'

It's then that I realise Stella has left the room. She is my only constant, and I depend on her. It's all my fault she feels uncomfortable about Ryan listening to family secrets, and now I'm trying to understand how to put it all right.

I rush out. When I reach the stairs, I know it's a fool's errand to go after her. She's right. Ryan is a stranger, and as much as I want to ask him about Zane and Nic, I can't do it in front of my daughter. It's an effort to make sure what we say doesn't verge on salacious gossip. Restraining anything I say to him about myself in confidence is becoming harder to manage.

Ever since Zane left, Stella has been tight-lipped and remote, as if some part of his departure weighed heavily on her. I remember when she heard he'd died, tears rolled down her cheeks, which she made no move to wipe. We stood there in a hug, her heart beating painfully fast; I could feel every pulse.

Bizzy charges towards me with Ryan in tow. She kisses me on the cheek. 'Ryan's taking me to football practice.'

'Great.'

Ryan nods at me and says, 'I'll be back in half an hour. We should talk.'

Suddenly it's all too much, and I know that whatever he needs to tell me will turn my world upside down. After they leave, I walk around the deer park, squinting through spits of drizzle. I shove my hands in my pockets, my fingers brushing against my keys. Suddenly, The Forge looks terribly inviting. There's half an hour before Ryan returns from dropping Bizzy off at school. Just a quick look won't hurt anyone.

The stable door comprises two panels, both of which use the same key. As I unlock the door, I feel as if I'm violating someone's privacy until I remind myself the entire property belongs to me.

The kitchen is tidy, with not a single dirty plate in the sink, and the laptop is the only thing on the dining room table. I touch the mouse pad and use the same passcode we agreed upon. There is only a small list of files, plans for the grounds and weak points, detailed reports on the breaches and a list of replaced cameras. Nothing personal.

I move into the bedroom and expect to see the type of mess you find in any bachelor pad. The bed is made and there's not a stitch of clothing draped over the chair. His weights are stored on a dumbbell rack, and there are two magazines by his bed: *Men's Health* and *Architectural Digest*.

My phone buzzes in my pocket. I'm thinking it's probably the anonymous caller again, only it's not; it's Ryan, and I push him to voicemail.

I search through his drawers and wardrobe, all suits and shoes in a regimented row. What grabs my attention are photographs in a shoebox, one of family – I can see the resemblance in his father and sister – and another photo that makes my heart kick.

While he is the focal point in the composition, it's the woman with her back to the camera, standing on tiptoe, her arms reaching around his neck, that bothers me the most. One of his hands is splayed out against her shoulder, the other cradles the back of her head. The composition is so poignant it makes me shudder. If I recall correctly, his ex was blonde. This woman is dark.

Was the photo taken by a professional photographer, or candidly by a friend? How long ago was it taken?

I feel a tinge of curiosity that she has been singled out for reasons I don't understand and would rather not dwell on.

What makes me jump is the distant squeal of tyres peeling down the drive. The photos slip from my hand and fall to the carpet, scattering. I gather them up and shove them back where I found them. Locking both panels of the stable door, I run around the back of the house and enter through the French doors to my study. It alarms me to find Stella standing in the middle of the room, uninvited.

'Been for a walk?'

'Shit, Stella, why are you following me around?' I drop my keys on the desk. 'What was all that about in the kitchen?'

She sinks into a chair and draws a long sigh. 'Ryan may stroke your ego and do a few little favours now and then. But you don't understand where his loyalties lie.'

Suddenly, it's not just Stella's words, it's the way she's looking at me, like I'm in trouble or something. As if there are rules for me having employed a CPO, and I am a thousand miles outside those lines.

'I love you, Lilja, like a daughter. I won't let anything happen to you or Bizzy. It's my duty to investigate anyone who associates with family.'

Great. Now my house manager has started some type of surveillance of her own. Alarm zips up my spine, and I know something isn't right.

'I like to think I'm open-minded and forgiving, but there aren't many people on this planet I'd forgive for an oversight like this. There is one thing Ryan McKellan failed to mention on his resumé.'

'What thing?' I ask.

'You might be concerned to learn that he used to work for your ex-husband's best friend before he came here.' She says *best friend* as if he were far from it.

I know who she means. His face is on tube station walls and bus shelters and advertised on social media. The man with Pharaoh Akhenaten's perfectly sculpted lips, the same man who took over the new lead in *Play Him Play Her*.

'That's what you wanted to tell me? Ryan used to be one of Marschōne Robinson's many CPOs. I'm well acquainted with his resumé.'

'Come on, Lilja, you know what I'm trying to say. If he worked for Marschōne, he must have known *her*.'

The first pinpricks of understanding pierce through my skin. Her name squirms in my belly. I take a deep breath and blow it out slowly.

'Nicola Gatlin.'

# 30

# ZANE

The dawn turns to a vibrant hue of red and orange, and the truck growls beneath me as I wind down through the mountains. Every shadow looks like a patrol car, and every dip in the road feels like a trap waiting to spring.

There are signs to Terrebonne, Blainville and Mirabel, but they mean nothing to me. As far as staying off the main roads, minor routes that take me closer to the mountains and away from the Ottawa River are best.

Even though I've disabled the GPS device, I still glance in the rearview mirror. There's nothing but the smear of my taillights bouncing off wet asphalt on an empty stretch of highway. The police can still track the truck, and without a plug-in GPS blocker, there's no way to hide from them or jam their signals.

At least my stomach is full of burrito and coffee, and I can charge my phone. Using the stolen phone, I called a few numbers in England just to listen to their voices. If it felt creepy to them, it was doubly weird to me. Something about the whole thing made me emotional, as if life had gone on without me and no one cared.

Then I called Lilja. Her voice was expectant, as if she knew it was me. It gave me the confidence to call again. But the second time, she hung up before I spoke, and I hurled the stolen phone out of the window while crossing the Petite-Nation River.

HOLLOWAY

That was too close, Zane, too
damn close. You never learn!

My head is pounding, and everything is spinning. The thought of the police tracing the call sends a chill down my spine. My breath hitches as I inhale. Staying on Highway 50 might not be a good idea.

My attention swiftly departs from Lilja and returns to the truck. The best option is stealing plates off another vehicle, preferably parked down a back street. After about forty-minutes, I see signs to Thurso. The town appears all at once with its school and bistros, and I keep the truck steady, like I've driven this route a thousand times. One glance from a bored cop and I'm screwed.

My stomach twists at the sight of a hardware store with buckets and shovels stacked outside under bright halogens. No point in trying to steal any of those.

I turn down a side street, scanning every house and every back alley. My chest tightens when I spot a shuttered auto shop surrounded by a chain-link fence. The snow on the ground is a thin powder already turning to slush, and I don't want to leave any footprints.

I kill the headlights and open the window, my heart hammering. I study a row of rusting car carcasses and closed roller doors. There's nothing I can break into without using wire cutters. For a moment, the silence is so thick it feels like the world has stopped breathing. Then a dog barks somewhere behind me, and lights flick on in a nearby house.

I give up on the auto shop and drive down the road for about a mile before turning sharply into a back alley, passing the backs of houses on one side, and a drainage channel on the other.

That's when I notice a small pickup under a lantern, parked outside a padlocked garage. In the flatbed are buckets filled with storage boxes and safety gear, and a ladder hangs over the tailgate. As I walk towards the pickup, the air stinks of wet cardboard and oil. The bucket holds wooden paint stirrers and rags, and there's an old grey toolbox. I grab them both, taking a few cans of spray paint, a tarp, and a wrench to my truck.

A creaking gate makes me jump. I pause for a second, waiting for the sound of footsteps that never come. There's only a slight breeze in the air, not enough to blow a paper bag across the alley.

I swap the license plates with the wrench, and suddenly the truck isn't mine anymore – it belongs to some faceless worker, driving another rig in a town full of them. There's a noticeable dent on the right fender, which is gashed with red paint. A collision with another vehicle, perhaps. But a mark like that is too easy to identify.

I work quickly. The spray can hisses and masks the dent with dark grey paint. After covering the bed with the tarp, its rope cinched and solid, I hear the voice.

'Hey!' A man walks along the alley, his belly hanging over his jeans, and he holds a tyre iron. 'You stealing from me?'

I'm filled with bone-numbing horror as he slowly raises the iron above his head, and pressing my back against the truck, everything swims in front of my eyes. I can't breathe. I can't move. He rears back and swings it down hard. It meets the side of my truck with a dull clang, missing my shoulder by inches.

Something breaks inside me, and just as he raises the iron again, I lunge from side to side as I circle him. The move confuses him, but he steadies the iron and waits for me to settle. There's an awkwardness about him, a drag to one of his feet, that gives me a fresh surge of confidence.

Suddenly, I bend low and go in for the slam, pinning him up against my truck. I hear him grunt as the iron clatters to the ground and his head slams into the door frame. I swing one wild punch after another until he falls to the ground, strings of drool and blood spilling from his mouth.

I bend down and pick up the iron. His eyes lock onto mine, and there's a flash of something in them. Maybe shock, maybe resignation. Maybe he's committing every detail of me to memory. I bring the tyre iron down hard on his skull, and his body jerks and then goes slack. My chest heaves in the silence, and blood slicks the concrete. I stagger back, staring at a lifeless mound, his face turned sideways with one eye open.

I blink the world back into focus, and my heart thumps harder. Grabbing him by the collar and hooking my other hand under his belt, I drag him to the drainage channel and roll him into rainwater and mud.

I stagger back to the truck and shove the wrench over the tailgate. When I climb behind the wheel, my reflection stares back at me in the rearview, my eyes wide and my face pale. The engine growls back to life, and the truck rattles over potholes as I tear out of the alley. The smell of blood clings to me, as if it persists in following me.

'He gave me no choice,' I whisper.

HOLLOWAY

> Choice? We always have a
> choice. You're still breathing
> because he isn't. That's the
> sum of it, Zane. One life for
> another. Clean and simple.

But it isn't simple. His eyes flash in my head, the shock and the fear before I swung. He was just a guy protecting his truck. Now he's a corpse, lying in a flooded trench because of me.

'It wasn't supposed to go that far,' I mutter, my throat raw.

HOLLOWAY

> Don't kid yourself, son. Every
> step forward is written in
> someone else's blood. You'll
> get used to it.

I blink hard, fighting the sting in my eyes, feeling the weight of the tyre iron in my hands. I tell myself I won't think about it again. But I already know I will.

<pre>
HOLLOWAY

Before I met you, I promised
myself I wouldn't kill again.
Killing is a lonely sport. But
now I have you and together,
we'll never get caught.
</pre>

I would have believed Holloway if it hadn't been for the blue-and-white patrol car easing out of a side street, headlights sweeping across me like a search beam. My stomach drops. For a heartbeat I consider gunning it, but that's suicide. The cop will grow instantly suspicious and, like a cat after a mouse, he won't stop chasing me.

As the sun crests over the mountain and breaks between the buildings, I keep my gaze fixed ahead. The patrol car pulls in behind me, close enough that its running lights burn in my mirrors. Any second now there will be sirens and the cold command to pull over.

But nothing comes.

I keep rolling through town, and my mind screams at every stop sign, every turn signal, that I'm giving myself away.

<pre>
HOLLOWAY

Relax. No sudden moves. It's
the easiest way to get caught.
</pre>

A tan-coloured van swerves out of a side street and into my lane. I'm forced to slam on my brakes to avoid rear-ending him. I angrily lay on my horn. The driver opens his window and flips me off, picking up speed to put some distance between us.

The cop swings around me and pulses his siren at the van. As they pull into a bank parking lot, I keep straight ahead, my hands trembling on the wheel.

The fake plates are holding up for now. But I won't get lucky twice.

## 31

# LILJA

My eyes snap open at 6.00 am. I flip on the lamp and unhook my phone from the charger, wishing the photograph in Ryan's drawer wasn't foremost in my thoughts. I've been under no illusion that he isn't here to dig deeper into Zane's involvement in Nic's death.

We still need to have that talk, so I send him a text, which he'll read after he wakes up.

I make a beeline for the kitchen and turn on the coffeemaker. The house is stiller and quieter than before. All I can hear is the sound of a ticking clock in the hallway and the gentle gurgle of the pot. Seconds seem to stretch into minutes, and I hear a sound outside, and I can tell from the look in the cat's eyes that he's heard it too.

Ted's tail brushes against my leg, and his nose points at the back door, his tail puffed. I can't figure out if he's scared or excited at the prospect of another cat on his patch. I peer through the blinds and see a blazing moon through the trees, beaming down on the flagstones with an almost impossible brightness. There's nothing out there.

The silence that follows suggests I must be imagining it. As I take one last look, I'm convinced I see something moving out of the corner of my eye. I want to rush out there, but I'm scared of what I might find.

The coffeemaker beeps, and I pour myself a cup. The sound of a patio chair scuffing the flagstones outside makes me flinch. I force myself to take a step closer to the back door. A loud expletive makes me shake my head. How many times is Burgess going to come home in the early hours and hope to stay alert during the day? I'm about to tell him to straighten up when there's a knock on the door. It makes me jump.

Ryan's shoulders are tucked up to his ears, eyes zeroing in on me. Just for a second, a tingling sensation rolls up my spine.

'Everything okay?' he asks, out of breath. His eyes dart around the kitchen, likely searching for a broken window, glass glittering like diamonds on the floor. 'I came over as soon as I got your text.'

I could make something up, like there was a shadow bobbing behind the juniper hedge, but he'd only search the grounds for someone who isn't there.

'Sorry, I was hoping you'd get my message when you woke up.'

The corner of his mouth twitches. 'Well, I'm awake now.'

'Coffee?'

'Coffee's fine, thanks.'

Ryan doesn't look tired at all. No coat. Shirt pressed; khaki trousers nipped at the waist with a brown leather belt. Shoes immaculate. I'm grateful he doesn't notice my bed hair, a scruffy t-shirt and pyjama bottoms. There's no point in lying about nosing around in his stuff, not if we're going to talk about Nicola Gatlin.

'Did you love her?' I ask.

He pulls out a chair at the kitchen table and sinks down, giving me a frowny look.

I press on. 'Were you and Nicola Gatlin intimate?'

He does a quick survey of my face, his eyes coming to rest on his mug. 'No. But I felt sorry for her.'

'In what way?'

'It can't have been easy being Marschōne's girlfriend, what with all the other women clambering for his attention.'

Anyone else would have been angry, but not Ryan. He waits politely for me to take the initiative. I don't know why I say it, but the words come right out.

'Why keep her picture?'

Wrinkles form at the corners of his eyes, and he smiles. 'I knew you'd been nosing around. You left muddy footprints on the tile.'

'Sorry. Tiny blunder. I should have wiped my feet on the doormat.'

He sits in a taut, edgy silence for a moment and sips his coffee. 'One of the makeup girls took that photo on her last day at work. Probably the saddest day of my life. I've never felt like that before. Or since.'

'Did she feel the same way about you?'

He looks startled and then shakes his head. 'No. I mean, I've never felt so utterly helpless over someone before. The hardest thing I did was tell her to be safe and happy. But that's not what happened, was it?'

I feel the colour draining from my face. I feel embarrassed for assuming it had been more. There's another charged silence before he speaks.

'One night, Marschōne asked me to drive them to a press junket, and I noticed the way her makeup was caked on one side of her face, the way she kept rubbing her jaw like it was numb. He must have hit her hard.' He shudders, hesitates. 'It was weeks before I ran into her again. She told me she was working for Zane and how excited she was. But it was the way she said it that made my blood run cold. I didn't want history repeating itself.'

'Well, it did.'

His gaze lingers on me for a moment. 'The only thing I'm guilty of, Lilja, is knowing that they were intimate before she came to work here. That's what I wanted to tell you.'

I can't meet his eyes. No one has ever crawled under my skin like Nic had. 'Did she keep in touch with you after she left?'

'She texted a few times. Of course, that stopped around the time she disappeared.'

I'm struck with a crippling fear. Had she said anything about me? 'Do you still have those texts?'

He leans back, slides the phone from his pocket, and starts scrolling. When he hands me his phone, I feel afraid, and yet I'm compelled to read them. They're dated a day before Zane's birthday party.

> He brings me so much pain; it's killing me. He says he
> loves me. But this isn't love. This is him crushing me
> so he can build himself up.

A shudder runs through me, disgust warring with dread. Internally, I'm imagining Nic sitting on a bar stool, flicking back dark hair. Her clothes were revealing enough to be considered a tease and classy enough to be high fashion. It's no wonder Zane fell for her.

> I thought he was one of the good guys. I thought he
> really loved me. He doesn't love me. He loves only
> what I can do for him.

She may have thought he loved her, but a bigger part of her knew Zane would never leave me. He didn't have the guts. But then she did something hellishly rash. She posted blurry photos of her and Zane on Insta for the world to see. And boy, did his fans speculate. They were running a sweepstakes.

> Ry, I'm losing him. I don't know what to do. Tell me
> what to do.

This is where my empathy falls short, and so clearly did Ryan's. His response was curt.

> You've gone too far this time. Having an affair with
> another celebrity is crossing a line.

And then hers:

> He can't just kick me out like nothing happened! I
> swear I'm going to make him pay for this.

Nic's voice comes rushing back, plaintive and mewling. It's clear she trusted Ryan enough to confide in him about her affair with Zane. What's sad is how she lapped up Zane's words and then loathed herself for loving a man whose easy, persuasive charm she fell for in a moment of madness. Yet she knew how evasive he was. It was all part of the game.

The one thing Nic did wrong was allowing Zane full control. All his romantic gestures were manipulative and fake, and yet she was fooled into thinking she was the love of his life; the one woman who could offer a different version of marriage, a more glamorous and sensual version, than the dowdy wife he already had.

The gears in my brain turn. If only Ryan knew Nic played me as much as she played Zane. If only he knew how dangerous and unpredictable she was. I try to calm myself, but my heart beats faster, a rhythmic drumming that rings in my ears. I try to drown out a question: How much does Ryan know? This was her last text to him, perhaps the last text she ever sent. She didn't mention my name, and the relief rolls off me in waves.

'I should have done something,' he says. 'I should have told her not to work for Zane before the abuse became a cycle. The bastard was heartless.'

A ripple of quiet falls in the room. He apologises repeatedly, though I've no idea what he's apologising for. Zane was a bastard. Still is.

'I feel nothing,' I say. 'Is that wrong?'

'No, it's not.' Ryan shakes his head. 'What Zane did was deeply wrong. He should feel profoundly ashamed of the pain he put you through.'

The roaring in my ears muffles his words, and I catch only fragments of sound. *The pain he put you through.* My eyes brim now, and I try to focus on something other than Ryan.

'You're an amazing woman, Lilja.' His breath eases from him, and he covers my hand with his. 'Don't you ever forget that.'

His touch knocks the breath out of me, and I try to keep my face neutral. I wish I could say thank you, but the words are stuck in my throat.

He takes his hand away and sips his coffee. 'You probably want to know if I ever saw them… you know, being intimate.'

'Did you?'

'Yes.'

Despite everything, I should feel relieved that he's admitted it, but the air still reeks of secrets. I've no idea how much Ryan knows, and that's what worries me.

'I want you to know I didn't condone what Nic did,' he says. 'My opinion of her fell even lower when she told me she wanted Zane to have you certified as mentally unstable.'

For a second, I can't move, I can't even think, and the kitchen swims before my eyes. My hands shake so much that some of my coffee slops over the side of the mug and onto the table. Everything goes silent and still for a second, as though the world has paused to see what will happen next. I feel completely disoriented. Lost.

'What?' Shock shudders through me. 'Zane told you that?'

'Yes.'

'Don't tell me it was to get control of my money.'

He shrugs.

There's so much more he must know about me. If Zane ever described me as *the bitch from hell* – a title he sometimes gave me – then Ryan might have wondered why. My stomach churns at the thought of Zane describing all my flaws in graphic detail, some exaggerated, some hinting at my fragile state of mind, anything to justify his affair. That I implicated him in Nic's murder in retaliation for what he did to me.

'Things got worse when Nic kept sending him nude photos of herself.' He stops when he catches sight of my face. 'Sorry. If you need me to stop, let me know.'

'No, it's fine.'

'She kept pressuring him to get a divorce. I could see he was cracking under the strain.'

I want to tell Ryan how wide and devastating the crack was. Because on the night of the murder at around 1.35 am, I was asleep or at least pretending to be, when Zane came into the bedroom and knelt beside me. He whispered, 'It's over, I promise. We're safe. She can't hurt us anymore.'

Something about what he said made the breath go out of me. I wanted to ask him, and I wanted to follow him downstairs, but I was too afraid to move. The words: *She can't hurt us anymore* carried a dreadful finality to them, as if he'd done something drastic to make it stop.

'Did you know something bad was going to happen?' I ask.

His face crumples a little. 'Maybe, somewhere deep down, I did. But I didn't know how bad.'

**BarbedWire - Trending #InZane**

@SherylAdams: Did you see that gorgeous man Lilja Osborne was with?

@CirceAtNight: Oh yeah, the dark one with the moody, broody eyes.

@SherylAdams: According to the brief interview someone did with him through the front gate, he's her bodyguard.

@HeyWhatsUp: He did an interview?

# PART III

# THE AWAKENING

# 32

# ZANE

The highway stretches on forever, grey tarmac cutting through endless fields and nameless towns. I don't know where I am, except that the road signs all point east. Toronto is out there somewhere.

I smell manure in the air as I pass dairy farms and fields, and my eyes continually dart from the wing mirrors to the rearview. The cars behind and ahead aren't in any hurry, and there are no light bars flashing in the distance.

HOLLOWAY

>Isn't it about time to ditch
>the truck? You're a walking
>headline.

He's almost convincing, but the thought of having to steal another car fills me with dread. These little towns are probably full of drifters and grifters, fraudsters and mobsters. I don't want to run into any of them.

HOLLOWAY

>I doubt there's anyone out
>there more dangerous than you.
>Just saying.

I turn the radio up to drown out his voice. Country songs, weather reports, then —

> '...police are asking for the public's help in locating a stolen vehicle believed to be linked to a violent incident in Lachute. The truck is described as a late-model black Dodge Ram, with possible damage to the right rear fender. If spotted, do not approach. Contact authorities immediately.'

My stomach drops. I fumble with the dial, but the voice hangs in the cab like smoke. Late-model Dodge. That's me. I'm about to panic when the gas gauge hits red. My stomach knots. I've been running on fumes, trying to stretch every mile, but I need fuel, or I'll be stranded out here.

The next exit spits me into Thurso, a small town with a school and café and, thankfully, a gas station. I pull in under the fluorescent canopy, which spills harsh light over the truck.

HOLLOWAY

> All it takes is one nosy atten-
> dant to remember your face and
> one camera lens to record it.
> Head down, pay cash, a quick
> in-and-out. What do you say?

What choice do I have? Since there's no one around, I kill the engine and tug my cap lower. I see a payphone hanging on the wall outside the store, and my mind goes into overdrive. It's my last chance to explain everything to Lilja, in a way that only she can understand.

If I buy a prepaid calling card, dial the toll-free access number and punch in the card's PIN, followed by Lilja's number, it will mask my location. My wife would only see the card service number, and not the payphone itself.

Inside, there's a man in his twenties slouched behind the counter. His head is buried in a car magazine, and he looks up and gives a polite nod. I wind my way around the shelves, keeping low and looking up occasionally to scan for any cameras. As far as I can make out, there's a dome in the middle of the ceiling and nothing at eye-level behind the front desk.

I'm craving coffee. I grab a cup and a couple of sandwiches from the fridge and four large bottles of water. When I approach the attendant, I ask for a full tank on pump 3 and a calling card. I pay in cash. He barely acknowledges me or the truck outside, too busy scanning my food and drinks and glancing occasionally at a plumb-coloured Dodge Challenger in his magazine. He tells me to have a good one and then flicks through a few pages.

Back outside, I grab the nozzle and jam it into the tank, and my eyes dart occasionally towards the store. The pump ticks slowly, and while the truck is filling, I walk towards the payphone, lights flickering across its scratched metal face. It feels like stepping back in time.

I slip the receiver off the hook, and the cord is sticky with old grime. I feed a coin in and then punch the toll-free access number from the prepaid card. The line clicks, and a mechanical voice asks for my PIN. I jab the numbers fast, eyes darting at the highway, and at the shadows, waiting for a car to swing in and spot me.

It rings. Once. Twice. My breath tangles in my throat.

'Hello?' Her voice is softer than I remember.

At first, I stay silent, willing her to know it's me. Begging her to be merciful, just for today. But her voice sounds enraged when she spits out my name. She knows it's me, knows I've been calling her all along, and senses how desperate I am. She says something about me killing my reputation, but I don't hear all of it. The worst of it is not wanting me to come home. Then she says the dreaded D-word.

*Divorce.*

My heart shatters into a thousand pieces. I know she's angry and confused, but I feel at a loss for words.

I can barely get a word in edgeways. When I do, I take a long, hard breath and tell her I'm not coming home, at least not yet.

Then there's a horrible twenty-second silence where she's probably in shock, thinking it through. I want her to believe me when I tell her I didn't kill Nic. I *didn't!*

She tells me to repeat it because she can't hear me, or she doesn't understand what I'm trying to say. I want to tell her how much I miss her and Bizzy, but the words don't quite make it out of my mouth. All I can manage is some garbled excuse about other method actors suffering from the same thing. After telling her what really happened, there's no response.

Maybe she's in shock, maybe she doesn't believe me, maybe she thinks I'm trying to pass the buck, I don't know. But I hang up, knowing that whatever I do now, whatever I say, won't change a thing.

I'm not blinking or breathing, and my heart is kicking it up a notch. Already I feel like consoling myself with a smoke. I perk up at the thought that if the police had been listening in to my conversation with Lilja, they might suspect how much she contributed to my leaving. I might have been verbally and physically abusive, but she wins hands down for her manipulative, psychological contribution.

Trudging back to the truck, I realise this isn't the first mountain I'll need to scale to get her to listen to me, and it won't be the last either. While I wait for the truck to fill up, my heart settles in my chest, as if resigning itself to the chasm I've created between us.

My attention quickly flicks back to the store because the attendant is watching me. My heart stops. Does he recognise me? Does he see a headline in my face—*violent incident, stolen truck?*

Then his eyes crest over my shoulder, and I realise what he's staring at. A sodding police car pulling in and parking outside the store. A knot settles in my core, and I try to quell my nerves. What is it with cops and gas stations? They're like fruit flies drawn to a honey jar. The cop doesn't get out, and he doesn't go in. He just sits there tapping his computer screen.

I yank the nozzle out and slam it back into the cradle. My hands are shaking. The pump reads almost full, enough to push me east. I'm back in the cab and driving slowly out of the gas station, its neon glow shrinking in the rearview mirror.

HOLLOWAY

Every garage stop is a coin
toss now. How many more before
your luck runs out?

I press harder on the accelerator, and the highway unspools into an endless monotony of green fields. I sip my coffee, but I can't escape the pounding in my chest. The road swims with images of cops and Lilja and dead people. For a second, I almost drift across the median before I wrench the truck back, tires screaming.

The radio slips back into country music, a catchy melody about a man on the run, a man with financial uncertainty like me. I study my breaths like Meggy, my therapist taught me… in for four seconds, hold, out for four seconds. I focus on the manic life I've crafted out of blood, sweat and murder, and an ironclad commitment to staying free.

As I drive, I keep seeing inevitable scenes of starvation and death in isolation. Because what I really need is a job that pays cash, no questions asked.

When I see signs to Linden Farm, that's when it hits me, the kind of work where an employer would willingly pay cash. Maybe I could feed animals and do a few repairs. Maybe I could help cover crops and truck out last year's grain; corn that was harvested last October. I know a little about farms. We had one near Barton Manor.

HOLLOWAY

You? Stacking boxes and shovelling shit for minimum wage
and for a farmer who'd sooner
shoot you than hire you. Face
it, you're not built for this
kind of life. You'll show them
who you really are. And when
you do, it won't be some poor

<pre>
bastard you'll just kill by
accident. It'll be deliberate.
</pre>

My hands shake on the steering wheel. I need a job, a cover, and a reason to keep moving. The farm is fifteen minutes outside town, down a gravel road lined with broken fences and skeletal trees. It looks shabby and tired even in the afternoon sun. I park the truck behind a red-painted barn and out of sight from the road. Mud clings to my boots before I even reach the front porch of a white house with a green roof.

I avoid my dilapidated reflection in the window by the front door, and I hope I don't frighten the people inside. The man who answers my hesitant knock looks me up and down like there's a foul smell under his nose. Mid-fifties, weathered face, and a scar running down his jaw.

'I'm Will,' I say, holding out a hand. 'I know this is a long shot, but do you need any help around here?'

'Ever worked on a farm before?' he asks, chewing on a sandwich.

'Er… no.'

'Lots of lifting and hauling.'

'I can do it.'

'Cash only,' he says, flatly. 'End of day. No questions, no complaints. You don't like it, you leave.'

'That's fine.'

'It'll be $20 an hour. Just so you know, we're wrapping up last year's harvest. Our sprayers will need repairing before spring, and we sell seed during the winter months. Name's Mick Morton. Glad to have you here.'

He hands me a pair of stiff gloves and jerks his head toward the barns.

The work is brutal. Stacking old hay bales, which are heavier than they look. Shovelling cow shit (thanks Holloway) and hauling sacks of feed that bite into my shoulders. By the second hour, sweat stings my eyes, and my shirt sticks to me like glue. My muscles burn, but it feels grounding, the type of pain I can manage.

                    HOLLOWAY

          Look  at  you,  breaking  your
          back  for  scraps.  Is  this  what
          survival  looks  like  to  you?


I slam another sack onto the pile harder than I need to. 'It's what keeps me alive.'


                    HOLLOWAY
              (circling like a vulture)

          For  now.  But  you  know  what
          happens  when  you're  tired  and
          when  someone  pushes  you  too
          far.  You  snap.  You  always  do.


The farmer's son – a kid, maybe early twenties, wiry and suspicious – watches me like I'm an intruder. When I grunt lifting another sack, something brews behind his eyes.

'Drifter can't hack it,' he says. 'Bet you'll be gone by tomorrow.'
'Bet I won't.'
A grin paints his face. 'I'll hold you to that.'
I bite back the reply boiling up my throat. So, he thinks I'm a drifter because of my tatty beard and dog-eared clothes. And because I stink like sewer gas.
Holloway chuckles, egging me on.


                    HOLLOWAY

          Go  on  Drifter,  show  him  what
          happens  when  you're  angry.
          Crush  his  throat,  watch  him…


I shut my eyes for a second and force air into my lungs and heft the sack towards the kid. 'Where do you want this?'

His mouth twists to one side, and he points to a corner of the barn. 'Over there, with the others.'

The day drags, but I don't break. When Mick offers me lunch up at the house, I tell him I have sandwiches, which I eat in the truck. By sundown, my arms ache and my hands are raw beneath the gloves.

Mick presses a small wad of bills into my palm without counting it. 'Keep the gloves. Be back tomorrow at four.'

'Four in the morning?'

'Yeah, four in the morning. What do you think this is? A pussy farm?' There's a hint of a chuckle in his tone.

A woman calls from inside the house. 'Mick! You want to watch the market?'

'Yeah, I'll be right there!' he shouts back. Then looking at me, he says, 'She monitors the commodities market, you know, for price shifts. Timing is everything when it comes to selling grain. Looks like you could do with a few good meals. Breakfast is at five. Lunch at one. Dinner at six. If you need somewhere to stay, take the cottage on the left. There's a fresh towel in the bathroom.'

I nod and pocket the cash, wondering if the fresh towel is some kind of joke.

His wide stare catches mine, but his lips fail to transform into a smile. 'You from around here, Will?'

'No, sir. From up north originally.' I opt not to mention where.

'No kidding. Scenery's different down here. Flatter. Well, I expect you want to get off to bed, so I won't keep you. See you tomorrow, I hope.'

'You will.'

As I head towards the truck to get my backpack, Holloway follows me, twirling a phantom dollar bill between his fingers.

HOLLOWAY

Congratulations. You've traded
murder for minimum wage. How
long before someone notices

you don't belong? You can't
hide those butter-soft hands
forever. Not from Farmer Giles.

I open the cottage door and, for once, I'm speechless. A bed, a fridge, a coffeemaker and a washing machine tucked under the counter. Best of all, there's a shower to scrub off the musk of grimy flesh.

Luxury.

I open the cupboards and drawers to find three of everything and wonder who may have lived here before me. How long did they stay? Where are they now? Out of every window I see fields, miles of them, stretching into the horizon.

Mick Morton might be a little rough around the edges, but he's a man with good intentions and a big heart. I won't cause him any trouble.

I'm here for one thing and one thing only. To make enough money to survive.

# 33

# LILJA

I'd normally spend the morning catching up with correspondence, but I realise employing anyone these days is never a good idea without digging deeper into their socials. Since Ryan's are non-existent, it leaves me to Google his past jobs.

I type his name in the search field. Ryan McKellan doesn't appear to be a common name in Dawlish. I ignore the first two; a landscape gardener and a commercial pilot and settle on the third. No Facebook, Insta or TikTok, and the thumbnail photo on LinkedIn is barely enough to make out his features.

When I open the page, his professional details, schools and college mirror the same credentials Lambeth's CPO's usually list. As I skim through his career history, there's a five-month gap between leaving the London Metropolitan Police and his joining Lambeth in Devon. It's not a missing job but a blank space where his timeline stops, as though someone had erased it.

Maybe he took some time off. People do that, right?

Then it hits me. I've heard the name before, but not in the context of him working for us, but something I'd seen on the news. I dig deeper and search public records. In an article from a year ago, the headline is so innocuous, I almost miss it.

*"Former police officer Ryan McKellan cleared of wrongdoing in internal investigation."*

I swallow, trying to dislodge the hard lump in the back of my throat. I skim the article, and disbelief crawls under my skin. Ryan, *this* Ryan, was thought to have accepted bribes from wealthy individuals, helping them to avoid prosecution in exchange for money. Something about his involvement in this case doesn't sit right. Is his clearing linked to his ability to cover his tracks or the influence of those protecting him?

Lambeth would have gone deeper than I have. If they found him a viable candidate, someone they could trust, then why can't I?

I lean back in my chair and try to make sense of the information that floods my brain. Is Ryan McKellan really who he says he is? Even though he appears devoted, none of it erases the nagging earworm whispering that maybe he's not as honest as I thought he was.

I text him to drop by my study before leaving today.

Less than two minutes later, he walks in, a scowl playing at the corner of his lips. He wears charcoal trousers and a blue shirt; his sleeves rolled up above the wrist. This is the best of Ryan. Ryan, the close protector, the perfectionist, the qualified professional for whom my family's safety is paramount. But he is too private to be this Ryan completely, and so Ryan the stranger creeps in.

I push aside the panic clawing at my chest and tell myself this is the perfect time. If I ignore it, the questions will eat away at me.

'Is there something you'd like to tell me?' I ask, pulling the collar of my silk shirt absent-mindedly.

'Sorry. I'm not sure what you mean.'

'I've been reading up about you on LinkedIn.'

His back stiffens. 'Okay.'

I know the façade he maintains to keep his job. What I want to know is whether he's ever used drugs or thought about hurting someone – but I can't quite go there.

'Do bribery and police brutality ring any bells?'

He follows my gaze to his restless fingers drumming unconsciously on his knee. He places his hands palm down on his lap.

'If you're asking if I know the difference between right and wrong,' he says. 'Obviously, I do.'

*Obviously.* The word jars inside me. 'Nothing is obvious. Far from it.'

He shakes his head, as if confused by my question. 'I believe I told you everything at our first meeting.'

'I don't think so.'

He looks at me, his eyes wide and earnest. 'I mentioned the police corruption incident.'

Fear bubbles up at the realisation that he may have told me something important. If I hadn't been staring at his ruggedly sculpted profile, I wouldn't have missed it.

'If you recall,' he says, shifting in his seat, his hands laced together, 'I said the police investigation was resolved and that it's now part of the public domain. If you'd like clarification, some guys I worked with accepted bribes all the time. It was their way of life. But to me, it was the difference between cowardice and stupidity, and I didn't want to lose my job. I thought the whole point of being a police officer was to help people. This wasn't helping anyone.'

'What happened?' I can hear a strain of desperation in my voice, but I need to know.

He runs a hand through his dark hair, immaculately clipped at the side and long at the top, like he'd barely styled it with his fingers.

'One evening, I was called to a disturbance outside a nightclub in Chelsea. When I arrived, my sergeant was talking to the owner outside, and there was a man lying on the ground with his hand over his face. There was blood everywhere. I thought it was odd there was no ambulance and that no one was attending to him. That's when I noticed one of the officer's hands was bloodstained and everything fell into place. They'd beaten the man because he owed the owner ten grand over a drug deal. When my sergeant handed me a wad of cash, I knew I'd been bought to keep quiet.'

The room sways, and the walls become less defined. I want to rush to the cloakroom, ram the lock shut and let the horror engulf me. It's too much to process, the admission of bribery and Ryan's failure to enforce the law. I grope for his answer, hoping that he refused the cash.

'Did you tell anyone?'

'My mistake was not only taking the money, but assuming an

ambulance had been called, which it hadn't. I should have radioed for help before I left the scene. But none of that matters now.'

I'm silent, trying to discern shades of a lie or any tiny omissions, and failing. 'Did you keep it?'

'Shit, no. The money was evidence. I misunderstood how messed up my sergeant was, but that's no excuse. This was unlawful use of force.'

For a moment, our eyes lock, and I struggle to find my bearings. There's no sign of him deflecting or wheedling his way out of this to outfox me.

Patiently and with unfaltering good humour, Ryan leans forward. 'Does that answer your question?'

'It does.'

'I'm going to earn your trust back. I don't know how, but I'll do what it takes.'

He's not a stranger who lies when it suits him; he'd been honest from the start. The failure is on my part, and I see that now.

He stands. 'If that's all, I'd like to finish up replacing the cameras on the east side of the property.'

'Thank you for explaining.'

I hear a phone vibrate, a noise I would usually ignore in a meeting, but its persistent sound seems to ruffle Ryan.

'Excuse me,' he says. 'I need to take this.'

I watch him as he hurries upstairs to the hall. I don't know why, but my feet follow him as far as the front door as it closes behind him. The familiar crunching of gravel tells me he's walking towards the stables with his phone pressed to his ear. I head into the sitting-room and follow him through the windows, trying to move the puzzle pieces until they fit into place.

He pauses beside one of the open windows, which is letting in a stream of cold air. Without thinking, I creep closer and strain to hear.

'I'm sorry. I couldn't talk yesterday.' His tone is warm. 'Is everything okay? Good, good... I was thinking the same thing. But yeah, let's do that.' He laughs softly. '*Yes!* You read my mind.'

He retreats towards the stables, and his words are too distant to make out. I've no idea who he's talking to. It doesn't sound like a mate or a colleague. The world seems to freeze for a second.

There is only one type of person he would interrupt a meeting for. A girlfriend. Sweat gathers at my hairline, even though I'm shivering from the draught. I feel stupid. Of course, he has a girl-friend. Any man looking like him would have several.

Stella walks through the sitting-room with her clipboard and throws me a smirk. Her attention zeros in on the window to see what I'm looking at.

'Looks like rain,' I say, trying hard not to shiver.

'Let me close that for you.' She reaches for the window, but not before looking me up and down. 'I'd put more clothes on if I were you.'

She disappears into the kitchen, where Paul is meeting with the chefs to go over the day's menus.

I look down at my silk shirt, which is see-through in all the wrong places, and flinch with embarrassment. What must Ryan think of me?

What must anyone think of me?

I run upstairs and rip it off, buttons popping onto the carpet. Angry groans escape me, becoming softer and softer, like a wound-ed creature slowly dying.

My phone rings and I accept the call.

When I say hello, there's no answer. The silence feels like a ticking bomb, and at any moment, everything could blow up in my face. It must be a reporter staying silent so they can learn some-thing worth printing. Only, it's not a tactic reporters use. Too many hang-up calls mean someone has something to tell me, and there's only one person I know with that type of determination.

'If this is you, Zane, it's not funny. I know you're out there, pretending to be dead and trying to ruin my life. But I won't let you. Do you hear?'

Still no response. I can't hear breathing or anything to give me a clue who it might be. So, I note the things I can hear – the occasional breath of wind, a passing car.

'There have been rumours about you living rough.' I let out an incredulous laugh. 'Ridiculous, I know. But rumours like that…' I pause for a few seconds. 'Could kill your pristine reputation.'

I'm confident that he understands the threat. The police are closing in on him.

'I know you can hear me because I can hear you.'

I expect him to say "Fine," and start talking, but he doesn't.

'Listen, Zane. You can be as quiet as you want so you don't give yourself away, but I want you to hear something. I want you to know that I've moved on. I'm happy. We're all happy. There's no need to spoil it by coming home.'

There. That should shake him.

The last thing I want is to drag Bizzy into the mess I've made. The last thing I need is for her to know the appalling sacrifices I had to make to get to this point. Zane doesn't get to break my heart continuously. I don't deserve it.

'While you're at it, give me an address so I can send divorce papers. All I need is your signature.'

Something changes in the air, as if the caller swaps hands and moves the phone to his other ear. A long exhale. A throat clearing. He's coming to his senses. He realises the importance of staying away from the family he abandoned and knows that the minute he sets foot on British soil, they will arrest him.

'I'm not coming home,' he says. 'I won't do that to do you or to Bizzy. But there is one thing I need from you.'

My breath hitches in my chest, and I can't breathe. *Oh God, he's alive. Please, no. Don't let it be him.* My worst fears are confirmed.

The white heat of panic threatens to overwhelm me. I pull the phone away from my ear and check the display. A private caller. This can't be right; this can't be happening. But it is Zane. I know his voice.

I feel sick just thinking about what he wants. What do I expect him to say? *Hey Lily, can we be civil about this and halve everything down the middle? Including the house. After all, I made most of the money doing films.*

What about my contribution? Isn't my putting up with his eccentricities worth anything? I would say it's worth more than half of what we own. He didn't suffer. I did.

I never thought I'd be this angry to know that my husband has tricked all his fans, his family and the police. Well, maybe not the police. I'm sure they're listening in on every call made to my number. But the point is, his fans mourned. His family mourned. We all felt abandoned.

My temper is already rising beyond what I would consider normal. If he doesn't hurry and get on with it, I might simply hang up. The only problem with Zane is that he is certifiably narcissistic, and whatever he asks will be unreasonable at most.

'I need you to believe me, Lily. I didn't kill Nic.'

The line has so much static; I have a hard time hearing. I tell him there's no way he can pin her death on anyone else. It's his fault he replicated Holloway's grisly behaviour, committed a crime and dumped his girlfriend in the sea. His fault and his alone. I won't be his accomplice or scapegoat, and I don't feel sorry for him. He's a con artist and not the person I thought he was.

He tries to bring up the past, as if this is merely a lovers' tiff, and that time can only move forward and past hurts fade. My memories are so different from his, and I remind him he's capable of killing anyone who comes between him and his success. I don't long for what we had. Zane isn't burdened with a sensitive heart. Where mine carries the scars of past hurts, his is as hard as stone.

'You left!' I shout. 'You hurt us and *left*!'

'I'm so sorry.'

I hear a sob in his voice, but I'm not moved.

He reminds me of Jared Leto, Christian Bale and Al Pacino, and how far they immerse themselves in their characters. It's not unrealistic for a method actor to become the character he portrays and cross a few lines. Which sounds as absurd as my pretending to be a timeless beauty like Gwyneth Paltrow and adhering to a macrobiotic diet. I might make waves in the press, but I'm no entertainer.

'I had to leave,' he says between sobs. 'I needed time… I needed to…' His sobs get louder and his words more incoherent over the wind. 'I couldn't let anything happen to her. I had to protect her. I had to.'

'Why? Why were you protecting Nic?'

Static fills the line, and all I can hear is the wind. Then the line goes dead.

### BarbedWire - Trending #InZane

@BantaBadger: Where's Zane then? He involved in this murder, maybe?

@CirceAtNight: He should be sentenced to De*th. End of story. #DeportHim

@MiloMorales: Not so fast. Something doesn't feel right about any of this.

@HeyWhatsUp: He's not playing Dr Death this time. He *is* Dr Death.

# 34

# ZANE

Morning hits like a hammer. I've barely shut my eyes when the rooster starts up, and the first smear of light crosses the fields. My body feels heavy and every muscle raw, and it's a miracle I haven't injured myself before now.

I walk out of the cottage and trudge over to the barn. The cold air bites through me, and I'm not looking forward to another freezing day outside.

Work starts before breakfast. Feeding the cattle and fixing a fence that looks like it's been broken for years. My arms burn. My back aches. But it's nothing compared to what's chewing inside my head.

The farmer's son, Callum, stares at me, all shoulders and smirk. Ginger hair peeks out from under his cap, and he couldn't grow a beard if he tried. He watches me wrestle with a feed bag and doesn't lift a finger.

'Careful, Drifter, you'll break your back before breakfast.'

I ignore him.

'Don't look like you know one end of a pitchfork from the other.' His expression is steely, and he glances over his shoulder at my truck. 'Nice ride. Bet it cost a lot.'

'More than you know.' His words are harmless on the surface, but they strike too close.

'Trust me, I know,' he says, grinning.

He's probing, testing, and sniffing out any weakness. I grit my teeth and heft another sack towards the nearest trough. My vision blurs at the edges, the world swimming with the sour churn of rage.

Callum leans against a stanchion. 'Man, you look rough.'

Holloway sidles up beside him in my mind, mirroring the boy's grin.

HOLLOWAY

```
He's right. You look like crap.
You didn't sleep last night
because you kept hearing some-
one outside. Now this little
bastard can see it too.
```

The pitchfork handle creaks in my grip. I force myself to breathe and to count slowly. My heart sprints faster with every insult the kid throws at me.

'What do you mean?' I ask.

Callum's body language is taut, and his shoulders are up. 'You don't think I've seen a dope peddler before?'

'I don't do drugs.'

'That's what they all say.' Callum jeers, his voice as sharp as wire. 'Or maybe you're covering for someone. Come on, Drifter. Spill.'

My hands twitch. For one long second, I see myself driving the pitchfork straight through that smirk, shutting him up forever. Instead, I slam the fork down into the dirt so hard the handle shivers. Callum's grin falters, just a flicker, but he doesn't back off. He knows he's getting under my skin.

HOLLOWAY

```
Give it a few days and you'll
be itching for a fight. An arse-
hole is an arsehole, Zane, and
the less this arsehole knows
about you, the better.
```

'First, I'm not a drifter,' I say, flexing my hand into a fist, 'and second, I'm not a dope peddler. Got it!'

His stance changes, and he looks furtive and somehow cowed. I assess the direction of his gaze, which seems to search for a way out. Some deep instinct tells me to bide my time. A high wind stirs the leaves in the trees and sends a flutter of snow across the yard. I see him shiver, and I doubt it's from the cold.

I leave him standing there, staring after me, as I walk towards the house. The kitchen smells of coffee and fried bacon, a welcome change from the sour taste of Callum's relentless bullying.

I sit at the rough pine table with a chipped mug clutched in both hands, trying to look like I belong. Mick grunts over his plate, already halfway through his breakfast when Callum comes in. He leans back in his chair, boots kicked out wide, watching me the way a dog eyes a stranger at the gate. I don't give him a second glance.

What surprises me the most about this family is Mick's wife, Amelie. Clearly, his second wife, as the image of the first, framed in silver, still lauds it over the family from the mantelpiece. Amelie is early thirties with soft brown hair clipped high on her head, and the palest eyes I've ever seen. When she sets a plate of eggs, bacon and toast in front of me, her fingers brush mine.

Callum takes it all in with a smirk. 'Careful, Amelie' he says, jabbing his fork towards her. 'Drifter here might not know how to use a pitchfork, but I bet he knows how to handle a cow.'

Mick frowns at him, faint but visible. 'Leave her alone, Cal. As for Will, he's here to do farm work, nothing more.'

'Yeah, right.' Callum narrows his eyes at me. 'You planning on sticking around long, or you just passing through like the rest?'

Amelie pours me more coffee, and I swallow it down in a gulp. 'I'm staying.'

HOLLOWAY

> That'll piss him off. But you
> feel it, don't you? The way he
> wants you gone. And her... She

                    sees something in you. That'll
                    twist the knife a little
                    deeper.

I can feel Callum's glare burning through me as she sets the pot down. The scrape of his fork against his plate is loud enough to raise hackles.

'Don't get too comfortable,' he says, voice sharper now. 'This ain't forever.'

Mick grunts again, as if to wave it off, but I can feel the weight of the words hanging in the air.

***

Every day is the same. Mick's young wife lingers at breakfast when she pours my coffee, asking if I slept okay. Callum snorts into his plate and mutters something about drifters and freeloaders. Mick ignores it, chewing slowly, but I catch the glint in his eye, and I know he's watching us all.

Out in the fields, Callum drives me harder. He makes the other farmhands give me double the work, and he stands close enough for me to feel the heat of his breath when he corrects me. Every word carries an edge, and the longer it goes, the smaller I feel, like he's whittling me down piece by piece.

That night I lie awake and Holloway whispers from the dark corner of the bedroom.

                    HOLLOWAY

               He hates you because Amelie
               likes you. We both know the
               danger in that.

          INT. BEDROOM - ZANE'S COZY COTTAGE AT
          NIGHT (DIMLY LIT)

Zane wakes, feeling the warmth
of a body pressed against his.
He traces her mouth with his
finger and then his lips find
hers. We are now close on the
kiss, seeing them coiled together, and we slowly retreat.
His hand slides down her neck
to her collarbone and rests
on her breast. She trembles.
By now we are far enough away
to realise that they are both
naked.

Shit, no!

I sit up in bed, sweating. The last thing I want to do is invite my boss's wife into my bed. I'd rather pin Callum to the cow stalls, knee him in the nuts and run like hell.

At every mealtime, Callum makes a point of telling dirty jokes about drifters not knowing how to handle farm girls. Amelie refuses to look at him when he says it, and she looks at me, a hot blush surging to her cheeks.

I'm willing Mick to say something, to beat the crap out of his gutless son, and I don't have to wait too long. Mick slams his fist down hard enough to rattle the plates and growls a warning.

'No one touches my wife, do you hear? *No one!*'

Callum flinches at his father's voice and grips the side of his chair. He doesn't move a muscle. It gives me the briefest sense of satisfaction to see Amelie's face crumple into relief. I wonder, not for the first time, if I could beat the crap out of him – even kill him – if it means shutting him up for good.

Could I do it so it would look like an accident?

HOLLOWAY

Oooh... Let me think. He'd need to
be struck by a moving tractor

```
or fall from a silo. Because
if it looked like murder, Mick
wouldn't hesitate to call the
police. Cal is his only son,
after all.
```

Each day I look for opportunities, but I don't want to cause trouble for Mick. He's been a good and fair boss to me, and I hate to disappoint him.

The following morning, I'm drained. Every creak of the old cottage kept me awake, and every shadow seemed to scratch the walls with its claws. Breakfast comes around again, and I take a seat at the long table with two other farmhands and Callum. Mick's already left to check the weather and inspect the livestock. My eyes burn, and my hands are stiff from pounding posts to make new fences.

Callum is sprawled like a king at his own feast. He smirks at his plate and at the way his fork cuts through the yolk and lets it bleed. When his eyes finally land on me, they're sharp and measuring.

'Sleep well?' His tone's too casual.

'Fine,' I mutter, though we both know it's a lie.

Amelie moves quietly around the kitchen, setting down more toast and pouring juice. She gives me a fleeting smile – kind, almost shy – and I glance away. Callum doesn't miss it, and his smirk hardens.

'You're up awful early for a man who worked himself half to death yesterday,' he says. 'Most drifters I've seen don't last two days. Soft hands, weak backs. But you… you like to come up to the house so you can sniff around her. Don't think I haven't noticed.'

The jab slides under my ribs. 'I come up here to eat. Got a problem with that?'

'No. Not really.'

Amelie stands between us. 'Let the man eat in peace.'

'Careful, sweetheart,' Callum says, smiling up at her. 'Don't spoil the hired help. He might get the wrong idea.'

Her face colours and our eyes meet briefly before the contact is broken.

'Look at him,' Callum says, jerking his chin at me. 'Doesn't swing a pitchfork like a man. He swings it like a poser.'

The men don't want to be caught between us, but they laugh anyway. I grip my knife even harder.

Callum's eyes glitter with amusement. 'Bet you never broke your back in the dirt before now. Bet you never earned a callus in your life.'

One of the men mutters, 'He pulls his weight. Puts in more hours than that lazy-arse manager you hired last month.'

But the comment dies in the air when Callum shoots him a look.

'Drifter here has no story and no past. Just a stranger who showed up in a shiny truck. Tell me, Will, what're you hiding?'

I force myself to breathe evenly. 'I'm not hiding anything.'

'Right.' He tilts his chair back, his eyes never leaving mine. 'A man without roots is like a weed. You never know when it'll choke the field.'

The farmhands around the table shift uncomfortably and trade glances. I feel the crack widening inside me, a fault line running through my chest and up into my head. While Callum presses on it, waiting for me to break, I simply carry on eating.

Amelie refills my coffee, and I mutter a thank you. She lingers for a second too long before returning to her chair. Callum's eyes catch the moment, his jaw twitching.

'You talk funny. Not from around here, are you?'

'None of us are,' I say, flatly.

He looks at the other farmhands, whose accents suggest a mixture of Mexican and Guatemalan, and he says nothing. But the room hums with his suspicion.

HOLLOWAY

```
      He sees you, son. Not for who
      you are but for the secrets
      you keep. He'll keep digging
      until he finds exactly what
      he's looking for.
```

I push back my chair and stand. 'Thank you, Amelie, for another wonderful breakfast.'

I trudge out of the house and into the barn, knowing it's only a matter of time before this house, this farm, and this fragile hiding place cracks wide open.

# 35

# LILJA

A lot can happen in a week. I've been wrapping my arms around my stomach, trying to keep down my supper. The dread I've been feeling rears its head again.

Zane's alive. The slimy, lying bastard is *alive*. How could he do this to us?

I will need my attorney to shine a light on where he is and for the police to bring him home. If he thought death was better than being a divorced, penniless recluse, then why hadn't he stayed that way?

Fear runs a fingernail lightly up my spine, and I feel as if I'm floating. My imagination fires into action. All I can think of are dead bodies and terrible publicity and police cordons all around the house. I don't know how to break it to Bizzy and to the rest of the family.

I open the study door and listen to see if any news is blaring through the house. I can't hear anything except the TV cycling through *Murder, She Wrote* episodes.

After I'd heard Zane's voice five days ago, I called DC Symonds. She told me he was clearly using a disposable pay-as-you-go phone. But if he was avoiding public Wi-Fi and had installed apps to block the police from tracking him, he was virtually untraceable. Also, he was probably changing his phone number regularly. But she confirmed they were monitoring all calls and texts from my phone, and Bizzy's, and that they were on it.

Wonderful. Fantastic. I haven't heard from them since.

Just as important, who was Zane trying to pin the blame on for Nic's death? A guest or one of the staff. We had a full house at the time. What scares me more is that without a motive, none of them would have any reason to have hurt her.

He can't have been alluding to the family. Their crimes, while perhaps not completely innocent, involve mundane offenses like parking tickets, a few little white lies, and smoking a few joints — not murder. Even I didn't see Nic as a threat until she became one.

I study each family member in my mind. Elin had nothing against Nic, nor did Paul. Of the two of them, he would be the most obvious. Dense and well-built puts him in the powerhouse category, though he'd never hurt a woman. Of that, I'm sure.

Then there's Burgess, our resident comedian, whose silky-smooth demeanour would be compromised by keeping such a secret. By the time I've gone around the house, I can't pick out one suspect.

I go upstairs to change into yoga pants and trainers. Bizzy's door is closed, which means she's changing or watching something she shouldn't on her computer.

I give the door a light tap. 'What are you doing in there?'

'Porn.'

She's on the bed, reading *The Kite Runner* by Khaled Hosseini. Her eyes slide over the top of the spine, and she lifts one eyebrow.

'I'm just going for a run,' I say. 'Want to come with?'

She glances at the window and at the trees bending in the wind and shakes her head. 'I'll pass, thanks. You are changing your routine.'

'Yes, I'm going up the hill behind the church. Be back in an hour.'

I wrap myself in a thick padded jacket and run downstairs. Peering around the sitting-room door, I notice Paul has fallen asleep on the couch with Elin half on top of him. When I cover them with a blanket, Elin opens her eyes.

'I'm going for a run,' I whisper.

She gives me a sleepy smile and closes her eyes again.

This time of year, the clouds are thick and grey, and there's often a golden glow to the trees. I study the garden and the front drive through the hall window, where a pair of hares are running across the lawn at sunset.

Outside, the melancholic sound of a wind chime comes from the stables, and I wonder briefly what Ryan is doing.

I break into a jog towards the front gate and lean into the wind. The church sits on the east side of Barton, looking like something out of a Claude Monet painting. Daffodils and crocuses grace the lawn between the trees and, looking through the rhododendrons, I see the family graves. Beside my grandmother's is a small headstone with the words, Oscar William Osborne, who was a tiny part of our lives. Sometimes I take a step back from myself and wonder if my baby would have looked more like Zane than me. My stomach lurches with grief. But I hold it in like I hold in everything else.

I cross the road and run along the lane behind the church. This is one of my least favourite routes as it's uphill all the way to the bridle path, and I'm often out of breath before I reach the stile.

A rush of cold air assaults me, and the wind slips inside my hood and makes me shiver. I hear someone shouting my name, and spin around.

I'm aware of pounding shoes behind me, trained breaths that tell me it's not a runner. Then a tiny head and shoulders appear over the brow of the hill, and the outline of a woman in a ski jacket like mine.

'Wait,' comes a voice.

I spy Bizzy's slender limbs as she pumps her way towards me.

'Hey,' I say, linking arms with her. 'I thought you didn't want to come. I would have waited.'

'It's okay. I changed my mind.'

Handing her one of my gloves, I tell her to put her other bare hand in her pocket.

'There's something I wanted to ask you.' She takes a few moments to catch her breath. 'I overheard you talking to the police a few days ago. Was it about Dad?'

A knot forms in my throat, and I try to swallow it away. 'It's about the silent calls I've been receiving. The police are taking the last one seriously.'

She jerks me to a stop. 'He called you?'

I can't keep her in the dark. She deserves to know. 'Yes. He did.'

'Oh, shit. *Shit!* She's turning in circles and flapping a hand. 'You're sure?'

'Yes.'

'Does Uncle Paul know? Stella?'

'No.'

She keeps shaking her head. 'What did he say?'

'That's the thing. None of it made any sense. He kept saying he hadn't killed Nic. He was trying to protect her.'

'From what?'

'I don't know. There was so much static on the line I couldn't hear him.'

I suddenly feel as if everything is distorted and unreal. I've always been in control of my life and Bizzy's, and now I'm floundering because nothing is as clear-cut as it seems.

Her grip is tight on my arm, and she looks at me in mild astonishment. 'Did you think he was alive? I mean, did it ever occur to you he might have been faking it?'

'No. Although I did fantasise about it. I had visions of him living on a tiny island somewhere with a different name. A different face. Did you?'

She goes quiet for a moment. 'No. I mean, the guys on *Barbed-Wire* kept talking about the sightings as if they were some kind of joke. What are they going to think now?'

'They're going to think he's an arsehole.' Then I cringe. 'Sorry, I didn't mean that.'

'No, you're right. They're going to hate him.'

'How will your friends take it?'

'They've been incredibly supportive. I don't see that changing.' We walk in silence for a moment. 'Has he done anything like this before? Gone missing and pretended to be dead.'

The frankness of her question hits a raw nerve and almost steals my air.

'He has, hasn't he?' she says, because of my delay.

I can feel myself drowning in the memory. 'When your baby brother died, your dad disappeared for three days. He never called, never told me where he'd been. I was nearly out of my mind.'

'Yes, but you knew he was okay. You knew he'd come back.'

I shrug. 'I don't see how.'

'Because it felt different.'

Then I see what she's getting at. Back then, Zane might have died inside, but I knew he'd come home, eventually. This time, I believed the coroner's report, even though he'd used the words *alleged bear attack*. It wasn't until his silent calls to me that I truly entertained the idea he could be alive.

The sob in Zane's voice stirred up all the emotion I'd felt after he left. This was the actor who had brought audiences to tears with his role in *Loving Alice*, where he played Harry Price, husband and caregiver to a wife dying of cancer. He was so good at it.

'I never expected him to do something like this,' I say, my breath clouding the evening air. 'I thought he was better than that. Allowing another woman into our lives and then killing her is not the way to end anything.'

'What if he didn't kill her?'

'Then he should have called the police.'

It seems too simple a solution and catches me off guard. Is telling me he was protecting someone else another ruse to make me believe he's innocent? If so, he played it expertly. Yet somehow, I keep picturing him in handcuffs, being escorted back into the country to a flash of cameras.

'Mum, listen.' She pulls me to a stop again and places her hands on my shoulders. 'I know Dad had affairs and how much it hurt. It would have pushed anyone over the edge.'

Our eyes meet, and I fight to hide a reaction.

'I saw how he treated you,' she says. 'Shit, I overhead some of it. We all did. No one would blame you if you'd—'

'If I'd what?'

'Nothing.' She drops her hands. 'I'm not saying anything.'

Her face is suddenly grave. The energy bristling off her is one that screams *don't make me tell you*. I'm confused by her statement and what she means by pushing anyone over the edge. Is she talking about me? As if I had somehow lost my footing and done something unimaginable.

I swallow hard, my saliva thickening. 'You can't think I had anything to do with it.'

'No.' She grabs my arm. 'I'm just saying… He hurt you, and he hurt me. I wouldn't blame you if you had.'

My hand goes to my mouth, and my knees almost buckle. She must feel it with me hanging on her arm, but she says nothing. Her accusation saddens me, and I take a moment to collect myself. She notices the tremor of emotion in my voice and lays her head on my shoulder.

'Bizzy, I would never… I hated Dad for what he did. If I had wanted to hurt anyone, it would have been him. But not like that. *Never* like that.'

'I know, Mum. I know.'

'It was terrible what he did. Now he's paying for it. *We're* paying for it.' I grimly plough on. 'No one else knows. They mustn't know, Bizzy. Not intimate family stuff. Not the things we know.'

It's stupid to worry about what the press thinks. It matters what it looks like to the public. However they spin this, the next few days will determine the next few months. I straighten and lock the anxiety away.

As we turn around and walk down the hill towards home, I can't help feeling sick with dread. And so very afraid.

**BarbedWire - Trending #InZane**

@BantaBadger: Sounds like Barton Manor is getting an award. They've been named the top restaurant in Devon.

@LostForWords: Meanwhile in Canada… Zane's living in a gutter somewhere.

@CirceAtNight: Er… no. He's probably shacked up with an heiress, living his best lie. #PunkOfTheDay

@HeyWhatsUP: Don't! Him being alive is scary enough to cope with.

# 36

# ZANE

Dust from the barn still clings to my throat when Mick finds me that evening. I'm sitting on the back steps of the farmhouse, staring out at the fields where the last of the light burns red across the horizon.

He lowers himself onto the step beside me with a grunt, and the wood creaks under his weight. He smells of hay and tobacco, a smell that never washes out.

'You did good today,' he says, his voice rough but kind. 'Don't mind Callum. Boy's always been sharp-tongued.'

I keep my eyes fixed on the horizon. 'I'm fine. It doesn't bother me.'

Mick chuckles. 'Course it does. You're only human. But he's my son, which makes me twice as responsible for his mouth.'

Silence follows, not the sharp kind that Callum leaves behind, but one I want to cling to like a warm blanket on a chilly night.

'You remind me of myself when I was young,' Mick says. 'I came here looking for work when I was fifteen. Wasn't easy, but folks were willing to give me a chance. I try to do the same for others now.'

I swallow hard, my throat tight. 'I appreciate it.'

'You ever think of going home?' Mick asks gently.

*Home…* The word is like a blade twisting in my gut. I picture my wife and her accusing voice, and I picture the life I screwed up.

'No. I burned too many bridges.'

Mick studies me, his weathered face soft with understanding. 'Well, you've got work here for as long as you want. I mean that, son.'

The word *son* knocks something loose in me, and suddenly it hurts to look at him. I feel an empty ache in my gut and a yearning I can't ignore.

HOLLOWAY

He doesn't know about the
blood on your hands. He'd put
you down like a sick animal if
he did. You can't stay.

I let Mick's words hold me together, because even if everything about me now is built on lies, it feels good to be seen as something other than what I've become.

He pats me on the shoulder and says goodnight, and I can still feel the warmth of his hand after he goes inside.

* * *

The sky breaks open the following day. Every animal on the farm is restless; stamping, shifting, snorting, as if they know a storm is coming. While I work into the late afternoon, my mind slides from Mick's compassion to Callum's animosity, wondering how on earth they could be related.

During the last hour, I'm out in the fields hauling feed when Callum finds me. Rain spits sharp against my skin, and wind tugs at my clothes.

'You've got him fooled,' he shouts over the rising wind. 'My old man thinks you're some kind of stray worth feeding. What is it about you?'

I grip the bag tighter and give him a leery look. 'Maybe I'm just a really nice guy.'

He doesn't miss the sarcasm and steps closer, rain plastering his hair to his forehead.

'You don't talk about where you're from. You don't talk about family. Yet you work like you've got the devil chasing you.' Lightning forks across the sky, illuminating his face in brief flashes. 'You're hiding something, and I'm gonna find out what.'

The wind howls, whipping through the fields, tearing the words out of his mouth and hurling them at me like stones. My chest feels like it's caving in, and my breath is caught between Holloway's laughter and the storm's roar.

HOLLOWAY

Do it! Grab the paunchy little
shit by the neck and squeeze.
There's no one watching.

I set the feed bag down slowly, and my hands are trembling, not from the storm but from the urge. Callum's eyes lock on mine, daring me, waiting for the slip he knows will come.

Thunder cracks overhead, and rain comes down hard and drums against my shoulders. In that moment, between the storm and Callum's stare, I feel the trap tightening. Instead of finishing him off right then and there, I stride across the fields to the farmhouse, leaving his short, stocky frame to shuffle after me.

This time, he doesn't join us for dinner, and I can't say anyone misses him. After everyone retires to the back porch for a smoke and a beer, I help Amelie with the dishes. Tears pool in her eyes, and she brushes them away with the back of her hand.

'What is it?' I ask.

Her voice is low, meant only for me. 'Be careful. Cal thinks you're a runaway.'

My heart beats faster. 'Why would he think that?'

'He knows that truck ain't yours.'

I draw a deep breath. I'd been careful to hide the VIN number on the dashboard near the windscreen with fast food wrappers. What else had given it away?

She glances at the door and then back at me. 'Covering a dent with grey paint with stolen cans in the flatbed, don't change anything. That's what I heard him say to Mick.'

So that's the noise that woke me last night, Callum snooping under the tarp over the flatbed. I'd imagined this moment so many times – someone ratting me out to the feds and the terror that follows.

'You're a kind man, Will Rivière, if that's your real name.' The warmth of her hand on mine takes me by surprise. 'Best you be gone by morning. Mick will understand.'

Callum steps into the kitchen just in time to see it. His eyes narrow, and I can see him taking in every detail, how close she's standing to me, how she snaps her hand back when she sees him.

HOLLOWAY

> Strictly speaking, you're screwed. You'd better get the hell out, old boy, before the police arrive.

My body is failing, and my nerves are shot. Callum circles me like a wolf, and his goading takes on a sharper, more threatening tone.

'Touch her, and you're dead,' he snarls.

I look at the knife he's holding, and I know he's not kidding.

Amelie walks behind him and stands by the door. From over his shoulder, she locks her eyes on me and shakes her head. If Callum's contempt is a blade pressed to my throat, I know it's only a matter of seconds before he drives it home.

'You know,' he says, 'I couldn't place your face at first.'

I try to force down the adrenaline and count my breaths.

'But then it clicked.' He's grinning now, teeth bared, like he's won something. 'You're him, aren't you? The bigshot actor from England who killed a woman and went missing.'

He presses the knife against my throat. 'They're looking for you. And here you are, playing farmhand and cosying up to my daddy's wife.'

```
                    HOLLOWAY

        Well, well. Curtains up, Zane,
        time for your big reveal.
```

'You don't know what you're saying,' I say.

Callum takes the phone out of his pocket with his free hand. 'Don't bullshit me. I've seen the news. I bet if I called the cops right now, they'd come running. Maybe I'll get that nice reward.'

My vision tunnels and my heart pounds. The panic curdles into rage. I shove him hard, and the phone flies from his hand and skitters across the kitchen floor. Callum swings wildly at me, pounding and punching, but my fist connects with his jaw, and the crack echoes off the walls.

He stumbles, spitting blood and roaring something that sounds like, 'You piece of shit!' but there's a front tooth missing and he can barely speak at all.

When he comes at me again, his fist slams into the side of my face and all I can see is a flash of white. I'm struggling to stay in the game. There's a second or two delay, giving my vision time to clear.

This time, he lunges at me, and my knee collides with his groin. But not before his elbow cracks down across my back. The greyout I've been dreading fills my mind. Somewhere within that frenzy of sounds, the action slows, and the kitchen is stippled in greys and whites.

A shout brings me back. Fearing Callum's knife is still poised at my throat or worse, I see him curled on the floor in a ball, his face covered in blood. Amelie hovers behind him, hands over her mouth, and I realise she has no intention of calling Mick.

I back away, my chest heaving and my knuckles raw. Callum's eyes are blazing at me with pure hatred, and I know I have to leave now.

I run to the cottage and gather my belongings, knowing that when Mick shows up, there will be hell to pay. As I drive past the barn, I glance at the house and see Amelie standing at the door, and I'm afraid to leave her behind.

As I bring the truck to a halt in front of her, something passes between us. Her shaking head and tear-filled eyes tell me she harbours no animosity towards me. Then her arm sweeps towards the open gate, urging me to hurry.

In that instant, I know what Holloway's been telling me all along. There's no safe place. No home. Only the road.

# 37

# LILJA

When I take a tray of hot chocolate into the sitting-room, everyone stops talking. Their eyes are on the anchor, whose voice is predictably deadpan, with minor traces of compassion.

> *'New details emerge in a manhunt for Devon celebrity Zane Osborne, accused of killing Nicola Gatlin before disappearing into the Canadian wilderness. Over a year after the body of Nicola Gatlin was discovered at Langstone Rock, law enforcement officials have confirmed that Osborne is the sole suspect. However, after several false sightings, authorities had conceded there were no new leads regarding his whereabouts. Until now…'*

The video leaves the studio and goes to a small shelter in the Canadian wilderness set back from the river and surrounded by trees. A voice-over continues.

> *Authorities are yet to release details, but there is a possibility that Zane could have travelled to Quebec under the name Theodore Oliver and may have changed his appearance.*

'Very original,' Bizzy says, googling plastic surgery. 'Typical Dad.'

'Seriously?' Paul weighs in. 'How did he do it?'

Paul's comment unsettles me, and something sinister seems to arrive in the room as I think of it. The help one would need to stay off the grid is unthinkable.

'It says here that a facelift costs anywhere between six and fifteen thousand quid,' Bizzy says. 'Where's he getting that kind of money?'

'It doesn't mention plastic surgery,' I say, electing not to tell Bizzy about the money Zane stole from one of our accounts. 'I doubt he has that type of cash.'

The image zeroes in on an old photo of Zane, wearing faded jeans and a leather jacket, leaning against a wrought-iron fence with his elbows propped on the top rail. Then the image goes to a Canadian news studio, where the anchor interviews a police lieutenant. It's a split screen with him talking about a hunter he'd questioned in Makkovik. CCTV monitoring the inside of a local coffee shop shows a man with sunken cheeks and a scraggly beard, wearing a baseball cap.

I stare at the image, at this monstrous betrayal, and I'm swinging between horror and rationalisation. It can't be him. It's a lookalike. Someone else with a similar face. Yet it is him, a thinner, almost unrecognisable version, and it's the only tangible evidence we have.

Then the image shoots to women's championship football, and Paul grabs the remote and mutes the sound.

I wonder what all this has set in motion, whether Barton Manor will suffer now that Zane is one of Canada's (and Britain's) most wanted criminals.

'Did you read the article in *The Quebec Chronical* about the reward?' Bizzy asks, looking up from her phone.

Heat travels up my chest. 'Go on.'

She reads it out to me. 'The Sûreté du Québec is offering a reward of up to $30,000 for information leading to Zane's arrest. They've warned the public that he could be dangerous, and to call the police immediately.'

'Dangerous?' I suddenly remember his psychotic behaviour the last time I saw him.

'The authorities spoke to someone called…' She scans her phone again. 'Jean-Marie Grenier, who insisted this was the same man who'd given him a broken nose *and* a broken jaw. Shit.'

How low had Zane stooped? His life, it turns out, is complicated. None of it started with the predictable hurting animals, nicking cars and selling drugs. He had a good upbringing, except that his father was mainly absent. But that wouldn't explain how he escalated to murder.

Frantically, my mind swings to the script from the Netflix series he did, and I know I'm on to something. I can feel it. Something so vile. Something he has never discarded.

Holloway.

Inside, my mind is racing. I recall Zane's expression that terrible night, when he looked at me through the car window as Bizzy and I tried to make it to the front gate. There wasn't a stitch of remorse in it.

'How horrible.' A tear tracks its way down Stella's cheek. 'To think I mourned him. I *actually* mourned him.'

'We all did,' Paul barks. 'Including his fans. Piece of shit.'

Elin looks from him to me, and then to Bizzy. We're both thinking the same thing – that this conversation shouldn't be had in front of her.

'I considered all kinds of theories about his death,' Stella says. 'That he'd gone on a drinking binge and fallen into the river. Or that a group of men living rough in the woods had killed him.'

'Let's not forget he was a survivalist,' Paul says. 'Let's also not forget that now he's alive, he can finally do time for murder. I'm going to make sure he never sees Bizzy again.'

I shoot Paul a look for her sake.

'Okay.' He shrugs. 'But he should be punished.'

Stella shakes her head as if trying to digest the information. 'When the police asked me what Zane was like, the first thing I mentioned was the drinking.'

'It's not like I'm teetotal,' I say. 'Or you.'

Stella meets my eyes. 'No. But he often drove under the influence. He could have caused a terrible accident.'

'Good grief, he killed Nic!' Paul sits bolt upright. 'Nothing can be more terrible than that.'

'It was a spur-of-the-moment decision.' Stella turns to face him. 'A stupid decision. It wasn't like he was behaving rationally.'

Then I realise what she's trying to say. If he'd been sober that night, he might not have lost his temper and lashed out at Nic. But my inner voice warns me not to believe it. Lies tripped off Zane's tongue too easily, and there's more to this story than she knows.

'When you get blackout drunk, you remember nothing. Nobody does,' she says.

'He wasn't *that* drunk,' Paul says. 'I don't remember him slurring his words or staggering about.'

'He didn't look well. He wasn't eating.'

'That's because he took Nic out for expensive dinners in Exeter,' he says. 'Might explain his loss of appetite.'

He took her to the Southernhay House Hotel with its spacious beds, freestanding baths and power showers. I saw the receipt.

Stella pulls a hanky from her sleeve. 'He was always pacing about and talking to himself, and he'd clutch his head like he had something sharp in it. Then he'd pass out on the couch in the afternoons. You don't think he was seriously ill?'

'Sorry,' Paul interrupts. 'But this might need a little clarification. He stayed at Nic's until four in the morning, nursing a hangover, before slipping back into the house without being seen. I don't think he needs your sympathy. You were the one who had to clear up all the mess. Wine stains on the carpet, cigarette ash on the couch and used condoms in the toilet.'

I almost die on the pot. Bizzy's face is screwed up in an expression of sheer disgust, and I wave my hand for Paul to stop talking.

'Paul's right. It needs to be said.' Elin's brow drops, and she shifts her weight on the couch. 'They fought a lot, him and Nic. It's not like we didn't overhear some of it. The last time she was so upset, I'd never seen her like that before.'

'Like what?' I ask.

'Like she was shaking so bad, I thought she was going to pass out. Please don't ask me when. I don't remember.'

There's something beneath the surface of her expression, a ripple of sadness, and I attribute it to her loyalty. He was kind to her, and he was charismatic and utterly charming. Elin adored him, hence her silence.

But it was Paul who followed Nic one afternoon and warned her to stay away from us. He'd had enough of her impropriety.

Elin glances out of the window at the trees at the edge of the property. She frowns as if there is something strange about a lawn peppered with frost, as if something about it is slightly off. Perhaps she's searching her mind for the one thing the rest of us might have missed.

'I can't sleep. I haven't slept in months.' She's sobbing now. 'It's awful. Everything's so awful.'

There's a loaded silence. Her fuse takes a long time to trip, if it ever trips at all, but I can see the dark circles under her eyes, and I know she's cracking under the strain.

When the police told us that Zane had died, I found Elin in the garden on her knees, hunched over a slick stain of vomit. The pressure had been too much. She had watched him sink into Holloway madness, and it must have been as terrifying for her as it was for me.

'I know you feel bad for everything,' I say, kneeling in front of her and taking her hands in mine. 'But you've got to let it go.'

'I wish Nic hadn't come to the house that night,' she says, wiping her eyes. 'I wish… Oh, God, I wish I could have stopped it.'

'How could you have stopped it?'

'I just think about it sometimes.'

I can see she's haunted by the horrible ordeal. Behind the sorrow, I can make out an emotion on her face that I haven't seen before, one that I can't read.

'Would you like me to call someone?' I ask. 'Someone you can talk to?'

'You mean a therapist?'

'Yes.'

'No. I don't think it would help.'

Her shoulders are tense, and she stares out of the window at the hydrangeas with their bare branches and brown blooms. After a few seconds, she looks at me, and that's when the hiccups of grief come.

I hold her until she hangs there exhausted, and I hope that every second of letting go will heal the pain Zane left behind.

When I wipe the tears from her cheeks, I hate him a little more.

**BarbedWire: Trending #InZane**

@Titmouse: This isn't Zane Osborne. If he were alive, which he's not, he's hardly the type to go around hurting people. Obviously, someone has set him up.

@BantaBadger: No one has set him up. He's guilty. Same as before.

@Titmouse: Seriously, put yourself in his shoes. What if it were your face splattered all over the tabloids for a crime you hadn't committed? You'd be running for the hills.

@BantaBadger: I'd turn myself in, hoping the right guy was found and convicted.

@Titmouse: What if the right guy wasn't found? What if it became another case of the police making a wrongful conviction?

@HeyWhatsUP: You've been watching waaaaay too many crime shows. #TheInnocenceProject NOT!

# 38

# ZANE

Holloway's incessant rendering of Gene Autry's *Back in the Saddle Again* is wearing thin. I need to ditch the truck and find something else, which is going to be hard with barely eight hundred dollars from my short stint at the farm.

My face is swollen and so is my back. I'm a walking disaster. The engine's hum should calm me, but it doesn't. I idly follow a grey convertible with a frayed top and peeling paint for about three miles before it veers into the turning lane. Then I'm alone on the road again, driving under an assembly of flickering stars.

A sharp feeling of sadness takes me by surprise. I wanted to thank Mick for taking a chance on me and offering me not only a job, but the use of a farm cottage as well. I feel frantic with guilt, and the desire to call him gets stronger by the minute. But my knuckles ache where they split Callum's jaw. Mick won't forgive me for that.

I flick on the radio, needing something – anything – to drown out a jumble of thoughts. That the truck might have a tracker jostles for first place. There's a bunch of static and then a nasal voice with a tone of moral superiority.

*'…authorities are still searching for former British actor Zane Osborne, wanted for questioning in connection with several violent incidents. The reward has increased to*

> *$40,000. People are slowly coming forward with believed sightings. A woman, who prefers to remain anonymous, is convinced she sat next to him on a plane bound for Sept-Îles… A man taking breakfast in a bistro in Old Quebec, thinks he may have seen Osborne stealing food from tables… Gare du Palais CCTV picked up a man stealing a phone from a passenger…'*

My stomach heaves. It's an absurd sum of money and gives more motivation for the public to find me. I want to turn the radio off, but I can't stop listening. At the same time, looking in my rearview mirror for a squad car with flashing lights.

> *'Police believe Osborne bought a ticket to Toronto and may have boarded the 6.20 pm train… Police pinged the phone to a tower near the Petite-Nation River, where Osborne made a long-distance call to his wife. But the trail doesn't stop there. He called her again from a payphone, insisting he was innocent of the crime of murdering Ms Nicola Gatlin. Mrs Osborne is said to be fully cooperating with the police in their enquiries.'*

The words *fully cooperating* make me tremble. How much has Lilja told them? The police are too close, and terror wraps itself tighter around me. The voice drones in the background, like a bee over a cluster of lavender.

> *'Stolen Toyota Corolla… Dodge Ram picked up by CCTV on Highway 50… Plates stolen in Thurso. Jack Ramsey's body was found bludgeoned to death in the alley behind his house.'*

There's the sensation of hyenas fighting over my internal organs, and it's all I can do not to double over.

                    HOLLOWAY

          Now, now, Zane. You can't
          escape the police. I told you
          all those phone calls would
          leave a trail, and I told you
          to stay out of sight. But you
          didn't, did you?

I twist the dial, but the next station picks up the same story.

> *"… a man has come forward to claim the reward. A transient, who goes by the name of Jean-Marie Grenier, was hospitalised after suffering a broken nose said to have been perpetrated by Osborne. He says he may have information about Osborne's whereabouts.'*

Bullshit! Jean-Marie doesn't have a clue where I am. He's slowly becoming every bit as loathsome as everyone else. I struggle to hear my own thoughts over the thudding of my heart.

                    HOLLOWAY

          But you are famous again.
          Front-page famous. How does it
          feel?

                    ZANE

          It feels like shit.

                    HOLLOWAY

          Cheer up, old boy. The dark-
          ness is particularly useful to
          you now.

As I slam the radio off, headlights flare in the rearview and a semi rolls up behind me, pressing me faster down the road. My chest tightens, and for a second, I'm convinced it's about to ram me, driver laying on the horn like it's about to rip open the night.

I tap the brakes, take the next exit, and dirt kicks up behind me. The semi barrels past on the main road, nothing but a trucker working the night haul. My breath rattles out, shaky and weak.

HOLLOWAY

```
You're such a snob, Zane. You
love this truck because it's
over four hundred and twenty
horsepower and it's fully
decked out. But you should
assume the police have a photo.
```

I know he's right. If they don't catch me in it, it'll burn me another way. I pull off onto a gravel track and haul arse between a stand of trees until I find the perfect spot and shut off the engine. The night folds in around me, and I open the window to hear the faint rustle of trees. If I abandon it here, no one will ever find it. If they do, it'll be some logger or a hunter delighted at finding a powerfully equipped truck at their disposal.

I check the window pockets for a torch and find one in the centre console. Leaving the keys in the ignition, I shoulder my backpack and step into the night. The first thing I feel is the cold, the biting sort that stings my cheeks and prompts me to take tiny sips of air. My toes curl inside my boots, anything to keep my circulation going.

I relieve myself behind a tree and take a good hard look at my surroundings. Saplings are bent at the root from the snow, and a layer of dead leaves litters the ground. I turn on the torch and walk downhill, stepping over roots and fallen branches. Somewhere in the distance I hear running water. After ten minutes, a small brook appears where thin shards of ice bob at the water's edge.

The sound of snapping twigs tears me from my thoughts, and shock ripples through me. Something small scurries past, dashing for the trees, which means either I frightened it or something larger is in pursuit. When nothing else emerges, I exhale loudly.

After stumbling around for an hour, the slope evens out and there's a break in the trees where a ploughed field comes into view. Moonlight streaks along the furrows, giving me enough light to turn off the torch. At the farthest corner, gravel crunches under my boots until it turns into a road. A glow on the horizon – orange against the black – tells me I'm getting closer to a town.

Headlights flicker in the distance, and I hunker to the ground as a truck flies past. Once it rounds the corner, I'm up again and walking along the main road. The town looks like the kind of place where people know each other, where a stranger walking at night sets dogs barking.

The gas station lot is empty except for a rusted sedan slumped by a chain-link fence, weeds creeping up its tires. It's a corpse of a car, but I circle it anyway and try the door.

Locked.


                    HOLLOWAY

        Dead  metal,  son.  You  need
        something that breathes.


I push deeper into the neighbourhood where pickup trucks glint under carports, and SUVs lounge in driveways. All too clean, too new, and far too risky. On one side of a house, I see it: an old Chevy, its paint oxidised to powder, and a hubcap missing.

I glance up and down the street. There's no movement, no dog walkers, and no sign of anyone hanging about. My pulse thrums as I walk towards it. All doors are locked, including the boot, and that's when I realise the rear passenger window is open about an inch. My throat tightens as I lean in for a closer look.

Inside, there's the scent of old vinyl and stale smoke. Fast-food wrappers are crumpled on the passenger seat, and there's a mug in the console. All of which tells me someone has used the car recently. If the window won't roll up or down, there's a chance the mechanism is broken. I try inserting my fingers and pushing down on the glass. But after a few tries, I give up. There's no way I'm taking this car tonight.

The sound of a roaring engine causes me to duck behind the Chevy. A white truck races into the short drive, its headlights glaring and driver's window open. There's a woman inside. What registers louder than the truck itself are the Ontario license plates *and* the conversation she's having on the phone.

'I've got Mia, and that's all that counts. Yeah, I got full custody.' She smiles and shakes her head from side to side. 'I'm just getting the rest of my things and then we'll be home. No, it's fine, Dad, I promise. The courts have ordered him to give me my stuff.'

Those words send ripples of potential through my mind. If I could crawl underneath the tarp, if I could just…

```
                HOLLOWAY
               (laughing)

    Is this a joke? You're going
    to hide in the back of that
    truck all the way to Toronto.
    Give me a break!
```

While I'm taking a moment to decide what to do, the lights go on outside the house, and a man comes out with a baseball bat, his voice low and threatening. The woman powers up her window and shakes her head. She looks over her shoulder at something in the passenger seat and then looks back at the man. I can see she's afraid.

This is my chance. My only chance to right so many wrongs and to do the chivalrous thing. I run towards him; my hands braced into two fists. He turns without warning, and with an expression of utter horror, raises his bat at me. Suddenly I'm on him, pounding, kicking, and snatching at that bat. I grip it with both hands and take a whack at him from all sides.

He's crouched on the ground, his hands over his head, as if shrinking into the concrete. I feel hands pulling me back and a voice yelling, 'Stop it! You'll kill him.'

While I'm thinking *that's the general idea,* the woman pulls me by the staps of my backpack and slaps a hand against my cheek, jerking my head around.

'What are you doing?' she screams.

'He... He was...'

I can't finish the sentence because she's staring at the man on the ground who hasn't moved. I'm staring at him too. There's no large puddle of blood, no crashed-in skull and no brain matter on the drive. His fingers twitch and then his eyes blink open. Somewhere within those precious few seconds, while the truck is idling, exhaust drifting in the cool air, I push her towards the cab and yell at her to get inside.

I hear the slam of a door as I run around the back of the truck, gravel spitting under my boots. Instead of launching myself under the tarp and over the tailgate, I knock on the passenger side window.

She pauses, looks over her shoulder and then stares at me. I freeze, my breath locked, my face begging. Then she leans across the seat and unlocks the door. I'm inside before she can change her mind.

There's a squeak of leather, the jangle of keys and the engine roars. The truck lurches backwards as we reverse with a squeal of tyres. My pulse pounds so hard I'm sure it's rattling my ribs.

I don't relax. Not for a second. Because every turn, every gas station, and every new town we pass through, I expect her to pull over and tell me to get out.

But she doesn't.

# 39

# ZANE

I keep my head low in the passenger seat, watching the dark ribbon of road stretch out in front of us. The young woman, who says her name is Sophie, has one hand on the wheel, the other tapping out a route on her navigation system.

That's when I realise there's a toddler in the back, soft snores muffled by a blanket. I should feel noble after what happened back there, but I feel my stomach twist like it's full of knives.

I can still hear her ex-boyfriend's teeth cracking when my fist connected. The way he dropped to the ground, choking on his own rage.

'You all right?' Sophie glances at me, her lips quirking into the kind of smile that would cut right through a man's guard. 'I'm sorry he did that to you.'

I realise she thinks the bruising on my swollen face was her ex's fault, and I don't correct her.

'I'm fine,' I lie. My knuckles throb where I hit him.

She doesn't know who I am. She doesn't know what I've done, or what they say I've done. To her, I'm just a stranger who saved her from her ex. But he won't lick his wounds quietly. He'll be calling someone. Friends, cops, anyone who'll listen.

The road hums beneath the tyres, headlights carving a path through the dark. Sophie keeps glancing at me, like she's still trying to figure out who I am.

'Back there,' she whispers, so she won't wake her daughter, 'If you hadn't stepped in… he would've smashed the window.'

I shift, the seatbelt cutting into my shoulder. 'I did what anyone else would have done.'

'No,' she says firmly, shooting me a sideways look. 'Most people would've turned away. Pretended they didn't hear, didn't see. But you—' She shakes her head, almost smiling. 'You didn't hesitate.'

I stare out at the road, black trees rushing past. If only she knew what hesitation had cost me before.

'I didn't think,' I admit. 'Just reacted.'

Her daughter stirs in the car seat, a soft sigh, then settles again. Sophie lowers her voice even more. 'It means everything.'

I nod, though inside my thoughts are running wild. If the cops come, they'll call it something else entirely. Assault. Battery. Fleeing the scene. She doesn't know it, but I'm no hero. Hell, I'm a fugitive, even if the charges haven't caught up with me yet.

The cab fills with silence, broken only by the hum of tyres on asphalt. Gratitude hangs between us, warm and undeserved. And beneath it, the cold certainty that the man I left bleeding in the driveway is dialling a number, giving a description, putting the law on my heels. I grip one side of the seat desperately, and for a moment I think I might faint. I've brought danger into her truck.

'He's not going to stop,' Sophie says after a beat, her tone darker now. 'Men like him never do. You give them a chance to make things better, but it only makes it worse.'

'I'm sorry.'

She glances down at my backpack in the footwell. 'I'm heading east if that's any good to you?'

'Actually, yes. I'm going to Toronto.'

'Do you have family there?' she asks.

'Yeah,' I say, without elaborating.

'We're going to stay with my dad for a while until we get settled. I can take you as far as Stratford. It's about an hour and a half from Toronto.'

'Thanks. I appreciate it.'

The gentle swaying of the truck and the warmth of the heater make my eyes heavy. I must have crashed out for a few hours because the clock on the dash says 3.26 am. I'm woken by a hand on my arm. It takes me a second to remember where I am.

'Thought you could use some coffee.' Sophie unbuckles her seatbelt.

I realise we've pulled into a highway diner, and my nerves, which so far have taken a rest, are now ramping up for another wild ride.

What if there are TVs inside, each blaring national news?

```
                HOLLOWAY

        A cop car in the parking lot,
        two trucks and a Nissan. Let's
        see how this plays out.


                  ZANE

        There aren't any cops. Stop
        jerking me around.


                HOLLOWAY

        Oh, come now. I'm only having
        a little fun.


                  ZANE

        This isn't the time or the
        place.
```

Inside the diner, the lights paint everything a sickly orange. Sophie juggles her daughter as we step inside, her arms wrapped around the small bundle of blanket and limbs. She glances toward the counter, scanning for a child seat.

'I'll get one,' I say.

The wooden frame is stacked with the others near the door.

That's when I see dried blood on my hands, and I pull my sleeve down. I feel the need to duck into the shadows, to get into a booth at the back of the diner. The need is so strong; I march to the farthest corner and set the seat down carefully. Sophie lowers her daughter into it, the child's head lolling, thumb still pressed to her mouth.

Something cracks open inside me. For a moment, I'm not in this diner. I'm years back, carrying a chair just like this for Bizzy. I can still smell her hair, sweet with baby shampoo, and I can still hear her giggle as she kicked her heels against the seat, impatient for pancakes. The memory burns sharp as a knife. I grip the edge of the table to steady myself.

The child seat shouldn't matter. It's just wood and straps. But it does. It means something I can't explain – something I've lost and will never get back. And the weight of it presses down harder than the fear of the cops, harder than the lies, and harder than the desperation I feel now.

'Thanks,' Sophie whispers. She looks curious, concerned, maybe. 'I'll just wash my hands.'

I push through the swinging door into the narrow corridor and the smell of disinfectant hits me like a wall. The bathroom is bright with fluorescent light. I grip the sink and stare at my hands. The blood's dried into the cracks of my skin, dark beneath the nails, a map of violence I can't scrub away. My reflection looks back at me, gaunt and hunted, like a stranger.


                        HOLLOWAY

        Something tells me you're
        going to back out of our deal.


                        ZANE

        What deal?

                    HOLLOWAY

          Isn't it rather obvious? You
          ditch Mummy and Kiddy here and
          take the truck.


                      ZANE

          There was no deal. I'm not
          leaving a young woman and a
          child stranded out here. I
          have a heart; you know.


                    HOLLOWAY

          Really. We both know you're
          hiding something big. She just
          doesn't know how big.

I twist the tap, and water gushes out, stinging as it hits the raw
scrapes on my knuckles. I scrub hard until the skin reddens and
burns, and rust-coloured rivulets snake down the porcelain.

Images flash behind my eyes – his teeth breaking under my fist,
the crunching of cartilage, and spit and blood spraying the gravel.
I press my palms flat against the basin, breathing hard. There's no
way he had time to see my face or what I was wearing.

A stall door creaks behind me. My head jerks up, and my stomach convulses with the sensation of seasickness. For a second, I'm
sure it's him, the ex, staggering in, ready for revenge. Or worse, a
cop, here to question me. But it's just a kid, twelve maybe, heading
for the urinal. He doesn't look at me, nor does he see the blood
circling the drain.

I leave the bathroom with my skin burning and the paper towel
shredded in my fists. Just down the corridor, tucked against the
wall, is a payphone.

I shouldn't call. Every instinct screams it. I should walk past,
go back to the booth, sit across from Sophie and her little girl and

forget all about it. But it's because of Sophie and her little girl that my hand hovers over the receiver.

One last call. One last chance to put words into Lilja's ear before the walls close in.

I take the phone card from my wallet. The dial tone hums and I punch in the long string of numbers, my hands trembling so badly I have to start over again. The robotic voice tells me to enter the PIN. My chest feels tight, like someone's pulling a wire around my ribs. Then the international ringing tone drones in my ear. Each pulse feels like a hammer blow. Any second, someone could push through the door and see me here, tethered to this phone.

When Lilja's voice cuts in, sharp and frantic, I close my eyes, and the ridges of the phone bite into my palm. I press on; the words tumbling out of my mouth, begging her to listen. Even though her angry words press in on me, I don't give up. I have no wish to blame her, but I feel I should.

She wants me to give myself up. But going to prison for the one person I didn't kill seems so unfair. Though, time should rightfully be served for the ones I did kill. I choke it all down because some truths will only make the goodbye harder.

There are so many things I want to tell her, so many questions I want to ask. The most important thing to say is how much I loved her. With so little time, the conversation is barely a summary of the one I'd rehearsed in my head. It seems like less than a minute before I hang up.

Squaring my shoulders, I force a smile as I go back into the restaurant. Sophie looks up, her daughter fully awake, and scribbling on a mat with a yellow crayon. For one dizzy second, I almost believe I could be part of something ordinary again. Then I catch the two men at the far table. One of them glances over and scowls, and the illusion shatters.

The server comes over with menus, pad poised. 'Coffee?'

I nod, though my stomach's a tight knot of dread. Sophie orders pancakes for her daughter, and two full breakfasts for us.

'I'll get this,' I say to Sophie. 'It's the least I can do.'

For a moment, the fear drains away. All I see is her. The soft glow of the fluorescent light brushes her skin and a strand of hair slips down her cheek until she tucks it behind one ear. She looks younger like this; her face open, almost luminous. I shouldn't be staring, but I can't help it.

When the coffee arrives, I wrap my hands around the mug and try to steady myself. But I can't swallow past the lump in my throat.

'Better?' Sophie asks.

'Much better,' I say, taking a long sip.

She feels guilty for what her ex did to me, or what she thinks he did, and that's why she's helping me. I'm grateful for all the kindness she's given me.

I meet her eyes. They're warmer than I deserve, holding me in a way that makes the room blur for a moment. I want to tell her the truth, that I'm not a man worth trusting, and that the past is closing in fast.

'This is Mia,' she says, looking proudly down at her daughter.

'Hello, Mia,' I say.

The child looks up for a moment, cornflower blue eyes assessing me for a second before resuming her drawing. I'm relieved she doesn't see the wolf behind my smile. I dig into my meal and ask Sophie if she's enjoying hers. She smiles between bites and nods.

The door to the restaurant opens, and my pulse slams as two men walk in, baseball caps low, jackets zipped. They don't look at me, but I feel their presence like a gun pressed to the back of my neck. One of them has the build of a cop. He has broad shoulders and a square jaw, the kind of man who's used to carrying authority. I imagine myself running for the back door, slipping and sliding over spilt sauce in the kitchen in my hurry to get away.

Sophie is radiant in the way people are when they've finally stood up to something ugly. She tells me that everything is going to be okay. I wish I could borrow her certainty. She studies me for a moment, her eyes narrowing, and I know she can sense it, that I'm not just some good Samaritan who showed up at the right time. I'm the man in the news.

I look out of the window and study the parking lot. A cruiser could roll in at any second, its blue and red lights spilling across the asphalt, officers running towards me with their hands resting on their holsters.

The door opens again, but this time it's a couple, shuffling in with linked hands. Relief floods me so hard it's almost painful. I take a gulp of coffee, scalding my tongue, forcing myself to look calm.

I'm not calm. I'm cornered. Every sound of cutlery scraping, a baby wailing, and a woman's shrill laugh, feels magnified.

I wish we were sitting in the darkness of Sophie's living room, watching movies on the comfort of a sagging sofa, without my forged identify rearing its ugly head and reminding me I'm out of time.

# 40

# LILJA

I look around at the stands. Everyone's gaze seems to be on the players, except a blonde woman in a crimson puffa jacket on the opposite side of the field, her phone lifted in her hand. I wonder if she's videoing her daughter or mine.

We're leading 1-0 against a neighbouring school and approaching the last sixty seconds of the game. Bizzy, dressed in navy cycling shorts underneath white football shorts, stands at the halfway line, her focus trained on the ball.

Ryan sits beside me and focuses on the goal, no doubt calculating how far it is. A tiny gust of wind whispers, *It's too far. She'll never make it.*

Then it happens. Everything goes still, and I can't breathe as the ball hangs in the air – one second, two seconds, three… and it drops inches under the bar and into the back of the net.

I'm on my feet, screaming and yelling as if I'm going to burst out of my skin. Ecstatic parents, whose girls are all on the same team, pat my back as voices cheer and shout. It's the third win of the season. I'm so proud of my Bizzy.

Ryan anchors me with an arm around my waist to stop me from falling, then steps away from me. I follow the direction of his eyes and see the woman in the crimson jacket, her phone scanning my row intentionally. Her phone stops at Ryan, fingers pinching the screen as if to magnify his image. He ducks into his seat behind the standing row in front of us and pulls me down with him.

'Press,' he warns.

'They don't allow the press in here.'

'She's press.' He grits his teeth and lets out a frustrated sigh.

The man in front turns and looks down at us briefly before facing forward again. Crimson Jacket is walking through the spectators towards the car park, her job done, her day over. Whoever she is, she's rattled Ryan.

'What's the worst that can happen?' I ask, as the teams congratulate each other.

He looks down at me, his eyes sparkling at full beam. 'Tomorrow's headlines will read: *Lilja Osborne's bodyguard? Or new squeeze?*'

I try to speak, but my throat is too dry to make any sounds. So, I roll my eyes, as if it couldn't be further from the truth.

Except that I thought about him last night. Dreamed about him. The hellish little voice in my head won't let go. I don't want to think about it. I *won't* think about it. Ryan is here to look after us.

My phone rings, bringing me back for a moment. I check the screen to see an international caller.

'Don't hang up.' Zane's voice comes out in a sad, strained whisper, as if he's scared someone close to him might hear. 'Just listen, okay? *Please* listen.'

I feel tiny goosebumps rise on my skin, and my gaze bounces from the field to the parents in my peripheral view. Ryan urges me out of the stands, and we find a quiet spot behind the playing field.

Zane tells me how Nic tormented him, how turning up at his party convinced him she was going to ruin us. The word *us* infuriates me. It was never about us.

My disgust over what he'd done to Nic and how he tried to cover it all up consumes me, a pin-sharp pain that will ambush me for years to come. Added to this, a dull ache in the back of my throat that he'd done something so despicable in my house. Doesn't he care that calling me has opened an invisible line for the police to trace?

'Just tell me you didn't hit her.' I hear the anguish in my voice, but I need to know.

'I pushed her. I didn't hit her.'

'I worry you did because you were angry and because you wanted it to stop and she didn't. Maybe she made you mad. Maybe you didn't mean to lash out. Maybe you thought the only way to stop her talking was to shut her up for good.'

'You know me better than that.'

'How was it, then?'

'She was yelling at me and punching me. She kneed me in the groin.'

'She was terrified, Zane. It was her against you. What did you expect? Had you paid enough attention – had you stopped to think about what you'd done to her? She was barely out of school.'

'She was twenty and an adult. She knew exactly what she was doing.'

'No. She didn't. There's a difference between you swearing undying love to her to develop your character and then dumping her.'

'I didn't love her, Lily.'

Hell, I was the one who loved Zane. Now I'm feeling sorry for Nic, the poison that still runs through us.

'I wonder if I did the right thing,' I say. 'Letting you believe Holloway was the best role for you.'

'He was every actor's dream, the most stimulating character I'd read in years. You… you, who rejected every romantic role they offered me, insisted I play him. Except I took it too far.' When he speaks again, his voice is quieter but unmistakably bitter. '*We* took it too far.'

Holloway may have stripped all layers of human decency from Zane, but it's not as if I held a gun to his head and said, play him or die. Yet my eyes sting with self-pity.

I can't disagree with him. I had screwed up someone else's life just as much as he had screwed up mine. But if Zane hadn't been so weak, if his head hadn't been turned to every woman in sight, we wouldn't be in this situation. He still believes that his version of the truth is the only one that matters. I can taste the bitterness in my mouth.

'So, you're implying that some part of this was my fault?' I say. 'Yet you were the one who drove her body to the beach. You were the one who ran halfway around the world, drew your own blood, enough for the police to think you were dead. You, who tormented the press, your fans and your family. God knows you've tormented the Gatlins.'

'I can't believe you'd say that. After everything I've been through. After all I've done to protect the family. I'm sorry about Nic. What happened to her was tragic.'

'It was devastating. That's why you need to tell the truth, if not for her family, for ours.'

'Listen to yourself. They've got to you, haven't they? The good old Devon and Cornwall Police.'

'No, they haven't. It's common decency to own up to what you did. She's dead, and nothing's going to change that.'

Zane has always done whatever he wanted, and I've been stupid enough to go along with it instead of confronting him. What must he think of the new Lilja? The assertive ex-wife, who no longer feels sorry for him. Shame flares in a way it hadn't since last year, before Nic's death, and before I was thrown right in the middle of it.

'So, you want me to confess to something I didn't do?' he asks. 'So that people can brand me a murderer and send me to prison? Is that what you want?'

'No. I want you to turn yourself in.'

'You don't know what you're saying.'

'Enough!' I scan a stream of parents walking towards the tea tent and craning their necks to see where the sound is coming from. Panic flushes my skin, then it suddenly goes cold. I lower my voice. 'I'm sick of going round and round and getting nowhere.'

'Lily. I'm sorry for us. I'm sorry for everything.' His voice cracks on the last word. 'You will tell Bizzy I called, won't you?'

I don't want to, but I know I will. Yet my precious daughter will forever by tormented by his admission, the crucial details of what happened to Nic, the one person she absolutely adored. Most of the time she carries this memory quietly, stoically, and with resignation. But I know her heart is aching.

'Yes, I'll tell her.'

'We… We loved each other, didn't we?'

Despite everything, I feel sorry. It's as if I'm standing over a grave with the headstone bearing the dates of our marriage and the words *Gone but not forgotten*. I stagger against Ryan. The rhythm of my breathing fractured with grief.

'But you left us.'

'I *had* to, don't you see?' His voice shakes as if saddened by my question.

Deep down inside, a question nudges. Why was he protecting Nic? *Protect*. The word lodges in my mind, like a tick burrowing into a vein. I wish I could wrap up my anger and box it away, but I can't manage that yet.

'You said you were protecting Nic. What did you mean?'

'No. Not Nic.' He makes a quiet, anguished sound, like someone trying to keep secrets. 'Lily, do you remember that two-mile walk we went on? The one from Lynton around the Valley of Rocks. There was a star in the sky, and we both saw it at the same time. We both said how bright and clear it was and how it seemed so out of place in the morning sky.'

'The shooting star?'

'Yes.'

'That was years ago, when I was pregnant with Bizzy.'

Something jars inside of me. For the first time since hearing his voice, I have a heavy feeling in my chest. I can hear my breathing, and it's too fast. I walk away from Ryan, my feet dragging in the grass towards an old oak tree.

'I want you to think about that,' he says. 'Someday, it will make sense.'

His voice falters, and I know there's something he's keeping from me. He knows the police are listening in, and he knows that the shooting star is significant enough to jog a memory. This time I don't ask questions. I accept his decision to keep it a mystery, unsure what it is or how it will affect me.

I pull out a tissue and mop my tears. The irony of it is I still long for the fierceness of his hugs, his warmth, and his wicked sense of humour. I can't believe I'm talking to the man who took it all away and broke me into a million pieces.

'Are you okay?' His question is soft.

'No, I'm not.' The words spill out in tight, sharp sobs.

'You will be. You and Bizzy will be okay.'

I hear the finality in his voice, the urging for me to say goodbye. I know if I don't say it now, the chance will be gone.

'And, yes, we loved each other,' I say. 'We did. So very much.'

'Yes. We did.'

Then his voice is snatched away by silence.

I know he would have extended his love to Bizzy, and he would have asked for her forgiveness, too. Now we must build our lives away from Zane's shadow. We must brave the outside world, the whispers and the faux smiles. The world knows he has cheated and lied and killed, and now we're tainted with the shame.

Ugly sobs blotch my face, and I clutch a sodden tissue. I look back at where Ryan is standing, hands in pockets, his back to me. I watch parents strolling across the lawn towards the marquee for tea and sandwiches. Most are successful bankers, estate agents and doctors, and a whole list of other brilliant careers. Some are entrepreneurs, like me. But do they have any big secrets? I doubt they've had more than a few parking fines. At the very most, a little white-collar fraud.

But have any of them been charged with murder?

What was I thinking coming here? Exposing myself to questions, judgement and ridicule. Will they ask, 'Did you believe he was innocent? Or was there ever any doubt in your mind?'

I will play the devastated, loyal wife, as I will need to do for his fans and the press. I will do it for Bizzy.

'Muuuuuumz!

The sound of her yelling makes me shrug the thought aside. My gaze snags on my daughter's infectious smile, her brilliant goal and the effusive praise that bubbles from my mouth.

Ryan claps and whoops and gives her a side hug. But it's me she runs to; me she envelops in two sweaty arms; and me who tells her she is the brightest star in my universe.

**BarbedWire: Trending #InZane**

@Titmouse: The way Ozzie's been depicted in the news #ConArtist #UnDead is killing me. I'll never forgive him for doing that to us.

@MiloMorales: I think you all need a lesson in Grudge Management.

@Titmouse: It's all about examining Holloway's effect on Zane through a surrealistic lens. #TakeOverBid. Serious chemistry and so convincing.

@BantaBadger: What's @Titmouse wittering on about?

@HeyWhatsUP: You're telling me Zane Osborne transformed into an entirely different human being and is therefore not accountable for his actions? Utter bollocks!

# 41

# ZANE

All the way to Stratford, I'm left wondering why Sophie trusts me. We stop at a park, and she lets me play with Mia. When we find a restaurant, she asks me to look after her handbag while she takes Mia to the bathroom.

How disjointed life is. It tears holes in friendships, splits open marriages and wrecks careers – an endless cycle of disappointments that never, never ends. Here I am, dragging my baggage around as if shedding it would destroy my identity. When in fact, it would give me freedom, a fresh start. A new life.

I gaze out of the truck window as we pull out again, watching the sun, hazy in the winter sky. Clearly, my life isn't over yet. I'm still here, maybe not completely me, but I will be.

On the way, Sophie can't stop talking about Stratford. Everything is Shakespeare, from the theatre to the gardens, and I should take in a play while I'm there. I must try the pizzas at Jobsite Brewing and, of course, the beer. She insists I stay with her and her dad for one night to get my bearings. I want to tell her I won't be staying, but refusing clean clothes and a shower seems so ungrateful, and I tell her I'll think about it.

But in all our conversations, she never once asks me where I'm from. What type of accent I have and why I look grubby like Tom Hanks in *Castaway*. Well, maybe not quite as dishevelled. I have washed my face.

The streets of Stratford are quiet, a small town that feels

crime-free. Sophie pulls into a driveway, and Mia snuffles softly in the back seat. Her father's house is a cream brick building with a two-car garage. There's a lawn in the front with a mulberry tree, and rows of freshly trimmed box hedges along the drive.

I get a sense that her father is detail-oriented and takes pride in his surroundings. He's probably a jolly, rotund, TV binge-watcher, and I'm feeling more at home than I have in months.


HOLLOWAY

```
Bet he's got one of those black
leather  recliners.  The  type
with  cup  holders  and  a  tray
for your popcorn.
```


'You'll stay,' she says, more a command than a question. 'It's late, and you look done in.'

I should refuse. I should already be halfway down the highway, a nameless, faceless fugitive. But my body aches from the fight, and my nerves are shredded. The idea of four walls and a bed – even a couch – sinks its hooks into me.

'If you're sure it's okay,' I hear myself say.

The house is warm, with lights glowing from every room, and the smell of cheese and beef clinging to the air. Sophie carries her daughter upstairs, leaving me in the living room.

I leave my backpack against the couch and drift toward the mantelpiece, where framed photographs line the shelf, catching the glow of the lamp. Sophie at sixteen, braces flashing in a crooked grin. Her mother in a garden, hands buried in soil.

My eyes slide over them without sticking. Just family snapshots, lives I don't belong to.

Then I see it. A photograph, larger than the rest, in a polished silver frame. A man in a suit, shaking hands with someone at a podium. His smile is tight and professional, and there's a banner behind him with the crest of the Department of Justice.

The name hits me a second later, the caption from some news article floating up from memory.

David Steele.

My throat closes and my pulse kicks against my ribs. I've seen his face before on courthouse steps, in headlines about corruption trials and convictions. Assistant District Attorney David Steele. A man who built his reputation on hunting people down like me.

And now, he's Sophie's father.

The room tilts. The air is too hot and too heavy. I step back from the mantelpiece, bumping into the arm of the couch. Upstairs, a floorboard creaks. Sophie is moving around and humming softly to her daughter.

If Steele walks through that door and sees me – if he recognises me – the game's over.

As if conjured by the thought, headlights sweep the room, and the sound of a car pulling into the driveway jolts me. I peer through the blinds at a black SUV with dark tinted windows and government plates. I freeze.

A door slams and keys rattle at the lock.

'Dad?' Sophie calls from the stairs, cheerful, oblivious.

And then he's there, stepping into the living room. Still in his suit, tie loosened, briefcase in hand. He looks tired, but his eyes sharpen the instant they land on me.

Recognition hits like a gunshot. His expression changes in a heartbeat from polite host to predator who's just spotted prey. My blood turns to ice. Sophie's kindness has become a trap without her even knowing it, and now her father is fastening the net with a terrifying snap.

Sophie frowns, glancing between us. 'Dad, this is—'

'Get upstairs,' Steele snaps. He drops the briefcase, his hand already going for his phone. 'Now, Sophie.'

'Dad, what—'

'Do it!'

Instinct takes over. I bolt for the back door, crashing through the screen, and my boots hit the patio. Behind me, Sophie shouts my name, while her father barks orders into his phone.

The night air slaps me in the face as I sprint across the lawn. Behind me, Steele's voice roars, words I can't make out. Roses tear at my clothes as I crash through them, and then I see a fence. Five feet at most and easy to vault over. My lungs are already on fire as I cut across a playing field, barking dogs exploding into the night.

I hear sirens – two, maybe three – coming fast from different directions. I duck into an alley, and the stink of damp brick and garbage closes around me. My shoulder smacks into a wall, and pain blooms, but I keep running. My chest heaves, and every inhale cuts deep.

Blue light floods the street ahead. A cruiser screeches around the corner, tires shrieking, spotlight swinging. I dive into the shadows and press myself flat against a fence, heart hammering so loud I'm sure they can hear it. The cop car rolls past, the beam missing me by inches. I can't stay here because they'll box me in, and then it's all over.

I cut down another alley, jumping a chain-link fence that rattles under me. My hands slip, still raw from scrubbing blood off them at the diner, and I drag myself over and drop hard on the other side. My ankle jolts, and there's a hot flash of pain. I stagger into a vegetable garden and take a rest.

Sirens blare too close, lights strobing against houses, chasing my shadow across brick and asphalt. I walk faster now; my vision tunnelling and every sound is amplified. The crunch of gravel, the metallic slam of a car door, and voices shouting.

I burst onto a street lined with shops, their windows dark and a Starbucks sign flickering at the far end. I skid around a corner, nearly losing my footing. Headlights flare. Another cruiser is blocking the road.

I veer left and spot a narrow gap between two buildings. Barely wide enough for me to squeeze through. I shove myself into the space, brick scraping my arms, and the walls pressing close. I fight my way to the other side and stumble out into an open lot.

For a moment, there's silence, just the pound of my pulse. Then the distant crackle of a radio as I sprint across the asphalt, my boots slapping the surface and echoing off the walls.

A spotlight sweeps the darkness and pins me for a beat.

'Stop right there!' a voice booms.

I dive for the shadows of a loading dock, my lungs burning and my muscles screaming. The cruiser skids to a halt behind me. Doors slam and heavy boots thunder after me.

I scramble up the metal steps and hurl myself at the dock door. It's locked.

A shout splits the air. 'Hands where we can see them!'

I turn, chest heaving. One uniform, his gun drawn and his face pale in the pulsing red-blue light.

Panic takes over. I hurl myself sideways, down the steps, into the gap between a pile of pallets. He lunges towards me and grabs my arm.

I twist and drive my elbow into his face. Bone crunches, and his shout is muffled by blood. He falls on his side, clutching at his face, as I rip free. I can hear him howling like a dog at the moon as he rolls to his feet.

He's after me, flailing at my back, his fingers skidding down the nape of my neck as he tries to grab my collar. For a brief second, he catches it, and I twist wildly to one side, yanking myself free.

I tear towards a gate and vault over before he can line up a shot. The crack of a pistol splits the night, and concrete chips spray near my feet. I look over my shoulder through a tangle of hair and see he's coming after me.

Sirens converge, echoing off the brick walls like a pack of hunting dogs closing in.

I don't think. I just run.

The dark yawns open onto a car rental lot, lines of SUVs looming like silent giants. I throw myself into the shadows, ducking low, sliding under one car. My chest heaves, and gravel bites into my palms.

Boots pound past, and a spotlight sweeps across the parking lot. I flatten myself to the ground, every muscle screaming, until the sirens fade and voices scatter in frustration.

Only then do I dare breathe.

I've bought myself a little time. That's all. But Stratford knows my face now.

I crawl out from beneath the car, gravel sticking to my skin, and blood streaking my arms. If they had dogs, I'd be toast.

I slip into the back streets, hugging the shadows. My legs feel hollow and ready to give out, and I remember my backpack and my ID, everything left behind. At this moment, I know I'm beaten.

That's when I see it. A steeple rises over the rooftops, its bell tower black against the night sky. At the end of a cobbled street, a small floodlit church emerges, surrounded by a wall and a well-kept graveyard. It reminds me of the church near Barton Manor. The spire, the bell tower and the great oak door. In the summer, I'd light a cigarette and go for an evening stroll down the lane and listen to the choristers practicing. Sometimes I'd meet Nic on the corner in my car, out of range of our security cameras.

I can still see her tiny figure in the camelhair coat, hands in pockets and a wide grin. She'd launch herself into the passenger seat, her lips puckered for a kiss. There would be times when she'd coil her arms around my neck and say, 'I absolutely adore you.'

I shouldn't have let it continue. It wasn't fair to her.

My mother always said churches are where you find clarity and healing. Perhaps after everything, that's what I need right now. Over the lynch gate are decorative carvings and the words:

> *Come to me, all you who are weary and burdened, and I will give you rest.*

A sharp gust of wind carries the scent of damp fur, something decaying. If only Holloway would stop darting around like a trapped animal who would rather chew off his own foot than follow me inside.

Then he shoots me a look with his dark eyes and scowling brows, one that would cause a gargoyle to crumble.

HOLLOWAY

We can't go in there.

                    ZANE

     Why?


                  HOLLOWAY

     Because of what we've done.
     Because of what we are.


There's something in his expression – a secrecy, a smugness – that reveals a far darker and more complex side to Holloway. He belittles me when I refuse to do what he asks, and he takes pleasure in undermining me. Despite my reluctance to kill, he has persuaded me that every threat must be eliminated, or I risk capture. He's always been such a trooper.

Now, he's afraid of a church.

His heels tap against the pavement behind me in rapid staccato, as if his mood is about to bloom into a rage.


                  HOLLOWAY

     You're not guilty. None of
     the deaths were premeditat-
     ed. By all accounts, it's a
     lesser charge than homicide,
     if you can prove it. It's your
     decision.

                    ZANE

     I'd like to turn myself in.


Holloway's response to my internal statement is an exasperated exhale. That he isn't coming up with a sarcastic quip bothers me. Shouldn't he be advising me? Shouldn't he be telling me to run from the police?

I'm scared and lonely, and he's not talking to me at all.

Over the past two years, I've valued his unique friendship, his willingness to be frank with me, even when our thoughts were not aligned. Knowing him made my world less lonely. I feel cautious in telling him this. He might judge me and tell me I'm chickenshit for depending on him. He might say, as my father once did, "Get a life!" I've rarely encountered moments of indecision. Yet it's he who has led me down this dark labyrinth. Now it's my turn to find my way out.

A disturbing thought strikes me. I was not only listening to everything Holloway said and doing everything he instructed of me; I had offered it as an excuse for my behaviour, even in private with my therapist. No credible judge would believe in a figment of my imagination.

Despite everything, I should have resisted him. If I hadn't played his character, he would never have played me.

HOLLOWAY

```
Well, my friend, if you're
giving yourself in, here's
where I make a detour. Remem-
ber, without my expertise, the
next victim could be you.
```

I hear a distant rustle, like the beating of wings. I look up at the church roof and expect to see a bird launching from a gutter. But there, rattling down the cobbled street, is Holloway, shoulders hunched, arms clasped behind his back.

Then he turns and looks at me for a few seconds and brings two fingers to his lips to blow me a kiss. At first, I think I'm imagining it. When he smiles and turns away, I sense the air thinning as he fades into the gloaming.

I could have sworn his arms became long, articulated bones, each veined with a layer of feathers. But I know I'm seeing things that aren't there. The street is empty, and for a moment it feels as if the dark paternal hand that once clasped mine has abruptly let go.

My eyes fill with angry tears. Doesn't he realise how broken I am, an innocent victim deceived and betrayed? Or was that the whole idea?

Something in me takes over, some kind of animal determination. I walk through a cluster of headstones towards the church door. In the vestibule are candles flickering on the votive stand. I stumble down the aisle and find a pew near the font.

My heart roars in my ears as if I've just run a marathon. It's a nervous wait. Just when I was thinking I was alone, a man steps forward from the shadows of a side aisle. A tall man with a head of grey hair and the air of a job to do. He introduces himself as Father Francois and talks to me about the sacrament of reconciliation.

'I'm not here to make a confession, Father.' I look around as if it's the first time I've ever seen the inside of a church. 'I didn't plan on ending up here. I just kept walking. I didn't even know where I was going.'

'Sometimes our feet know what our minds won't admit.'

I try to smile, but I'm spiralling mentally, barely holding it together. 'I've done something terrible.'

'Haven't we all,' he says, spreading his hands. 'May I?'

I nod, and he sits beside me.

'If it helps,' he says. 'I volunteer in prisons. There's nothing I haven't seen.'

There's something about him that makes me want to talk; at the same time, holding on to a sliver of hope that he won't hate me for it. It suddenly occurs to me he's speaking English rather than French. Perhaps he already knows what I've done.

'Are you going to call the police?' I ask.

'Do you want me to?'

'I don't know.'

'That's usually the first honest thing a man says after he's done something terrible.'

I look down at my hands, the instruments of so much cruelty. 'I suppose you're going to tell me that God still loves me.'

'God's love isn't a shield from consequences, but a path through them.'

The candles and the arches fade into my periphery, and I feel as if I'm about to black out. Except my vision doesn't narrow to a pinhead; it expands, the curtains of my life sliding wide open. It all comes gushing out, every sordid little morsel. Afterwards, I have a giddy sense of elation, like I'd unblocked an artery and the blood is flowing again.

I want to tell him that even though every bit of running I've done signifies guilt, it also signifies someone without a choice.

I close my eyes. Maybe because it's the last place left and because I wanted walls around me for comfort. Maybe some part of me is stupid enough to believe there's a way out. I let myself sag against the pew. The candles blur, and my heartbeat slows.

Outside, faint at first, then rising, I hear the distant wail of sirens. And I know there's no way out at all.

# 42

# LILJA

I dress in a cable-knit sweater and jeans and run downstairs.

The kitchen is softly lit with a night light as coffee gurgles on the counter. I pour myself a cup of espresso. Anything to distract me. Once I'm on my second, I feel awake and ready to face the day.

The newspapers are obsessed with Zane's arrest. There's a photo of him outside a church, head down and hands cuffed behind his back. His hair is long, and his beard is uncombed, contradicting the indelible image of him preening on the front cover of *PEOPLE Magazine*.

Heat creeps up my neck when I think of the terrible events leading up to his capture. The words swarm around my head like echoing shots from a gun. Had Zane fallen into a life of crime? Had he killed someone else? If so, what will I tell Bizzy?

The press will sniff for dirt outside the house today, and his fans will want to hear from their beloved celebrity in his usual blasé tone. They'll overlook the way he plays with words through omissions and half-truths.

The impending court case might affect my business, although I'm not legally responsible for Zane's wrongdoings. Perhaps it would be beneficial to stay out of sight until the whole thing blows over.

I catch movement outside. Ryan is standing on the patio; his phone pressed to his ear. His shoulders stiffen while he attends to whoever is on the line, and the pitch of his voice drops to a snarl.

This is a side of him I've not seen before, and now I want to know who he's talking to.

I pull on a coat, grab two mugs of coffee and go outside to join him. 'Everything okay?'

He tenses but manages a dimpled smile. 'There are a couple of developments I wanted to talk to you about. Is now a good time?'

'To be honest, I was just coming out to—'

'It won't take long.'

He places a hand below my elbow and steers me to a patio chair. I catch the flick of his eyes, a quick sideways sweep. I wonder what he wants to tell me, and whether I should feel nervous.

'It's about Zane, obviously,' he says, sitting beside me. 'They were hoping to extradite him back here for Nicola Gatlin's murder. But…'

'But what?'

'They think he might be responsible for another murder.'

I'd just taken a sip of coffee and had to slap my hand over my mouth to stop myself from spraying it on the table. 'What?'

'It gets weirder. A lieutenant out there interviewed a hunter in a coffee shop about another case. During the conversation, this hunter mentioned he was travelling to Montague, Prince Edward Island, to stay with a friend.'

'And?'

'Something didn't sit right with the lieutenant. So, after dropping off the guy at a hotel, he called the police department in Montague. It took a few hours to get a call back from a sergeant, who confirmed the hunter's story was false. There were other things that bothered him, such as paying a helicopter pilot in cash and using what he later found out was a fake ID. So, he searched through a list of national and international fugitives, and he was certain the man he'd had coffee with was Zane.'

I gasp and shake my head. 'Shit. Just when you think you're having a rough day.'

'We all have those.' Ryan shuffles about in his seat. 'The difference is yours is all over the tabloids.'

I pull a face. 'Wait, who do they think Zane killed?'

'Some guy down an alley, but there were no cameras or witnesses and no murder weapon. I don't have all the details yet.'

Something shifts in my stomach, and the surrounding air feels cold. I feel sorry for Bizzy, so excruciatingly sorry that I want to scream. What on earth possessed Zane to do such a terrible thing?

I'm having trouble looking at Ryan. I don't want my contempt to show. When he meets my gaze, all I see is concern, the type that causes an icy chill to course through my veins. Panic hammers at my temples, and I feel as if I'm going to be sick.

'I wanted to update you in case they keep him in Canada,' he says.

'Is that likely?'

'We don't know yet. It could be months before police gather enough evidence and build a case to present to the Crown Prosecution Service once he's been charged. The defence will need time to gather evidence against the prosecution. Before this, he'll need to attend Magistrate's Court to offer a plea.'

'What if he pleads guilty?'

'It'll result in immediate sentencing and no trial. A not-guilty plea will result in the case moving to the Crown Court, where more hearings might take place.'

I rub my temple wearily with a hand. 'How long will this take?'

'Six months. A year, maybe. It will be up to the court whether Zane is remanded in custody while awaiting trial, or if he's allowed out on bail.'

'What happens if he's remanded?'

'That time will be removed from his sentence or suspended. So, if he gets twelve years, it will be twelve less however many months served on remand. He would be expected to serve around eight years, two-thirds of the sentence per the Sentencing Council.'

We shift into silence, and I try hard to ignore the lights in the upper rooms of the house as my family stirs. Zane is on my mind all the time. Zane, the husband, the father, the actor. How he might appear in the courtroom when the time comes. I'm not sure which aspect of him I'll remember in the long run. There are ghosts of him everywhere, pushing toddler Bizzy on her swing, weeding his beloved hydrangea bed, and working a room while a gaggle of women doughnut around him.

An icy breeze plays on my face, and I promise myself that when all this is over, I will replace the old memories with new ones. While I'm inwardly mulling it over, Ryan gazes at me for a moment, long enough that I think he might see through my skin. There's something I've been wanting to ask him and now seems like a good time.

'How many times were you Zane's CPO?'

He looks down, but I catch the sudden shift in his expression. 'Off the top of my head, eleven, twelve times. Usually for two weeks at a time. But it was the best fun I'd had in years.'

I don't ask what kind of fun he's alluding to. Hopefully, it didn't entail a few drunken parties, where women curled their fingers around his arm and tugged him into a bedroom.

The kitchen window is open, and from inside comes the sound of voices mixed with laughter. Stella and Paul, I think, grabbing coffee at the start of a new day.

'You and Zane must have got to know each other pretty well,' I say.

He frowns and takes a beat, as if processing the information. 'He was good to me. Always polite, always wanting to know if I was okay.'

'Zane wasn't one for small talk, though, was he?'

He falls silent and stares at me. 'There were a few occasions he'd say some deep shit and then laugh, and I was never sure if he was serious.'

'He liked you.' I feel the rigid hang of hesitation, as if his relationship with Zane is something he'd rather not share. 'That's why he kept asking for you. He said confidentiality like yours is hard to find.'

It's a lie, but I need to draw him out. What was to stop Ryan from witnessing some of Zane's transgressions? What was to stop his being dragged down in the undertow?

'I assume you drove him up to our house in London a few times?'

Ryan clears his throat. 'A few times, yes.'

'Was he alone?'

He looks at me properly now, blue eyes alert. 'No.'

'Who was he with?'

He looks down at his coffee, fingers clasped tightly around the mug. 'Nic.'

'How did that make you feel?'

'That he was with her?' He tilts his head sympathetically. 'Like I said before. Awkward.'

'Tell me about it.'

I listen, transfixed, as he describes the lavish dinners they had, the movies they watched, and the champagne they drank. I force myself to be pleasant and amenable. Not to let him see how stiff my smile is. The garden closes in, suffocating me, and I bite my lip to stop myself from bursting into tears.

Zane invited him up to the roof of our Holland Park house to watch the stars, their bare feet resting against the lead flashings, their backs against the slates. I can almost hear their laughter drifting across the lawn, exactly as Zane and mine had done many years before. Had Zane loved spending time with Nic as much as he had with me? Had they spent nights in our king-size bed, unable to keep their hands off each other?

Here I am thinking Ryan's obligations were confined to driving them from A to B. I'm suddenly ambushed by nausea.

His face twitches, a tiny spasm he seems to get when he's stressed. He tells me about the time when Nic was passed out on the couch and Zane was too drunk to carry her upstairs. So, Ryan, good dependable Ryan, carried her to bed.

*Our bed.*

I shudder as my thoughts seem to find their way onto darker paths. Why has Ryan convinced himself that he was being loyal to Zane, and that he was honourable in keeping his secrets?

Then I tell myself he was only doing what Zane asked him to do. What he was paid to do. I don't know why I settled on this tiniest of betrayals. It's all in the past now. Yet anxiety wells in my throat, and I try to calm myself.

'I'm sorry. I know how bad this must sound,' he says, his

expression growing more concerned. 'Is there anything you need?'

I turn my face away before he can see my eyes shimmering and mull over the question. What do I need?

I look up at grey clouds drifting past as the lump in my throat grows. I need Bizzy to enjoy the breezy comfort of life at Barton Manor, not have it crashing into the horror of her father's conviction. I need her to feel safe and loved and stable. I need job security for my staff and family. I need people to stop staring at me when I go shopping. People I know would do anything to swap places with me because they think I have everything. Millions in the bank and a business that will guarantee status. Though I'm clearer-sighted about Zane's court case, navigating the future fills me with dread.

Then, the image of Zane carrying Bizzy over a rock pool at the beach, frightened of a tiny crab, crosses my mind. One of me hugging him so tightly before a trip, trying to keep hold of him as if I'd never let go. I can almost feel his cheek against mine, the ghostlike whisper of his voice telling me how much he loved me. These are the flashbacks that spool through my mind at night, yet I don't want to be reminded of them.

Will the court question my motives? The classic woman scorned.

What are my next steps?

It's time to make a choice for both me and Bizzy, a decision that makes sense considering what Zane has done.

'I'll tell you what I need,' I say, taking a sip of coffee. 'A good divorce lawyer and a very long holiday.'

**BarbedWire - Trending #InZane**

@CirceAtNight: So... ZaneO has finally been captured. That's one hot inmate.

@BantaBadger: Stupid bastard deserved everything he got. #Twat

@HackedOff: What do you think, Zane? Got any computer privileges yet? Come and join the chat.

@HeyWhatsUP: Rumour has it, he'll be out in ten years.

@CirceAtNight: Six, if he plays his cards right.

# 43

# ZANE

**Three months later.**

Being in the remand centre is a bit like being at boarding school. No space, no privacy, and no choice, although I am familiar with the structure and the lousy food. The guards call me by number, not by name, as if I've already been erased.

As I lie on a sagging mattress, which groans whenever I change position, thoughts of escape bounce around in my head, and I plan a mental assortment of what-ifs. There's nothing else to do.

When they arrested me, the cold snap of handcuffs was terrifying. So were the frisk and pat-downs. But not half as intrusive as the strip search I endured during the intake process, guards ordering me to squat and cough, while my skin crawled under their stares. Afterwards, they cut my hair and told me to shave. It was a shock seeing my sharp-jawed face for the first time.

That morning, I had an odd sensation in front of the mirror. I thought I saw Holloway perched on the bunk behind me, only he deteriorated into a waft of dust motes and could barely hold a shape.

I realise the recklessness of our choices and understand that we would never survive if the unvarnished truth of all those hidden bodies ever comes to light. My future would be in jeopardy. More importantly, my wife's career would be dead in the water. The truth must never surface because Barton Manor is just as important to me as it is to her. After all, where will I go when I get out of here?

To this day, Holloway's myth continues. He is still referred to as my alter ego and likely always will be. It doesn't stop me from daydreaming about our time together and how attached I was to him. But he has deserted me now, the same as everyone else. Perhaps that's a good thing.

I'm escorted to the interview room, which is colder than my cell, with bare walls and a metal table bolted to the floor. She sits across from me, blonde and dangerously beautiful, a set of pearls shimmering against a silk shirt. She offers me a steaming cup of coffee.

'Mr Osborne,' she says, sliding a slim folder onto the table. 'I'm Carol Sanchez, retained to contest the British extradition request.'

She averts her eyes for a moment, and I realise I'm staring too intently, and she recognises the predatory nature of that stare.

She turns a few pages over in her file. 'Britain says you've more to answer for there. If you go, it won't be just prison walls you face. They'll tear through your past, through every connection you've ever had, and they'll dig until there's nothing left.'

'And you're here to stop that?' I ask.

'I'm here to offer you a choice. Fight the extradition and stay here where the system is predictable, where you still have… anonymity. Or let it go through, and risk never having a voice again.'

The silence stretches. I hold her gaze, searching, but she doesn't flinch. For a moment, I wonder if she's for me or against me. But then I think of Britain and what waits there. Angry press, a hateful wife and a daughter who would rather I was dead. I know my answer.

'Let's fight it.'

'Good.' She writes something in the folder and then snaps it shut. She leans forward and I catch her perfume, delicate and flowery. 'One more thing: in here, the walls have ears. With me, they don't. Use that wisely.'

'I'll remember that,' I say, smiling.

Her eyes, which until now have been fixed on mine, drop to the papers in front of her. She slides a newspaper across the table, and the headline glares:

## POLICE PLEAD FOR PUBLIC'S HELP IN TRACKING DOWN PERSON OF INTEREST IN LACHUTE DEATH.

A grainy closeup shows a man inside a truck, his face half-hidden under the brim of a baseball cap. It could be anyone.

'Does this ring any bells?' she asks.

'No.'

'CCTV captured the truck at a nearby intersection.'

So, the police don't have sufficient proof I was there or that I'd killed anyone. Still, I feel my throat tighten. I admire her persistence, and I'm almost convinced she's going to get the truth out of me. Maybe I should confess, spin it as self-defence, say he jumped me for my wallet.

'It's not me. That guy doesn't even look like me.'

Sanchez remains unconvinced. 'It's the same baseball hat you were wearing when they arrested you. Same logo.'

'Half the population wears hats like these.'

She sits back in her chair and crosses her arms. 'Any idea where that truck is?'

'No. Because I wasn't driving it.'

If the police find it, my fingerprints will be all over the place, in the same way as the DNA they will find on the guy in Lachute. But the truck is well-hidden in a stand of trees, and provided there is no way to track it, the police are shit out of luck because someone will steal it first.

She gives me a faint smile and stands. 'See you in court.'

When she leaves, I sit in the humming silence, her words echoing through me. For the first time in months, I let myself believe there might be a way forward. A crack in the walls. A chance. It's the only hope I have.

In the yard that afternoon, men circle me in packs, watching for an opportunity for a fight. One shouts, 'Big shot actor. Let's see if you bleed the same as the rest of us.'

A guard stands between us, his voice loud and steady. It serves as a reprieve for now.

Court is no safer. They dress me in an ill-fitting suit and tie and drag me to the dock. The Crown attorney lays out the evidence from the UK, a thick dossier of reports, signed warrants, and affidavits.

'The Crown respectfully submits that the accused must be returned to the United Kingdom to face trial.'

There are a few seconds where I'm thinking… where will they send me? Isn't there a prison in Dorchester? I doubt it has plush cells with ensuite bathrooms, but if it's close enough to Dawlish and I'm eligible for family visits, it could work to my advantage.

The judge nods, ready to rule. I lean forward, my palms damp with sweat. This is it. I'm going home.

Then the courtroom doors open, and a detective strides down the aisle, and drops a folder on the clerk's desk. I break out in a sweat, and I'm thinking, *holy shit*, what now?

'Your Honour, Canada has its own interest in this man.'

Murmurs ripple through the benches. The judge frowns, irritated. 'Explain.'

The detective opens the folder and flips it around. It's the same grainy photo of a man who looks more like Hagrid from Harry Potter than me. I barely hear the judge's gavel pounding for silence.

Sanchez's voice cuts through the din. 'This is highly irregular—'

But I'm not listening. I'm squinting at the shape in the shadows sitting at the back of the courtroom. A man with his arms crossed and a faint smile curving at the mouth. Holloway, my old friend, and not a waft of smoke, as I'd previously imagined.

I want to point and shout and say, 'That's your man! He's the killer.'

While I'm trying to process the visual, my brain knows that he is simply a mental image I'd created, the other half of me, the darker half, bubbling out of my imagination.

I barely bear the words, 'Bail is denied.'

The words hit like a fist. I clench my jaw and force myself not to react. The courtroom is louder now, tension coiling in the air like static before a storm. I don't remember being dismissed, but I hear heels echoing along the corridor as the guards escort me outside to the bus. I press my face against the window, watching sunbeams as they funnel down across the buildings, and there's a sense of something evil creeping towards me, like a fine mist gathering at the edge of the trees, ready to pounce.

The years I'd spent with Lilja spin like leaves in a gust, the love we'd had, the joy and the pain. Every betrayal had built a wall between us, and neither of us were willing to scramble over it, let alone knock it down. I wish I had been a more loving partner. Things got out of hand, and I'm not proud of it.

Back at the remand centre, I lie on my bunk, succumbing to intermittent bouts of claustrophobia. There's no sense of normality here, what with all the yelling coming from the next-door cell at night. I suspect it's the prospect of being moved to a federal prison that drives him to it. I'd be head-banging the walls if I had to do life. If I follow the rules and sweet-talk the screws, I could be out in six years.

The hunter I killed lies beneath the roots of an old tree and is unlikely to be found. Same with Pederson. The elements and wildlife are on my side, as is the sheer remoteness of the region. Their remains are hidden for now.

As for my capture, I have Lt Tulimaq to thank for that. I'm convinced he remembered the yellow fletching in my pocket and put two and two together. Fortunately, I doubt he'll find the bow or the rest of my arrows, unless he has some kind of supernatural powers I don't know about.

As for the police knowing I was heading for Toronto, it was simply because I'd stupidly told Jean-Marie. I should have known he was a hustler and an informant from the many questions he asked.

Sometimes in the dead of night, nightmares come and go. The icy touch of Nic's fingers under my shirt, travelling like ants up my chest. I keep dreaming long after her words fade away. I realise with absolute certainty that none of this was her fault. It was all mine.

That terrible, stupid night was an alcoholic blur, a desperate-to-get-away-from-Nic blur. I can still hear her howling like a woman possessed, tears of rage cascading down her face. Her eyes shone with defiance, and her teeth were clenched, erasing all softness from her face.

Even though I can still feel those punches, it was when my head collided with the brick wall that I saw grey pinheads dancing around behind my eyelids.

But I saw something else as well.

I saw someone else behind her that night. Someone who is no longer trapped in a memory and now whispers my name. The face that has skirted around the edge of my consciousness suddenly reappears in my mind, and the echo of a familiar voice adding clarity to each feature. Her lips, her eyes, her hair, a complete person coming to life.

She kept screaming for Nic to stop beating me, but her cries went unheard. While I tried to shield my head and chest and reassure myself that I could handle it, I knew I couldn't.

I don't know if she grabbed Nic by the collar and jerked her backwards, or if she wrapped her hand around Nic's hair. There was a greyed-out moment where I saw Nic's body arcing towards the cellar steps and my mind couldn't process why or how she was airborne, only that she was.

Afterwards, we both stood there, the air thick with her questions.

*Why isn't she moving?*

*Is that blood?*

*Oh, God, please do something!*

I remember smelling the alcohol on her breath and hoping it would all be forgotten in the haze of a hangover in the morning. I remember telling her that Nic was knocked out cold and I would wait with her until she came to. I asked her to do me a big favour. To go back to the party and not to tell anyone that Nic was here.

She nodded in that stoic way of hers, as if acknowledging that everything that had happened that night would remain between us. I couldn't bring myself to tell her that Nic was already dead. I refused to let her go down for a crime she committed to protect me.

Lilja may think Bizzy is her brightest star. She's certainly mine. But that's not where I was going with the analogy. Names are everything, and this analogy refers to a celestial star, the most steadfast I know. There's only one person with the passion to protect both my wife and my daughter and to do what needed to be done.

And that is Stella.

Her name hits me in the chest, her face fractured by the tremor in my voice. She knows now that Nic had died that night. That I drove Nic's body to the beach and waded out into the sea in an ebbing tide. I dropped the body like a stone, where it surfaced near Langstone Rock a few weeks later. She knows I tried to cover it up and pretend Nic was simply missing. I wonder if there is a kernel of grief, knowing that I'd done it for her.

As for my time here, I've decided to play the humble inmate, a role not unlike James Stevens, the butler in *The Remains of the Day*, dedicated to pleasing the screws. I'll help my fellow prisoners form a book club and win a few brownie points if I can.

I lie back on my bunk and watch the news. They're running my story, showing a manor house in Dawlish with green lawns and majestic views of the sea. There's my wife, strolling through the grounds, long hair hanging loose down her back, smiling for the cameras. Looking on in blue-eyed concentration is Ryan McKellan, my dearest friend and confidant, standing by the front door wearing my lambskin leather jacket. I said he could borrow a few of my clothes but not the David Beckham collection. Sneaky bastard.

I doubt it was hard for him to plant the seeds of insecurity in her mind, little hints that there was an intruder about; a door left open here, a muddy footprint there, and a spray of my old cologne. Then there were the cigarette butts on the gravel, the same brand I always smoked. Ryan does light up occasionally, no matter what he told my wife.

He also turned off the CCTV, so Lilja didn't know it's him skulking around the gardens at night. If anyone could convince Lilja she needed security, it was him. I promised him a lump sum on condition Lilja hired him – which she did – and any proof he could find of unlawful activity.

Just because Ryan didn't have a key to the house didn't mean he couldn't find an opportunity to roam the corridors unseen and hack into Lilja's computer when she was busy in the kitchens. But he found nothing to incriminate her. No diary, no strategic blow-by-blow account of how she enticed me to take the role of Ethan Holloway. Or how she – my ingenious, calculating wife – came up with a pen name for the script of *Play Him Play Her* that no one would think to investigate. I couldn't believe she would go to such extremes to get rid of me. But she wanted me gone after the last and final affair, and I don't blame her.

When Ryan told me Lilja knew Nic before she came to work for us and that she knew about our affair, it got me thinking. My wife had artfully employed Nic, knowing I'd fall for her. But without Nic to corroborate all of this, there's no evidence.

Ryan gives snippets of information to a reporter when he can. But the reporter is adamant they must have proof before writing a story, which Ryan has yet to give. No one knows she created the character of Ethan Holloway, master manipulator and killer, as an elaborate plan to destroy me. Although a jury might find it hard to believe on hearsay alone, a video recording is so much more convincing.

Ryan has the resources to video her confession through a tiny camera hidden in his shirt collar. Everything is transmitted remotely to a tape recorder in his flat, copies of which he sends to my attorney. So far, she's said very little. But she won't be able to resist his good looks for much longer. Ryan is slowly wearing her down layer by layer, and she's trusting him a little more. While my wife continues in blissful ignorance, there will come a time when the illusion shatters. She should stay clear if she wants to outwit him and elude whatever else he has planned.

As I make my way to the computer room, I think about how grateful I am for this one last chance. I will send a letter to DC Symonds and, hopefully, in due course, taped conversations between Ryan and Lilja showing how she set me up. If I can't put things right, it will sow the seeds for further investigations.

I open the link for the Devon and Cornwall Police website,

click on REPORT and then CRIME. There's a window that says:

> *Is a crime happening now, is the suspect still at the scene, or is someone seriously injured or in immediate danger.*
> YES
> NO

I don't know if it will open a form that needs to be filled in. I don't know if it will give me the number I need to call. But I do what any man would do in my position.

I hit YES.

# 44

# LILJA

I've been sleeping a little better since Zane is locked away. I've refused all calls from him so he can't inflict himself on me, and I won't respond to any of his letters. It's safer that way.

But safety is fragile. Although my family appears to be back to their jovial selves, playing board games in the evenings, and movie nights on Sunday nights, I see the cracks in Ryan.

At first, it's the little things. The way he looks at me too long, his bright blue eyes staring into mine, unblinking. The way he smiles a little too much. He asks questions that don't sound like questions and then asks them again in a different way. At first, I think once a police officer, always a police officer. It's in his genes.

But now I'm not so sure.

Then, the strangest idea clatters from the back of my mind to the front. Is he watching me? By watching, I mean following me in the car when I go to the bank or to the hairdresser. Or when I have lunch with Stella on the beach, my wonderful house manager, whose words about him selling our conversations to the press keep hounding me. I glimpse him sometimes in my rearview mirror, and I wonder why he does it.

I've always known the lengths Zane would go to punish me. I've already pictured how he'd get off with a lighter sentence with no actual evidence of what he's done. That he'd escape like the three men who escaped from Alcatraz – through the ventilation ducts. But I'm on the tenth chapter of my tell-all book, putting the ghost to rest, and giving the fans the closure they need. He won't escape this.

Sometimes I wonder if he has access to my thoughts. Proof that the psychosis that blossomed in him was all my fault. I don't know for sure, but I know I need to be more careful around Ryan.

Tonight, it's just the two of us in the study. The patio doors are open to let in the warm July air, and the curtains flutter. This time, I was the one who opened them. Of that, I'm sure.

'Do you think I'm being mean not wanting to talk to Zane?' I ask, leaning back in my chair and using my desk as a barrier between us.

Ryan looks down at the signet ring on his finger and twirls it twice. 'It can't be easy for either of you. He's inside. You're here.'

I give a brittle laugh. 'He's inside for good reason. We both know that. But prison won't stop him.'

'What do you mean?'

I keep my tone light, though a cold thread of panic twists inside me. 'It wouldn't surprise me if he had a little help on the outside, someone close enough to nudge me into talking, into trusting, so he could build a case against me.'

It's the quick downward glance, the rubbing at the corner of his mouth with a thumb, and the slight inhale he does when he's trying to deflect any sincerity. 'Then he'd be wasting his time.'

Zane may be thousands of miles away, but he still creeps into my house. Not in the flesh, but in Ryan's questions, which are always so gentle, reasonable, and patient.

For months I've let it pass, grateful to have someone at my side. But the longer I watch him, the clearer it becomes.

He isn't mine. He's Zane's.

That's when I know Ryan is not just listening; he's *recording*. Carrying my words to Zane via telephone or email.

I need to call DC Symonds to ask whether covertly and obsessively filming me inside my house amounts to harassment or stalking. I suspect it violates a reasonable expectation of privacy and could be a criminal offense. It would be prudent not to let a single word slip that Zane could twist into a rope around my neck.

'You ever think about the series?' he asks. 'What drove Zane to do it and you to agree to it. Sometimes going back over it, detail by detail, helps. Like lifting a weight.'

I school my features into a tight smile. 'You're beginning to sound like a therapist.'

He smiles, and for the first time I see how smug he is. Not kind. Not loyal. Just smug.

'I think you'd feel better if you told someone,' he says. 'Even if it's only me.'

The silence stretches. I want to let him believe I am considering it, weighing whether to hand him the confession he's been hoping for.

Then I smile. 'You think there's a story there. Something worth printing.'

'No. No, that's not what I mean.'

'What do you mean?'

'There's so much more to it than that. Holloway wasn't fabricated out of thin air. He was meticulously researched and created. He was written by someone who knew Zane well enough to know he'd fall for it. I don't think he would have done it if he knew—'

'If he knew what, Ryan?'

'If he knew who'd written the script.' His hand subconsciously goes to his collar, where I suspect the hidden mic is.

I can't help thinking that if Ryan had hacked into my computer, if he had gone through all my files, what would he have found?

Absolutely nothing.

The script and all my *well-researched* details, originally saved to a USB drive, have long been deleted and any handwritten notes destroyed. There were no Google searches made on my laptop, and nothing was saved to the hard drive. No character profile for Holloway and no tracking history of either Nic's or Zane's whereabouts while they were having the affair. Or any conversations I'd had with her prior to employing her. There's no proof that I'd devised any such plan at all. He could have got the information from Zane himself. And it's hypothetical at best.

I fling an annoyed look at the ceiling. 'You know what I think. I think I should trust my instincts. So, you must give me credit when I smell bullshit.'

He looks over his shoulder at Paul, who is standing in the doorway, arms crossed like a bouncer. Ryan knows he's been caught, and he knows what's coming next.

'I applaud you for your stamina,' I say, rising. 'But I think it's time we ended our agreement.'

His eyebrows lift. 'Lilja—'

'There's no need for you to say anything more. I've made my decision.'

The command in my voice startles him. He straightens, and after a moment's hesitation, he collects his jacket from the back of the chair. His eyes linger on me, searching for weakness or guilt, and he finds neither.

When Paul escorts him out, the relief I feel comes in a long, drawn-out sigh. In the quiet that follows, I sense something harden inside me.

I'm still here. I'm unbroken and untouchable.

That's all I can hope for in life.

**BarbedWire - Trending #InZane**

@CirceAtNight: The sad part is, when *Celebrity UK* asked Zane Osborne if on-screen roles bled into off-hours, he said 'Sometimes.' Makes you wonder if his faculties were compromised. If playing Holloway pushed him over the edge?

@Titmouse: It was an off-the-cuff remark... not serious. Not an issue.

@BantaBadger: Admittedly, I always thought this man was a joke (simply because of his bad acting). But I couldn't have been more wrong. I know he probably won't see this, but if he does, Mr Osborne, I sincerely apologise for what I thought of you. You're a brilliant actor. You fooled an entire nation.

@SherylAdams: I was thinking this too @CirceAt-Night. Instead of people saying Ozzie was one big, unhinged person, maybe he was so broken down, he fell apart.

@HeyWhat'sUP: You're all missing the point. He's been arrested for murder. His disappearance and "death" were one big con.

Let that sink in.

# NOTE FROM THE AUTHOR

Like other small-presses and independent authors, I rely heavily on word-of-mouth recommendations to reach new readers. A positive review on Amazon, Barnes and Noble, Waterstones, or any of your favourite bookstore websites, would mean the world to me. All you readers are the champions of our industry, and if you loved the book, then you are the ones I wrote it for!

Preordering from your favourite author helps build buzz and is so important to the success of a novel. It sends a message to the publisher that readers are excited about an author's work, characters, and the series. Thank you for your support, and I hope you love *Hidden Remains* as much as I do.

If you haven't read the first book, *Play Him Play Her,* in this two-part series, you can read it here.

# ACKNOWLEDGEMENTS

As always, I owe an enormous debt to so many people without whom this book would not have been possible. My sincere gratitude to everyone who gave their time, talent, and support.

Thank you to my developmental and structural editor, A.J. Humpage, who advises, edits, proofreads, corrects and, most of all, makes me a better writer. Your passion and dedication have been amazing. Thank you.

I owe a special debt to Jane Dixon-Smith for the amazing cover and for her incredible work on the book's behalf. You really are a lifesaver! There isn't enough space to acknowledge every actor I have met, interviewed, or simply watched in awe from the sidelines. Thank you for everything you've taught me. I'm sure you are all keen to tell me what I got wrong about The Method. I respectfully refer you to the (fictional) Zane Osborne for his advice and expertise, thereby saving me from abject humiliation. Special gratitude to film and stage producers and directors Charlie Lepper and John Schlesinger CBE for giving me the inspiration.

To Kelly Lacey at Love Books Tours for doing such a wonderful job and so many heartfelt thanks to all the fabulous bloggers who make up my street team. It takes a village, and these are mine. You guys rock!

Most of all, thank you to my readers. Whether you've been with me from the start or whether this is the first of my books you've read, you are the reason I can make a small living doing what I love. Please keep leaving reviews, keep supporting independent bookshops and indie authors, and most of all keep reading! Three cheers for putting up with Zane's #inzanity. I hope you know how grateful I am.

Finally, thank you to Jeff for telling me not to sweat the small stuff and for loving me the way I am. For Jamie, my coffee and walking buddy, for always making me howl with laughter. To my twin brother, Mark, for just being there. Our hilarious convos back and forth across the pond have made me feel less isolated and alone. To big bruv Giles for telling me not to let the bastards grind me down. And to Edward, my darling boss, who provides hourly interruptions in the hope I will serve and buttle for him as if my life depended on it. Meow to you too!

# ABOUT THE AUTHOR

Claire worked in the hotel and catering industry, and as an executive assistant for companies in the UK, US, and Hong Kong. She loves doing writing courses with Curtis Brown, and her award-winning novels owe much to her years as a member of the Albuquerque Police Citizen's Academy, where her focus was the impact of violence towards women.

Originally from Bradfield, UK, Claire worked in London before moving to Utah, where she now lives with her family and her cat, Edward.